Cupcake Girls - Part 5 of The Vixen War Bride Series

The Vixen War Bride

Thomas Doscher

Published by Thomas Doscher, 2023.

CUPCAKE GIRLS - PART 5 OF THE VIXEN WAR BRIDE SERIES

First edition. February 1, 2023.

Copyright © 2023 Thomas Doscher.

ISBN: 979-8215669440

Written by Thomas Doscher.

Also by Thomas Doscher

The Vixen War Bride

To my sons.

Common Acronyms

- AAFES – Army Air Force Exchange Service
- AO – Area of Operations
- BX – Base Exchange (on-base department store, Air Force)
- CID – Criminal Investigation Division
- CJTF – Combined Joint Task Force
- COC – Combined Operations Center
- DFAC – Dining Facility (Nice way of saying "chow hall.")
- DFAS – Defense Finance and Accounting Service
- DLI – Defense Language Institute
- DPAA – Defense POW/MIA Accounting Agency
- DV – Distinguished Visitor
- ECP – Entry Control Point
- EOD – Explosive Ordnance Disposal
- FARP – Forward Air Refueling Point
- FOB – Forward Operating Base
- GO – General Officer
- ID – Infantry Division
- JDOG – Joint Detention Operations Group
- LT – Lieutenant (pronounced "El-tee.")
- LTV – Light Tactical Vehicle
- LZ – Landing Zone
- MEDEVAC – Medical Evacuation
- MOS – Military Occupation Specialty
- MRE – Meal Ready to Eat
- NASA – National Aeronautics and Space Administration
- NCO – Noncommissioned officer
- PA – Public Affairs
- PX – Post Exchange (on-base department store, Army)
- QRF – Quick Reaction Force
- RIF – Reduction in Force

- RIP/TOA – Relief in Place/Transfer of Authority
- SeaBee – United States Naval Construction Battalion. (Heterograph of "CB," for "Construction Battalion.")
- SGLI – Servicemembers Group Life Insurance
- SNCO – Senior Noncommissioned Officer
- TOC – Tactical Operations Center
- TTP – Tactics, Techniques and Procedures
- UNCLASS - Unclassified

Va'Shen Pronunciation

- Aderen – *Ah-dur-en*
- Alacea – *Ah-lah-say-ah*
- Alva'Rem – *Al-vah-rem*
- Alzoria – *Al-zor-ree-ah*
- Aru'Dace – *Ah-roo-dah-say*
- Azarin – *Ah-zah-rin*
- Bao Aren – *Bou Ah-ren*
- Bao Sen – *Bou Sehn*
- Basilla – *Ba-sih-la*
- Boso – *Boh-soh*
- Boto – *Boh-toh*
- Dan Huun – *Dan Hoon*
- *Dara Tang* – *Dah-rah-tang*
- Donya'Ta – *Dohn-yah-tah*
- Garan'Sel – *Ga-ran-sell*
- Goto – *Go-tow*
- Hesmea – *Hez-may-ah*
- Hestean – *Hes-stay-en*
- Kasshas – *Ka-shas*
- Kastia – *Ka-stee-ah*
- Ketra – *Keh-trah*
- Mezina – *Meh-zee-nah*
- Mikorin – *Me-kor-rin*
- *Myorin* – *Me-yor-in*
- Nadro – *Nah-droh*
- Na'Sha – *Neh-shah*
- Nazea – *Nah-zay-ah*
- Pavastea – *Pah-vah-stay-ah*
- Pelle – *Pel*
- Posha – *Po-shah*

- Runa – *Roo-nah*
- Sho Nan – *Show Non*
- Tasshas – *Ta-shas*
- Tenzeta – *Ten-zeh-tah*
- *Tesho – Teh-show*
- Toka – *Toh-kah*
- Toki – *Toh-kee*
- Turean – *Too-ray-en*
- Turan – *Too-ran*
- Va'Shen – *Vah-Shen*
- Voro – *Voh-roh*
- Wenlin – *When-lin*
- Ya'Jahar – *Yah-Jah-Har*
- Yarl – *Yah-ril*
- Yasuren – *Ya-soo-ren*
- Yunhee – *Yoon-hee*
- Zaishin – *Zy-shin*

Prologue

Six months ago...

Va'Sh was a fairly temperate world. The planet itself was tilted by only seven degrees where Earth was tilted by 23.5. This meant that, unlike Earth, which experienced varying degrees of sunlight and seasons depending on the time of year, Va'Sh's seasonal shifts were less dramatic. Warm places closer to the equator tended to remain warm, even in "winter."

But the further north or south you went from the equator, the colder it got, and it tended to stay that way. The poles, of course, were frozen year-round. But areas that might enjoy a warm summer and a heavy winter on Earth would, on Va'Sh, remain somewhere in between.

It was this knowledge that made the Army major sitting in the command seat of a light tactical vehicle curse under his breath. Outside the window, the sky was a sickly grey overcast. It was wet. It was chilly. And it was going to stay that way.

That's just how it was this far north on Va'Sh's main continental landmass.

It wasn't quite raining yet, but it felt like it wanted to. A drop here and there hit the LTV windshield. The vehicle was parked, so there was no need to run the windshield wipers. It was merely a place to review some paperwork while his troops outside finished their preparations.

He sighed and tiredly rubbed his high-and-tight as he reviewed the personnel files in front of him. Outside, someone was shouting, but he didn't pay it any mind. He was more concerned with the screwed-up personnel situation he faced in this new assignment. While, thankfully, most of his personnel were holdovers from his previous command, practically all his senior noncommissioned officers had been poached to fill spots at the headquarters level. His new terp was fresh out of the Defense Language Institute, and the closest he had been to any action was a two-day seminar on basic infantry tactics.

The situation was, as his commander had put it, "less than ideal."

There was a knock on the LTV window, and he cracked it open. One of his men, Staff Sergeant Brandon Castillo, gave him a quick nod in greeting. No one saluted him. That was standard operating procedure and had been since he took command.

"Sir, we're ready for you."

"Thank you, Staff Sergeant," the major told him. "Give me a few moments."

"Yes, Sir."

Castillo left, and the major looked over one more record before returning the stack to the manila envelope and tossing it on the dashboard next to the now-useless command interface terminal normally used to coordinate forces and direct convoy movements.

Taking a breath, he opened the door and stepped out, pausing only to put on his patrol cap. Red, gritty mud squelched beneath his jump boots, and he felt a few drops of chilly rain hit his face and hands. He took a quick look at the overcast sky above him. It was simply an ugly, disgusting ass day. He started marching forward, and two armed soldiers fell into step on either side of him, escorting him to where the rest of his troops were waiting.

When he arrived, he surveyed the scene before him. His troops, armed, armored and intimidating as hell, stood in a line in front of him, facing off with a group of perhaps three hundred aliens who looked back at the troops with angry tails whipping about. Behind them was the main road that led into their village of simple houses, storefronts, and a tall, ornate temple that reached up to the very sky.

As he approached, two soldiers stepped aside so he could break through the line and stand between the Va'Shen in front of him and troops behind him.

He looked at the Va'Shen before him for several moments, letting them get a good look at him. They were simple folk, dressed in drab colors. Some had faces covered in coal dust, having come directly from the mine where they had been working when he arrived. Intermittent drops of rain cut streaks across their blackened skin as they stood there and glared at him.

When he finally spoke, the aliens' ears all stood up in surprise.

<I am the War Leader, Elkanah Keyes> he boomed in near-perfect Va'Shen. <By the orders of my people and your Emperor, I am now overlord of this village.>

The Va'Shen said nothing.

<I want peace!> he shouted at them. <But if you force me, I will give you war!>

Again, the Va'Shen said nothing. Some looked down at the ground. Some held one another in worry. And some stared at Keyes defiantly.

<To make peace,> he continued. <We will make it so you cannot make war.> He turned and gestured for the soldiers to begin. Every third troop in the line, stepped forward and moved toward the group, causing some of the Va'Shen to back up in panic. <You will not be harmed!> Keyes assured them. <They will look at you and make sure you carry nothing dangerous items.>

While the remaining troops in line watched, their weapons not quite pointed at the villagers, the rest went from Va'Shen to Va'Shen, patting villagers down and checking bags. One tod stepped forward to object to the way one of the troops was patting down a vixen, perhaps his wife or sister, and three more troops stepped up, rifles raised and pointed at his head.

The tod raised his hands and obediently stepped back while the search of the vixen continued.

Keyes watched silently as his men conducted their search. Down the line to his right, one of the troops called out.

"Glass!"

The major turned and found three soldiers, their weapons raised and aimed at the head of a tod in a faded blue monpei. His hands were raised to show he meant no harm.

One of the soldiers, the one who had called out, took a leather satchel off the tod's shoulder, holding it carefully at arm's length. Another troop, this one equipped with what looked like a pair of plastic, hand-held toy robot claws, opened the bag with the claws and looked inside. Turning to Keyes, he nodded and, using the claws, very carefully took the bag and started down the line and away from the group.

Keyes watched him go and turned to the tod who had been in possession of the glass grenades. The Va'Shen stared back at him, his tail waving quickly back and forth behind him in fear, anger or a mixture of both.

The major turned his head toward the man who found the glassers.

"Corporal," he said, his tone all business. "Shoot that thing."

Without a word or moment of hesitation, the soldier raised his rifle to the villager's head and pulled the trigger. The villagers in the group screamed as parts of the tod's brain and skull splattered onto them. The Va'Shen man fell down, his tail twitching once before going completely slack.

Keyes turned to Castillo and gave him a nod. The staff sergeant waved his hand, and half of the troops remaining in the line rushed forward, weapons raised. Each of them grabbed a Va'Shen woman or child and pulled them, kicking and screaming back to their original line. The Va'Shen adults and men reached out, screaming at them, begging the humans to let their loved ones go, but the soldiers maintained an iron grip on the frightened villagers.

Keyes raised his hand, beckoning for silence.

<If you try to kill us, you must now also kill some of them,> he told the remaining adults. <If any of you have more weapons, put them down in front of the you and back away!>

A few tods hesitantly stepped forward and placed glassers or satchels down and then backed up to their original place in the line. More soldiers with toy claws checked the bags and carefully picked up the Va'Shen ordnance, taking it away for disposal.

Keyes eyed those tods. <I thank you for integrity,> he told them. He nodded at Castillo, and the search of the villagers continued. Every so often, one of the soldiers would call out, "Glass!" The search would pause, the weapons taken away, a gunshot, and more screams from the crowd.

The major said nothing, his face revealed nothing. After three more gunshots, the search came to an end. The soldiers returned to their line, and the Va'Shen women and children were released, all of them rushing headlong back to their loved ones. Keyes raised his hand for their attention.

<We will search your homes. You will stay here. When done, you may leave.>

Two-thirds of his troops started into the village, opening doors and moving carefully inside, checking for traps or hidden commandos the entire time. Some of the doors were locked, prompting the soldiers to kick them in before proceeding inside.

The search took several hours, and the Va'Shen were forced to stand there the entire time. Some held each other for comfort while many more stared down at the ground in fear and shame, afraid to lock eyes with the Dark One, Keyes, lest he decide to kill them too. Although it was not raining hard, they had been standing out there longer and were already becoming soaked.

The bodies of the Va'Shen who had been caught with glassers remained as they lay, their blood mixing with the muddy water around them.

Finally, the soldiers conducting the house searches returned. They returned to their spots in line as Castillo gave Keyes a brief on what they had found: hardlight rifles and glassers.

"Any uninvited houseguests?" Keyes asked.

"No, Sir," Castillo replied. "What do you want us to do about the weapons?"

Keyes knew exactly what the sergeant meant. He wanted to know if he wanted to try to find out who the weapons belonged to, but Keyes figured his point had been made.

"Dispose of them," he said simply.

"Yes, Sir."

"Any other concerns?"

"No, Sir," Castillo told him. "The FOB is secure, and we have people surrounding the vil at every access point. Nothing is moving unless we want it to."

"All right," Keyes said. "Let's wrap this up."

"Yes, Sir."

Castillo rejoined the line, and Keyes stepped toward the villagers.

<The weapons you hid from us have been taking,> he informed them. <If we see you with weapon, you will be killed. Your Emperor commands you to cooperate. Cooperate, and we are friends. Not cooperate, and we are enemies.>

He waited to see how the Va'Shen would react, but the villagers continued to look downward in fear.

<I am the Overlord,> Keyes told them. <I am Elkanah Keyes.> He paused for effect. <You will respect me... Or you will die.>

Chapter 1

Two months until contact...

The entrance to the cave was almost two stories high with the dark gray rock surrounding it chiseled and sculpted into the likeness of a hissing cobra with its mouth opened wide. The stink of death and decay wafted from the entrance, forcing the three members of the party to cover their noses for a moment lest they retch. Low moaning sounds came from within, the sources of which were unknown.

One of the party members, a very tall black knight wearing a horned helmet that completely covered his face, stepped forward and put his hands on his hips. "So, this is it," he rumbled. "Doesn't look that bad."

From his right the blonde woman in white cleric's robes rolled her eyes. "Only you could stand in front of something like this and say it doesn't look bad."

"Well, it doesn't," the black knight replied shortly. "At least I don't have to crouch."

A halfling pixie a third his height floated up to his left side, held aloft by fluttering diaphanous wings.

"It shore wooks scawy, d'ough!" the pixie squeaked, her hands under her chin in concern.

The black knight turned to her, and he took a deep breath before sighing. "Yeah. Yeah... it's totes 'scawy.'"

"Aw we weally going in dere?" the pixie asked, pointing at the entrance with her magic wand.

"Yes," the black knight told her. "We're really... Look, could you stop that?"

"Stawp what?"

"That. Could you stop talking like that?"

The pixie cocked her head to the side in puzzlement. "Bat dis is how I always talk."

"Okay, look, we get it, all right," the black knight said. "You're fucking adorable, okay?! We *all* know you're fucking adorable! Now, can you just talk like a normal person!?"

The pixie clutched her wand in fear. "I do'n awnderstand!"

"Yes, you fucking do!" the knight cried.

"Dude, calm down," the cleric said, holding her hands up as if to physically intervene at a moment's notice.

"No! He needs to talk like a normal person!"

"Bot I'mma girl pixie!" the pixie objected.

"Which brings me to my next point!" the black knight rounded on her. "What in the actual fuck, man!? You could have picked anything, but you picked the closest thing you could to 'magical girl!' Did you do this to fuck with me?! Are you fucking with me?!"

The pixie hung her head and sniffled. "Why aw you so mean?"

The knight stared at her for a moment and raised his gauntleted hand, pointing a black steel finger at her.

"I fucking hate you."

The pixie looked up suddenly. "Hey, what time is it?"

"Don't change the subject!"

* * *

"No, I mean seriously," Staff Sergeant Jared "Burgers" Baird asked from his seat at the long rectangular table in the center of the dining facility's main dining room. Maps and papers covered the table, held down by the weight of several dice, plastic figures and pencils. Most of the lights in the DFAC were off, giving the room an eerie feel. The other tables had chairs placed on top of them, and the floor was still slick with having just been mopped.

Glowering at him from across the table, his friend, Staff Sergeant John Ramirez, checked his watch. "Coming up on zero-two hundred," he said.

Burgers rose from the table and grabbed his patrol cap. "It's time," he announced. "You still wanna come with?"

"Anything is better than listening you talk in that baby-boo-boo voice," Ramirez told him, grabbing his own hat.

Sitting next to Burgers, Navy Corpsman Second Class Mina Fletcher stifled a laugh. "You want us to wait for you to get back?" she asked.

"Nah," Burgers told her. "You go on into the Cave of Woe, and we'll catch up with you when we get back."

The two stepped out of the DFAC and into the warm night air, putting their patrol caps on and walking briskly toward their target on the other side of the FOB. It was a clear night, and the stars shone brightly through the green and purples of Va'Sh's ever-present aurora borealis. Most of the camp was asleep, giving the FOB a creepy quality that made one want to instinctively walk a little faster.

"So, how you wanna do this?" Ramirez asked as they strolled toward the target. "Get some grappling hooks and some ropes? Go in all ninja style?"

The two stopped next to one of the FOB's many perimeter watchtowers, and Burgers placed his hand on one of the rungs of the wooden ladder that led to the top. The towers were made of plain, unpainted plywood, held aloft by four six-by-sixes that reached forty feet into the air.

"I'm just going to climb up the ladder like it's a regular day," the larger man said.

"Man, you are just no fun at all," Ramirez told him as Burgers stepped onto the ladder.

"*Quests and Corridors* was fun," Burgers pointed out.

"Sure, for Petunia Pixie of the Poopified Phorest," Ramirez shot back, climbing up the ladder after his friend.

The big African American Texan paused about halfway up the ladder and listened carefully for any sign of movement.

Nothing. Not a sound.

He frowned and started up again, not going out of his way to be loud, but not trying to be quiet either. He wanted this to be fair.

As he approached the top of the ladder, he slowed and cautiously peeked over the edge and into the guard post. His face scrunched up in a grimace at what he saw.

The two sentries assigned to the post were both fast asleep, one sitting on the floor in the corner. The other was sitting comfortably in a plastic DFAC chair, having the audacity to put his feet up on the edge of the window looking out over the countryside beyond the perimeter fence.

Burgers looked down at Ramirez and put his hand on the side of his face, miming sleep.

Ramirez grinned. "Oh man," he whispered. "This is gonna be great."

Now the two entered Ranger stealth mode and gingerly climbed up inside the tower. Burgers put his finger to his lips as Ramirez followed him and stood up inside. He pointed to an M-31 resting against the wall near him and turned to pick up the other one resting against the opposite wall.

Once both weapons were in their hands, they checked to make sure the weapons were on SAFE, removed the magazines and ejected the chambered rounds. Ramirez gave Burgers a nod, and the big man took a deep breath.

"WHAT THE FUCK IS GOING ON HERE?!" he bellowed.

The two sentries startled awake as if to a bomb going off nearby. The soldier who had been sleeping in the chair with his feet up fell over backward, landing on the floor with a crash. The other soldier jumped to his feet, saw Burgers and Ramirez holding *their* rifles and went deathly pale.

Scrambling to his feet, the other soldier turned, angry about what he thought was some kind of joke.

"What the fu…" Turning, he saw Burgers glaring daggers at the man and immediately went to attention, already knowing he was in *a lot* of trouble.

"You two up here getting your beauty rest?" Burger demanded.

"No, Staff Sergeant!" the two replied in near-perfect unison.

Burgers's eyes went wide in surprise. "So, I did *not* just catch you two asleep at your posts? I'm a fucking liar, huh?!"

"No, Staff Sergeant!" one cried. "I mean… Yes, Staff Sergeant!"

"What?!" Burgers continued. "You think because we happen to have it pretty good here, we can just kick back and relax? We ain't got *no worries* up here at FOB Leonard, huh?! We don't need any sentries because everything is just so goddamn peaceful and serene, huh?!"

"No, Staff Sergeant!" the two cried.

"Or do I got this shit wrong?" Burgers asked. "Maybe you two figure since you guys can't catch Tod coming into the base anyway, there ain't no point in even trying. Is that it? You two just say 'fuck it' and gave up?"

"No, Staff Sergeant!"

Burgers bit his lip and shook his head in fury while Ramirez watched from the side, content to let his friend handle it. Even so, he knew he had a role to play here.

"So, what do you wanna do with them, Staff Sergeant?" Ramirez asked him. "Extra duty? Confined to base?"

"Extra duty?" Burgers asked as if the very suggestion insulted him. "These two dirtbags just got caught sleeping on sentry duty. That's capital punishment!"

"You wanna *shoot* these guys?" Ramirez asked in mock surprise.

The two sentries went dead white. One of them actually started to shake.

"A sentry asleep on duty in wartime can be sentenced to death," Burgers went on. He turned to the two men in question. "You have any idea what could have happened while you were up here dozing? You know how many people could have *died*?"

Ramirez didn't say anything and let his friend roll with it. He knew this was the Texan's particular pet peeve, and he knew why.

When the war broke out, their Ranger outfit had been deployed to the third planet in the Epsilon Eridani star system. It was during those first few months that their camp had been raided by Va'Shen commandos in the middle of the night. The raiding party had managed to evade the mines, tripwires, infra-red cameras and the eyes of every sentry ringing the camp and went on a total rampage, burning, shooting and glassing everything they saw. They killed 24 Coalition troops, seven of them Rangers from their unit.

All this happened before the Coalition discovered the Va'Shen's particular talent for stealth, so in the aftermath of the attack, the immediate assumption was that someone had screwed up. An investigation was launched, and every troop pulling security that night got thoroughly interrogated by Army CID over and over again. The Army needed someone to blame, and they were going to find that someone.

One of those potential someones had been one Specialist Jared Baird, who had been manning an M-270 machine gun in Tower 6 that night.

It wasn't the investigations or the suspicion that had so deeply affected Burgers, however. It was that he didn't *know*. He had asked himself constantly, ever since that night that seven of his fellow Rangers were killed, "Did I miss them? Was I the one who missed those commandos?"

Later, as the Coalition learned just how good the Va'Shen were at stealth, additional measures were put in place to ensure security at forward bases, and most people understood that the attack on the FOB on Epsilon was just the first of what would become many more. But Burgers never stopped asking himself those questions.

So, when Burgers found troops not taking sentry duty seriously, he had a tendency to take it personally.

"So, yeah!" he said. "Death!"

Maybe a little *too* personally...

"Yeah, Staff Sergeant," Ramirez began, "I don't think we can authorize that at this level. I think executing people is more a Captain Gibson thing."

Burgers pretended to chew on this thought while the two sentries remained at attention and quietly prayed. Finally, the giant NCO nodded and turned to them.

"Okay, you two, here's what you get to do," he said, putting his knife hand in their faces. "You're going to go down to the NCO quarters, find Sergeant Carpenter and wake him up. You're going to stand there and explain to him *why* you're not at your posts and *why* you don't have your weapons and let him know that Staff Sergeants Baird and Ramirez are doing your jobs for you while he finds two replacements for you. Then, you get to tell him that Staff Sergeants Baird and Ramirez are eagerly awaiting his arrival here so we can discuss how this happened and what we're going to do about it. Then you two are going to report to the DFAC, pick up a mop and clean the floors for the rest of the night. And I swear, if those mops stop moving for even a second, I will have you cleaning urinals with your toothbrushes for the rest of this deployment. HUA?"

"HUA, Staff Sergeant!" the two cried in equal measures of fear and relief.

"Now," Burgers said quietly, leaning in close to the two of them and speaking in a whisper. "Run away."

The two took off down the ladder like a shot, causing the entire tower to shake as they fled the two NCOs.

"Very nice," Ramirez said, giving Burgers a golf clap. "Hell, *I* almost shit my pants." He stepped over to the chair the sentry abandoned and righted it, sitting down and leaning over the abandoned M-270 light machine gun. "Man, this takes me back," he said.

Burgers rested the unfortunate sentry's M-31 against the wall and sat in the other chair next to his friend.

"You really gonna give up all this?" Ramirez asked him, gesturing to the dark and dingy guard tower. "Just to go live on some colony and work at some IT company?"

It was a familiar argument. Ever since Ramirez had discovered his friend was considering leaving the Army, he had done his level best to convince him to stay.

"Oh yeah," Burgers replied sarcastically. "Nothing's better than staying up 'till two a.m. so you can go yell at a couple of idiots who fell asleep on watch."

"You love it," Ramirez replied. "Don't lie."

Burgers sighed. The sad truth was he really did love it. Most of the Army could be divided into two kinds of people: The people who enlisted to do four years and go to college, and the people who enlisted because they wanted to be *soldiers*. For most people, the stuff the Army did, "the suck," as it was called, was a chore one had to endure in order to get the paycheck and free college. You did it. You could even be good at it. But it was still work, and you would rather be doing anything else.

But Ramirez and Burgers fell into the second category. They truly *loved* sleeping outside, running around the woods and shooting guns. There would always be stuff they didn't like, sure, but being a soldier was the only life they ever wanted. Where else could you get paid for jumping out of a helicopter, landing in a lake, swimming to shore and then zipping back across that lake in a rigid inflatable boat? Shoot, that *never* got old.

"You know," Burgers said, "You *could* come with me. Go to some colony, open the galaxy's most awesome burger joint. You could mop or something."

"That is the most tempting offer I have ever heard in my life," Ramirez replied. "But I'ma pass."

They turned as the sound of feet... angry, pissed off feet... came rattling up the ladder to the tower. After a few moments, Sergeant Carpenter, Noncommissioned Officer in Charge of FOB Security, climbed into the look-out with them.

He looked at them both and took a resigned breath, running his hand over what used to be blond hair before he shaved it down to almost nothing. "I don't know what to say, Staff Sergeants," he said remorsefully. "I didn't want to believe it was happening."

"Neither did we, man," Ramirez told him.

There had been suspicions over the last week or so that sentries had been sleeping overnight at their posts, so Burgers and Ramirez had talked to Carpenter. Given the severity of the charge, Carpenter felt compelled to defend his people and challenged the staff sergeants for proof.

Proof that just came into his hooch and woke him up.

"They said you were going to kill them," Carpenter told Burgers with an arched eyebrow. "If so, I gotta be honest, I'm only a *little* against it."

"Oh, I wanted to," Burgers said. He sighed a moment later. There were plenty of options as to how to handle this issue. Burgers hadn't actually been joking. It was *technically* possible to execute sentries caught sleeping, though no one in today's Army would ever even consider it. He just wanted the two men to understand the severity of their actions.

"They're your troops," Burgers told Carpenter diplomatically. "What do you suggest?"

"Can't let them off with a warning," Carpenter answered immediately. "Too severe for that. We could Article 15 them, but honestly that would destroy any chance they have to go career, and this is their first cock-up. If you don't object, Staff Sergeant, I'd like to recommend to the captain that he take a stripe from them and put them on extra duty. That should send a message to the rest of the camp, and they could still recover from it."

Burgers chewed on that for a minute. An Article 15 was nonjudicial punishment. It was supposed to be a way that a commander could punish a troop without it going to the legal system so that the troop could learn from the experience and still go on to have a career. In the more modern "one-mistake Army," however, having one on your record almost automatically meant you were prevented from re-enlisting. The captain, however, could reduce them in rank, citing their unreadiness for the responsibility and give them "corrective training" so that the act wouldn't show up on a record.

He looked to Ramirez who gave him a shrug as if to say, "your call." Burgers nodded to Carpenter.

"Okay, Sergeant. It's all yours from here."

"Thank you, Staff Sergeant. I'll make sure it never happens again."

"I know you will, man," Burgers replied and reached out to shake his hand. It was important to Burgers that there not be any bad blood about this. He and Carpenter were on the same team.

"I got a couple of guys coming to take over," Carpenter told them. "I'll stay until they get here."

Ramirez hopped up and started for the ladder. "Cool."

"Have a good one, Sergeant."

"You too, Staff Sergeant."

The two staff sergeants climbed down the ladder and left the junior NCO alone in the tower. As Burgers's feet touched the ground, Ramirez patted him on the shoulder.

"Cave of Woe?" he asked.

"Cave of Woe," Burgers confirmed.

The Rangers started back toward the chow hall where, they hoped, their party hadn't gotten too far ahead of them.

"But seriously, could you knock off the cutesy voice?" Ramirez asked.

"It really bothers you, huh?" Burgers asked.

"It's creepy."

"Awww!" Burgers replied in his high-pitched fairy voice. "Den mawbe a'll tolk like dis all da time!"

Ramirez shook his head, but wouldn't look at his friend.

"I fucking hate you."

* * *

Captain Ben Gibson stood at the entrance of the small camp that the Va'Shen craftsmen and his SeaBees had been building for the last month and whistled appreciatively at what he saw. What had once been a strip of empty land butted up against a hillside with some red grass and a few purple trees was now a small neighborhood of small, interconnected houses. It reminded Ben of a row of townhouses back in Indiana but built with a mixture of Va'Shen and human styles.

He knew the SeaBees's reputation for working fast without giving up on quality, but even he had doubted they would be able to put together so much so fast.

With the arrival of hundreds of refugees from the Va'Shen village of Garan'Sel only a month out, Ben had asked the local council, the *Aderen*, if they had adequate food and housing for them. Upon hearing that housing was going to be an issue, the Ranger captain had offered the support of his Naval Construction Battalion sailors to assist, and the village leaders of Pelle agreed. While it might seem like a small thing, Ben understood that it had, in fact, been a huge win. Unlike last time the American troops had offered aid, the villagers had taken his offer in the spirit in which it was given and agreed.

That had been just over a month ago, right after he had returned from Jamieson Airfield with the survivors of the Pelle commando. With so little time to gather the resources they would need and to work with the villagers, whose language they still barely understood, Ben had considered it near impossible for them to have enough temporary housing for the incoming refugees. But here he stood on the far side of Pelle from FOB Leonard, with several completed buildings made from a mixture of local wood and imported human polymer, forced to shake his head in wonder.

Although impressive in its own right, the camp was still incomplete, and the sounds of hammers and sawing filled the air around him as Va'Shen and sailors milled around the buildings, doing their best to coordinate their efforts through their mutual language issues. Looking up on the roof of one of the ugly but sound buildings, he saw Azarin nailing a board into place.

As if he could sense the human's eyes on him, the one-eyed former commando officer turned and looked down at Ben. The Ranger saw this and waved in greeting. Azarin turned back to his job without responding.

Ben was still uncertain as to how he should feel about or interact with his brother-in-law. They had managed to cooperate at Jamieson enough to get him and his tods freed from the detainment facility there, but now that he was free, the Va'Shen man seemed to want little to do with him.

A part of him was thankful for that. It was one thing to interact with villagers who had no idea what the war had been like, who had no say in it or influence in how it was carried out. It was quite another to face an alien who literally used shooting medics as an example of how he had killed human soldiers.

The war was over. That was what he had told Azarin. He had also told him the end of the war couldn't really come until both sides could at least potentially become friends. The fact that such a thing seemed more possible to Ben than Azarin was strange to the Ranger, given how many nights he awoke in a cold sweat from nightmares. Then again, he had had several months of "peace" where the mission had been to work with and understand the Va'Shen. For Azarin, he had been at war until literally a month ago.

"Sir!"

Ben turned and found the SeaBees's senior noncommissioned officer, Senior Chief Petty Officer Chase Warren, walking up to him. Unlike his usual five-pointed camouflage cap, the sailor sported a bright yellow hard hat on top of his head, and the dirt and grime on his uniform told Ben that the man wasn't just there drinking coffee and telling junior enlisted sailors what to do.

"Senior Chief, this is amazing," Ben told him right off.

"I told you we could do it," Warren told him with a smile. "You have to stop doubting me."

"Never again," Ben promised. "How is it looking?"

"We'll be done in time," Warren informed him. He gestured to the buildings and the hideous hybrid of Va'Shen and human architecture and materials that made them. "They're not pretty, but they're warm and they'll keep the rain out until the villagers can build proper houses for them."

"Hey, Chief!"

They turned to find another SeaBee in a yellow hardhat trotting up to them.

"Chief, the power saw just gave out on us," the sailor told him. "We need the other one from the shop."

Warren nodded. "Okay, I'll get it. I need to check in with the shop anyway." He looked around the various hard hats and furred ears until he found the pair he was looking for. "Turean!"

The one-armed Va'Shen teen had been carefully using a power driver to screw a section of plywood wall into place. Hearing his name, he looked up, put the driver down and trotted over.

"Yas, Senor Jeef?" the boy asked.

Warren paused to make sure he knew the words he wanted to say. <I must return,> he said. <You guide me in "gator" and return here with big tool?>

The boy's ears began to flutter happily through the holes in the top of his hardhat. "Yes, Senor Jeef!"

The chief fished a set of keys from his pocket and tossed them to Turean, who caught them easily. Warren pointed down the road where a green, four-wheeled tractor the size of a golf cart waited.

<Bring to here. We go,> he said.

The youth dashed off to retrieve the vehicle, and Ben smiled. He remembered watching Warren teaching the Va'Shen boy how to drive the gator, the two of them careening all over the FOB at top speed with Turean howling in glee. Since then, the boy took any opportunity to drive.

"Well, Sir, back to work for me," Warren said, giving the captain a salute.

Ben returned the salute as Turean brought the gator to a skidding stop next to them. "Let me know if you need anything."

"Will-do, Sir," Warren replied as he hopped into the passenger seat of the green cart. "Turean, haul ass."

"Holing da ass, Jeef!" Turean cried as the two zipped off back to the FOB.

* * *

As Warren and Turean drove down the main drag of the new camp, they passed two vixens in colorful hanboks, who stepped closer to the buildings as the unknown vehicle went by.

Alacea watched the two go by, and her purple-furred ears twitched a smile. She was glad to see that the Va'Shen boy and the alien engineer were still friendly. When the commando had returned without Turean's father, she had worried that their growing friendship would be suddenly aborted. That didn't seem to be the case, however. After a week spent mourning with his mother, the Va'Shen boy had returned to the SeaBees' workshop and got back to work.

<What a noisy thing,> her friend, Hestean, commented as she watched the gator quickly turn a corner behind them and disappear.

Alacea was forced to agree with her friend, although, it did look fun.

The spiritual leader of Pelle had, ostensibly, come to the new camp to look over the progress, but she had invited her friend along so that they could have a conversation about something troubling the young vixen. As the two meandered down the street, Alacea decided it was time to get to business.

<How goes the war history?> she asked the other Mikorin.

Hestean gently moved her blue and white hair back behind her shoulder. <It goes well, Na'Sha,> she said, switching to business mode with the change in topic.

Alacea studied her friend critically. Hestean's eyes were cast downward, and she wouldn't meet the other vixen's gaze. The delicate fingers of her hands were folded in front of her, and her tail twitched nervously from side to side. <Your interviews with the commandos have been fruitful?> Alacea asked casually.

<Quite fruitful,> her friend replied.

<Was their captain able to help you narrow down the list so that you would know what to ask about?>

Hestean lost a step with this question, and Alacea knew why.

<I... have not yet interviewed their captain, Na'Sha,> Hestean confessed.

<If I am not mistaken, the captain is the *first* interview that should be conducted when commandos return from battle, is it not?> Alacea asked.

Hestean continued to look at her feet as she walked. <Yes, Na'Sha.>

Alacea saw her friend's ears fold down in sadness. <I am not so stupid as to be unaware as to *why* you would avoid such an interview,> she said. <That said, you are the Mikorin Aru'Dace. Many thousands of years from now, future Aru'Dace will look to your writings for guidance from the past. A gap in this guidance may deny them the exact piece of wisdom they seek in a time of strife. You are *obligated* to perform your duties in providing that guidance as completely as possible.>

<You are correct, Na'Sha,> Hestean said sadly. <I am sorry. I placed my feelings before my duty.>

<Your feelings have a place in this situation,> Alacea told her. <One need not come before the other. Your feelings should fuel your duty.>

<I understand, Na'Sha,> Hestean replied. <I will seek out Azarin at his earliest convenience.>

<Good,> Alacea said. Her ears fluttered, and she took the other Mikorin's hands in her own, giving them a reassuring squeeze. <Then we shall speak no more of this.>

With the issue resolved, the two began to walk again, but Alacea paused when she saw her Tesho speaking to two soldiers near one of the new houses. Her violet-colored eyes lingered on the human as they walked. A lot had changed since their near-disastrous first meeting, and the fear and disgust she had felt back then no longer appeared when she looked at him. Without realizing it, her ears twitched the tiniest bit.

Hestean saw this and, perhaps out of revenge or just wanting to troll her friend, she spoke up.

<Have you decided whether or not to have the Facilitation?> she asked.

As usual when it came to discussing the more intimate aspects of her marriage with the alien overlord, Alacea's tail began to flail about nervously. Hestean's question wasn't exactly rude or out of the ordinary. Alacea, herself, had told her she was considering inviting her Tesho to a Facilitation.

While, to human eyes, the Mikorin presented themselves as a religious organization, the truth was somewhat more complex. Above and beyond their duties to the Gods and souls of the Va'Shen community in their charge, the Mikorin also served several vital roles in how the community functioned and the positive relationships between the Va'Shen themselves. Sho Nan, for instance, served as the head cook for the Mikorin, but also as the village's approving authority for food and water sources. If a new spring was discovered, it was her job to inspect it and ensure that the water was clean enough to drink. Other Mikorin had other such duties, some dealing with very intimate aspects of the villagers' lives.

<I would like to have a Facilitation,> Alacea admitted. <I think it would propel our relationship a great deal. It is just... I am a little embarrassed due to *whom* would conduct it.>

The comment confused the Mikorin historian. <Has Pavastea done something inappropriate to cause this embarrassment?> she asked.

<No...> Alacea replied. <But also yes.> At her friend's curling ears, she explained. <Just after we were wed, I came upon Pavastea saying very offensive things about my Tesho to Sho Nan. She said them out of concern and in my defense, but I still found it

inappropriate. So, in a bit of immature retaliation, I spun her an overexaggerated story about my Tesho's... um... mating practices. She then fled in embarrassment... possibly terror.>

Hestean's ears fluttered madly. Were she a human, she'd be doubled over in laughter. <And now you are afraid she may approach the Facilitation with the wrong ideas.>

<I am afraid so,> Alacea admitted.

It was now Hestean's turn to gently scold her friend. <I think if you explain to Pavastea why you found her words offensive and ask her to help you, she would be both honored and happy to do so.>

<Perhaps,> Alacea allowed.

<I also think a Facilitation would benefit you both,> Hestean continued. <Your interactions with each other are always so... formal. At some point the Overlord and the Na'Sha must move aside so that BanKipson and Alacea may meet one another.>

Alacea thought on her friend's words and found them wise. As political as their marriage was, the key to its endurance would be both of them finding happiness in it, and she believed it had the potential for it. She thought of how they had laid quietly together in his den and of the gift he had given her of the book with images from other worlds. The kindling was there, but their positions and doubts seemed to prevent a spark from ever igniting it.

<Why not ask him now?> Hestean suggested.

Alacea's ears touched the sky. <I don't know,> she said. <I think I should give the matter more thought.>

<More thought would only give you more reasons not to ask him,> Hestean told her. <There is a certain courage in ignorance.>

Alacea's tail swished from side to side as her friend looked at her with stern ears, and she realized she was trapped. She had just gotten done lecturing her friend on the need to push through her feelings to do what must be done. If she waffled now, it would undermine her whole argument.

<You will make a very good Na'Sha one day,> Alacea commented bitterly.

<I hope such a day never occurs,> Hestean said with an amused twitch of her ears. <For that would mean I have lost a very good friend. One, I would point out, who knows the value of my advice.>

Alacea finally decided to surrender and raised her head regally. <Very well. Please go on without me, and I will speak with him.>

<I shall wait here in case you need assistance,> Hestean pledged instead with twitching ears.

Alacea's own ears folded down irritably at her friend's insistence on staying, as if she expected Alacea to wait until she was out of sight and then run off.

<Very well,> Alacea said with a stiff turn. As Hestean watched with fluttering ears, her friend crossed the road to the house Ben was inspecting.

As if sensing her approach, the Ranger turned, and the corners of his lips turned upward in what Alacea had come recognize as happiness. He gave her an abbreviated bow, what he had come to refer to as a "casual bow" or "casbow."

<Blessed day, Myorin,> he greeted.

She bowed shortly to him in return. <And blessed day to you, Tesho. I thank you again for your people's help in building these shelters.>

<They are very ugly,> he told her. <But they will be warm, and they will be dry.>

<Then I am sure our new guests will be grateful for them,> she replied.

<That is book.>

She didn't react until she saw his smile widening, and her ears began to flutter at the joke. <Quite 'book,' I think,> she said.

Her Tesho's speech had become much better in the month since the commando's return. The fact that he could joke with her made her more confident in regards to what she was about to ask him.

<Tesho,> she began, <I would like to have a Facilitation with you.>

<Facilitation?> he sounded out the word slowly. <What is Facilitation?>

It took almost ten minutes for Alacea to explain the concept to Ben using the most simplistic language she could, but in the end the Ranger thought he had a decent grasp of it. A Facilitation was, if he was interpreting her speech correctly, a "guided courtship." He and Alacea would have dinner at the Mikorin shrine together with another Mikorin who would provide entertainment but also guide the conversation so that the two could learn more about each other in a much more relaxed atmosphere.

Ben looked down at his alien wife and saw the fur on her ears bristling. He had recently come to learn that it was a sign of nervousness or embarrassment, the Va'Shen equivalent of blushing. It made him imagine the fox woman blushing and found the idea incredibly cute and disarming.

When they had first met and were unwittingly married, he had been overly cautious around Alacea. He knew she wielded a great deal of power in the village, enough power to make the American soldiers' lives very dangerous and miserable. As time went on and they learned more about one another, those fears had evaporated, and the priestess no longer appeared to him as a dangerous public official who needed to be "handled," but as a very sweet and beautiful young woman. The kind of woman, he believed, his friend and official ex-wife, Jessie, would have tried to set him up with. It was with that thought in mind that he answered her.

<I agree,> he said.

Her ears twitched and popped upward at hearing the simple answer. She had been certain this would require a bit more explaining or cajoling. His quick acceptance made her happier than she thought she would be.

<Good,> she said. <That is good. I will make the arrangements.> She bowed and started back down the road. After a few meters, she turned back to him. <Tomorrow night?> she asked, realizing she hadn't given a time.

<That is good,> he said with a smile.

<Then tomorrow night,> she promised. She turned to leave but stopped again. <Sundown,> she specified, turning back to him again.

<That is good,> he said, holding back an amused chuckle.

<Good,> she replied. This time, she started down the road and didn't turn back again.

Ben grinned at the display. Normally, the strait-laced Alacea was always so composed and seemed to always know what to say. To see her stumbling over, what he believed to be, her asking him out on a date was downright precious.

It had been a month since the night she had laid down with him in his quarters and nervously slept next to him, and like the night they spent together in the wilderness following her kidnapping, it seemed like the occurrence had knocked down another barrier between them. Since then, his Va'Shen language lessons with her had seemed warmer, more comfortable and more enjoyable. He finally felt he was getting to know Alacea as a woman rather than a spiritual leader.

His smile touched his ears as he kicked the dirt at his feet and turned back to his inspection. Unbeknownst to him, one particular Va'Shen woodworker was looking down at him from the roof of the house he was working on, his single eye tracking him like a predator studying a meal... or a threat.

Chapter 2

Two months until contact…

Ben had just walked into his office and removed his patrol cap when Lieutenant Patricia Kim stood up at her desk. The simple plywood and polymer shack would not have looked out of place on any other forward operating base on any other planet aside from the lack of computers and technologically advanced equipment made useless by Va'Sh's strange electromagnetic interference.

The "Fuzz," as it was called, was unlike any kind of electromagnetic phenomenon any human had ever seen. It seemed to obey no strict rules in regard to its behavior. One piece of equipment would work while another, similar piece wouldn't. It was as capricious as it was frustrating, forcing the humans occupying the planet to operate at a technological level more befitting the mid twentieth century.

"Welcome back, Sir," Patricia greeted. "Everything good at the refugee settlement?"

"Better than expected," he said as he prepared to sit down.

Before he could, the Korean-American interpreter cleared her throat and pointed behind him. Turning, Ben saw an older tod with coffee-brown hair standing in the corner. He wore a tan monpei and a short beard, and the captain had no idea if he had ever actually met the alien man or not.

"This is Notaro," Patricia said. "He arrived about an hour ago and asked to speak to the Overlord."

"Oh yeah?" Ben asked as he took stock of the man. "He say what about?"

"No, Sir. He wanted to wait for you to return."

"Gotcha." He bowed to the Va'Shen man, who bowed low in return. <I am Ban Kipson,> he said in introduction. <What can I do to attain your trust?>

<I am Notaro, son of Hutarin, brother of Motaro and uncle to Alzoria, daughter of Motaro.>

<You are family to Alzoria?> Ben asked. When the tod's ears folded in the affirmative, Ben smiled. <Alzoria is good vixen.>

<Yes... She is,> Notaro replied hesitantly. He straightened his shoulders and looked Ben straight on. <I have come to offer Alzoria to you.>

The phrasing struck Ben as odd, and he turned to Patricia.

"Uh, yeah, he said 'offer' in a way that denotes marriage," Patricia told him.

Ben turned back to the man. <Um... I am wed to Na'Sha,> he informed the tod.

<I am aware,> Notaro said, and, again, something about the man's speech gave Ben a weird vibe. <As you are wed, I offer her to you to unite with one of your corporals.>

<One of my corporals?> Ben repeated. He knew the word "corporal" wasn't meant literally. In the Va'Shen commando rank structure, the term was used to denote just about every noncommissioned officer rank.

<Yes,> Notaro confirmed.

Ben paused, realizing he was standing in the middle of a minefield. <You wait little?> he asked. <I must speak at my captain.>

Notaro bowed. <As you wish, Overlord.>

The Ranger gave Patricia a nod of his head, and the two moved to a corner of the office to convene. Although he was pretty sure the tod couldn't speak English, they spoke in hushed tones regardless.

"Okay, what's this about?" he asked.

"It looks like he's offering up his niece to marry one of our troops," she said. "It's actually pretty common in some cultures back on Earth. Probably the same here."

Ben arched an eyebrow. "I bet you just want to tear into this guy," he noted. Patricia had had some issues with the Va'Shen views on gender roles in the past, issues that had sometimes conflicted with Va'Shen traditions that she found somewhat backward and demeaning. He imagined that this new development made her want to hoist the feminist flag and start slitting throats.

Her response, however, stunned him.

"Actually, I don't think this is his idea."

"What do you mean?" he asked.

"Look at him," she whispered, nodding subtly in Notaro's direction. "The tail. The ears. He *hates* this."

Looking at the Va'Shen man carefully, Ben could see the telltale cues of discontent, which only raised even more questions. "So... Why?"

Patricia grinned at him. "I think Alzoria put him up to it," she said. "She's making her move on Staff Sergeant Ramirez and probably thinks this is the most surefire way to go around having to wait for him to make the first move."

"She gets her uncle to offer her to us, and I *order* Ramirez to marry her, is that it?" Ben asked.

"From a Va'Shen standpoint, it's not a bad plan," she said. "After all, it's pretty common knowledge that we participate in political marriages."

"But we don't," he corrected her.

"Tell that to Alacea," she said with a smile.

"Ah," he said, his lips forming a thin line. "So, what do I do?" he asked.

"Something tells me you turning down the offer isn't going to hurt this guy's feelings as long as you do it in a way that's respectful to his niece," Patricia advised.

Ben thought for a moment and then nodded. "Okay. I'm going in. Cover me."

The two returned to the waiting Va'Shen man, and Ben began by bowing to him.

<I thank you,> he said. He signaled to Patricia that he wanted her to take over translation and continued in English. "I am honored that you would ask us to join your family," he continued, pausing long enough for Patricia to translate. "But I am forbidden from ordering someone to marry." Another pause. "Should Alzoria and one of my corporals wish to marry, we would all support their union and be happy." Pause. "But until that time, I cannot interfere." He ended the statement by bowing again. "I ask for your understanding."

Hearing this, Notaro visibly relaxed. It was like watching a tightened spring uncoil. He bowed to Ben.

<The Overlord is wise, and I thank you for your kind words.>

The tod's relief was obvious, and Ben wondered what Alzoria did to make her uncle agree to this in the first place. It would, however, be rude to ask, so he let it go.

With his business seemingly concluded, Notaro bowed to both of them and left without another word. Once he was gone, Patricia smirked and leaned against her desk.

"So," she began, "Do we warn Ramirez?" She still remembered the first conversation she had ever had with the Ranger NCO and how he wanted to be the first man to get a vixen for a girlfriend.

Ben looked at her. "We probably should," he said. "Then again... that wouldn't be very funny, now, would it?"

Patricia walked around her desk and sat down again.

"He's in so much trouble."

* * *

It was a combination of factors that had prevented this event from happening for the last month or so. First, there were the celebrations that ate up the first week. Finding the families of fallen comrades and telling them how their son, brother or father had died had taken time as well. And the immediacy of the arrival of the refugees from the north meant everyone who could help build the new shelters was called upon to assist. And by that time, the weather had become poor.

But it was now time, and the Huntresses were very excited to be going on their first hunt with their brothers and fathers in the Hunters guild since they left for the war three years ago.

There were perhaps 40 of them altogether, preparing to hop into the wagons that waited outside the lodge that would take them to the hunting grounds. The sun was just beginning to rise over the forested hills to what was looking to be a beautiful day.

Bao Sen, the leader of the Huntresses, looked at the collection of tods and vixens with bows and spears, and her ears wiggled a smile. Turning her head, she addressed the tod standing next to her. <I have dreamed of this day for three years,> she told him.

The tod, Dan Huun, touched the back of his head reflexively, trying to feel the hair that was no longer there. With the deep red that ran in his family, the long hair he had grown out during his time as a prisoner of war had made him look like a vixen from a distance. Cutting it was one of the first things he had done upon his return. But like a phantom limb, he could sometimes still feel it back there.

<I never thought I would hold a bow in my hands again,> he told her. <I only wish that Father and our brothers could join us.>

Bao Sen's ears drooped at the reminder. Her father and five of her brothers... gone. She and Dan Huun were all that remained of their family. She had asked Dan Huun about the particulars, how her father and brothers had died, but he hadn't wanted to talk about it, claiming it would be difficult for a vixen to understand what battle was like. She had almost thrown her own experience against the Windsabers into his face in anger, but she could see in his ears and tail that what he said wasn't the true reason.

It pained him.

It pained him visibly, and if he did not want to relive it by telling her about it, she did not want to hurt him by forcing him to.

<We will have to tell them about this day when we arrive in the Glade,> Bao Sen told him supportively.

She worried for him. What he needed was a myorin to support him, but he didn't seem interested in pursuing any of the farmers' daughters who have been eyeing him recently. Perhaps she would subtly push one of her Huntresses in his direction...

As she was pondering which of her Huntresses would make the best myorin for her brother, Alzoria approached them, her bow slung over her shoulder.

<The wagons are ready, Bao Sen,> She said. <John should also be here soon.>

<Thank you, Alzoria,> Bao Sen said. <We will leave when he arrives.>

Dan Huun looked at her in puzzlement. <Ja-on?> he asked. <Who is Ja-on?>

"Sorry I'm late!"

<To speak of a demon is to wish for his presence,> Bao Sen remarked as she turned to the man walking up to them from the road.

As he passed a group of Huntresses milling around one of the wagons, he gave them a quick bow. <Grand morning hunting, gentlevixens!>

"Hola, Rah-mee-raz!" the vixens called back as one, their ears twitching.

Seeing the display, Alzoria's ears flattened, but she said nothing.

Hers weren't the only ears digging against their skull. Dan Huun looked at the human in surprised anger, wondering if he was dreaming.

<What is that and why is it here?> he demanded.

Bao Sen looked at her brother and suddenly felt extremely stupid. How could she not have anticipated this?

She cleared her throat as Ramirez approached, a scoped, bolt-action rifle slung over his shoulder and a floppy boonie hat threatening to cover his eyes.

<Brother, this is Rahmeeraz,> she said. <He is a friend to the Huntresses.>

Ramirez saw Dan Huun's red hair and made the connection immediately. <You brother to Bao Sen?> He held out his hand. <My name is Ramirez. Good hello to you.>

Dan Huun ignored the Dark One and looked at his sister. <Did you invite this thing to hunt with us?> he asked.

It is important to note one of the differences in the Va'Shen language here as compared to English. In English a "thing" could be anything that is not alive. In Va'Shen, however, there were different tiers of "thing," each tier with a different form of the Va'Shen word for "thing." The differences between the words were subtle, and human ears could only barely catch them when they were listening for them. As such, Ramirez, who had only a basic and tenuous grasp of the language, was unaware of the form Dan Huun had used.

That form was used for "things" that were disgusting, such as sewage.

<That was very rude!> Alzoria cried at the Hunter.

Bao Sen, understanding quite well that this situation was her fault, raised a hand to bid Alzoria to calm down and faced her brother.

<Rahmeeraz protected Alzoria during a dangerous time,> she told him. <And so we allow him to hunt with us. I apologize. I should have considered this before inviting him.>

<Consider what?> Alzoria argued. <What's wrong with inviting John? He always hunts with us!>

Ramirez looked from one Va'Shen to the next, very much aware of the sub-zero vibes he was getting from the former commando. A quick look at some of the other male Hunters, almost all of them former commandos, waiting near the wagons and the glares they were giving him, made the issue painfully obvious. "Oh..." He said with a nod. "I get it."

<You go hunting with one of the very Dark Ones who might have ended Father or our brothers' lives?> Dan Huun hissed to his sister in amazement. <Are you serious?>

Bao Sen looked at the ground, chastened. Her ears drooped in embarrassment. A lot of things had happened in Pelle before her brother's return. How was she supposed to explain it all to him in a way that *didn't* sound like she had betrayed her family?

<John didn't kill your father or brothers!> Alzoria shot at Dan Huun. <You know nothing about him!>

<How do you know that?> Dan Huun snapped back.

That question shut Alzoria's mouth. She honestly *couldn't* say that Ramirez hadn't killed Bao Sen's family. All she could say was that the odds of it were very low.

<I beg consideration for interruption,> Ramirez said, breaking into the squabble. The three angry Va'Shen looked at him, and he chucked a thumb over his shoulder. <I go. You hunt.>

<You don't have to leave!> Alzoria replied.

<Yes, it does,> Dan Huun growled.

The younger Huntress turned heated eyes toward Bao Sen. <Bao Sen! You named him a friend of the Huntresses! This is not how friends are treated!>

The red-haired Huntress said nothing in reply. No matter what happened here, she was going to feel ashamed.

<Alzoria, it good,> Ramirez said, putting himself between his friend and the siblings. <Family thing. Should be fun. I stay. Make bad. I go.>

<John,> Alzoria said quietly. <You don't have to go.>

Ramirez chucked his thumb over his shoulder again and took a step back the way he came. <I go. Talk later.> He smiled at the group and gave a quick bow as he started back up the road.

<Come,> Dan Huun said, hefting his bow and starting for the wagons. <Let us go.>

Alzoria's gaze turned toward Bao Sen, her ears pointed straight at the other Huntress, but she didn't say anything. She started walking toward a separate wagon, leaving Bao Sen alone.

* * *

"CEASE FIRE! CEASE FIRE!"

The sound of the order coming over the bullhorn prompted the Rangers on the target range's firing line to lower their weapons and begin clearing them for safety. Walking up and down the line, Burgers looked at each weapon through his mirrored sunglasses, sometimes kneeling next to a firing position to doublecheck that everyone's chamber was clear. Once he was satisfied, he raised the bullhorn again.

"RANGE IS CLEAR. CHECK YOUR TARGETS."

The shooters started down the line to look at the paper targets tacked up on wooden frames. The targets were the typical black and white human silhouettes used for centuries, though one smart-ass Ranger had drawn in fox ears on the head of his with black marker.

While the shooters were checking their targets, Burgers turned and did a double-take as he saw Ramirez approaching the off-base live-fire range the SeaBees had constructed for them.

"The hell you doing here?" Burgers asked. "Thought you were going hunting?"

"Eh, it was a family thing," Ramirez told him good-naturedly. "Felt like I was intruding."

"Uh huh," Burgers replied knowingly. "Let me guess: some of those Huntresses' older brothers didn't like the look of you hanging around."

"In fairness," Ramirez said, "I do look like trouble."

"I've said that for years," Burgers agreed. He raised the bullhorn to his lips again. "OKAY, FOLKS. THAT'S LUNCH. BE BACK AT THIRTEEN HUNDRED."

"Wanna get lunch?" Ramirez asked.

"Sure thing."

The two started down the road at the back of the gaggle of troops heading back to the FOB.

"Are you pissed?" Burgers asked him seriously.

"What? Naw!" Ramirez replied. "Don't get me wrong, the conversation wasn't pleasant, and I'm pretty sure there were some ethnic slurs thrown in there, but man, you should've seen Alzoria go off on them. I don't know that much Va'Shen, but I'm pretty sure at one point she told me to hold her weave."

"So, what is *the deal* with you and Alzoria, anyway?" Burgers asked.

"What do you mean?"

"You know what I mean!" his friend snapped. "Does the carpet match the ears?"

"Aw, dude, it ain't like that," Ramirez said casually. "Alzoria's great, but she's a little young, you know?"

"Don't tell me you're still after the redhead," Burgers said.

"Bao Sen?" Ramirez asked. "Naw, man. I'm pretty sure she just wants me for my security clearance if you catch my meaning."

"Track'n, track'n," Burgers said. "Alzoria seems to like you, though," he continued, getting back on the original track. "What's the age of consent on Va'Sh, anyway? Some of these girls getting married in the village look a lot younger than her."

"Don't get me wrong, she's great," Ramirez said.

"Great, huh?"

"Yeah. Great."

Burgers watched his friend in intense silence for several moments before stopping and removing his sunglasses. "Holy shit," he said quietly. "You're really into her, aren't you?"

"Whaaaaaaat?!" Ramirez replied. "Me? *You're* the one who's supposed to be into legal-jailbait anime characters, not me."

Burgers smiled, not willing to let his friend get off the hook. "So, you use that 'beautiful tail' line on her yet?"

"Dude, I'm telling you, you got it all wrong."

"The fuck I do," Burgers told him. "The last time you said a girl was 'great' and then got all quiet, we were talking about Mac..."

"Dude, more than one girl can be great. It doesn't mean anything."

Burgers grinned at him and put his shades back on. "Okay," he relented. "You hold onto your adorable little delusion."

"Thank you, I will," Ramirez replied before starting down the road again.

As they approached the main gate to the FOB, everyone dug out their ID cards and showed them to the bored-looking sentries. Since they were all human, they didn't exactly have to worry about infiltrators. Turning the corner and walking toward the DFAC, they stepped into the lunch line and waited for their turn to wash their hands.

Once they had picked up today's delicious Salisbury steak combo meal, Burgers spotted Fletcher at a table by herself, reading the latest command newsletter, and nudged Ramirez, indicating they should join her. The Navy medic didn't even bat an eye as the two Rangers sat down opposite her at the table.

Looking up from the paper, her eyes narrowed at Ramirez. "Thought you were hunting today."

"Yeah, me too," he replied simply. He stabbed at the spongy meat object while nodding at the paper in her hands. "Anything new?"

Fletcher sighed and turned the paper around. "They went ahead and did it," she told them.

Ramirez read the headline. "'Water slide construction starts at Jamieson,'" he read. "No fair. I want a water slide..."

"No, below the fold," Fletcher corrected.

He looked downward at the other headline. "'DoD begins RIF.'"

"There it is," Burgers grumbled.

Fletcher turned the paper around again and read from the article. "'The Department of Defense has begun its first round in the Reduction in Force process to right-size its troop numbers in order to provide the nation with a lighter, more agile and more lethal force.'"

"Translation," Burgers broke in. "'Thank you for your service. Now, go fuck yourselves.'"

It wasn't exactly a fair assessment. Congress determined the exact number of personnel each branch of the military was allowed to have. When the war broke out, many troops were "stop-lossed," a measure used to retain troops by preventing them from separating from the military whether they wanted to stay or not. That, combined with temporary increases in troop numbers, meant that now that the war was over, the military found itself with too many troops, and Congress wanted things back to normal.

Never mind that DoD was currently doing its regular day-to-day mission *and* trying to occupy an entire planet at the same time. Troops cost money. Paying, equipping, feeding, housing... that money had to come from somewhere.

But for the troops who wanted to stay in, particularly after fighting a brutal war for three years, to suddenly be dismissed after enduring so much was a kick in the teeth. One which made all the talk from generals and politicians about "a grateful nation" sound decidedly hollow.

"I still got a spot open at Burgers' Burgers for a guy who can flip burgers," Burgers told Ramirez.

"Just get a robot to do it," Ramirez said.

"One, that's sacrilege," Burgers told him. "You can't have a real hamburger made by computer. It's wrong. Two, robots are expensive, and *you* are cheap."

Ramirez's lips curled in thought. "I *am* pretty cheap…" he mused. "But, no, man. I'm staying. If they want me out, they're going to have to kick me out."

"What about you, Fletch?" Burgers asked. "You gonna try to stay?"

The corpsman shrugged. "Dunno yet. I figure I can at least wait until this deployment is over."

"Not necessarily," Ramirez said. He turned to Burgers. "Remember Animal Man?"

"'Animal Man?'" Fletcher asked.

"Animal Man was a friend of ours," Burgers told her. "A couple of years ago they merged two MOS's together; Animal Man's and something else. But he didn't have the qualifications for the other MOS."

Ramirez took over the story. "So, we're in this firefight on Epsilon, right?" he said. "Shooting and moving, shooting and moving… Suddenly, the tablet attached to Animal Man's M-31 gets a pop-up message *while the dude is shooting*, telling him he's been selected for mandatory separation. They literally kicked him out of the Army *while in combat*."

Fletcher looked at them in amazement. "Your branch isn't very good at tact, is it?"

"You can't spell 'tactical' without it," Burgers said. "And yet, behold, for we have none."

"Well, at least the Persephone survivors can take the deal," Fletcher said. "That's something."

The U.S. government had promised any military member from the doomed Persephone colony could separate early and receive the funding for a fresh start on the colony of their choice.

"Even so," Ramirez mused. "They would still be starting with almost nothing. All their stuff was back in the barracks at Fort Accetta. Some of them don't even have civilian clothes to change into."

"It'll work out," Fletcher assured them.

"Oh yeah?" Burgers replied.

"Yeah," Fletcher returned. "Come on, man," she continued. "You talk about how much you love the Army. Try having a little faith in it. *Someone* in command has to care. Don't be so ate up."

Burgers suppressed the urge to roll his eyes and concentrated on forcing the Salisbury steak down. When he was done, he stood up and grabbed his hat.

"Gotta go. Y'all have a good one," he said.

"You too," Fletcher replied.

Faith in the Army... he mused as he walked out the door. *Why does that sound so... wrong?*

Chapter 3

Two months until contact...

As was usual, it was the blue-haired Mikorin, Sho Nan, who opened the door. He had only knocked on the temple door a few seconds ago, exactly as Va'Sh's sun, Bellatrix, was beginning to disappear behind the western horizon.

The young vixen looked over Ben as if assessing his worth, her light blue hair cut shorter than other vixens, hanging down to no lower than her shoulders. Other Va'Shen, Mikorin included, tended to treat Ben with an overwhelming amount of respect, like if they said the wrong thing, he might kill them for it. But he and Sho Nan had bonded a little during their stay in the FOB clinic, and the Mikorin was much more likely to treat him like... well... just another guy. It was in this spirit that she spoke to him now.

<You have come to call on young Alacea, have you not?> she asked. She crossed her arms over her chest and looked down her nose at him, her bright blue tail swishing back and forth behind her.

Ben knew Sho Nan well enough by now to suspect some kind of trap. <Yes,> he said simply. <This is truth.>

<As we Mikorin have no mothers or fathers, we see each other as family,> she said. <As such, I have elected to take on the role of Alacea's father tonight.>

<Father?> he repeated stupidly.

<Yes,> she confirmed. <You are calling on her?> she asked again.

<Yes,> he said cautiously.

<I see,> she replied. <I will require a stout stick with which to thrash you. Please wait right here...>

<SHO NAN!>

She turned as Alacea appeared in the doorway behind her, out of breath as if she had just run the length of the temple.

<Na'Sha, you have a visitor,> she announced deadpan.

<Yes, Sho Nan, thank you! I am aware!> Alacea replied. She bowed quickly to Ben. <I apologize for her sense of humor, Tesho,> she said. <She means no harm.>

<It well,> Ben said with a smile as the two made room for him to enter. He turned to Sho Nan and bowed his head very slightly to her. <I would win,> he assured her good-naturedly.

<You would not,> Sho Nan replied.

<Thank you, Sho Nan!> Alacea interrupted. <I will escort the Overlord from here.>

<As you wish, Na'Sha,> the blue-haired woman said, before turning and gliding elegantly down the hall from which she had come.

<I am sorry, Tesho,> Alacea said again. <There are times when she lacks any decorum at all.>

For the first time, Ben took a good look at his alien wife. She was, as always, dressed properly in a hanbok, but this was one he hadn't seen before; deep blue with dark pink sleeves like the color of a sunset over an ocean. Her braided side ponytail fell down over her left shoulder.

Alacea saw him looking, and her ears fluttered. <Is something wrong?> she asked.

<No,> he replied. <Myorin looks well.> He silently kicked himself. He had forgotten any word that came close to "beautiful."

<I am indeed well,> she said. She gestured down the hall. <The Facilitation is this way.>

She led the way, and Ben dutifully followed. There were other Mikorin moving about, their dinner time just having ended, and each bowed to them as they passed. Reaching a door situated at the far corner of the temple, Alacea paused and turned to him.

<From this point onward, the roles, positions and ranks we hold are not acknowledged,> she told him. <We are simply Alacea and

BanKipson, 'tesho' and 'myorin.' Our Facilitator will speak to us as equals, with neither subservience nor authority. Do you understand?>

Ben worked through the translation in his head, and decided he caught enough of it to see where Alacea was going. No "Overlord" or "Na'Sha" here. Just two people having dinner.

<I understand,> he told her.

With that, Alacea opened the door and gestured for Ben to precede her. As he stepped inside, he recognized a young vixen with pink half-up twin-tails the color of strawberry ice cream in a white and brown hanbok.

Ben smiled and bowed to the young alien girl. <Blessed evening, Pavastea,> he said. <You are well?>

Pavastea's ears fluttered as she bowed in return. <Blessed evening, BanKipson,> she said. <I am honored to be your Facilitator tonight and hope the evening is enjoyed by one and all.>

<Pavastea is Fashimilader?> Ben asked.

<Facilitator,> Pavastea corrected. <I will provide entertainment and make certain all that needs to be said is said and said well.>

<Yes, good,> Ben said, reasonably sure he had gotten all of that.

Pavastea bowed to Alacea next. <Alacea, thank you for honoring me with your trust.>

Alacea bowed in return. <I am honored by your presence here, Pavastea.> Truthfully, Alacea had been concerned about including Pavastea in this. While it might seem odd to outsiders to see such a young vixen perform such a role, it was actually more odd to have a Facilitation for a couple as old as Ben and Alacea. Facilitations were most likely to be requested by young married couples who had married before learning everything there was to know about their significant other. As such, the couples preferred to be with a Mikorin closer to their own age.

<Let us sit,> Pavastea invited, taking a seat on a cushion on one side of a low table, leaving the two pillows on the other side for Ben and Alacea.

Taking up a crystal decanter with a blue liquid inside, Pavastea poured three small cups and offered them to the couple.

Alacea sniffed at hers, taking in the fruity fragrance of the drink. Ben, however, looked at the glass almost suspiciously.

<What is?> he asked.

Alacea took a sip before answering. <It is *mura*,> she told him. <It relaxes the drinker.>

Va'Shen alcohol? Ben thought as he examined it. He took a sniff. It didn't smell like any alcohol he had ever had. And while he had never been a heavy drinker, Jessie had introduced him to so many different cocktails and drinks during their time together, he could consider himself an expert.

Still, he didn't want to get wasted.

<Is it strong?> he asked the two vixens.

Pavastea's ears fluttered. <Oh, no!> she said. <This is a very gentle beverage.>

<Even Va'Shen children are allowed to partake of it on special occasions,> Alacea said. <There are more powerful drinks, but we would have to have someone go and fetch some as we don't have any here at the temple.>

<No. Is good,> he said. He took a cautious sip, and his eyebrows arched upward. <Is very good!> he said. It was sweet, but not overpoweringly so. It kind of reminded him of raspberries, and there was none of the burning from a strong drink. He figured the alcohol content was probably very low.

Well, that's too bad, he thought. *It might be fun to see Alacea drunk.*

He took a longer drink, finishing what was left, and before the glass left his lips, the door opened, and Sho Nan appeared, carrying a tray with several Va'Shen dishes balanced upon it.

Ben had expected Sho Nan to make some joke or crack, but there must have been some rule against it because she remained silent as she gracefully placed each dish in front of them.

"This looks great." Ben said in English as he looked at the spread in front of him. At the two vixens' questioning looks, he dropped back into Va'Shen. <Appears wonderous,> he said.

<Here, Tesho,> Alacea said, holding a bowl out to him. <Try this. It is like the meat you gave me at your dining hall, but different.>

Ben took the bowl and stabbed at the small shreds of meat with the two-prong fork that had been provided. He took a bite and nodded in appreciation of the taste. It had a smoky flavor to it. He washed it down with another drink of *mura*.

<BanKipson, I have not had the chance to speak with one of your people like this before,> Pavastea said. <I have so many questions.>

<I have questions also,> Ben said. <What is that?> he said a second later, pointing at the stringed wooden instrument resting against the wall behind Pavastea.

<That is my *domshir*,> she said. <I will play it if you like!>

"I... would... LOVE THAT!" Ben replied eagerly. <Apologize,> he said. <I say yes, to yes very good.>

<Wonderful!> Pavastea said, turning and picking up the instrument. <Please, the two of you enjoy your meal, and I will play for you.>

Pavastea closed her eyes and began to play. Ben had expected something like a banjo, but the notes played were much softer and more subdued.

<Pavastea is a very talented player,> Alacea told Ben. <I envy her abilities.> "Talented" was something of an understatement. For her age, Pavastea would have been considered a savant on Earth. The priestess took a sip of her drink and watched as her Tesho finished his own.

She picked up the decanter and refilled it for him.

<Thanks be to you,> he said in appreciation. He put a piece of some red, pickled vegetable in his mouth and chewed. <Good,> he said. He picked up another piece with his fork and held it up to Alacea. <You try? Is good?>

<Oh! Um...> Alacea wasn't sure what to do here. He wasn't handing her the fork, so she leaned forward and took a bite. Her ears fluttered. <Yes, it is quite good.>

<Right?> Ben asked in what sounded like amazement.

They continued to eat, and as the end of the meal approached, Pavastea put her *domshir* down and addressed them.

<Tell me, Alacea, what do you and your tesho do when your schedules let you have time together?>

<Oh!> Alacea replied, her hand going to her mouth in thought. <I have been teaching Tesho more of our language. Um... we've been discussing the coming refugees...>

<Myorin rubs my chest,> Ben broke in suddenly.

Alacea froze. <Wh...Wh...What?!>

<That is sweet,> Pavastea told him. <Is that how your people show affection?>

Ben took another slug of *mura*. <No. I have wound on my own chest. Myorin put good stuff on it.>

<Oh! I see!> Pavastea said, hiding her mouth behind her palm. She eyed Alacea meaningfully.

<He was hurt and refused to see a healer!> Alacea countered indignantly.

<Then we slept as one,> Ben added nonchalantly.

Alacea's tail puffed out in shock. <Why would you tell her such a thing!?>

Ben gave the question some honest thought. <I do not know,> he finally replied.

<But it's so sweet!> Pavastea gushed to Alacea. <I was often concerned that your marriage may not be loving, but it seems I was wrong!>

Ben poured himself another *mura*.

<Tell me, BanKipson, what was the first thing you thought when you first saw Alacea? Did you think of her beauty?>

<Pavastea,> Alacea said in embarrassment, but with no heat.

Ben thought for a moment before replying.

<I think... 'She has sticks in the hair.'>

Alacea blanched.

<Sticks?> Pavastea asked in confusion.

The head priestess heard her question even as she was covering her ears in embarrassment. <I was quite disheveled when we met,> she explained.

<She yell at Kasshas,> Ben continued. <I like that.>

<Um, Alacea,> Pavastea said quietly, <BanKipson seems somewhat... different than normal.>

<I've noticed that too,> Alacea said. <He can't be intoxicated, though. It would take a dozen glasses of *mura* to become inebriated.>

Pavastea clapped her hands together. <Even so, I like him this way!>

<Pavastea!>

<Come now, Alacea,> Pavastea whispered to her. <Now is your chance to learn sensitive information.>

Alacea's ears pointed down. <If you mean information about his people's def...>

<BanKipson, I was wondering, is Alacea beautiful to your people's eyes?>

<PAVASTEA!>

"That's the word!" Ben cried, pointing at Pavastea. "Thank you! That was going to bother me all night!" He cleared his throat. <Alacea is much beautiful.>

The fur on Alacea's ears stiffened, and she covered them with her hands again. <T...Tesho...>

<But why?> Pavastea asked. She continued a moment later. <I mean, your people don't have ears or tails.> Her own pink tail waved behind her as she said this. <What does a tod of your people look at on a vixen?>

"Oh!" Ben said, readjusting his seat. "That's easy!" He held his hands out about six inches from his chest. <Tods look for chest things!>

<Chest things?> Pavastea asked. <Does he mean a vixen's breasts? What a weird thing to look at...>

Alacea placed her hands at roughly the same distance from her chest and looked down, seeing a rather unappealing gap between her breasts and her hands. She sniffed in indignation and looked away.

<Also!> Ben continued, turning in his seat and pointing at his rear. <We look to tail!>

<But you have no tail,> Pavastea pointed out.

<No, no,> Ben said. <Not tail-tail. Back portion.> He slapped his own butt in emphasis.

<The buttocks?> Pavastea asked. <That's crazy!>

Alacea looked behind her at her tail. She wasn't so naïve as to not realize it was slightly longer and fluffier than many other vixens' tails, but it also obscured what lay under it.

<And also, there are legs,> Ben told them.

At this, the high priestess perked up, and her tail waved back and forth in interest. Thanks to years of dancing, her legs were quite strong and probably the most attractive asset on her Tesho's list.

<Your people are very strange, BanKipson,> Pavastea told him.

<Yes,> he agreed. <We are strange.> He held his *mura* up as if toasting this and took another drink.

Without missing a beat, the pink-haired vixen turned to her other target. <Alacea, what about you? What do you find attractive in a tod?>

The priestess's ears pointed at the roof. <Me?>

<There must be something about your tesho you find attractive.>

<Oh... Well... Um...> Alacea hesitated. She looked at Ben and then down at the floor. <He is kind.>

Pavastea's ears fluttered at the answer. <Kindness is important.>

<Myorin is kind,> Ben agreed as he poured himself another *mura*. Alacea's fur stiffened at the praise.

<BanKipson, were you always a commando?> Pavastea asked him.

<I was a... um...> He struggled to answer, more to a lack of vocabulary than the *mura*. <One who learns things.>

<A student?>

<Student,> Ben repeated. <I was student of... um... things that happen before.>

Pavastea's ears pointed upward. <History? You were learning history? Just like Hestean?>

<Yes. Learn history. Learn fighting. When learning done, become commando. Now commando.>

Alacea looked down at her lap. It was starting to seem that, in her Tesho's eyes, she was not as attractive a myorin as she first believed. To alien eyes, she was not as physically attractive as she thought she was to her people and when it came to common interests, it now looked as if he would have much more to talk about with Hestean than her.

Pavastea saw Alacea's reaction out of the corner of her eye. <BanKipson,> she began, <Have you ever seen Alacea dance?>

The question made Alacea's tail twitch.

Ben looked up at her. <No,> he replied. <I know she was dancing. Not see her.>

<Would you like to?>

<Pavastea!>

<Yes, I would like!> Ben told her.

<She is quite good,> Pavastea went on, ignoring the pleading looks from her boss.

<I want see,> Ben said before downing another *mura*.

<Um...> Alacea pressed her index fingers together nervously. <It has been quite some time since I danced for an audience...>

Pavastea held something out to her, and Alacea looked down at them. A pair of folded fans were in the small vixen's hands. Pavastea's ears fluttered, proud of having thought to bring them.

<Very well,> Alacea said in defeat, taking the fans and rising to her feet. She moved off away from the table and faced them as Pavastea picked up her *domshir* again. <Pavastea...>

<I shall play something appropriate,> the younger Mikorin told her, and before Alacea could object, she began to play a song.

Almost automatically and from instinct, Alacea began to move her body to match the notes Pavstea played. For the Va'Shen, the dancing of an Alva'Rem was not for entertainment purposes, but to remember and honor the Gods. So, each piece of music matched to a specific dance for a specific reason. Alacea knew each dance by heart. She could still, even after three years as Na'Sha, perform them in her sleep. Even now, with no forewarning or preparation, she performed the dance that matched Pavastea's song instantly and flawlessly.

The fans in her fingers snapped open as she turned and raised her arms over her head. The song's tempo increased, and Alacea began to lose herself in the movements. For her, dancing was more than an art form, it was a religious experience.

But as she moved this time, she realized she was now dancing for a specific person. She had only done so once before, when she had danced with other Alva'Rem for the Emperor. She could not stop the dance or divide her attention to look at Ben's face, to see if his eyes approved or disapproved of her performance, and she was suddenly nervous about which it was. She found, now more than she ever had before, that she wanted to perform perfectly.

It was in these thoughts that she finally, consciously, realized what Pavastea had done. The song she had chosen to play was one matched to a dance from early Va'Shen mythology. One of the twin Goddesses of the Moons, Nareana, wed the War God Odorin. Nareana performed this dance for him on the night of their wedding to entice him before marking him.

Another dancer may have missed a step from that revelation, but not Alacea. While it made her self-conscious, it also gave her performance an added significance, and she did not want to ruin it with self-doubt. As the tempo increased again, she whirled around, the hem of her hanbok rising just the smallest bit to reveal her ankles.

The song ended with Alacea dropping to her knees with her head bowed and her hands outstretched, offering the now-closed fans to Ben.

Ben looked at her, his eyes wide.

"Woooooow..." he breathed. "That was awesome..."

And then he passed out.

* * *

Most of the Mikorin were asleep in their rooms already, so Alacea did not have to worry about any of them seeing her Tesho being carried down the hall by three vixens.

As the smallest of them, Pavastea was selected to lead the group, checking each hallway they passed for prying eyes, while Alacea and Sho Nan each took one of Ben's arms over their shoulders and hauled him bodily through the temple.

Having passed out, the Dark One appeared to be sleeping peacefully, blissfully unaware he was now being hauled about like a large sack of vegetables.

Pavastea reached another intersection and checked both ways before turning and leading them down the hall that led to the right. Alacea and Sho Nan stopped at the intersection, and the high priestess called to her.

<That is the wrong way,> she called softly.

<Your den is this way,> Pavastea told her.

Alacea froze. They hadn't really discussed where they were going to take her Tesho, and she just automatically assumed they would take him out of the temple and somehow haul him all the way to his base. Pavastea's idea, however embarrassing and panic-inducing it might be for Alacea, certainly made much more sense.

<R... Right,> she said, and the two started hauling the sleeping Ranger after the singer.

<Na'Sha, if you prefer, I can have him rolled up into a carpet and have the acolytes dump him outside his camp,> Sho Nan suggested.

<No, that won't do,> Alacea replied seriously. <We must safeguard his dignity. No one will think ill of him spending the night in our den. It is simply... uncomfortable... for me.>

<I see,> Sho Nan replied. <His den is much more comfortable for mating...>

<Sho Nan!> Alacea hissed as her tail began to thrash about.

<Forgive me, Na'Sha,> Sho Nan apologized. <I was thrown off by being called to haul an inebriated alien overlord out of our temple.>

<You make it sound so... *indecent...*> Alacea bit out. <He shouldn't be inebriated at all! He didn't have that much *mura*!>

By benefit of her position, the thought occurred to Sho Nan before anyone else. <Did you check to see how his people react to *mura*?> she asked.

Alacea's ears pointed skyward at the question. <React?> she asked. <Well... No... It's just *mura*.>

<Hmmm,> Sho Nan replied as they continued dragging/carrying the unconscious human forward. <It is possible that their bodies do not react well to it.>

<Do you think he is sick?> Alacea asked worriedly.

<Probably not,> Sho Nan said. <Having seen the other things these people put into their mouths, I doubt a little *mura* will do much. All the same, you should keep an eye on him for awhile in case anything odd happens.>

<Like what?>

<Like dying.>

<WHAT?!>

<Na'Sha! Sheeeeeee!> Pavastea hissed back at her. <You will wake the others.>

<Among other, less severe, things,> Sho Nan amended.

Alacea felt like whapping her friend with the very fans she had been dancing with earlier. But as she couldn't, she said nothing.

The three brought Ben into Alacea's room and, as gently as they could, lowered him to the futon-like cushion the Va'Shen used as bedding. The unconscious man rolled onto his back and continued to slumber.

<Enjoy the rest of your night, Na'Sha,> Sho Nan said as she turned to leave.

Pavastea bowed to her. <If it means anything at all, I think tonight went quite well. I think you both are fumbling toward each other in a dark room, but you will eventually find each other.>

Alacea's ears fluttered even as she sighed. <Thank you, Pavstea.>

As the other two Mikorin left the room, Alacea looked down at her sleeping Tesho and sighed. To the night's credit, they had managed to say and do things they would not normally have done, and wasn't that the purpose of the Facilitation?

<I imagine you will be quite confused when you wake up tomorrow,> she whispered.

She stiffened a moment when she realized he was sleeping in *her* den, leaving her the option of sleeping on the floor... or sleeping next to him.

The priestess quashed the embarrassment down. It would not be the first time nor was it in any way inappropriate. Also, it wasn't like he was in any condition to mark her anyway.

She removed her clothes and quietly lay down next to him on her side and facing him.

I suppose it is at least a step in the right direction, she thought.

Her ears fluttered once, and she closed her eyes, settling in to sleep.

Ten minutes later she would leap across her room in fright and run out the door in a panic.

Five minutes after that, the entire temple would be awake and terrified.

Chapter 4

Two months until contact…

At first, she thought she had dreamt it, but when the knock came a second time, Patricia knew something bad just happened. Clicking on the light in her hooch, she rolled out of her bed and went to the door. When she opened it, she found a fully geared up specialist standing there.

"Sorry to wake you, Ma'am," the soldier said. "Specialist MacGregor from ECP One. There's a Va'Shen woman at the gate asking for you."

"What time is it?" Patricia sleepily asked.

"2310, Ma'am," the sentry reported.

"I don't suppose you have any idea what it might be about?" she asked.

"No, Ma'am," MacGregor told her. "But she sounds scared shitless."

"Did you wake the captain yet?" she asked with a little more urgency.

"No, Ma'am. He signed out around sundown and hasn't signed back in yet."

A million different terrible scenarios ran through the lieutenant's mind in that instant.

"I'll be there in a minute," she said. "Let me get dressed first."

"Yes, Ma'am." With that, the sentry started back for the gate.

Patricia dressed quickly and strapped her weapon belt around her waist before dashing out the door, letting it hit the frame on the way out. Trotting to the entry control point, she immediately saw a young, green-haired vixen in a simple monpei waiting in the bright lights of the inspection point.

She walked up to the girl and gave her a short bow. <I am Patricia Kim. You ask for me?>

<Yes!> the girl responded frantically. <I am from the temple! The Na'Sha says you must bring your healer there immediately! The Overlord is very sick!>

Patricia turned to MacGregor. "Find Corpsman Fletcher! Tell her to grab her medical kit and meet me at the front office!"

"Yes, Ma'am!" replied and ran off.

<Go. Tell Na'Sha we arrival soon,> Patricia told the girl. The vixen ran off, and Patricia went to their office where the LTV was parked. She was warming up the engine when Fletcher came running up, in uniform and with her medical bag over her shoulder.

"That was fast," Patricia commented.

"We were in the chow hall assaulting Mt. Badass," Fletcher explained.

Patricia threw the LTV into gear. "I'm just going to pretend I know what that means."

"Any details?" Fletcher asked as the LTV took off for the gate. Expecting her, the sentries already had the sallyport gates open for them, and they rolled right off the FOB.

"Just that he's really sick, and the Mikorin are really freaked out by it," Patricia replied.

"Okay, well, I brought everything in my emergency pack," she assured her. "What was he doing at the temple, anyway?"

Patricia cleared her throat. She knew that Captain Gibson was there on, for lack of a better word, a date. He had to tell her in the event there was an emergency. And while his marriage to Alacea was now common knowledge on the FOB, until she knew more of what was going on, she decided to be vague.

"Key leader engagement," she fibbed.

"Quality time with the wife?" Fletcher guessed. When Patricia didn't answer, Fletcher smiled. "'Key leader engagement...' Never heard it called *that* before..."

They pulled up to the temple and found Sho Nan waiting for them at the entrance. The two human women rushed to the door, and the Mikorin led them immediately inside.

<We do not know what it is,> Sho Nan told them, dropping the usual humor. <At dinner, he drank a beverage we call '*mura.*' It is used to relax the drinker but does not inebriate them unless taken in extreme excess. And I have never known it to cause this... sound.>

It took a little back and forth before Patricia caught on to the Va'Shen word for "inebriated." Once she did, she explained to Fletcher.

"And he passed out?" the corpsman asked they turned a corner.

<Yes,> Sho Nan explained. <He appeared to be sleeping.>

As they approached a room at the end of the hall, there were several vixens gathered around the doorway in various states of dress, their tails whipping about in concern. Patricia could just make out a low growling sound rising and falling within.

<Is that the 'sound?'> Patricia asked.

<Yes,> Sho Nan replied as they reached the back of the crowd. <It woke the entire temple.>

<Lady Patricia!>

They looked up to find Alacea pushing her way through the crowd between them. The priestess was wearing a long teal-colored robe, and her tail was moving a mile a second. She grabbed Patricia's hand and began to pull her back toward her room.

<I did not know what it was, so I was afraid to wake him lest it worsen his condition!> she explained quickly.

They entered the room to find Ben laying on his back on a futon... snoring.

<What is happening to him?> Alacea asked the two women, her voice overflowing with worry. <I gave him *mura*. Did that do something to him?> she continued asking.

Patricia and Fletcher shared a look.

<Alacea,> Patricia began gently. <Is this noise the only wrong thing you of know?>

<Is it not enough?!> she asked.

<Peace, peace,> Patricia said, holding her hands up to try to calm the vixen. The other Mikorin were looking through the doorway, watching with rapt attention. <Need know all things.>

Alacea took a deep breath. <He passed out at dinner,> she explained. <He seemed inebriated. We carried him here and laid him down. Not long after, he began making this horrible snarling sound."

Fletcher grinned and tried to hold it back.

<Can you help him?> Alacea asked.

<Er... Yes,> Patricia told her. <No concern.> She gestured for Fletcher to do... something... and the medic knelt next to the captain. Reaching under his arm with one hand and grabbing his belt at the hip with the other, she pulled and rolled him over onto his side.

The snoring stopped.

"Ask them where I should send the bill," Fletcher joked as she stood up.

<That... That is all?> Alacea asked. <He sounded like he was...>

"Snoring," Patricia informed her.

<Su-no-ra?> Alacea sounded out.

<It happens sometime,> Patricia explained. <Sometime when drink lots.> When she was a child, her father would sometimes come home late after drinking soju with his coworkers and would spend the rest of the night snoring loud enough to wake the dead.

<I have never heard him do this before,> Alacea admitted.

Patricia smiled. *Just how often have you spent the night with him, anyway?*

<He is well,> Patricia assured her. <If does a second time, turn him again.>

The fur on Alacea's ears stiffened in embarrassment as she realized she had woken the temple and sent a plea for help over something that was so simple. She bowed to Patricia. <Forgive me. It seems I overreacted.>

<No forgive,> Patricia said gently. <Did not know.> Truthfully, the Va'Shen reaction was fascinating, and she was already trying to fit the new tidbit into what she knew of them. Perhaps the Va'Shen had evolved in a way that made them incapable of snoring because of the threat it presented. The Va'Shen were already so naturally stealthy, it seemed absurd that they would be so unnoticeable during the day only to wake the entire forest at night with snoring.

As Alacea spoke to the Mikorin and assured them everything was all right, Fletcher gave Ben another quick once over just to be sure. It looked like the Ranger captain was having the best night of sleep in his life, and that was all. She went back to Patricia and smiled.

"Okay," she began, "the question I have is, 'what do we tell him tomorrow?'"

Patricia's urge to tease her boss mercilessly warred with what she thought of as the right thing.

"Let's not say anything," she finally decided. "Everyone did the right thing here. Let's leave it at that."

Fletcher grinned. "You're no fun," she commented.

* * *

Ben entered his office whistling a tune he couldn't remember hearing before but liked all the same. As the door closed behind him and he jauntily tossed his patrol cap on his desk, Patricia looked up from her own desk and grinned.

"You look happy," she declared. "Sleep well?"

"Slept *great*," he replied, almost astonished by his own answer.

"Really?" Patricia asked, wondering how much of last night the captain actually remembered and what he would be willing to explain. "I saw in the log you didn't check back in at the gate last night."

"Yeah," Ben said with a smile. "I had drunk a little, so the Mikorin put me up for the night. I don't know if it's the futons or what, but that was the best night of sleep I've had in a long while."

Something about his behavior clicked in Patricia's mind. "You're not hungover," she noted.

"I guess I didn't drink enough," Ben said with a shrug before sitting down. "There's always next time."

Patricia knew there was no way that could be true. He had drunk so much Va'Shen alcohol he had passed out. Yet here he was, bright-eyed and (figuratively) bushy-tailed. Maybe she should try that *mura* stuff...

"Anything new in the dispatches?" Ben asked, getting down to business.

Patricia held out the stack of papers that came in with the last convoy to roll through. "Big thing is that the refugees are three days out," she reported. "They're bypassing Jamieson completely."

"Hmm," Ben replied as he took the documents and breezed through them. "I wonder why."

"Probably to keep from freaking out the villagers," Patricia guessed. "Helicopters, jets, heavy orbital transport launches... It's so loud they'd probably think the place was Hell."

"I suppose so," he relented. "I'll let Kasshas know. Let's arrange for one of our people to meet them a few hours out and guide them in."

"Good idea," Patricia agreed. "We should bring them into the village instead of the FOB. That worked pretty well last time."

"Okay, as soon as I hear from Kasshas where he wants them delivered, we'll send them out," Ben told her. "Anything else?"

"Just the usual stuff," Patricia said.

"What about this thing in the ECP One log you answered last night?" he asked as he was looking over the security logs from the previous night.

"Oh, that," Patricia said as nonchalantly as possible. "It wasn't a big thing. The Mikorin had a quick question about how we do things."

Ben nodded and, to Patricia's relief, let it go at that. "Okay. What's next?"

"Sir?"

They looked up and found an armored Ranger in the doorway. "There's a tod at the gate asking to see you. Should we let him in?"

"Second time in two days?" Ben asked Patricia. "Same guy, you think?"

The terp shrugged, and Ben gave the sentry a nod. "Send him down."

"Think he's offering to throw in a dowry this time?" Ben asked with a smile.

Patricia rolled her eyes. If it was Alzoria's uncle again, she had a feeling it would be harder to get rid of him this time. So, she was both relieved *and* surprised when a familiar silver-haired tod with an eyepatch over his right eye entered the office and bowed.

<Azarin is welcome,> Ben told the Va'Shen man as he returned the bow.

Patricia gave the tod a once-over. Since returning from his time as a prisoner of war and then a more ambiguous "detainee," he had cleaned up rather well. His hair was shorter and tied back in a pony-tail that went no further down than his shoulders. He had replaced the government-issued medical eyepatch with one made of dark leather. His white and tan monpei fit well, and it appeared he had slimmed down some since his captivity and added some more muscle. Patricia thought he looked like a samurai out of an old period drama. To be quite honest, she found him rather attractive and dashing.

<Brother,> Azarin began, utterly ignoring Patricia and focusing solely on Ben. <I need help building a house on my parents' land.>

Ben worked through the translation. By now he was a much better speaker, but he still thought twice before saying anything. Especially given what had happened the last time he had taken an initial translation as gospel.

<My people is working for new villager houses,> he told Azarin. <Cannot stop for them to help you. I am sorry.>

Azarin's tail twitched with a twinge of annoyance. <I did not come to ask you to send minions,> he told Ben. <I am asking my brother to help me build a house.>

"Oh," Ben replied in English as he worked it out. <You want me help?> he asked, pointing at his chest.

<Yes,> the tod told him simply.

"Um... well..."

"Why don't you?" Patricia suggested suddenly. "Do some male bonding. I got things here."

Ben cleared his throat and scratched his eyebrow as he turned to her and lowered his voice. "What if he's trying to get me alone so he can kill me?" he asked.

"Then... I guess... he's happy, and I get a promotion," Patricia replied.

Ben narrowed his eyes at her. "Fine," he said. "But you better avenge me."

"Just as soon as I'm done moving my stuff into your hooch," Patricia promised.

The captain ignored that last promise and turned back to Azarin. <I get tools. Be on other side of door.>

<Good,> Azarin told him. <I will wait for you there.>

"Have a good time!" Patricia called to him as he left.

* * *

Alzoria was on the hunt.

One of the first things a Huntress learns about hunting is that meat could not be taken without persistence. Meat will always be persistent in preserving its own life, and so a Huntress must be even more persistent in taking it. So, if one attempt or tactic fails, a Huntress cannot simply give up. If she does, she does not eat.

A smart Huntress finds a tactic that *will* work.

One such tactic was to seek the aid of other Huntresses and hunt as a pack.

And so it was as a pack that she and two of her sister Huntresses sat around a small table in the Huntress lodge on the edge of the village, planning their next move as the heads of previously killed trophies looked down at them as if they, themselves, were participating in the "war council."

Ketra and Mezina were both, like Alzoria, younger Huntresses and had both played a part in her rescue from the Windsabers. As they were young and had more experience working with the Dark Ones than some of the other, older Huntresses, they were both somewhat more accepting of Alzoria's intentions to snare one as her tesho. For them, Alzoria's excuse of there being so few males from which to choose was a reality, but neither of them wanted to be the first to attempt courting a Dark One. They wanted to see how Alzoria would fare first.

While it was true that there were villagers from Garan'Sel coming, there was no guarantee that those villagers were in any better shape than those of Pelle. If all their tods had been lost in the war, then that meant competition for mates would actually increase. While the social castes occupied by Huntresses and farmers were very close, the rung held by Huntresses was just a little higher, meaning if a Huntress was not beautiful enough or skilled enough to attract a tod from the higher castes, they would be forced to look downward if they wanted to marry. In rural villages it was *just barely* acceptable for Huntresses to do so, but it still sent a message that they were not worthy of a more affluent male.

And so, when Alzoria explained her intentions, the two Huntresses decided to assist her. For four thousand years, marrying and having children was considered a holy duty for vixens. So much so that if they could not do so with Va'Shen males, then perhaps marrying into Dark One families could satisfy the requirement.

<Your uncle's request was denied?> Mezina asked, her light green tail twitching behind her. Her long green hair, flecked with small black spots, was tied up in a pony-tail that bounced with every move of her head.

Alzoria's ears twitched an affirmative. <I suppose I cannot fault him for not pressing the case,> she said. <He was not exactly supportive when I asked him to help me.>

<It is good that you got his promise to help *before* you asked the favor itself,> Ketra pointed out. Although her teal hair was as long as Mezina's, she kept it in two tight braids that rested on her shoulders.

<I did feel guilty about it,> Alzoria confessed. Alzoria's father had been a Hunter and was killed by a *toka* a few years before the war. Per custom, Alzoria was permitted to request from her uncle an "act of familial love," something that could not be denied. She had used this custom to get her uncle to propose the marriage to the Overlord. He had been less than pleased by her request. However, now that he had done as she had asked, she could not ask him to do more.

<So, what now?> Mezina asked.

<At least we now know that the Overlord will not intercede in an engagement,> Alzoria told them. <That is one concern that no longer applies.>

<Perhaps you should appeal to Rahmeeraz in a more traditional way,> Ketra suggested. <Wear your hanbok, cook something he likes...>

Alzoria's ears folded downward. She had never considered herself a "traditional" vixen, and she couldn't remember the last time she had worn a hanbok. They were difficult to move in, and she much preferred the red, blue and purple shorts and shirt that concealed her from prey while letting her move quickly. In fact, one of the reasons she liked Ramirez so much was that he seemed to respect the way she lived and the things she liked to do.

Then again, that could be the reason he didn't seem to look at her as a vixen, but a "buddy."

<Ketra, Mezina, may I speak with Alzoria privately?>

The three looked up in shock to find Bao Sen standing in the lodge doorway. The chief Huntress was so stealthy that none of them had any idea she was there or for how long.

Ketra looked to Mezina, and she rose to her feet. <Of course, Bao Sen. We will go get something to eat.>

Bao Sen kept her eyes on Alzoria as the other two Huntresses left. Her long, bright red hair caught the light from the window, making the other Huntresses wonder how it was they had missed her approach.

It was only after the door slid shut that she stepped forward and sat down across from the younger vixen.

<So,> the redhead began. <You intend to go through with this.> It wasn't a question.

Alzoria's ears curved inward, and her tail slapped the floor defensively. <I do.>

<I ask you to reconsider,> Bao Sen requested gently.

<I refuse.>

<Of course you would,> the Huntress leader replied wearily. <Have you considered the difficulties you will face?> she asked. <You remember how my brother reacted? Do you think he will be the only one to react negatively? We have been blessed here in that

our experiences with the Dark Ones have not been as bad as others have experienced.>

<John and his people have not harmed us,> Alzoria retorted. <Or are you suggesting, as your brother did, that of all the Dark Ones who fought our people, *he* was the one who killed your kin?>

<I am not suggesting that,> Bao Sen replied, still feeling guilty about how the earlier encounter turned out. <And Rahmeeraz *is* a friend to the Huntresses. But you must look at this critically. You two can barely speak to one another. You can't even tell how he feels as he has not tail nor ears. And our world is full of tods and vixens who would look at your union as a betrayal to all those we've lost, *including* members of your own family.>

Alzoria said nothing to this, but her tail slowed and her ears uncurled as she considered her guild leader's words.

<Alzoria, I do not say these things to be cruel, but because I want you to be happy,> Bao Sen continued. <Please. Do not walk any further down this path. I will help you find a suitable tesho. Please... Let him go.>

Alzoria stared down at the tabletop, her ears now drooping.

<No,> she finally muttered. Raising her eyes to look at Bao Sen, she continued. <When I met him, I hated him. I berated him. And the entire time we were imprisoned together, he was trying to comfort me, to protect me.> The tips of her ears pointed at Bao Sen. <I am supposed to give up a tod who treats me well no matter what... so that other people who would treat me bad feel better?>

<It is not about making them feel better,> Bao Sen corrected gently. <It's about not incurring the anger and bitterness of a great many people.>

<Their anger and bitterness are their own!> Alzoria snapped back. <And it has nothing to do with me!>

It was at this point that Bao Sen decided to give up for now. Once Alzoria dug in her heels, there was no changing her mind.

Even as she thought this, the look on her brother's face when he saw Ramirez entered her mind. The way he looked at *her*, as if she had committed the greater crime. She knew that look would be plastered on the face of almost every Va'Shen Alzoria came into contact with if she went through with this bizarre plan.

The lead Huntress rose to her feet. <I hope you are right. I truly do,> she said. <But if you are not, I want you to know that your sisters here will support you.>

Alzoria's ears drooped again. <Thank you, Bao Sen. I hope I am right too.>

Chapter 5

Seven weeks until contact...

Burgers hopped off the hood of the LTV and adjusted the M-31 slung over his shoulder as the first deuce-and-a-half truck turned the corner ahead of him and slowed to a stop. The dirt road was surrounded on one side by a fenced-in pasture and a steep, forested rise on the other, giving the trucks very little room to maneuver. Fortunately, it was a sunny and dry day. Rain might have made the roads a muddy mess.

He raised his hand and gave the lead truck's driver a wave, and the uniformed driver casually waved back. The Ranger could hear the sound of truck doors opening and closing as passengers and gunners exited the trucks. As he got closer, Burgers heard someone call out to him.

"Holy shit! Burgers, is that you?!"

Burgers looked up and found the man who called out to him. The Ranger grinned as the other man, a soldier with three chevrons on the front of his uniform, walked up to him.

"Two-Time Mitchell!" Burgers called out, holding his hand out to shake. "Ain't this a small galaxy?!"

The sergeant, a short and slim African American man shook his hand with a smile. "Damn, man, where have you been?! I haven't seen you since boot!"

"Oh, you know," Burgers said jovially. "Jumping out of helicopters, winning wars, shit like that." He pointed at the infantry badge on his friend's uniform. "What's this infantry shit, man? I thought you wanted to drive tanks."

"Yeah," Mitchell replied. "Then they found out 'tank' is just another word for 'big-ass coffin,' and they pushed us into infantry. Man! It is good to fucking see you! So, they got you at Pelle, huh?"

"Yup," Burgers replied. "Captain asked me to come out here and guide you guys in the last few miles. Any issues?"

"Nah!" Mitchell said. "They've been pretty quiet the entire way."

"Cool. Can I talk to their chief? I need to brief him on what comes next."

"Well, they don't got one of those," Mitchell said, turning and gesturing for the bigger man to follow as he made his way to the rear of the first truck. "But there's a furry woman we work with. You can talk to her."

"Yeah, okay," Burgers said as he fell into step with his old friend. The part about the village not having a chieftain threw him for a moment. Then again, these people were coming from another part of the continent. Their ways might be different from Pelle's.

* * *

Wenlin felt the truck come to a stop, and her hands began to shake. It wasn't time to stop for a meal or one of the pre-arranged rest breaks, which meant that they must have arrived at their destination. She could hear the sound of booted feet approaching on the other side of the canvas that covered the back of the truck.

Reaching into her pocket, her trembling fingers grasped the small glass vial within and took it out, fumbling with the stopper before knocking it back like a tequila shot.

She felt the liquid's warmth spread through her, and her breathing slowed. The other Mikorin sitting near her looked at her with pity but said nothing in response to the flagrant display of her addiction.

There were two Dark Ones approaching, going by the sound of their voices. She recognized one of them as a corporal who was in charge of their convoy and a frequent visitor to the bakery her Mikorin ran. The other she had never heard before, and she wondered if it was their new Dark One overlord.

As the two Dark Ones turned the corner, she looked down at them from her seat at the edge of the truck. The new Dark One was huge compared to Meetchall, and he hid his eyes behind mirrored glass. She swallowed nervously.

"This is her," Mitchell said, pointing his thumb at Wenlin.

Burgers paused, waiting for more. Like an introduction or even a name, but Mitchell provided neither. Left on his own, Burgers cleared his throat and bowed to the woman.

<I greet you,> he said in passable Va'Shen. The vixens in earshot responded with surprise, their ears pointing up at the sky. <You come down? We speak?> he asked.

Wenlin looked to Mitchell as if for permission, and the other soldier waved for her to climb down.

"Come on, princess, don't keep the man waiting," he said.

The raven-haired vixen started to climb down from the truck, and Burgers offered a hand to help her down. The vixen didn't take it but was soon standing in front of him. She bowed low.

"Greetings to you, *Aridesho*," she said in English.

Just as surprised as the vixens were a moment ago, Burgers came up short. Aside from Alzoria, he had never heard a Va'Shen speak English... and polite English to boot.

<My name is Baird,> Burgers continued, using Va'Shen to be polite. <I come take all of you to Pelle. Ask questions I may can?>

He realized he was butchering her language and waited for her to say something about it, but she only bowed again.

<Please ask your questions, *Aridesho*,> Wenlin said. <I will answer the best I can.>

Burgers brought out his clipboard and clicked his pen. <How many Va'Shen are you?>

<There are three hundred and twenty of us,> Wenlin supplied.

Burgers checked his Va'Shen-to-English numerical chart and made the proper notation. <How many sick are you?>

<There are no sick,> Wenlin told him.

The large man paused. <No sick?> he asked again.

<There are no sick,> the Na'Sha repeated.

Burgers was surprised at the answer, and, for the first time, took a good look at the Va'Shen woman. Her ears were pointed straight up and hadn't moved once since they started talking. Her azure blue eyes were wide and round, and her pupils were slightly dilated.

"Problem?" Mitchell asked.

"Uh, no," Burgers said, still a little surprised. "It's just that the indig doctor here at Pelle was so worried about getting people with radiation sickness that we built her a whole new clinic to treat them, but she's saying no one is sick."

Mitchell shrugged. "Sorry, man. Don't know anything about that."

Again, the flippancy of his friend's answer bothered the Ranger. He noted Wenlin's answer on his clipboard and faced her again.

<We take the all of you to Pelle,> he said. <Na'Sha also the others will meet you there.>

Wenlin bowed. <As you wish, *Aridesho*.>

Burgers nodded. "Okay." He pointed back at the truck. <Thank you. Please sit. We depart soon.>

Without another word, Wenlin climbed awkwardly back into the truck and retook her seat, and Burgers and Mitchell started back to the front of the convoy.

"Okay," Burgers told him. "You guys are going to follow me to the center of town. We unload the pax there and then you will follow me to the FOB."

"How much security do we got?" Mitchell asked.

"None," Burgers told him plainly. "Captain wants the Va'Shen to welcome the new folks themselves, so they'll be more comfortable. No troops. We drop them and we go."

"So, we're rolling into the middle of the vil with no additional security?" Mitchell asked, somewhat amazed.

"It's not needed," Burgers assured him. "The villagers here are pretty cool."

"Well, if it's that mellow, I'm going to have a good time here," Mitchell replied with a grin.

"I thought you guys in Sector Six had things pretty pacified," Burgers commented as they stopped at the front of the lead truck.

"Sure," Mitchell told him. "Eventually." The sergeant put on a pair of ballistic sunglasses and shook Burgers's hand. "See you at the FOB."

"See you there," Burgers said and started for his LTV, his mind reviewing everything he had just seen and heard.

He couldn't shake the feeling that there was something weird happening in the background.

* * *

There was a festive atmosphere in the crowd not seen in Pelle's main square since the Arbor Day festival more than a month ago. Almost the entire Va'Shen community had shown up to welcome the newest members of their village. Tables with food and drinks had been set up, and others with piles of clothing and other supplies the newcomers from Garan'Sel might need lined either side of the street.

Conspicuous by their absence, however, were the Dark Ones. There were virtually no mottled green uniforms or black guns to be seen. The one exception was at the very center of the crowd, speaking with Alacea and Kasshas, the village chieftain.

<You have all needed things?> Ben asked for what must have been the third time. <You need things, you please tell to us.>

The black-haired chieftain, his hair falling over his eyes almost to the point where it looked like just another part of his long, black beard, swished his tail, inadvertently striking two people behind him.

<Overlord,> he said in clear exasperation. <Again, we thank you. We have all we need.>

Seeing that Kasshas's frustration was beginning to emerge, Alacea took Ben's arm in her hand.

<I believe what our Chieftain means to say, Tesho, is that all is prepared and there is nothing more that can be done except wait.>

Ben saw Kasshas's tail, normally still, twitching and realized he had managed to annoy the man. He smiled. There was a time when the Va'Shen man wouldn't dare show such emotion in front of him out of fear that Ben would retaliate against his people. The fact that he was now comfortable enough to do so showed a kind of progress that made Ben happy.

<I understand,> he told Alacea and bowed to Kasshas. <I shall depart.>

<Are you certain you wish to do so?> Alacea asked him. <You do not want to meet the newcomers?>

<I will not meet them now,> he told her. <They are scared, uncomfortable. Need to see happy Va'Shen people. Meet later.>

<How about tonight?> Alacea suggested suddenly.

<Tonight for dinner?> Ben asked.

<Yes,> Alacea replied with a twitch of her ears. <It is customary for the Na'Sha to host the new Na'Sha for a meal. Surely, that would be an appropriate time.>

Ben thought about it for a moment. <Yes. Good. When?>

<Sundown. At the temple,> Alacea instructed.

<Yes. Good.> Ben repeated. He gave her a short bow. <I see you at that time.>

Alacea bowed back, and the human started walking down the road away from the crowd.

Sho Nan suddenly appeared next to Alacea.

<Your tesho will dine with us tonight?> she asked.

<Yes,> Alacea told her. <Please make the appropriate arrangements.>

<Yes, Na'Sha,> Sho Nan replied. <An additional meal and a wheelbarrow. I shall see to it.>

<One of those things will not be necessary,> Alacea told her firmly.

Sho Nan paused. <Which one?>

Alacea was saved from having to answer the trollish question by the arrival of several large Dark One trucks. Unlike those that had carried the Pelle villagers from the mountains back to their village, the backs of these trucks were covered with drab, green fabric, concealing from view the Va'Shen inside. The trucks parked in a semi-circle before them, and the crews got out, banging on the sides of the beds as they moved to the rear.

The crowd watched as several Va'Shen in simple clothes, some with bags in their hands, descended from the vehicles and looked around. Some searched with suspicious eyes or bewilderment. Others kept wary eyes on the Dark One crews who had brought them there.

As one, Kasshas, Alacea and Yasuren stepped toward them, and the bearded tod raised his hands over his head.

<I welcome you to Pelle,> he called out, grabbing the group's attention. He bowed to them as part of his greeting. <As Chieftain, I greet you and welcome you to our home, and now yours.>

By protocol, this was the point the Garen'Sel chieftain would come forward and return the greeting, but no tod stepped forward. Instead, a raven-haired vixen in a simple brown and white hanbok approached them and bowed.

<I am Wenlin,> she said. <Na'Sha to the people and minerals of Garan'Sel.>

Alacea stepped forward and bowed. <Greetings, Na'Sha. I am Alacea, Na'Sha to the people and animals of Pelle.>

<Was your chieftain delayed, Na'Sha?> Kasshas asked Wenlin respectfully.

<We have no chieftain,> Wenlin replied. <I speak for the community.>

The other three Va'Shen looked at each other in confusion. A Na'Sha was never a chieftain. She was the personification of the community, not its leader. For ages it was agreed that a chieftain led the community in worldly affairs while the Na'Sha led it in the spiritual. Even the Emperor, himself a God, had a Na'Sha.

Alacea studied the young vixen in front of her. Although seemingly calm and collected, she could sense something beneath the surface. Not hidden, per se.

Dampened. Restrained.

Wenlin's eyes didn't seem to move. Her large, blue irises resisted any attempt to read into her spirit, like curtains thrown up over a window.

Alacea did not know what Wenlin and her people might have been through during the war, the invasion, the destruction of their provinces and the occupation, and so she did not wish to make judgements. Her own experience was a perfect example of just how insane things could become.

Her ears wiggled a smile, and she took the other woman's hands in her own.

<Then, please, let our people serve you a meal and provide for your comfort. Then we will show you your temporary lodgings.>

<Do the Dark Ones not wish to inspect our belongings?> Wenlin asked.

<Is that what your former overlord did?> Yasuren asked, taken aback by the question.

<He was very concerned that we may have weapons,> Wenlin explained.

<It is not an issue here,> Kasshas assured her. <The Overlord has not given any orders to that effect.>

<I see,> Wenlin replied robotically.

<Come,> Alacea said, holding out her hand.

* * *

The dark-haired tod who climbed down from the truck took a look at his new surroundings and couldn't believe his eyes. It seemed to him that the Dark Ones had never even been to this village, yet he had been assured that it had been occupied almost as long as Garan'Sel had.

<Uncle Goto?>

Goto blinked the disbelief out of his eyes and turned, holding his hand up to help his teenage niece down from the truck. The petite girl, her long, blue-green hair worn in a braid, took his hand and hopped down from the truck. Taking a moment to adjust her blue and white hanbok, she joined her uncle in taking in their new home.

<I don't see any Dark Ones,> she said.

<Just because you cannot see them doesn't mean they are not there, Posha,> Goto told her. <They are probably watching us from the tops of the buildings.>

They looked up as the Pelle villagers began moving as a formless mob toward the newcomers. They all held baskets of food and small gifts to welcome them.

They look... happy, Goto thought.

The older man was suddenly hit by several conflicting emotions. That these people seemed excited to see them puzzled and unnerved him. He was expecting his people to join another village in its misery. It was so unexpected that he became immediately suspicious. Despite what he said to his niece, he saw no signs of any Dark Ones anywhere.

Was this village even occupied?

He was pulled from his thoughts as two villagers approached and bowed to him. One of them, a young tod who appeared to be in his teens, was missing his right arm. The other, an older woman he assumed was the boy's mother, pointed toward two long tables that had been set up nearby.

<Welcome,> Basilla told them. <I am Basilla. This is my son, Turean. Come! We have prepared a feast to welcome you to our community.>

<A feast?> Goto asked. <The Dark Ones allowed a feast?>

Posha's reaction was quite different. <A feast?! How wonderful!>

The mother and son, likewise, reacted in two different ways.

<The Dark Ones did not say it was forbidden, nor did they say we should have one,> Basilla replied to Goto.

<We... We have spice buns!> Turean told Posha, his tail whipping about nervously.

Goto grunted noncommittally, and Posha's ears twitched. <Then, please, lead the way,> Goto said.

* * *

"And that's about it, Sir," Sergeant Mitchell concluded from his chair on the opposite side of Ben's desk. "No issues to speak of." He finished by reaching out and handing Ben a thick, sealed manila envelope.

Ben took it and put it on his desk for perusal later. "Thank you, Sergeant. I'm guessing your guys are probably looking forward to hot showers, warm food and real beds," Ben told him with a smile. "We already got places for you set up. Get your folks squared away, and we can worry about the inprocessing briefings starting tomorrow morning."

The new NCO sighed in relief. "Thanks, Sir. It's been a long haul."

"C'mon," Burgers told him, cocking his head to the door. "I'll show you what's what."

Both Ben and Mitchell stood up and reached out to shake hands. "Welcome to Sector 13, Sergeant," Ben said with a smile.

"Thank you, Sir."

With that, the two NCOs left the office, leaving Ben, Patricia, Warren and Fletcher alone.

"Thoughts?" Ben asked them.

Leaning against one of the staff desks to Ben's left, Warren folded his arms over his chest. "More than enough temp housing for them. No worries there."

"I'm a little surprised that there are no radiation cases," Fletcher spoke up from her seat next to Patricia's desk. "Did they just get really lucky or did they find their own way of treating it?"

"Maybe they got moved before the radiation could reach them. I can ask at dinner tonight," Ben promised her. "I'll be meeting with the new Na'Sha."

"It didn't sound like there were any intel issues," Patricia said. "I'm not going to really know if there are any language or dialect barriers until I have a chance to talk to them myself."

"They speak regular Va'Shen, don't they?" Warren asked.

"Yes," Patricia agreed hesitantly. "But accents and regional dialects could make communication hard."

"Like a guy from Boston talking to a guy from Jamaica," Ben threw in. "Yeah, technically they're both speaking English..."

"Gotcha," Warren said in comprehension. He had known a sailor from Negrille when he was a young petty officer. Never had trouble understanding him until he saw him speaking to another guy from

Jamaica and had dropped back into his accent. He still had no idea what they had been talking about.

"Okay," Ben said, summing up the meeting. "Let's get Mitchell's folks bedded down and inprocessed, and we'll see how things go from there."

"So, they *are* staying?" Fletcher asked.

Ben nodded. "With the Garan'Sel villagers moving here, Admin Sector Six has been drawn down to almost nothing. It made more sense for Mitchell and his forty troops to just stay here until their deployments are up than try to farm them out everywhere else."

Fletcher nodded.

"Okay, dismissed," Ben said casually. Warren and Fletcher headed toward the door.

"I hope things are going as easy for the Va'Shen as they seem to be going here," Patricia commented to Ben.

"I wouldn't worry," the Ranger captain said. "Alacea and her folks pulled out all the stops. I'm sure they'll have no problem integrating the newcomers." He paused and pointed at Patricia's chest. "By the way, that looks really good on you."

"Huh?" Patricia looked down at her uniform shirt before looking up again and smiling. "Yeah, thanks."

Sewn just above her linguist badge on the left breast of her shirt was a small rectangular patch of a combat knife surrounded by a wreath. Her actions at Jamieson Airfield during the Va'Shen attack a month before had qualified her for the Combat Action Badge, awarded to any soldier who fires their weapon in the course of a battle with enemy forces. She had sent two of her uniform shirts to Jamieson with a Ranger making a supply run to have them sewn on.

"Ramirez keeps asking me if I have a date for Ranger school," Patricia remarked.

"You want one?" Ben asked with a grin.

"Hell no!" Patricia cried in near-panic. "I have *no* desire to do something like that!"

"Awww, you'd do great!" Ben needled her.

"Yeah, sure I would," Patricia replied. "More importantly," she continued, eager to turn the tables on her boss, "Are you ready for your date tonight?"

"It's not a date," Ben assured her. "It's a..."

"... Key Leader Engagement," they both finished in unison.

"Uh huh," Patricia said with a grin. "You and Alacea have been having a lot of KLEs lately."

"Because she is a *key leader*," Ben emphasized.

"That is the worst pet name ever," Patricia told him. "How're things with her brother?"

Ben paused at this question, unsure of how to reply. "I... don't know," he confessed. For the past several days, Ben had been leaving work early to help his Va'Shen brother-in-law build a house on the outskirts of the village. "Mostly, he tells me to hold something, or carry something or something like that, and that's it. We don't really talk."

"Why not?" Patricia asked.

"I'm not really sure what to say," Ben replied with a touch of embarrassment. "It's not like we have a whole lot in common."

"You're both officers, aren't you?" Patricia asked. "You fought in the same war. You have a lot in common."

"How am I supposed to talk to him about something like that?" Ben asked seriously. "We may have that in common, but the memories aren't exactly great."

"Well," Patricia said, "If you can't talk to your brother about stuff you went through, who can you talk to?"

"Literally anyone else," Ben replied with a wan smile.

* * *

Wenlin led the small group of Mikorin down Pelle's main road toward the temple with a sense of cautious optimism. Their first meeting with the Pelle villagers had gone incredibly well. After a small feast where both communities spent time introducing one another, the Pelle Mikorin and other members of the community led them to the temporary housing they had prepared for them, stressing that it was only until the Garan'Sel population could establish their own homes.

The houses, large buildings with multiple dens inside, had looked positively hideous with their blend of Va'Shen and Dark One architecture, probably what prompted the Pelle villagers to repeatedly stress its temporary nature. But in truth it was much more than Wenlin and the villagers had anticipated. Although ugly, it was quite obvious that a great deal of work went into making sure they were dry, warm and secure.

Before the Pelle villagers left to allow the newcomers to move into their temporary quarters, their Na'Sha, Alacea, had invited Wenlin and her Mikorin to dine with them that night.

Perhaps it was the utter lack of a Dark One presence, but for the first time in a long while, Wenlin felt safe. Her fears of facing unwelcoming glares from already-hungry villagers had evaporated, and the associated fears of armed Dark Ones walking the streets, leering at her, were fading as well.

She had elected to bring four other Mikorin with her. The rest of them were busy helping establish their community in their new homes. Wenlin understood the next challenge she would face would come from Alacea's generosity and the expectations of Va'Shen custom.

As if reading her thoughts, the Mikorin walking on her right spoke up.

<What do you intend to say when they invite us into their temple?> The vixen's snow-white hair had ribbons of black running

diagonally down her back, and her red eyes and pale skin would have made a human think of her as an albino.

<We have time for now,> Wenlin replied quietly. <We will tell them it is more important for us to remain with our people. Though I would prefer the younger Mikorin move in with them immediately.>

<I wish this meal was held somewhere else,> another Mikorin behind Wenlin sighed. <It is... uncomfortable.>

<I know,> Wenlin told her, not even bothering to turn to face the other vixen. <Endure.>

<Yes, Na'Sha.>

When they arrived at the temple, they found Alacea and a blue-haired Mikorin they had met earlier that day waiting for them outside. Alacea's ears twitched when she caught sight of them, and she glided down the steps to meet them halfway. The blue-haired woman followed her, and they both bowed to them.

<Warm welcome and a blessed evening, Wenlin Na'Sha,> Alacea said.

<A blessed evening to you as well, Na'Sha,> Wenlin replied, bowing deeply to the other woman, her raven-black hair falling to just above the ground like an obsidian waterfall.

<I believe you have met our Aru'Dace, Hestean,> Alacea continued, gesturing to the other woman.

<Of course,> Wenlin said courteously. <My other Mikorin are assisting our community as they settle in, but I have brought four of my most trusted Mikorin.> She gestured to the tall, white-haired vixen. <My Roroa'San, Yunhee.>

The albino-like woman bowed to them.

<My Ya'Jahar, Tenzeta.> Another Mikorin, this one with red hair speckled with yellow splotches in an almost leopard pattern, bowed. <My Donya'Ta, Hesmea.> The vixen who bowed this time was a head shorter than Wenlin with dark blue hair with black spots.

<And my Aru'Dace, Runa.> The Garan'Sel historian was in her mid-teens, younger than the others, and bowed nervously, her pale, minty-green hair worn up in a bun.

Hestean stepped forward, her ears twitching. <I look forward to working at your side, Runa,> she said. <I am very interested in learning the history of your community.>

<And I yours, Honored Aru'Dace,> Runa said with another bow.

Wenlin's ears twitched once. <Runa Aru'Dace has only recently assumed her position among us. I hope you will mentor her to become as talented an Aru'Dace as you, Hestean Aru'Dace.>

<Well, please, come inside,> Alacea invited, turning to lead their guests up the stairs. As they reached the entrance to the temple, another blue-haired vixen, this one with her hair in a collarbone-length bob, appeared.

<Na'Sha, the others have been seated.>

Alacea gestured to the vixen. <Our Ya'Jahar, Sho Nan.>

Sho Nan bowed, and they went through the introductions again. It was obvious that *She Who Feeds* was busy, and so she didn't have time for small talk.

<Your tesho has arrived as well, Na'Sha,> Sho Nan told Alacea. <The wheelbarrow is at the back entrance near the garden.>

<Sho Nan!> Alacea hissed, her tail slapping the floor.

<One thing does not necessarily have anything to do with the other,> Sho Nan replied calmly.

The purple-haired woman growled in annoyance. Before she could chastise Sho Nan further, however, Wenlin spoke up.

<You are wed?> she asked Alacea, the amazement plain on her ears.

<Yes, I am,> Alacea replied, caught a little off-guard. <I suppose I should have explained... but really it is probably easier if you just meet him.>

<I see,> Wenlin agreed even as the wheels in her head turned. Some things, she thought, were starting to make sense, and a part of her admired Alacea for her resourcefulness. Only a noble of high rank, a count at least, could marry a Na'Sha, meaning that her tesho probably had a fair bit of political clout. Enough clout, perhaps, to blunt the Dark Ones' influence in her village.

Wenlin's cautious optimism began to grow. If such a noble were protecting Pelle at the Imperial Court, then that would benefit her own community by extension. Even if Pelle's overlord did have some vendetta against the Va'Shen, it was possible that Alacea's political maneuvering and marriage had defanged him. It was a longshot, she knew, but one worth hoping for.

<This way,> Alacea said, leading them into the temple.

The Garan'Sel Mikorin hesitated at the door, but Wenlin's tail slapped the floor, and the four of them followed her inside without complaint.

<Your temple is beautiful,> Wenlin complimented Alacea.

<Thank you,> Alacea told her. <But please, I hope you will soon know this as your temple.>

<Soon, I hope,> Wenlin replied with only a hint of the sadness she felt.

They walked down the hallway until they arrived at a sliding wooden door. Sho Nan, took hold of the handle and prepared to open it as Alacea gestured for Wenlin to precede her inside.

The Garan'Sel Na'Sha stepped forward as Sho Nan opened the door. She froze in shock as, on the opposite side of the room at the head of the table, a Dark One rose to greet her.

Wenlin was rooted to the spot in shock. Her heart began to pound in her chest. Her Mikorin around her made sounds of surprise as well, but Wenlin began to actually shake.

Her legs gave out from under her, and she hit the polished wooden floor as Alacea and Hestean gave cries of alarm.

The Dark One rushed from around the table toward her, and Wenlin began to panic.

<Wenlin Na'Sha! Are you all right?!> Alacea cried, kneeling down to help her. <We'll get you a healer! Hestean, find Kastia!>

The raven-haired vixen's eyes never left the Dark One as he approached her, but she quickly spoke up.

<No!> she told Alacea. <That is not necessary!> She quickly found her footing and stood up, her Mikorin all touching her arms and shoulders, ready to assist at any moment. <I was merely surprised,> she said in what was practically a gasp. <I did not know a... a Dark One would be here.> She tried to give her voice a little levity, as if she weren't shocked into terror a moment ago.

<I am so sorry!> Alacea said quickly. <I should have said something!>

<All is very well?> Ben asked, not getting *too* close to the group of Va'Shen priestesses.

Wenlin swallowed and bowed to him. <Forgive me,> she said. <I was surprised at your presence, Lord.>

<Perhaps the Na'Sha should have a moment to collect herself,> Hesmea suggested.

<Of course,> Alacea agreed immediately. <I shall show you to the washroom. Sho Nan, could you see to the others?>

<Of course, Na'Sha.>

Alacea took Wenlin's hand and gently guided her to another room down the hall.

<Forgive me,> Wenlin begged. <I am afraid I have always been somewhat skittish.>

<It is no problem,> Alacea told her supportively. <I forget, sometimes, that not all Va'Shen have had as much exposure to my Tesho's people as we have.>

Wenlin nearly lost a step. <Your tesho's people?> she repeated.

<Yes,> Alacea said, her tail waving in chagrin. <That Da... that tod... is my Tesho, the Overlord of Pelle, Ban Gibzon.>

Wenlin said nothing, shocked into silence. Her mind reeled at what she was hearing.

<I... would like a moment alone, please,> she managed to mutter as Alacea opened the door to the water closet.

<Of course. I will wait out here for you.> Alacea punctuated this by gently placing her hand on the other young vixen's arm.

The touch didn't even register to Wenlin. She stepped inside the water closet and slid the door shut behind her. She found the blue ceramic cleaning basin filled with clear water and splashed some into her face with shaking hands.

Collect yourself! The part of her that was Na'Sha chastised the part that was the young woman. *Endure!*

<Endure,> she whispered to herself. <Just endure.> Reaching into her pocket, she withdrew the familiar glass vial and pulled the stopper, taking a quick shot.

Wenlin took a breath as she felt her fear and surprise deaden inside her, along with all the other emotions she had begun to feel today. Her tail slowed, and her ears rose slowly to their more normal position.

There was no mirror in the water closet, but if there had been she may have seen her pupils slightly dilate even as the light left her eyes.

<Endure,> she commanded herself.

* * *

When the two vixens returned to the dining room, Wenlin's four Mikorin looked up from their seats with worry, a worry that did not dissipate even as the Na'Sha glided to her seat with the utmost grace and sat down on her knees. She bowed to the center of the table.

<I apologize for my outburst,> she said evenly. She turned to Ben at the head of the table and bowed again. <I ask for your forgiveness, Overlord.>

<No forgive,> Ben replied clumsily with a bow. <Nothing for forgive.>

Wenlin bowed to him again and faced the center of the table as Sho Nan and two of her acolytes began to hand out bowls of a thick vegetable soup. She watched as Alacea knelt and sat on Ben's left and poured a cup of tea that she then presented to him with both hands.

<Oh... Um... Gratitude,> Ben told her as he took the cup. <*Mura?*> he asked.

<No,> Alacea told her pointedly before Sho Nan could say something. <Tea.>

<Yes, good.> Ben said, taking a sip.

Wenlin watched the simple domestic byplay and reassessed her earlier thoughts on Alacea. Though her emotions were weighed down by the drug, she still felt sympathy and sadness for the vixen. She had thought her own situation was bad, but here Alacea had spiritually chained herself to the Dark One overlord. When Wenlin died, her pain would end, but Alacea's would follow her for eternity.

The Pelle Na'Sha had tempered the evil impulses of the Dark Ones, but at an extreme cost to herself. Wenlin found herself respecting Alacea all the more and suddenly felt twinges of shame and guilt that she had so lamented her own situation.

I and my Mikorin will do our part, Alacea Na'Sha, she vowed. *You will not endure this alone.*

<Houses adequate?>

Wenlin's head slowly turned to the source of the question, and she bowed as she answered Ben.

<The Overlord's mercy is generous,> she said evenly. <We are most grateful for what he has provided.>

<If problem,> Ben told her, <... please tell. We fix. Build other.>

The other four Garan'Sel Mikorin watched the conversation nervously. Wenlin had shared Keyes's warning about the Pelle overlord, and they each wondered if he was setting some kind of trap for their Na'Sha. If she complained now, would he lash out at them for her ingratitude?

But they had faith in Wenlin. She had navigated the fraught relationship between them and the Dark Ones before. She would do so now.

<I thank you for your consideration,> Wenlin replied as woodenly as before. <I am quite certain that the Overlord's preparations were far greater than we deserve.>

Alacea, Hestean and Sho Nan watched the conversation with concern but not for any possible punishment. Wenlin's formality was certainly polite given the current company, but there was something about the way she spoke that made their ears tremble. As if they were not listening to a vixen speak, but something that had taken her body as a marionette.

It was Hestean that decided to come to the rescue. Facing Runa, who sat across the table from her, she adjusted her seating and spoke up.

<Runa Aru'Dace,> she began, <I have begun to make space in our archive and library for Garan'Sel's books and documents,> she said. <We can begin to move them in as soon as tomorrow if you like.>

The green-haired vixen's tail whipped behind her nervously, and she looked down at the table in shame. <There are none, Hestean Aru'Dace.>

Hestean's delicate ears popped upward. <None?>

Wenlin's almost ghostly voice replied for Runa. <Our temple suffered a fire,> she said. <We lost all of our records.>

<And our Na'Sha,> Hesmea added in a sad voice just above a whisper.

<That's terrible!> Alacea cried. <I am so sorry!>

<Was it during the war?> Sho Nan asked.

Alacea cursed Sho Nan's bluntness, though she knew, in this case, Sho Nan did not mean anything by it. It was the obvious question to ask, but someone more diplomatic would have realized that asking such a question in the presence of a Dark One overlord only invited awkward recriminations.

The Garan'Sel Mikorin immediately saw it that way and looked to Wenlin nervously to see what she would say.

<It was a tragic accident,> Wenlin told them and wouldn't say more than that.

<I see,> Hestean said uncertainly.

Runa decided to try to help, herself. <I... I believe the Gods foresaw the union of our communities,> she told Hestean quickly. <And wished to encourage us to leave our old pains behind and look ahead as part of your community.>

<Well said,> Yunhee agreed.

<And I am certain our union will be a happy one,> Alacea told them. <To that end, we have rooms available in our temple for all your Mikorin.>

<That will not be necessary,> Wenlin replied firmly.

Alacea's tail nearly puffed up in surprise. <It will not?> she asked.

Wenlin looked at her, and Alacea swallowed nervously at the expressionless visage. <I mean no insult,> Wenlin said. <And it would be more correct to say, 'that will not be necessary *yet*.' We simply prefer to remain close to our community during this time and not assume the comforts of our new homes until our people can do so themselves. Once they have found permanent homes, we will revisit the matter.>

<Of... Of course,> Alacea replied. <If that is your wish, it will be honored.>

Wenlin bowed her head to her. <I thank you, Na'Sha.>

Ben could see the troubled look in his wife's ears and wanted to ask what was wrong but remained silent, not wanting to inadvertently shove his foot into his mouth. Instead, he focused on trying to remember all the newcomer's names and faces. Though he was no expert on Va'Shen language by any means, he thought he could detect an accent to the new Mikorins' speech, but nothing that seemed to interfere with his ability to understand them. No more, anyway, than his usual lack of vocabulary or understanding.

The biggest thing he learned came from meeting the Garan'Sel Mikorin, Hesmea. Until now, he had not heard of the position of "Donya'Ta."

<It means, '*She Who Nurtures*,'> Hestean explained to him. <She is like a mother to the young acolytes and any orphans the temple takes in.>

That made sense to Ben. The way he understood it, vixens joined the temple when they were young girls, so it stood to reason they would need someone to look after them.

<Your doings sounds good,> he told Hesmea.

<Thank you, Overlord,> was all Hesmea would say in reply.

Despite Ben's best efforts, he couldn't seem to draw any of the new Mikorin into a conversation. Any question he asked was answered by Wenlin, who gave the most direct reply possible and then promptly stopped talking.

Ben wasn't the only one who found the experience strange. Alacea also felt there was a wall placed between the Garan'Sel vixens and the Pelle villagers. The priestess, however, chalked it up to cultural differences. Garan'Sel was quite a distance from Pelle, and it was natural for their people to have different feelings on communicating with others.

The dinner proceeded with chitchat making its way back and forth over the six-foot-high wall of protocol for about two hours until the lateness of the evening prompted its end. Both sets of

Mikorin faced each other in two lines and bowed to one another in farewell.

<I look forward to many more conversations with you and your Mikorin, Wenlin Na'Sha,> Alacea told her respectfully.

<You honor us,> Wenlin replied with a bow. <And we shall endeavor to properly honor you in return. Blessed evening to you.>

<And to you,> Alacea said with a bow.

Wenlin turned to Ben and bowed. <Blessed evening to you, Overlord. I remain your humble servant.>

Ben bowed back. <I enjoy our meeting,> he told her.

With a silent nod to the other vixens, Wenlin led the entourage out the door and into the light of Va'Sh's two moons.

Alacea, Ben and the Mikorin watched them go. None spoke for a moment. Alacea wanted to ask Hestean and Sho Nan what they thought of the night, but she felt doing so in her Tesho's presence might affect their answers. It was Sho Nan who spoke first, bowing to the group.

<I will begin cleaning up,> she told them. <A blessed evening to you all.>

<Thanks to you, Sho Nan,> Ben told her.

Hestean was next to make her exit. <If you will excuse me, I have a great deal of work to begin tomorrow.> She bowed to them both. <Blessed evening.>

Ben and Alacea bowed to her in return, and the blue-haired woman glided down the hall toward the back of the temple, leaving the two of them alone.

A few awkward moments of silence passed between them before Ben remembered there were still things he needed to speak with Alacea about and so couldn't quite yet leave. Turning to her, he cleared his throat.

<You, me, talk some?> he asked.

<Of course,> Alacea said. <Would you like to speak in the garden?>

<Garden?> Ben asked, searching his mind for the word. Alacea waited expectantly for him to remember it without her help. <Garden! Yes! Garden,> he said. <Where the things enbiggen...>

<I suppose that is accurate enough,> Alacea said with a flick of her ears. <Come. This way.> She started down the hall, and Ben followed after her.

After a few turns, Ben found himself in the temple garden. He had never been here at night and found the place lit by colorful waterlamps, giving the plants an ethereal quality. The garden was lovely by day, but at night it was a completely different kind of beautiful.

<You wish to speak?> Alacea prompted as the two began to stroll slowly on the circular path that led through the garden.

<Wish to know certainty,> Ben told her. <Hear told there are no sick in new Va'Shen.>

<That is true,> Alacea confirmed. <Kastia was very relieved.>

<It is strange,> Ben told her. <Fletcher say should be some.>

<Perhaps the Gods offered them kindness,> Alacea said. Seeing his confused look, Alacea tried again. <Gods nice to them,> she explained simply.

Ben bobbed his head up and down. <Perhaps. Good,> he replied.

<Was that all you wished to discuss?> Alacea asked.

<No,> Ben drawled out somewhat nervously. <I want to tell you that I liked previous nights. The... um... Facibination...>

<The Facilitation?> Alacea corrected. Her ears twitched a smile. <I did as well.>

<I do not remember some,> he continued. <Um... I do things bad?>

It was hard for Va'Shen to tell when a Dark One was nervous, but Alacea was learning based on her Tesho's behavior in context. It seemed now that he was concerned that he had done something untoward.

<No,> she assured him. <In fact, I think you had a better understanding of the purpose than I did.>

<Um... So... Good?>

<Yes,> she said. <I am sorry. I did not know *mura* would affect you like that.>

<*Mura* is good,> Ben replied. <Slept very good.>

Alacea said nothing for a good long while. <What do you remember?> she asked.

<I remember you dance,> Ben told her, causing Alacea to miss a step. <Very, very good.>

<Oh... um... thank you,> she said. <I had not danced in a long time. I was worried I would look foolish.>

<Not look foolish,> Ben assured her. <Myorin never look foolish.>

Alacea's ears pointed toward him. <Not even when I have sticks in my hair?> she asked pointedly.

<Sticks make Myorin look nice,> Ben responded immediately.

The priestess paused and looked at him. <Is... that true... or a joke?> For all she knew, it was true.

Ben stopped and turned to her, taking a breath and thinking hard for a moment. <Yes,> he finally said.

Her ears twitched a little, then more, until finally she had to turn away and cover them with her hands.

<Myorin.>

Alacea turned and found Ben leaning down toward her.

She gasped in realization. *This is it! He's going to nip me! My first nip!*

Time seemed to slow down for her as he continued leaning over, past the tips of her ears.

Where is he going? she thought.

Before she could come up with some logical answer to her own question, his lips ended up in the last place she ever would have thought they would; planted over her own.

The vixen sputtered and stepped back, looking up at him with her tail snapping back and forth behind her.

Ben looked at her in near-horror, wondering if he had misread the atmosphere and overcommitted. <Um...>

<What was that?!> she demanded.

Ben looked at her. Her ears were flattened in panic.

<Um... a 'kiss,'> he said.

<Kisu? What is kisu?> she asked, still keeping a good step away from him.

Ben swallowed, both nervous and mortified. He reached up and scratched the back of his head.

Well, I really fucked this one up, he thought.

He cleared his throat and searched for a way to explain. <Tesho and myorin,> he began. <Um...> He touched his lips. <Touch their lips. Show... um... good feeling for them.>

Alacea's tail continued to whip back and forth as she digested the explanation.

<Don't do that. I don't like that,> she announced.

<I am sorry,> he said. <Much remorse.>

The priestess's tail slowed, and she began to realize that she, too, had made a major miscalculation. She should not have shot down his attempt to show affection to her. She rather *wanted* him to show her affection, and she wanted to show him affection in return. Everything had been going so well, and she had just acted as if he had tried to suck her brain out through her mouth.

She straightened and took a breath. <I apologize,> she said. <You surprised me. I did not know that was how your people... um... show care.>

<Yes, sorry,> Ben repeated. <To ask you how to be better.>

Alacea cleared her throat nervously. <You... You could nip me.>

<'Nip?'> Ben asked.

She turned her head so she wouldn't have to meet his eyes, the hair on her ears beginning to stiffen. <We show care... by nipping,> she explained. <Um... Little bites,> she said. Her ears shook nervously. <On our ears.>

<Oh,> Ben said a few moments later as he worked through the translation. <I... bite your ears?> he confirmed.

<Not hard!> she clarified quickly. <Just... little bites.>

Ben swallowed. <I...I understand,> he said. A few moments of awkward silence went by before he continued. <I... um... try?> he asked.

Alacea turned away and tried to play cool. <If that is what Tesho wants,> she told him, trying very hard to not flee the garden right then and there.

She heard his footsteps as he approached and tried to contain her excitement. She was a 27-year-old vixen, a Mikorin, a *Na'Sha*... She had to be dignified in all things. Even this. Yes, it was her first time. And, yes, she was woefully unprepared for this. But those were not excuses.

He rested his hands on her shoulders.

REEEEEEEEEEEEEE!!! Her mind screamed, but her feet remained planted on the ground.

Ben swallowed nervously. He felt like a middle-schooler about to kiss his first crush. But it wasn't some freckle-faced girl with braces, it was an alien priestess from another world. Leaning down, his breath touched Alacea's delicate ears, and he paused as they fluttered as a result.

After they slowed and stilled again, he continued, moving down and gently putting his teeth on the very tip of her right ear.

Stars exploded in front of Alacea's eyes, and she let out a small squeak despite her heroic efforts to keep it back.

<That... well?> he asked nervously.

<Quite well, quite well,> she replied quickly, her hands folded together to keep them from covering her ears in embarrassment. For a moment, she thought that would be it, a single nip, a formality between two married people who...

Then he nipped her again.

It was just a little harder and a little lower down her ear. Alacea inhaled a deep breath while at the same time trying to hide the fact that she was taking a deep breath. Her lips disappeared as she bit down on them.

<Is also well?> he asked.

<MMM HMM!> she replied.

<Not hurt Myorin?> he asked.

<MMM MMM!> she assured him, biting down on her lip as much as she could stand.

Two bites, and they had been gentle and tender, but she could swear she could feel the tip of her ear burning. She felt his teeth land on another part of her ear and suddenly stepped away, grabbing the hem of her hanbok and rushing back toward the temple.

<IT WAS A WONDERFUL NIGHT IT'S VERY LATE HAVE A BLESSED EVENING!> she cried as she disappeared into the temple without another look back at him.

Ben watched her run off and swallowed nervously. He put his face in his hands and took a deep breath. Chuckling to himself, he started back into the temple send toward the exit. He was a little worried that he had done something wrong, but he knew if he had, Alacea would have corrected him. She was good at understanding that the mistakes he made were exactly that: mistakes.

As he approached the front entrance of the temple, Sho Nan bowed to him and opened the door, allowing him to pass.

<Not bad,> she said just before the door shut behind him.

He whirled around but found the locked door to the temple staring back at him. The Ranger gasped out a laugh and then a few more as he shook his head and started toward the LTV.

* * *

The five Mikorin walked in silence toward the temporary housing that had been arranged for them. Wenlin led the way, and she could almost feel the gazes of her subordinates on the back of her head.

<Speak,> she ordered as she walked, wanting them to just get it out of their systems before they reached the others.

<I thought it was quite insensitive of them to pry into the past,> Tenzeta spoke first. <How did they *think* our temple was lost? Yet they try to manipulate us into either falsely confessing our fault or telling accusatory truths to the new Overlord in our first meeting.>

<I found it puzzling,> Yunhee confessed. <They seemed almost naïve, as if they weren't aware there had ever been a war.>

<I thought they were nice and were trying their best,> Runa told them. <But...> she continued more quietly, <... it wasn't nice to not tell us the Overlord would be there.>

<Agreed,> Hesmea chimed in. <It was as if they were looking forward to watching us grovel. Almost as if they knew of our sacrifices and wanted to push our faces into them.>

Wenlin stopped suddenly, and the other four vixens nearly crashed into her back. The Na'Sha did not turn to them as she spoke, her voice still in the ghostly tone of one devoid of emotion.

<Did you not take note of Alacea Na'Sha's position?> she asked.

The four came up short. It was so difficult to believe that they had seemingly put it out of their minds. A vixen, a Mikorin, a *Mikorin Na'Sha* had allowed a Dark One to take her. Their minds could not wrap around it. It was if they were staring at something their brains knew could not exist and therefore could not process.

<You complain of the sacrifices we have made,> Wenlin continued, prompting Hesmea, in particular, to lower her ears in shame. <While that vixen has given her own *eternity* to protect her people. When we die, our suffering shall end, but hers will continue until the end of all time.>

Wenlin finally turned to them, meeting their gazes with dilated, bloodshot eyes.

<I weep for her,> Wenlin continued. <I weep as she sits next to that monster and pours him tea. I weep to think of the things he subjects her to once the lights of the temple go out for his own sick amusement. I weep... because until now I thought our sacrifice was as much a Mikorin could possibly give and wallowed in self-pity even as I congratulated myself, and us, for making it. I am shamed. And so are you.>

The four Mikorin stared down at their feet, their hands covering their ears in humiliation.

<We will not allow her to endure this burden alone,> Wenlin declared. <Tenzeta...>

At the sound of her name, Garan'Sel's *She Who Feeds* raised her head. <Yes, Na'Sha?>

<Tomorrow, you and the others will seek out new equipment and space,> Wenlin told her. <We shall reopen the bakery.>

The four Mikorin covered their ears again and shut their eyes, their tails shivering in dread at Wenlin's proclamation. She was the Na'Sha. They trusted her to see them through to the next world. There was nothing they could say in opposition.

<We will protect our own people,> Wenlin told them. <We will not burden our hosts. If we can save even one of them from shame, we shall do so. That is our role.>

The remained quiet, and Wenlin took their silence as defiance.

<Say the words,> she ordered, her voice emotionless and cold.
<It shall be done, Na'Sha,> they said in sad unison.

Chapter 6

Six weeks until contact...

Ben looked up at Bellatrix and silently cursed her. She might *look* cooler than Earth's sun with its barely perceptible blue tint, but if you were sitting on the roof of a half-built house, she felt every bit as hot as Sol on an Indiana summer day.

Taking another nail from the box he had borrowed from the SeaBees, the Ranger carefully placed it against the wood plank resting on the roof ridge and prepared to hammer it into place. After a few whacks, Ben checked his work and smiled, satisfied. He looked up at the other end of the house and found that his partner, in the time it took him to nail one board, had already completed four.

"It's not a race," he muttered.

And since it wasn't a race, he felt justified in stopping for a minute and taking a swig from the hydration bladder strapped to his back. It was the only thing he was wearing between his belt and the patrol cap on his head. He had soaked through his uniform shirt in the first hour.

He looked up again and saw that Azarin had also stopped and was taking a drink from a wooden canteen that looked like a small barrel. Like him, Azarin was shirtless. And also like Ben, the tod's body boasted scars from his time at war.

Ben took it as a sign that it was break time and stretched his muscles. The house was coming together quite well, he thought. He was no carpenter, but Azarin, apparently, was, and he had to admit he was learning a lot about how the Va'Shen built structures to last.

The officer looked out at the overgrown fields of red and purple grass. In the distance, he could just make out a wooden fence marking the edge of the property. Apparently, this was not the first house to sit on this land. A pile of stone rested near where they were working, the only remaining indicator that a building had once stood there.

Ben looked at his brother-in-law, but Azarin was looking out at the property as Ben was a moment ago. They barely spoke. Azarin would explain what he needed him to do. Ben would do it. Azarin would explain what he did wrong. Ben would do it all over again. Wash, rinse, repeat.

Weirdly enough, Azarin never seemed to get angry or annoyed with him. He had been working with the former Va'Shen captain part of most days for the last week or so, but so far it had been all business.

Ben decided it was time to change that.

<What do you will grow here?> he asked suddenly.

<What will you grow here,> Azarin corrected.

<Apologies,> Ben said. <What will you grow here?> he repeated.

<Nothing,> Azarin replied.

The answer puzzled Ben. This had obviously, at one time, been a farm, and there was plenty of good land. <No farm?> Ben asked.

<You tell me,> Azarin volleyed back.

<I do not understand,> Ben said. He knew *that* phrase was correct. He used it all the time.

<You are the one who will live here,> Azarin said. <The land is good. Grow whatever you want.>

Ben was certain he was mistranslating something. <I live here?> he asked, pointing at himself.

<I will live here,> Azarin said.

<You will live here?> Ben said, thinking the mistake was cleared up.

<No,> Azarin's ears flattened. <You mean to say, 'I will live here.'>

Ben and his brother-in-law looked at one another in silence for another moment.

<I will live here?> Ben asked again.

<Yes,> Azarin replied carefully and with the patience of a Na'Sha.

<Why I live here?> the Ranger continued.

Azarin didn't bother correcting him this time. <Your camp is not a proper place to raise a family,> Azarin told him. <And neither is the temple. So, you and my sister will live here.>

Ben was so shocked he didn't know what to say. First, the gesture was incredibly kind and had come completely out of left field. Second, how was he supposed to decline such a gift without thoroughly offending the tod?

<Kind,> Ben said finally. <Very, very kind.> He paused. <I could need leave Va'Sh,> he said with trepidation. <May not be able to remain.>

<You are a commando,> Azarin admitted. <Alacea and the children will live here until you return.>

<I...> Ben stopped and took a breath. Whatever happened to him wasn't in his hands, and there had been no indication from the U.S. government as to who may be allowed to travel to or remain on Va'Sh once the occupation inevitably ended.

Would I even want to stay on Va'Sh?

There was also a chance he would have to stay past his initial deployment. He still hadn't heard anything about where the Persephone survivors would go next. He might be asked to stay on in Pelle or sent to another part of Va'Sh entirely.

It all added up to say that there was really no point in trying to refuse Azarin's offer since he had no idea where he would be a year from now nor any control over it whatsoever.

<Thank you,> he told Azarin quietly, adding as deep a bow as his position on the roof would allow.

Azarin bowed back. <I leave my sister to your care. It is not my preference,> he added. <But my sister has made her decision.>

<I understand,> Ben replied.

<I stand ready to aid my sister however she may need,> Azarin told him pointedly.

Translation: Hurt her, and I'll fucking end you, Ben thought before bowing again in acceptance. Big brothers were the same on every planet, it seemed.

<Please excuse me for interrupting!>

The two looked down at the source of the sudden intrusion on their male bonding and found a familiar blue-and-white-haired vixen in a pale blue and white hanbok looking up at them from the ground.

Azarin tensed suddenly while Ben gave the Mikorin a wave.

<Blessed day, Hestean Aru'Dace,> Ben called down.

The historian looked away suddenly, her blue and white tail moving quickly back and forth.

<Might I trouble you both to put on your shirts?> she called over her shoulder.

"Oh, shit, yeah," Ben muttered in reply, looking for where he left his uniform top. Azarin stood on the roof and walked back to his own brown and white, loose-sleeved shirt, throwing it on without a word before heading toward the ladder.

Now that they were fully clothed, Hestean turned back to them and bowed regally.

<Blessed day,> she said to them both.

<You need me?> Ben asked, pointing at himself.

<No, Overlord. Thank you,> Hestean replied. <I must speak with Azarin.>

The former commando looked at her with his single, predatory eye but said nothing.

<Yes, good,> Ben said. He pointed at where they had left their pre-made lunches. <I go to there.>

Hestean bowed again as Ben walked off. He wasn't quite outside of earshot, but, in a way, Azarin preferred that.

The Va'Shen carpenter bowed to her. <How may I assist the community?> he asked her formally.

Hestean replied in an equally formal tone. <I must speak with you concerning the commando's time spent away from Pelle. The history must accurately reflect the events as they happened and, most importantly, why they happened that way.>

<I recommend you speak with Tasshas,> Azarin told her plainly. <He is much better with words than I am and has a good understanding of everything that happened.>

The historian, however, would not be swayed. <As you were their captain, I am bound by duty to speak with *you*,> she told him.

<And you have no concerns with doing so?> he asked her.

<Of course not,> she assured him.

<I do.>

Hestean's tail whipped against the ground in pique. <And why is that?> she demanded formally. <Am I to believe you are incapable of behaving as a civilized tod in the presence of an unwed vixen?>

Azarin's eye met hers and narrowed at the implication. <It would wound me greatly to hear you believed that,> he said.

<As well it should, and I would add it is impossible for me to do so.>

<Others would not think so,> Azarin said. Realizing he was stepping ever so closely to the line between the formalized speech they hid behind and his true thoughts, he paused a moment. <Some... who believe they know much about me... would see us alone together and suggest an ulterior motive.> He paused again. <I would not see your honor stained by such a thing.>

<If my honor could be stained by such a small thing, then it must not be that great to begin with,> she returned.

<All the same, I will not allow such a thing,> he told her. <My... respect... for our Aru'Dace is far too great to tolerate it.>

<Your respect is acknowledged and appreciated,> Hestean replied. <But my duty remains. Would you interfere with it? That would be a far greater stain on my honor, to be known as an Aru'Dace whose role is considered so inconsequential that a commando captain could not spare her a little of his time.>

Azarin's tail was beginning to move a little faster in irritation. Why couldn't she see that he was trying to protect her?

<Then I must insist on a chaperone,> he told her.

<A chaperone?!>

<Yes,> Azarin held firm. <No one could suggest impropriety then.>

From off to the side, Ben watched the back and forth with the same interest a tennis fan watches a match. His eyes moved back and forth with each volley as he silently observed while eating a ham sandwich.

Hestean's ears were digging into her skull. <Your argument has a fatal weakness.>

<How so?>

<You say we need a chaperone to avoid the appearance of impropriety, yet the very presence of a chaperone, when one has not previously been used, implies a desire for impropriety.>

Hestean's tail slapped the ground, and the change in Azarin's ears made Ben think the historian had won an important battle.

And he was right. Azarin was trapped. How could they have a chaperone to show that everything was right and proper when the very presence of a chaperone suggested the need for one? As the silence persisted, the former commando could hear the sound of chewing, and his eye turned until it fell on his brother-in-law.

Azarin's ears twitched a smile.

<Brother,> he suddenly called, making Hestean's ears pop up in puzzlement.

Ben looked around and pointed at himself as if to say, "Who? Me?"

<Hestean Aru'Dace must speak with me to learn about what we did during the fight with your people,> he explained slowly. <Would you like to listen and learn?>

The Mikorin looked away, her ears once again flattened against her head. Azarin, on the other hand, seemed cool and collected.

Ben wasn't stupid. He understood he was being dragged into a fight. But as an officer, a soldier, and a historian himself, he *really* wanted a briefing on what the Pelle commandos did during the war. It could provide enough background information to help him in his relationship with them as a group.

<When you do this?> he asked.

Azarin looked over at Hestean for the answer. The blue-haired vixen, it appeared, was ready to give up.

<Tomorrow. Three bells after midday. At the temple.>

Shit...

Ben shook his head. <I must go to speak with my field cornet,> he said. A new commanding general had just taken command of the combined joint task force, and Ben had been asked to come for a face-to-face meeting.

Azarin's ears fell, and Hestean's rose.

<Um... Patricia Kim can go?> Ben asked. In a way it made more sense for her to go as she was their intelligence officer and better able to follow the conversation anyway.

Once again, the placement of the two Va'Shens' ears switched.

<That would be more than acceptable,> Azarin told him. The fact that Patricia was a female, if anything, made her a better choice for a stealth chaperone anyway.

<Yes, good,> Ben said. <I will tell her.>

It was obvious by her ears and tail that Hestean didn't like this, but she nevertheless bowed to Ben. <Thank you, Overlord.> Rising from her bow, she gave Azarin a sharp, but disappointed look, turned on her heel and started down the path toward the main road.

The two veterans watched her go, and Ben turned to Azarin. <Azarin and Hestean good friends?> he asked.

<Hestean is a Mikorin,> Azarin replied, walking back toward the ladder.

Ben waited for more, but Azarin seemed to feel that those four words explained everything about what just happened. He wondered if he should pry a little more but then smiled.

Whatever it was, he bet Alacea knew what was up. He'd ask her. Although, she *had*, it seemed, been avoiding since the night he kissed/nipped her.

Ben was far from a virgin. But with all the differences between his culture and Alacea's, he kind of felt that way, fumbling around while trying to figure out if the things he said and did were romantic or cringe-inducing.

The nip, he was afraid, could have gone either way. He still wasn't sure why he had done it. He just... wanted to. They were in the garden, the moons were out, she was beautiful... It was a perfect set-up for a first kiss, so he went for it.

He looked up at Azarin and wondered, given their most recent conversation, how he would feel if he knew about it.

The answer, he decided, was "not very good."

* * *

Blllbblblblblblblblblblblblb...

<So... this again,> Sho Nan announced as she and Pavastea slipped into the bath and watched their Na'Sha, sitting low with the water up to her nose, visibly pouting.

<But everything was going so well!> Pavastea cried, amazed. <What could he have done to ruin it!?>

<Nothing,> Sho Nan answered. <It's her fault.>

<It is not!> Alacea cried suddenly, the water in the bath splashing outward as a result of her outburst.

<It is?> Pavastea asked, acting as if Alacea had said nothing at all.

<The Overlord, Dark One though he may be, cannot be accused of not trying,> Sho Nan said.

Alacea's glare and ears turned to the blue-haired woman. <What do you know of it?>

<I am the Ya'Jahar,> Sho Nan told her as she dabbed a wet cloth on her neck. <I know of all things that occur in this temple.>

<YOU WERE PEEPING?!> Alacea cried, leaping to her feet.

<'Peeping' is a childish word used to describe young tods hiding in trees to look in at vixens' bedrooms,> Sho Nan countered. <I, however, was hiding behind a bush.>

<SHO NAN!> Alacea cried in complete mortification. <That is so inappropriate!>

Pavastea looked at Sho Nan in awe. <You must tell me everything,> she said.

<PAVASTEA!>

Alacea covered her ears and fell back into the water in shame. As soon as she had run off that night, she had gone straight to her room, thrown herself onto her futon and rolled around while silently chastising herself for her behavior.

Why did you do that?! her mind had screamed.

I don't know!!!! another part had screamed back.

Everything had been going wonderfully! They were on the precipice of a world-shaking change in their relationship!

And then she *ran!*

<Why did you run?>

For a moment, Alacea thought she had asked the question of herself. It wasn't until Sho Nan repeated herself that she realized it had come from her friend, who was now looking at her questioningly.

Alacea looked down at the water. <I don't know,> she said. <I was just... overwhelmed... by all of it.>

<I see,> Sho Nan said.

<Do you think he is angry?> Alacea asked them.

<I cannot imagine the tod I met the night of your Facilitation being angry with you for something like that,> Pavastea told her. <I do believe, however, he would be rightfully confused.>

<The Overlord is incredibly patient for a male,> Sho Nan added. <*I* would have put an end to your nonsense weeks ago.>

<Well, that is why I didn't marry *you*,> Alacea said in reply to her friend's joke.

<For which you will live forever in regret,> Sho Nan continued.

<Why don't you just nip him the next time you see him and let him know everything is fine?> Pavastea suggested.

<How am I supposed to do that?> the Na'Sha demanded. <I can't just walk up to him and nip him!>

<Why not?> Pavastea volleyed. <Do not other married couples do so?>

<Yes, but...> Alacea sank deeper into the water in an effort to escape the embarrassing line of questioning.

<Alacea,> Sho Nan said, stunning the other two Va'Shen. Sho Nan rarely used the Na'Sha's name. Though the two had grown up as friends and still considered each other thus, protocol demanded Alacea be referred to with respect.

Apparently, Sho Nan intended for this to demonstrate how seriously she took her next statement.

<This is not the courageous vixen who drew a knife in an attempt to defend my life,> Sho Nan told her frankly. <Nor is it the

conviction of the Na'Sha who bared her throat to the enemy for her people. You demonstrate courage for the benefit of everyone around you, but when the time comes to harness that courage for yourself, you falter. If you are strong enough to die for other people, you can surely brave a few moments' embarrassment for the sake of your own happiness.>

Alacea and Pavastea stared at her in shock.

<I think that is the most I have ever heard Sho Nan say at once,> Pavastea commented.

<And, as usual for Sho Nan, her words are pointed, barbed... and true,> Alacea relented.

<Good,> Sho Nan said, settling back into the water. <Now bare your fangs and hunt him like a proper vixen. The ambiguity of your relationship is beginning to bore me.>

<Sho Nan,> Pavastea muttered in disapproval.

<No, she is right,> Alacea said, rising to her feet. <The time has come!>

<The time has come!> Pavastea cheered.

<Go forth and do not falter,> Sho Nan ordered.

Properly motivated, Alacea climbed out of the tub and went to change, leaving the other two vixens alone.

<Do you think she will do it?> Pavastea asked.

Sho Nan did not reply.

* * *

A few hours passed, and as it did, Alacea began to wonder if, perhaps, the time has *not* come. After all, she reasoned, you shouldn't just nip someone without a reason...

Right?

She had just managed to convince herself of this when an acolyte came to her room and announced that the Overlord had come asking for her.

<Shall I bring him here?> the young vixen asked her.

Alacea thought for a moment. If she met him here, she could be reasonably assured that Sho Nan was not secretly peeping on them. If she met him downstairs, she wouldn't be able to be very intimate with him.

<I will meet him downstairs,> she said, quietly kicking herself for her cowardice. In her mind's eye, she could see Sho Nan, her arms folded across her chest as she looked scornfully down at her.

The acolyte had left before she could change her mind, however, and Alacea simply had to accept that, no, the time truly had not come.

Pausing only long enough to check her appearance in the mirror, the head priestess went downstairs and found that the acolyte had shown her Tesho to a meeting room where he was standing with his hat in his hands. As she entered, he smiled and gave her a short bow.

<Blessed evening, Myorin,> he greeted.

<And to you, Tesho,> she said with a bow of her own.

They stood there awkwardly for a few moments, neither quite sure what to say or whether to address the events that occurred during their last meeting.

Finally, Ben decided to just get down to business. <Wanted tell you,> he said, <Will be gone two, three days. Must see big overlord.>

<Ah!> Alacea said. <I see. Thank you for telling me.>

More awkward silence.

<Um...> Ben continued after several uncomfortable moments. <Ask... discomfortable thing?>

Alacea's tail twitched. Here it comes...

Why did you run from your Tesho?

She braced for the question, but what came instead surprised her.

<Azarin and Hestean,> he began. <Um... They talk today. They will talk tomorrow. Patricia there for talk.>

<Oh!> Alacea replied. <Hestean must interview Azarin. So, Patricia will be there as well? That is... interesting...>

She knew Hestean was hesitant to speak alone with her brother, but she thought she had gotten over it. She wondered why she would ask Patricia, of all people, to chaperone them...

Ben watched her reaction carefully before starting again.

<Azarin and Hestean... big friends?> he asked.

Alacea was taken aback by her Tesho's question. Was it really so obvious that even someone from another world had noticed? Her ears folded inward as she thought about how to respond. She did not want to lie to her Tesho. At the same time, was it really her secret to tell?

As she considered it, though, she found that there was no reason to not tell him. It was a *family* secret. He was her Tesho. And he was the Overlord. If he was asking her, he might have a good reason to need to know.

She gestured to the table, prompting him to sit, and she knelt down on the opposite side of the table from him. As she waited for him to get comfortable, she tried to think of a good way to word it.

<Azarin and Hestean... care for each other a great deal,> she said. <After our parents died, I went to the temple where I met and became close friends with Hestean and Sho Nan. My brother was worried about me and came often to the temple to check on me.>

Her ears twitched at the happy memories of growing up in the temple with her Mikorin sisters. She paused for a moment to make sure Ben was following the story before continuing.

<As we got older,> she went on, <I began to sense that my brother was coming to the temple more to see Hestean than to check on me. And Hestean was finding reasons to be present during his visits.>

Ben nodded his head. <I see,> he said. "Puppy love."

"Poopy lahv?" Alacea repeated.

The Ranger switched back to Va'Shen. <Nice love,> he said. <Um... young love.>

<Yes,> Alacea said with a touch of sadness. <Sho Nan and I pretended we did not see. I wish now we had not. They became rather... careless... about it.> She looked up at him. <I have said before... Mikorin cannot be taken by common tods. They belong to the community. A noble may take them, but it is normally a noble from outside the community.>

Ben stopped her to clear up a translation, but she soon continued her story.

<The stone that broke the jar was when Hestean gave Azarin a lock of her hair,> she said. At Ben's questioning look, she explained. <A gift of hair from a vixen to a tod is like saying she is in love.>

<Oh,> Ben replied. <I understand.>

<Jemenista Na'Sha took them both into private and berated them. She told Hestean that Mikorin are forbidden from such relationships. But she was much more harsh with my brother.>

Alacea paused again to make sure Ben was keeping up, but he quickly gestured for her to continue, wanting to hear what happened next.

The priestess looked down at the table, her ears drooping. <She told him that even just the appearance that he was pursuing a Mikorin... and that that Mikorin was receptive... stained her honor, that it risked destroying the respect Hestean would hold in the community.>

<Really bad?> Ben asked.

Alacea thought on his question, trying to determine what he really meant to ask. <For us,> she replied, <When you love another, the worst thing you can do is bring shame to them, to darken their honor.>

Ben didn't reply, and she assumed that answered his question.

<My brother is an honorable tod,> she told her Tesho. <And the thought that he was bringing dishonor to Hestean shamed him greatly.> She looked down at the table again. <He stopped coming to the temple and even when he and Hestean crossed paths, he spoke to her only in the most formal way, a way befitting her station. Not because he didn't love her anymore... but because he did... and does... greatly.>

Ben listened to the sad story and sighed. It was a Va'Shen "Romeo and Juliet," the kind of story someone could turn into a romance novel like the one Dr. Morant had lent him.

<Why no run away as both?> he asked. He knew that was what humans would do. Run off and start over in some other place and be happy.

Alacea looked like the very question was scandalous. <To be a Mikorin is to live a life of service and sacrifice,> she told him. <How could she ever face the Gods if she abandoned it?>

Ben nodded sadly. The world he came from did not place much value in the few religions that remained, so it was hard for him, sometimes, to realize just how powerful a force the Va'Shen gods were for them. They were not just some way to teach morality or a way to explain away the meaning of a person's life. They were living, breathing things that created the Va'Shen... and demanded their respect.

Her words and the thoughts that followed brought up an uncomfortable question for him.

<Um... You... will be well... With...> He stopped and just pointed at her and himself.

Alacea seemed to get what he was asking, and her ears twitched a smile. <Our situation is different,> she said. <When I let you take me... it *was* as a sacrifice for my community.> She looked at him, and there was something sad in her eyes. <I assumed... that you would spend the rest of my life... hurting me. And that when I died,

the Gods would allow you to continue hurting me... forever.> She looked down, somewhat ashamed of her previous fears. <That was the sacrifice I was willing to make for my community.>

<I am sorry,> Ben said quietly. When she looked up at him, he continued. <I did not want for you to be afraid. I just wanted to find and help Pelle people.>

Her ears twitched again. <I know that now. And what I once considered a sacrifice, I know now was a gift.> She reached across the table and took his hand in hers. <You were gifted to us by the Gods... and to me.>

<Alacea,> Ben whispered, feeling a lump in his throat. There, in that moment, he understood Azarin's feelings. The woman in front of him triggered something in him, something that made him want to protect her... from *everything*... and in every way.

But that also made him feel guilty.

<I may need leave one day,> he told her. <You... could not come with me.>

Her ears twitched. <I know,> she said. She looked up into his eyes. <I am the Na'Sha. This is my community. I belong to them even as I belong to you. If I sacrifice one... it must only to be for the greatest good of the other.>

Ben understood. The work she did here in Pelle, what she *was* to the villagers here... There was no way being a dependent spouse living on an Army base somewhere on Earth or the colonies could ever rise to that level. If she were ever forced to choose... to sacrifice... she would sacrifice him.

The same way, he knew, he would be asked to sacrifice her.

<But we would meet again,> she said as if she could read his thoughts. <This life is only the prologue to eternity. Even if you left, we would see each other again in the Glade... and then forever.>

That was according to the Va'Shen religion, their belief in gods that the overwhelming majority of humans would scoff at in disdain as primitive and stupid.

But in that moment, Ben never wanted to believe something more than he did right then.

<It is late,> she said, rising to her feet. <You must travel tomorrow, yes?>

<Yes,> he agreed quietly, almost disappointed.

Looking up, he found her looking down at him with twitching ears and happy eyes. <Then I shall see you when you return.>

He smiled.

<Yes. Yes, you shall.>

Chapter 7

Six weeks until contact...

As Ben exited the well-decorated office of Va'Sh's highest-ranking U.S. military officer, he sighed in relief. One never knew what kind of general officer you were going to get when a new commander rotated in. Ben's star had been on the rise at headquarters considering Sector 13's progress, the release of the Pelle detainees and his own actions during the recent glasser attack on the base.

But all of that happened before the new general had come in. He hadn't seen it. Ben wasn't *his* guy.

So, realistically, none of it meant anything.

And that was the gist of the speech he had gotten. "You're doing good work. Keep it up. But remember to respect the chain of command."

He was already bracing himself for the litany of "good ideas" that were ready to fall on his command from the new leadership. Ben was so fixated on it that he almost didn't respond when, passing the executive officer's desk, the man sitting there called, "Have a good one."

"Yeah, you too," he said, turning his head just briefly to acknowledge the man. But in that quick look, he saw something that made him stop and turn back.

"Executive officer" meant something very different in the Army and Air Force than it did in the Navy. In the Navy, the "XO" was the second in command. But in the Army, Air and Space Forces, "the exec" was, for all intents and purposes, the commander's secretary. Well, *one* of the commander's secretaries. They would also typically have an actual secretary as well. It usually meant very long hours doing work that ranged from the actually important to the downright menial, and the payoff was, sometimes, you got some mentoring. It was still seen as a stepping stone to higher command, though most execs Ben had known would have chopped off their left hand if it meant going back to a combat unit.

The man behind the desk had short dark hair, but not a high-and-tight. He had obviously grown it out a little. A bright gold oak leaf sat firmly on the front of his uniform jacket, but his desk was rather spartan.

But it was the nametag on his uniform that made Ben stop.

"Major Keyes?" Ben asked. "Elkanah Keyes?"

The major looked up. "That's right," he said. He saw Ben's name tag and stood up, offering his hand to shake. "Captain Gibson, Sector 13, right?"

"That's right," Ben confirmed with a smile as he shook the man's hand. "It's nice to meet you. I heard a lot about you and your folks up in Sector Six."

"I understand you actually ended up with some of them," Keyes said.

"Yeah, Sergeant Mitchell and about forty others," Ben said.

"Mitchell's a good NCO," Keyes told him. "Just a little young for the additional responsibilities."

"Aren't they all?" the Ranger quipped. "You'd think they could spare us *one* senior NCO."

"But then who would run the coffee machines here?" Keyes joked.

Ben laughed. "Hey, would it be possible for you and me to talk over lunch or something?" he asked. "I'd like to pick your brain about the Garan'Sel folks we have now."

"Sure," Keyes told him, checking his watch. "I was just about to go on lunch now. You available?"

"Definitely."

Keyes smiled and grabbed his patrol cap off his desk. "Then lead on."

* * *

One day every week was reserved for Market, when the villagers of Pelle would gather in the village's main thoroughfare and sell their wares. Most villagers had some form of side-employment where they would craft or scavenge or produce something that might fetch them a few extra ears, and most other village activity stopped during Market so everyone could participate.

Because of the wide array of crafts, food and potential souvenirs, it was also the day most troops on FOB Leonard liked to go out into the village. At first, many of the villagers were concerned to see Dark Ones coming out of their base in groups and looking around their little town. Although the relationship between the two races in Pelle was fairly good, anytime the humans did something new, the Va'Shen were nervous. They wondered if the Dark Ones would simply go around taking what they wanted or would just rudely gawk at the villagers as they sold their wares.

Then they found out the Dark Ones had *money*.

Not only that, the Dark Ones wanted to *spend it*.

The Overlord's plan to send his troops into the village to both improve relations and the local economy worked better than he could have hoped. The troops were bored, and there was an entirely new alien world out there for them to explore.

Of course, there were some growing pains. Humans found out rather quickly that the Va'Shen didn't haggle, and the first time someone tried to get a better deal on a piece of hand-crafted leather jewelry, it almost caused an incident. The Va'Shen, it seemed, saw haggling as an insult to all concerned. An honorable merchant, farmer or craftsman had an obligation to sell their products for a reasonable amount to cover the materials, labor and enough of a profit to adequately benefit the merchant. An honorable buyer had an obligation to respect the efforts of the merchant in bringing the product to market and the price the merchant set. To haggle was to imply that the merchant's efforts were either inadequate or that they were attempting to cheat the buyer.

Fortunately, those first few days Alacea had had the Mikorin out and about to defuse such situations, and they and Ben's NCOs had quickly made public announcements explaining the newly-discovered rules. By this point, most Va'Shen were willing to accept that the Dark Ones needed a learning curve, and as long as bad behavior did not persist, they were willing to let it go.

Since then, Market had become the busiest day of the week in Pelle for the Va'Shen *and* the humans, who would walk around searching for some new shiny to spend their money on.

Alzoria, however, was not shopping today. She was on the hunt, weaving her way through chattering crowds of Pelle and Garan'Sel villagers in search of a certain alien soldier. The Huntress wasn't a very tall vixen, and Ramirez was short for a Dark One, which made it difficult for her to find him in the crowd. But being the clever Huntress she was, she knew the trick wasn't to look for Ramirez himself, but his much larger, darker friend.

That's how she zeroed in on her target, strolling down the main street, looking over the leather crafts at one of the stalls nearby.

The peach-blonde's ears twitched, and she made her way stealthily through the crowd until she was standing behind Ramirez and Burgers, examining a grey strap of leather and asking questions of the dark-haired tanner on the other side of the table.

"John!" she called out.

Ramirez jumped in surprise and turned, his lips turning up as he recognized her. "Hey, Al!" he said.

"Hallo Bahgers," she greeted the taller man with a wave.

Burgers smiled and waved back. "Hey, Alzoria." <You are doing well?> he asked in passable Va'Shen.

"All good an da hood," Alzoria assured him in similarly passable English.

Burgers looked quickly between Ramirez and Alzoria and cleared his throat. "I'ma go get something to eat. I'll be right back."

Before Ramirez could say anything, the other Ranger was making his way through the crowd, leaving Ramirez there holding the strap and Alzoria looking at him with her hands behind her back.

"What'cha doo'in?" Alzoria asked him.

Ramirez held up the strap for her to see. "I want to use this to hold my rifle," he said, not sure "sling" would translate well.

"Oh," she replied, taking a close look at the leather strap. "It is good made. *Datsu* skin strong."

"Yeah, I think I'm going to get it," Ramirez said, turning back to the tanner. <Three ears?> he asked.

<Three,> the merchant confirmed. Ramirez searched his pocket and produced three triangular metal coins, offering them to the tanner.

The merchant bowed, and the Ranger bowed back. Transaction honorably completed. With that done, Ramirez turned back to Alzoria.

<You look for thing?> he asked her.

<I was looking for you,> she replied, her tail swishing behind her as the two began to walk. "I make you thing for you," she added in English.

"Me?" he asked.

Alzoria pulled her hands from behind her back and held them up to him. In her fingers was a small loop of braided material that shimmered red and gold in the light. The braid ran through several black and red beads that could move freely along the length of the material.

Ramirez took the familiar item and smiled. "A pace counter?" he asked, fingering the material.

"Like what you have," she said, pointing at his left wrist.

The Ranger held up his wrist, showing her a similar-looking piece of "jewelry." Rangers used pace counter beads to measure distances travelled on foot during night when visibility was an issue.

"Thank you so much," he said, holding the bracelet up to the light and examining it. As he fingered the material, he wondered briefly what it was made of before his eyes went back to Alzoria, who was looking away and playing absently with her hair.

Her gold and red hair.

"Did you make this with your hair?" he asked, pointing at her head.

The fur on the vixen's ears stiffened in embarrassment. "Vixens do for tods," she explained, her English skills abandoning her in her nervousness.

"Wow!" Ramirez said. "Al... I don't know what to say." He smiled. "It is beautiful."

Alzoria looked down at the ground, her tail whipping around spasmodically.

"Thank you," she said quietly. She was glad he liked the gift but was still somewhat disappointed that he didn't seem to understand the significance of it. A vixen's hair was her pride. Myorin, sisters and mothers would often give items made from their hair to the tods in their lives. During the war, vixens donated their hair to make ropes or tripwires for their commandos. When an unmarried vixen gave her hair to a tod, it was a grand gesture of emotional interest. It was essentially an open invitation for the tod to take her as his myorin.

Ramirez, of course, understood none of this, but he still appreciated the gift. He removed his old pace counter and immediately replaced it with the one Alzoria had given him.

"Thank you," he said again and bowed to her.

Standing not far away, a young Va'Shen woman watched the exchange with great interest.

<Turean, who is that vixen?> Posha asked, her ears pointed at Alzoria as if in emphasis.

The one-armed young man looked, and his ears twitched. <That is Alzoria. She's one of the Huntresses.>

Posha looked down at the fire-glazed clay bowl she had been considering as she continued speaking. <Is it common for her to behave so... indecently?>

Turean's tail twitched in confusion. He had happened upon Posha at the market, who had come into the village proper to post a letter. Turean had escorted her to the mercantile where messages came and went through Pelle. Afterward, she had asked him to show her around the different stalls. The young man had immediately agreed. As a cripple, vixens tended to not pay him much attention, but as a young tod, he wished greatly for it.

<Indecently?> he asked. <What do you mean?>

<I mean look at her,> the Garan'Sel villager replied. <A vixen shouldn't be hanging all over a Dark One like that. People will think she's seeking a tesho.>

<Oh,> Turean said, his ears twitching again. <I think she is.> At Posha's startled look, he continued. <That is Corporal Rahmeeraz. They are close. I heard her uncle even sought an arrangement on her behalf.>

<I see,> Posha said noncommittally.

Her eyes left the bowl and found Alzoria again, and this time they did not leave her.

* * *

"So, what do you want to know?"

Ben sat on the opposite side of the small chow hall table from Keyes and took a sip of his coffee as the other officer began to put various condiments on his cheeseburger.

"Basically, just a little about your experience with the Garan'Sel folks," Ben told him. "I've spoken to a few of them, but they're not very talkative."

"Well, that's good, actually," Keyes told him as he shook some pepper onto the burger. "If they're not talking, they're not lying to you."

Ben pursed his lips at the response. "I heard things up north were pretty intense," he said. "I take it you had some issues with them."

"Plenty... at first," Keyes replied with a shrug. "Who hasn't? But after a while, they figured out we weren't going anywhere. Show a little weakness, and they'll go after you hard. Show some strength from the jump, and they'll reassess their situation. You know how it is. I'm sure you had your own problems with them."

"Most of our problems have come with communication," Ben said. "We've been fortunate in that we haven't had any violence."

"Well, we had plenty of that," Keyes told him. "The Va'Shen like to talk a big game about their honor, but that doesn't stop them from knifing you as soon as your back is turned."

Ben bit his lip. He felt like he wanted to defend the Va'Shen, but it was difficult considering his first encounter with Kasshas had resulted in the chieftain lying through his teeth at him. In fairness, he might have done the same in his position, but remembering how angry he was back then, it was hard to take issue with Keyes's feelings on the matter.

"I had some early issues with their chieftain," Ben admitted. "Speaking of which, I was told that Garan'Sel didn't have one."

Keyes looked at him and gave him a resigned look. "That's the kind of thing I'm talking about," he said. "Lots of assurances of cooperation and peace. Then, one day, we start taking fire from a ridgeline overlooking our FOB. Lob some mortars in reply, and, lo and behold, whose body do we find up there? The chief."

"That's disappointing," Ben sighed.

"I expected it would happen eventually," Keyes told him. "Their viciousness walks hand-in-hand with their duplicity. We learned after that, kept a much tighter leash on them and let them know there would be consequences for attacking our people."

Again, Keyes's attitude gave Ben pause. "What kind of consequences?" he asked.

Keyes took a bite of his burger and chewed before answering. "Stuff I'm sure civilians back home wouldn't care for," he said. "But necessary all the same. You can't judge the Va'Shen by human standards. Those ears and tails aren't just for show. They're more animal than man. And sometimes you have to treat them like that. The Slovaks, the Koreans in the neighboring sectors... they never got that. They were trying to deal with the Va'Shen like the would the Albertans or the Martians. They didn't understand that the Va'Shen *think* differently."

Ben noticed that Keyes hadn't actually answered his question, and he let the silence hang in the air for a moment before asking his next question.

"What happened to their temple?" he asked.

Keyes looked up from his meal and gave the Ranger a half-smirk. "Wenlin trying to pin that on us too?"

"All Wenlin said was that it burned down and some people died," Ben answered. "She didn't blame anyone."

Keyes wiped his hands on a napkin before replying. "A couple of insurgents with laser rifles took a few shots at one of our safehouses in the downtown area," he said. "My troops went after them, and the insurgents ran into the temple, declaring 'sanctuary.'"

Ben listened with a cold feeling growing in the pit of his stomach.

"Out of respect," Keyes went on, "We didn't go in after them. We surrounded the place and decided to wait them out. We sure as hell weren't going to just shrug our shoulders and let them slip out." He took a sip from his soda before going on. "Well, 'sanctuary' means something a lot different for the Va'Shen then for us, I guess, because our guys started taking laser fire from the top floor of the temple. We returned fire."

Ben took a breath. Under the rules of war, some places were protected from military attack. Religious buildings were among them. But if that building were to be used for military purposes, it lost that protection.

"My guess is some of the tracers hit some paper doors or something, and the place went up," Keyes finished.

Not an ounce of regret in his voice, Ben noticed. Keyes could have been talking about some weeds he pulled in his garden. Legally, the major was in the right, but even so, surely he could have foreseen the immense emotional cost to the Va'Shen for losing their temple and how that would translate to his relationship with them.

"Unfortunate," was all he said.

"In some ways," Keyes told him. "In others it was a boon. Their religious leader, the 'Na'Sha' they call her, died in the fire. That's when Wenlin took over. She was much more cooperative than her predecessor or their chieftain. Things got easier after that. But you still gotta watch her."

Ben thought of the short, dark-haired vixen and her evasive answers to his questions. The vixen had looked at him in absolute fear, and he was beginning to see why.

"Hey, I gotta go," Keyes said suddenly, looking at his watch. "The commander has meetings this afternoon. I hope this helped."

"Yeah," Ben replied with a nod. "Yeah, thanks." He stood up and shook Keyes's hand.

"Good luck, Captain," Keyes told him. "Just keep a tight rein and you'll be all right. I let Wenlin know that you weren't one to be fucked with. Hopefully, that will start you off on the right foot."

"What do you mean?" Ben asked.

"I told her about Persephone," Keyes said as he gathered up his hat and empty lunch tray. At Ben's silence, he went on. "I hope that's okay. I didn't think it was a secret."

"It's not," Ben said. "We just don't make it a big deal down there."

"You should," Keyes advised him. "The Va'Shen have a 'right of vengeance.' It can justify just about anything you may have to do with them, and they can't say boo about it."

"You know a lot about the Va'Shen," Ben commented.

"Yeah," Keyes said as he turned to go. "And it was all learned the hard way." With that, he walked away toward the exit to drop off his tray, leaving Ben there alone with his thoughts.

"I don't doubt it," he whispered.

* * *

Patricia could hardly contain her excitement as she placed her notepad and pen on the polished purple wooden table in front of her. There were intelligence officers all over the galaxy who would kill for the opportunity to listen in on a debrief of a commando captain about his actions during the war. There were still things the Army didn't understand about the Va'Shen. They had a good handle on their organization, but some of their tactics, their way of planning, their technology were still a mystery. It didn't help that the Va'Shen captured and interrogated had been, like Azarin, almost completely silent about anything the humans might ask them, no matter how benign.

Even their technology refused to offer them any clues. Their hardlight rifles, for instance, still had scientists pulling their hair out on Earth. There didn't seem to be a single screw or machine mark on any of them, as if there were forged from a single piece of... well... whatever they were made of. That, too, was still a mystery. To add insult to injury, whenever one was cut into by laser torches or drilled into, the internal components *liquified*. It was as if the weapons' creators wanted to ensure that no one, not even the troops who carried them, would ever know how they worked.

Glassers were even worse. It seemed that if they came into contact with any living thing that wasn't a Va'Shen, they went off. They still couldn't even figure out how the Va'Shen activated them. After the war was over, a Va'Shen soldier demonstrated their use, running a finger along the smooth crystal side in different patterns for differing effects. No buttons, no switches, no pins. For humans, it may as well have been magic.

So, for an intel officer like her, the prospect of being the one to solve these mysteries excited Patricia to no end.

Sitting on opposite sides of the table in front of her, however, Hestean and Azarin appeared less than enthused. The Mikorin's blue and white tail would gently slap the floor every so often, while Azarin sat motionless, his arms crossed over his chest as if deliberately trying to appear standoffish.

<We shall begin,> Hestean announced quietly, dipping her pen in an inkwell. <You are Azarin, son of Forazin, the most recent elected captain of the First Prince's Storm Rifles, drawn from the village of Pelle.>

<I am,> Azarin confirmed.

<Your commando was assigned to the Thornbush under Field Cornet Dao Fun.>

<It was.>

<I am sorry excuse please,> Patricia interrupted, her hand raised. The two Va'Shen looked at her and waited patiently for her to continue. <What is the Thornbush?>

<It is one of the holy realms the Va'Shen were charged with protecting by the Great Ones,> Hestean replied.

<A world?> Patricia asked. <Like Va'Sh?>

<Yes,> Hestean told her. <I do not know what your people would call it.>

<Thank you. I am sorry,> Patricia said.

The two Va'Shen continued, and Patricia listened carefully, taking notes as quickly but as thoroughly as she could as Hestean probed deeper and deeper into the Pelle commando's activities.

<How many battles with the Dark Ones did you fight?> Hestean asked him.

<Twenty-six separate battles,> Azarin told her.

The historian made a note. <I would like to ask about the weapons and equipment the Dark Ones used against you,> she said.

Patricia listened as Azarin described human weapon systems with rapt interest. At one point she interrupted again.

<This is not right,> she said.

<What do you mean?> Hestean asked.

<Weapons we use,> Patricia told her. <Not deliberate loud. Just loud because they are loud.>

Azarin looked at her, his tail twitching in surprise. <Truly?> he asked with interest. <We assumed they were made that way to damage our hearing.>

Patricia shook her head, forgetting for a moment that the gesture meant nothing to the Va'Shen. <Have used for many many years. They are just loud. We have ways to make them quiet, but... um... cost more.>

<Interesting,> Azarin commented. <Is it the same for your flying vehicles?>

<Yes. Just loud. Would like them to not be loud,> she admitted. <But they are loud.>

Hestean was furiously taking notes, and Patricia realized she may have just given military information to their former enemies. It's not like it was sensitive information, but as an intelligence officer, it made her feel guilty all the same.

The historian looked up at Azarin and continued her questioning.

<Did you fight *tanpuki* during your time there?> she asked.

<No,> Azarin replied. <We trained to fight them, but they never appeared.>

<*Tanpuki*?> Patricia asked.

<Again, I don't know your word for them,> Hestean said. <But they are animals your people use to hunt us.>

Working dogs, Patricia's mind filled in for her. With a nod, she made a note.

<They did use a different kind of animal,> Azarin told her. <Small, with four legs and fur. They were fast. Similar to *toka*.>

Hestean made a note as Patricia looked up in confusion. Azarin was describing military working dogs, but the way he talked about them made it sound like they were different than what they had expected.

<Do you have a name for these animals, Lady Patricia?> Hestean asked curiously.

<Um... you describe 'dogs,'> she said. <Not *tanpuki*?> she asked.

<No, *tanpuki* are very different,> Azarin told her.

<You tell me about *tanpuki*?> Patricia asked.

<Big as a tod,> Azarin told her. <With six *sudai* and a long *boda*.>

The inclusion of two totally new words made the explanation useless to Patricia.

<Don't know *sudai* or *boda*,> she admitted.

<Here, I shall draw one,> Hestean told her, quickly doodling a quick sketch and passing it to her.

Patricia looked at the drawing and blinked in shock. She wasn't sure if she was looking at a giant spider or an octopus, only this drawing had six either legs or tentacles and a long beak like a petrel.

She shook her head. <I do not know this animal,> she told them.

<Your people have used them to attack us,> Hestean assured her.

<No,> Patricia replied. <We do not have these animals. We did not use them in war.>

Hestean seemed annoyed by the argument, but Azarin interjected with a suggestion.

<They may not have used them in this war, so she would not have seen them used,> he told Hestean.

The historian's ears popped up as she realized what the mistake must be. <I see,> she said, turning to face Patricia again. <I was also referring to the first war. Our records say they were used quite often back then.>

Patricia froze as she worked through the translation in her mind. *That couldn't be what she meant,* she thought to herself.

<You say again?> Patricia asked. <Not understand.>

<I said the *tanpuki* were used during the first invasion of our world by your people,> Hestean explained.

<First invasion?> Patricia repeated. The Coalition invasion of Va'Sh had proceeded in phases, yes, but when troops began landing in great numbers, it was mostly done as a single operation.

<Yes,> Hestean replied, her voice betraying her growing frustration. This was supposed to be a simple interview with a commando officer, but she was now being constantly sidetracked by the inclusion of this Dark One. <The first invasion during the war four thousand years ago.>

<A moment,> Patricia said. She pulled out her numerical note card and looked at it intently, sure that she could not have heard the number she just did. <Four thousand?> she asked.

<Yes.>

<Years?>

<Yes,> Hestean answered, her ears now folded downward. Azarin looked back and forth between them, and unlike Hestean, he seemed to sense something was wrong.

<What is wrong?> he asked Patricia directly.

<This number?> Patricia asked, holding the card out and pointing to the Va'Shen numeral for one thousand. <But four of them?>

<Yes,> Azarin said.

Patricia looked at them both in bewilderment. Four thousand Va'Shen years was equal to about four thousand, five hundred Earth years.

<We did not fight Va'Shen four thousand years ago,> she told them. <We fight other us, use sticks and rocks.>

Hestean stared at her intently.

<Your people have fought us twice,> she said, half in question, half in assurance.

<We fight once,> Patricia replied. <Did not know of Va'Shen before three years of past.>

Azarin said nothing, his one eye moving back and forth between the two women as he thought on Patricia's words himself.

Hestean was the first to reply, however.

<You are mistaken,> she said.

<I am not,> Patricia said in growing excitement. The more she thought on it, the more things about the Va'Shen and the war made sense.

<You are mistaken,> Hestean repeated. <You and the Dark Ones who invaded four thousand years ago are one and the same.> She said this a little louder, and her tail began moving behind her faster and faster, sweeping the floor in growing panic.

<No,> Patricia said. <We are not. Could not travel... um... realms... four thousand years ago.>

<Hestean,> Azarin said quietly. <If what she says is true, it would explain a great many things...>

<It explains nothing because it is not true!> Hestean cried, practically leaping to her feet. <You are the Dark Ones! We know this is true! The Emperor, himself, has said it!>

<Hestean,> Azarin began softly, trying to calm the priestess down.

<Hestean *Aru'Dace*!> she corrected him with some heat. <I do not know what game Lady Patricia is attempting to play, but her suggestion is... is... it simply cannot be!>

Azarin stared at her with his one grey eye, refusing to be cowed by the vixen's rank. He had seen field cornets use the same tactic before, falling back on their rank when it was obvious their decisions no longer made sense but could not accept it.

<Then why did the Great Ones not come to our aid?> he asked her bluntly.

<I do not know,> Hestean replied.

Patricia watched the exchange and swallowed. She had stepped on a land mine and she knew it.

<Why do the Dark Ones not try to exterminate us as they did before?> Azarin asked.

<I do not know!> Hestean cried.

<Why are the descriptions passed down of their equipment, their animals, their ships not match *anything* commandos like me have seen?>

<*I do not know!*> Hestean shouted at him, her hands balled into fists and her ears digging into her scalp. <What would you argue?!> she demanded. <That the Emperor lied to us? That he was wrong?! You know that is not possible!>

Azarin could say nothing to this. For the Va'Shen, to suggest either was the absolute height of heresy. The Emperor was a god. If he said something, that something was fact.

<It is much more likely that this Dark One woman is lying to us!> Hestean continued, pointing at Patricia and causing the human woman to jump in her seat.

<For what purpose?> Azarin asked her.

Hestean's mouth opened to reply and shut just as quickly.

<Hestean,> Azarin said gently, rising to his feet. <If the Emperor had not made the declaration himself... what would the evidence tell you?>

<You believe her?> Hestean gasped.

<Why try to prevent our release,> Azarin replied, <If *not* to keep us from sharing what we had seen? If *not* to prevent something like *this* interview from occurring?> Hestean didn't answer, and he continued. <Everything... *Everything*... we were trained to expect from the Dark Ones turned out to be wrong. If *anyone* but the Emperor had told me these were the Dark Ones... I would have thought they were lying to me.>

<I will hear no more of this!> Hestean cried, snatching her notes up from the table. <You have always been an unruly and incorrigible tod, Azarin, but I *never* would have thought you would risk the Frost with such foolish heresy! Good day!>

With that, the vixen stormed angrily from the room, leaving Patricia and Azarin alone.

<I... am sorry,> Patricia said. She looked up at Azarin. <We did not know.>

<No,> Azarin replied softly. <I don't believe you did.>

<Can you tell me,> Patricia asked. When Azarin looked down at her, she continued. <Can you tell me about this first war?>

* * *

Ben found Master Sergeant Jacob Marcus exactly where he expected to, leaning over the shoulder of an Air Force two-striper in the CJTF Operation Unified Resolve Public Affairs Office. The Ranger had a complicated relationship with military Public Affairs. When they were good, they were really good. When they were bad, they were really bad, and it was those times that Ben found happening more often than not during the war.

To be completely fair, it wasn't necessarily Public Affairs' fault. Like every staff office in the military, they were restricted by the often-capricious nature of their leadership, the well-earned paranoia with all things media of the unit commanders and a slow, plodding chain of command that made it impossible for them to be as responsive as they wanted to or could be. Ben's own bad encounter with the media made him vow never to work with Public Affairs again, but a kind gesture from Marcus, who had found the very last video-recorded messages from Persephone before it was destroyed, had gone a long way to repairing that relationship.

"Look, I don't want to sound like an asshole," Marcus was telling the airman, "But you *have seen* a Va'Shen, right?"

"Yes, Sir," the airman replied. "I mean... from a distance..."

Marcus sighed, and Ben smirked at his discomfiture from the doorway.

"Okay, look," the senior NCO said. "I want you to go with Dr. Sinclair next time he has a meeting with the Va'Shen. Just sit there and look at them, okay? Don't try drawing them until then, all right?"

"Yes, Sir."

Marcus stood up and turned, and the airmen returned to work. Seeing Ben, the man smiled and extended his hand, which Ben shook.

"Trouble?" Ben asked.

"Not really," Marcus said. "This is Airman Lynch, the *first* illustrator to come from the Defense Information School in more than two hundred years."

"Illustrator?" Ben asked.

"Can't use holocams or vid recorders here," Marcus said with a shrug. "So, the Air Force took some artistic types, taught them to draw and are sending them to us to hand-draw pictures instead."

"That's actually kinda cool," Ben said.

"It is," Marcus agreed. "He just needs a little more exposure to the Va'Shen. This is his first deployment."

"Where are you coming in from, Airman Lynch?" Ben asked.

Realizing he was being addressed by an officer, the young airman leapt to his feet. "Fort Meade, Sir!"

"Well, welcome to Va'Sh," Ben told him. "You'll have a good experience here."

"Thank you, Sir!"

Marcus grinned at the young enlisted man's response. "They sent him straight out of tech school," he told Ben. "I don't approve, myself. An airman needs time to adjust to the military, realize that it's not anything like basic training, but... that's where we are."

"If you want him to get a good look at Va'Shen without worrying about safety, you could send him to us," Ben offered. "We'll put him up for a few weeks."

Marcus looked surprised at the offer. "That would be great, Sir. Give me a few weeks to get him situated, and I'll take you up on that. In the meantime, what can I do for you?"

Ben handed him a thick manila envelope. "Here's that background info you asked for. Lieutenant Kim went around and got some quotes from our people and a few Va'Shen about what we're doing down there. Hope it helps."

"Oh, outstanding!" Marcus said, taking the envelope from him, cradling it like a newborn baby. "This is going to make my life tons easier."

"While I'm here," Ben began tentatively, "I was wondering if I could ask you if you've heard anything about Sector Six."

Marcus froze, just for a moment. "Sector Six?" he asked. "That was Major Keyes's AO, right? You know, he's the new exec here. Have you talked to him yet?"

"I have," Ben admitted carefully. What he was doing wasn't, strictly speaking, the military way of doing things. Asking a senior

NCO for information on a fellow officer put both of them in an uncomfortable situation. But his discussion with Keyes had set off alarm bells in Ben's mind, and he didn't have many contacts inside the CJTF headquarters.

Also, while Public Affairs wasn't the most respected office on the staff, it benefited from the fact that it was included in almost all of the meetings and, by virtue of its mission, talked to almost everyone.

"And what did he say?" Marcus asked, and something about his tone made the alarm bells in Ben's mind ring stronger.

"He gave me some advice," Ben said. "Sector 13 got a bunch of Va'Shen from his AO, and we're settling them in. I thought he could give me some insight. But he's pretty busy, and I know you hear a lot..."

"You got his Va'Shen?" Marcus asked. At Ben's nod, the senior NCO tapped the manila envelope with his fingers in thought. "I could go for a milkshake. You?" he asked.

"Sure," Ben said immediately, sensing the change in the tone of the conversation.

"Let's go for a ride," Marcus said, starting for the door.

"Can I have a milkshake?" Lynch asked from his desk.

"You finish that press release?" Marcus asked.

"No, Sir."

"Then no."

Marcus gestured for Ben to precede through the door, and Ben obliged, silently bracing himself for something he hoped was benign.

Something, however, told him it wasn't.

* * *

Marcus brought the LTV to a stop in a parking area on top of a hill overlooking the Jamieson Airfield space launch center. From here, Ben could see the entire length of the titanium launch rails from the hangars where orbital launch vehicles were horizontally loaded, across nearly the entire length of the base, and finally the gentle curve upward that would orient the vehicle into a vertical climb as it left the rail to achieve orbit.

At that moment there was a roar from the horizontal end, and Ben watched in awe as one of the vehicles raced down the rail, powered by four giant rocket engines, before whipping upward and disappearing into the sky above them.

Marcus watched the launch pensively and took a sip of the milkshake the two had gotten through the drive-thru ice-cream shop on the other side of the base.

Headquarters really was a different world.

"They've been doing three or four launches a day for a week now," Marcus told him. "*Neil Armstrong* is headed for home in a few weeks, and a few of the Air Force units are going with them."

Ben nodded casually. "You didn't bring me up here for the view, though," he said.

Marcus's face scrunched up in thought. "Look, Sir, I wanna make it clear that I don't make it a habit of shit-talking officers to other people. Only reason I'm telling you any of this is because it sounds like you're inheriting Major Keyes's shit-show and no one's warned you."

"Warned me about what?" Ben asked.

"How much you know about Keyes?" the Air Force man asked.

"Nothing, really," Ben said. "Just what I read in the intel reports from his sector."

"Keyes is... complicated," Marcus told him. "On paper, the man is an American hero. Everyone loves him. But then you hear from some of the guys who spent time attached to his unit." Marcus looked at him. "So, this part is just rumor," he said. "I can't confirm any of it. But, from what I *heard*, Keyes was pulled down here as a result of leadership hearing some 'concerning' rumors. And whatever they heard, it must have been big, because they broke up his entire unit and scattered them to the four winds as a result. Major Hampton, the guy Keyes replaced, wasn't supposed to leave the exec job for another four months, but they cut him loose and sent him down to the wing."

"There are always rumors," Ben argued with a shrug. "They're usually just that. Rumors."

"Normally, I would agree with you," Marcus said. "But... there's also the stuff I *do* know as a fact. Because I saw it up close."

"What do you mean?"

"You know about Debby?"

Ben smiled and gave a short chuckle. "My fr... late wife..." he corrected with a smile, "... was an astronomer. I've heard *all* about Debby."

About ten years before NASA began finding multiple Earth-like planets all over the galaxy, what astronomers like Jessie had dubbed "The Time of Plenty," the American space exploration organization had had severe budget troubles. To try to raise money as well as a little attention, the organization offered people the opportunity to name stars. For a few hundred dollars, you could choose a star and name it whatever you wanted as long as it wasn't obscene. This wasn't one of the schemes you saw on the vids, either. The star's name would be used on official U.S. star charts, and the buyer would receive a framed certificate with the star's numeric designation, new name and coordinates signed by the director of NASA.

Fast forward a decade, and NASA began finding habitable worlds left and right. The rule that was established was that once a star was confirmed to have a habitable planet, it was given a proper name. One star, Gamma Delta 152-5, was found to have one such planet, and NASA gave it a name from British literature, "Galadriel."

And that's when the problems started. Upon announcing the new planet, its location and name, a man from Macon, Georgia, stepped forward and declared that Galadriel was "his world" and demanded that NASA use the name he had given it. Ten years before, the man had paid NASA $300 to name Gamma Delta 152-5 after his wife, Debby. NASA refused, and the man took them to court. Assuming the lawsuit would be thrown out as frivolous, NASA's legal team didn't take it seriously.

At least, not until the judge held up the certificate, pointed at the NASA director's name, and asked the team, "Is that the former director's signature?"

Forced to admit that, yes, that was his signature and that, yes, they did say that the name would be official, the legal team watched in horror as the judge brought his gavel down and officially declared Gamma Delta 152-5 "the Debby system."

NASA tried to buy the naming rights back from the man, offering millions of dollars, but he refused. And since then, spaceship captains, those associated with the U.S. government at least, have been forced to look at their navigators and order them to "set course for the Debby system."

Debby's third planet was home to a weather research station. The winds in the southern continent were consistently extreme, giving meteorologists and climatologists an opportunity to study its effects for most of the year. Ben seemed to remember there being some action there as well.

"Keyes was on Debby 3?" Ben asked.

Marcus nodded. "It's where he was nominated for the Medal of Honor."

"The *Medal of Honor*?" Ben repeated, slack-jawed.

The senior NCO nodded again. "Distress call from the researchers came in, saying a force of Va'Shen had set up shop nearby and was shooting them up on the regular. On Debby 3, there's a semi-regular two-week window when the winds are calm enough for air operations. After that, you gotta wait another three months before the birds can get back in. Keyes's infantry company was choppered in to provide support and the whole thing went sideways."

Marcus took a sip of his milkshake as another launch down at the launch center made it too loud to continue speaking for a moment.

"Whole thing was a trap," Marcus went on after a moment. Once they were on the ground, Va'Shen started shooting up the choppers from the tree-line, and there were a helluva lot more than the researchers reported. For the next week, any rotary asset that tried to go in was shot up. Whenever close air support came in, the Va'Shen went to ground and waited it out. They played hide and seek until the window closed, and then they started hitting the research station in force. Whole thing turned into a siege."

"Sounds like Dien Bien Phu," Ben muttered.

"Deeya beeya whatta?" Marcus asked.

"Not important," the Ranger replied. "Go on."

"So, at first, command thinks it's no big deal," Marcus went on. "They decide to send in an armored column to relieve Keyes. By the way," Marcus remarked dryly. "This is how we learned tank armor doesn't work against hardlight rifles."

"Holy shit," Ben muttered.

Marcus nodded. "Column gets torn to pieces a few miles from the station. Air window is closed for the next three months. Keyes is essentially on his own. They try resupplying with high altitude flights, but the drops just get blown all to Hell and gone. Food, ammunition, water, it all starts running out. Keyes keeps requesting *any* kind of support, and then someone at command advises him to *seek acceptable terms for surrender.*"

Marcus paused to let that sink in. No large U.S. unit had surrendered in more than two centuries.

"They told him to *surrender*?" Ben asked in disbelief.

Marcus nodded and took a sip from his milkshake. "Guess some two-star in a headquarters building somewhere decided that a surrender of living troops would look better on the news than a massacre they couldn't prevent."

"So, what did Keyes do?" Ben asked. As much as Keyes's attitude concerned him, he found himself rooting for the man now.

"Well, Keyes just spent the last month seeing how the Va'Shen treated guys they captured," Marcus told him. "His patrols were finding guys with their ears cut off and their throats cut. So, he tells command to shove it and, instead, decides to go for it. He figures since they don't know anything about the Va'Shen, the reverse is probably also true, including how we construct our buildings. So, he orders his guys on the perimeter to stop returning fire, and in the middle of the night, pulls them all back to the research station. By now, their ammo is real low anyway. He has his guys fix bayonets and then hide in every closet, subbasement, ceiling access and cabinet they can find."

"A trap?"

"He made it look like they had snuck out in the middle of the night. Va'Shen sent some scouts, who saw an empty building and reported it was clear. When the Va'Shen showed up to take the building, Keyes's guys burst out and start killing 'em, up close so the Va'Shen's range advantage doesn't mean anything, real 'war-to-the-knife' kind of stuff. Keyes lost a hundred guys, but they almost completely obliterated the enemy force."

"So, they put him in for the Medal of Honor," Ben concluded. "Sounds like a slam dunk."

"Army thought so too," Marcus told him. "Enough that they had me and a PA team go there after it was all over to get interviews and imagery while the investigation was going on."

Ben nodded. Getting a Medal of Honor was still, all these centuries later, a huge deal. A nomination had to be thoroughly investigated to make sure everything that was alleged to have happened actually did. The Defense Department understood what it would look like if they awarded someone something so precious only to have to take it back later because someone embellished their story.

"So, what happened?" Ben asked.

"All of a sudden, out of the blue, the investigation stopped," Marcus said. "We were pulled out. Award was downgraded to a Silver Star."

"What?" the Ranger asked in amazement. He had to pause as another heavy lift take-off roared down the launch rail.

"People think our job is a joke," Marcus told him. "But I don't like it when people waste my time, so I decided to do a little looking into what happened. At first, I figured DoD didn't want anyone to know that one of their generals told an American hero to surrender. That would be pretty embarrassing. Then, I found something. A discrepancy in the records."

"What kind of discrepancy?"

"According to the report Keyes sent up to command, they took twelve Va'Shen soldiers prisoner," Marcus explained. "But when I looked through the interview notes my photojournalist made, I saw that *several* enlisted soldiers told him that they had been guarding *thirty-seven* prisoners."

Ben froze at the implication. It was *possible* that there was a legitimate reason for the discrepancy. Perhaps fifteen of the prisoners had been severely wounded and died of their injuries. Perhaps the guards were wrong or someone fat-fingered the report.

But, usually, you didn't feel the need to *hide* stuff like that.

"Could the guards have been wrong?" Ben asked.

Marcus shook his head. "They told my guy they had to count them every half-hour given how slick the Va'Shen are when it comes to sneaking around."

"The report was wrong?"

Marcus looked him right in the eye. "I thought so too. But the pax manifest for the flight off Debby 3 matched the report."

"You realize what you're saying?" Ben asked in shock.

"I know exactly what I'm saying," Marcus replied. "Sometime between Keyes's capturing them and them being moved off-world, fifteen Va'Shen prisoners just vanished."

"Did you report this?" Ben asked him.

"To command *and* the IG."

"And?"

"First, it was 'we'll look into it.' Then, after a while, it became 'shut up and color.'"

"Why?" Ben asked in amazement. "Why cover for Keyes? If they escaped, that would explain losing the Medal of Honor... But if he *did something* to them... That would be a war crime. At the very least, there should have been an investigation."

"You ever hear of Thaddeus Keyes?" Marcus asked.

Ben paused. "That name is really familiar," he admitted, almost bracing himself for another bombshell.

"It should be," Marcus told him. "He's the Chairman of the Senate Armed Services Committee... and Elkanah Keyes's father."

"Son of a bitch," Ben gasped. "So, they covered Keyes's ass so they wouldn't make an enemy of his dad and shipped him off to Va'Sh where there's no media presence to ask him uncomfortable questions. Son of a bitch..."

"And, apparently, even that wasn't enough," Marcus told him. "Because all of a sudden, he's down here, *literally* in constant eyesight of the commander, his troops are scattered all over the planet, and the Va'Shen he's been 'looking after'... well, they're now *your* problem."

* * *

<It is an absolute disgrace,> Goto told the three tods sitting around the tiny table in the small, temporary home he shared with his niece. The home was connected to several others in a row, more like an

apartment complex or motel one would find on Earth. Each had a small room with whatever furnishings the Pelle villagers were able to share with their new Garan'Sel neighbors, but that wasn't all that much. A table for meals and a small stove for cooking and keeping the home warm were the only things they had in this room. There were two additional rooms in the back for sleeping, only one of which had bedding, which Goto had insisted go to his niece.

Posha knelt next to her uncle with a small kettle and began to pour tea for the four tods as her uncle continued his rant.

<We have seen the Dark Ones do terrible things,> Goto continued. <But to hear of a vixen throwing herself at one is shameful in the extreme.>

<Perhaps she has been forced?> one of the tods at the table suggested.

Goto's tail slapped the perfectly cleaned floor behind him. <No, since hearing about it, I have asked others. The stupid little vixen even tried to make a formal arrangement, and the Overlord forbade it.>

<Another level of shame,> another tod commented.

<Perhaps the Overlord knows a shameless vixen when he sees one,> another quipped.

<Do you know what my niece asked me?> Goto told them angrily. <She asked me if *she* would be expected to do the same thing!>

<Obviously not, Posha!> one of the tods cried at her in alarm. <How could you ever think that?!>

The vixen, Posha, lowered her head in shame. <It just seems to me that the peace these Va'Shen have has come at a price. If we are to have that peace too, will we be expected to pay a similar price?>

<Such a peace is too dearly bought!> spat the tod at the far side of the table opposite of Goto. His ears were folded down into his dark brown fur, and his tail whipped about in agitation.

<I know that I am not the only vixen asking this question,> Posha added guiltily. <I have talked to several who wonder if they should learn the Dark One language or how they prepare their food.>

Goto felt rage well up in him, but, for his niece's sake, he pushed it back down, deep into his chest. All this vexation over a shameful vixen who had forgotten the value of her own virtue.

The thought of Posha going through something similar made Goto sick. After everything she had been through, everything she had been forced to endure...

Goto's sister, Nazasha, had left Garan'Sel when she was young, going to the regional capital in the north to learn the arts of healing. Goto had been a teenager at the time, and he had been so proud of her, to have enough of a gift to be accepted to learn the healing arts.

Travel for Va'Shen of Goto's class was difficult due to its expense. As a result, he had never seen his sister again, but they exchanged letters often. Goto had gone to the temple to learn to read just so he could read her letters and write ones of his own. It was through those letters that he learned his sister had been taken by a young city bureaucrat and that the two were very happy together. It was not long before a letter came announcing the birth of their first daughter.

When the war broke out, Goto wrote more often, worried for Nazasha and the young niece he had never met. Unlike other communities, most of Garan'Sel's tods were required to remain in the village to help mine coal and iron for the war effort. Nazasha's husband, however, had been called to the commando and was sent to another realm to fight. Nazasha's letters spoke constantly of her worry.

Then, one night, the dawn broke in the middle of the night, the sun seeming to rise from the north instead of the east before fading away. Then another sun rose and fell. And another. Va'Shen from the northern towns, some with horrific burns and other injuries began streaming through Garan'Sel, speaking of powerful explosions that had all but erased their towns and cities.

Including the regional capital.

Very few Va'Shen were heading north, but Goto shoved a letter in the hands of each one as they passed, begging them to ask for Nazasha and her daughter and deliver them. He even tried to go himself, but the other tods of the community stopped him, the Na'Sha begging him for patience and to allow the Gods an opportunity to answer his prayers without endangering himself.

Then, one day, several weeks after the "Night of Six Dawns," a young vixen with a dirty face and hair, holding a single small bag, entered the village. Goto, on his way to the mine that day, saw her and stopped, finding something strange about the young vixen. He asked if she needed help.

<I am looking for Goto,> she told him. <Do you know him?>

Upon confirming that he was Goto, the girl's ears popped straight up, and her tail swished furiously.

<U... Uncle Goto?> she asked with trembling lips.

The Gods had delivered a miracle to him. His niece lived. She had been in a root cellar when the bombs fell, and when she emerged the next day, the city was simply gone. She had searched for her mother, who had been working at the local clinic that night, helping an expecting mother give birth, but there was no sign of her. The clinic where she worked was little more than a charred stain on the ground. She continued searching, hoping she would somehow find her, but her search was fruitless.

With nothing left for her in the city but ruin, she took a bag she found in the rubble, filled it with whatever food she could find, and ventured south, hoping to find the only kin she still knew of; the uncle she had never met.

She was the last piece of family Goto had left.

And he would be damned by the Gods if he allowed her for one second to worry that she might be married off to a Dark One.

<Something needs to be done,> Goto told them.

Before someone could suggest what that "something" should be, there was a scratching at the door. The tods tensed. Visitors in the middle of the night, they had come to know, usually ended with a group of Dark Ones kicking in the door and pointing rifles at all of them.

Posha, however, walked right to the door, commenting over her shoulder, <Dark Ones do not scratch. They bash their fists.> The four tods relaxed but also felt shame well up in them at the young vixen showing courage where they had immediately felt fear.

The aqua-haired vixen opened the door slightly and looked out. A Va'Shen, their head and face concealed by a dark robe and hood, looked back at her.

<Go to the back,> Posha told her. <I will help you there.>

Without a word, the black-robed visitor turned and started toward the end of the block of apartments to circle around to the back entrance.

<Problem?> Goto asked her.

<Someone is in need of healing,> Posha told him as she started toward her room.

Goto's ears twitched, what on a human would be, a proud grin. His niece had inherited her mother's brilliance and often helped the village healer and others in need.

The young vixen entered her room and shut the door, locking it behind her before turning to the door that led out back and waiting. A minute later, another scratching came, and she quickly let the robed Va'Shen in.

Posha said nothing, instead going to the small worktable she had acquired where clay jars of crushed herbs sat.

<It has not been that long,> Posha said as she began mixing ingredients. <Be careful that you do not take too much.>

<I take what is necessary,> a flat but feminine voice replied. The visitor pushed back her hood, revealing her jet-black hair and ears.

Posha turned and held out her hand. <The bottles?>

Wenlin pulled three small glass bottles from a pouch on her waist and handed them to her. <Thank you,> she said quietly, almost timidly.

<If you take too much over too long, the effects may become permanent,> Posha cautioned as she mixed some herbs with water and poured the compound carefully into the thin-necked bottles.

<The Gods would never reward me with such grace,> Wenlin assured her bitterly.

<Have things been so bad?> Posha asked her.

<Outwardly, no,> Wenlin told her. <There is a veneer of happiness in this village, but I have learned the cost for it. It is... more than I have been willing to pay.>

Posha carefully regarded the Na'Sha for a moment before her ears twitched a smile.

<I am told you will reopen your bakery,> she said. Wenlin stiffened at the comment. <The people, I am certain, will be thankful for the bread you provide them.>

<I am sure,> Wenlin said absently.

Posha held out three now-filled bottles, and Wenlin took them. <I know you walk a delicate cliff's edge,> she said. <Baking bread for Va'Shen in the day and cakes for the Dark Ones at night. I know it earns much goodwill from them.>

Wenlin wasn't sure what to say and so said nothing. Posha watched her intently as if searching for some crack in the Na'Sha's defenses that she might exploit.

<Thank you for continuing to provide my medicine,> Wenlin said woodenly.

Posha bowed to her. <And thank you, Na'Sha, for all you do for us.>

Her cargo safely concealed in her pouch, Wenlin pulled the hood back over her head and turned to the door.

Posha watched her leave, her ears folding downward as her eyes narrowed.

Chapter 8

Five weeks until contact...

Patricia met him at the door of their office like an excited puppy happy to meet its master after a long trip. Ben had managed to catch a convoy heading south from Jamieson, but it hadn't gotten into FOB Leonard until about one in the morning. The Ranger had thanked the driver of the LTV for the ride and walked straight to his hooch where he collapsed into his bed and fell immediately to sleep.

The things he had learned during his trip to Jamieson concerned him greatly, and he had been racking his brain for a way to find out more and, hopefully, cut off any issues before they became real trouble. Because of that he had been looking forward to speaking with Patricia and back-briefing her on what he had learned. He hadn't expected, however, for her to have her own report, one that seemed so important that he let her go first.

"The whole war was a mistake!" she declared theatrically.

"They say that about every war," he countered.

"Yeah, but this time it's literal!" she said, leaning over and planting her hands on his desk as he took his seat. "That interview you asked me to sit in on? The one with Hestean and Azarin..."

"Yeah, how did that go?"

Patricia proceeded to tell him everything that had happened in that interview along with everything Azarin had told her afterward, sometimes speaking so fast that Ben had to ask her to back up and repeat things slowly. By the end of it, Ben was leaning back in his chair as if exhausted with digesting all of it.

"Well," he said quietly after a long minute. "Shit."

"I know, right?!" she cried. "Hestean flat out accused me of lying and practically branded Azarin a heretic! It was surreal!"

Ben didn't reply immediately, putting everything Patricia told him together in his head with everything else he had learned.

"So, they find us setting up shop on a world they say belongs to one of the Great Ones we had heard about," he summarized. "Assume that we're these... what did you call them?"

"Dark Things."

"... Dark Things," Ben continued. "And mobilize for war. And because their Emperor said it, it must be true."

"Which I do not get *at all*," Patricia told him. "I mean Hestean acted like she was personally offended by the idea that their Emperor might be wrong."

"But not Azarin?" Ben asked.

Patricia shook her head. "No. He seemed to think it made other things that happened make more sense."

"Maybe it did," Ben said. At Patricia's questioning glance he went on. "We still have no idea why Va'ShGov was so intent on letting the commandos sit in that detention center. Maybe it was because they had seen things that would have made them question what they had been told."

The more Ben thought about it, the more it made sense. He looked up at Patricia and tried a different line of reasoning. "If you had been taught, all your life, that one thing, just *one thing*, was absolutely true no matter what... what would you do if you found out that it wasn't true after all?"

Patricia thought for a moment before answering. "I'd question everything else I'd been told."

Ben nodded. "Va'Shen society is based on the *fact* that the Emperor is a god and a god is never wrong. Some Va'Shen ship captain reported that he saw Dark Things on some world, that report went to someone in the Imperial Court who then told the Emperor..."

"And the Emperor told the Va'Shen," Patricia finished. "So... someone screwed up and jumped the gun..."

"And now they have no choice but to hide it and hope no one finds out," Ben concluded. "That's why they were afraid of letting the detainees go. How do you argue that monsters have taken over your world when the prisoners they take come back better fed than when they left? With their wounds treated?"

An even more disturbing thought struck Ben at that moment.

How long has the Imperial Court known we weren't their enemy?

"Okay, that tracks a little bit," Patricia said. "Except for the occupation forces. We're not treating the Va'Shen badly."

Ben took a breath at that statement. Seeing his change in expression, Patricia stood up.

"What?" she asked.

"I found out a few things about the guy who ran Sector Six," Ben told her. He quickly went through his conversation with Keyes and what Master Sergeant Marcus had told him.

"You think he abused the Garan'Sel villagers?" Patricia asked quietly.

"I don't know," Ben replied, tapping the desktop with his finger. "But even if he was one hundred percent honest about how he responded to insurgent attacks, it would be *easy* for the Va'Shen to *see it* as monstrous. They get attacked, so they killed the chieftain. He says it was incidental, but the Va'Shen could see it as deliberate retaliation. Same thing with the temple burning down. What Va'Shen, told for years that the people occupying them are evil, would believe that the temple burning down was an accident and not a deliberate act?"

"Keyes brought down the hammer," Patricia concluded, "And doing that reinforced what the Va'Shen in Garan'Sel already thought."

"And that's just assuming he was telling the truth," Ben said. "From what Marcus said, this guy has a real axe to grind with the Va'Shen."

"We almost did the same thing," Patricia commented quietly.

"Huh?" Ben asked.

"When we first arrived here," she went on. "I mean, we learned a lot since then, and we know better now, but... could you imagine what would have happened if we had actually done something to Alacea? I don't mean abuse her... But... even keeping her locked up or sending her to Jamieson... Heck, I'm pretty sure that, at the time, Kasshas would have killed you if he thought he could have done it before being shot."

Ben considered his deputy's words and let out a breath. "There but for the grace of God, huh?" he asked quietly. He remembered how angry he had been when Alacea had falsely confessed to ordering the Persephone strike. If she hadn't been a priestess... if she had been a tod wearing an officer's uniform... Ben couldn't say for certain he wouldn't have drawn his sidearm and shot him right then and there. "Keyes told me that he told Wenlin about Persephone as a way of letting her know not to fuck with us."

"So, she thinks *you* have an axe to grind too."

"Shit," Ben sighed, leaning back in his chair and looking up at the ceiling. "So... to sum up... the Va'Shen think we're evil for a reason, we might be sitting on a timebomb when it comes to the Garan'Sel villagers, and, to top it off, there are at least *two* other alien races out there we know nothing about."

Patricia nodded. "And I don't know where these Dark Things are now, but I hope we never meet them. Remember how I said I thought there might be something in the Va'Shen past that made them so baby crazy?"

"Yeah?"

Patricia swallowed. "Azarin said that when the Va'Shen first united under their emperor, they did a world-wide census. At the time, there were about seventy million Va'Shen. After the war was over and the Dark Things left Va'Sh, there were *two million left*. They practically wiped these people out."

"The Great Ones don't sound much better," Ben said. "They basically tricked the Va'Shen into being cannon fodder for them."

"They *did* help fight the Dark Things when they invaded Va'Sh, though," Patricia argued, not sure it was correct to put the two unknown alien races on equal moral ground. She pointed up at the ceiling. "The aurora? The Fuzz? Azarin called it 'The Blessing.' Apparently, the Great Ones put it around Va'Sh to help knock out the Dark Things' technology."

Ben, however, had a counterargument. "Yeah, and in doing so they made sure the Va'Shen would never advance out of the steam age. If the Va'Shen ever found out the Great Ones weren't actually heralds from their gods, there would be no way they could fight back. All their military tech came from the Great Ones. With that 'blessing' in place, they could never create the technology they would need to oppose them."

Patricia and Ben shared a moment of silence as they considered this.

"Wow," Patricia breathed. "Aliens are dicks."

"Yup," Ben agreed.

Patricia looked at Ben as another uncomfortable thought occurred to her. "I haven't spoken to Hestean or Alacea since the interview," she said. "How do you think Alacea is going to react when Hestean tells her what was said? Is it going to cause you trouble?"

Ben thought for a moment and took a deep breath.

"No," he said, looking up at Patricia.

"What makes you think so?" the intel officer asked.

"I think Alacea already knows."

* * *

Perched upon a throne of human bones, the demoness, Zathria, eyed the three intruders with amused curiosity. Standing at a full nine feet tall, with hellish flames for eyes, crimson skin and sharp horns that added another foot to her height, the scantily clad nightmare amazon had little to fear from the dark knight, the cleric and the fairy that floated nearby.

"You have intruded into my abode," Zathria informed them in a deep, sultry and dangerous voice as she stood and picked up the double-bladed battle axe that rested against her throne. "Have you anything to say to me before I kill you all?"

The three adventurers looked to each other as if silently deciding who should speak first. Finally, the dark knight stepped forward and cleared his throat.

"Um... Hey, girl," the knight said. "Are you a side quest? 'Cause I wanna do you for the experience."

"Oh my god," the white-robed cleric muttered, putting her face in her hands.

"Foking *weally*!?" the fairy asked him.

"What?!" the knight demanded, turning on them. "Maybe she'll be so charmed that she decides she *won't* murder us!"

"Dude, yor chawisma stat is *zewo!*" the fairy reminded him. "You gave up all dose points so you could dual-wield!"

The knight looked to Zathria as if asking for help. The demoness grinned. "No, I'm still going to murder you all."

"Well, fuck," the knight replied. "Now what?"

"Stawt wewolling new chawacters?" the fairy suggested.

The demoness snarled and took a step toward the trio, who raised their weapons warily. Suddenly...

"Staff Sergeant Ramirez?"

* * *

"Yes! I'm saved!" Ramirez cried, throwing his hands in the air in victory. The few other troops seated in the dining facility at this time of night all looked up at his table and shook their heads. The Ranger turned away from the murderous looks his friends were shooting him and saw the soldier in full gear and armor, his rifle slung over his shoulder, approaching him. "What's up?" he asked.

"Staff Sergeant, there's a Va'Shy girl at ECP One asking for you," the young private told him.

"Blonde and orange-haired girl?" he asked, his assumption instantly going to Alzoria.

"No, Staff Sergeant," the sentry told him. "Green."

Ramirez's face scrunched up, trying to come up with which of the green-haired vixens he knew would be coming to see him at this time of night.

"You guys okay with me taking this?" he asked, rising to his feet and grabbing his patrol cap.

"We're all about to die anyway, so sure," Fletcher replied in a resigned tone.

"Nah!" Ramirez cried. "You guys got this!"

Burgers looked at him with a scowl, shook his head, and gave him the finger.

"Back in a bit," the marksman promised and started for the exit.

He followed the sentry into the night air and started the short walk to the main entry control point. His grin was still all the way up to his ears when he arrived and found a familiar Huntress standing in the center of the shining floodlights.

<Blessed evening, Mezina,> Ramirez called. <You doing the goodness in this night?>

The green-haired vixen turned to him, her tail whipping back and forth in agitation.

<Rah-mee-raz!> she said quickly. <You must come with me!>

The Ranger stopped as he worked the translation in his head.

<Alzoria has been attacked!>

* * *

Mezina opened the door without scratching, and Ramirez followed her inside. He had never been inside the small house that Alzoria, her mother and sister called home, and he found it so full of Huntresses that he would have been hard-pressed to describe the interior afterwards.

He looked up as one older vixen pointed at him and started yelling in his direction.

<You!> the orange-haired woman cried. <This is your fault! This wouldn't have happened were it not for you!>

Another vixen, this one a much younger blonde, took her by the arm and gently pulled her away.

<This is your fault, Dark One!> the older woman cried as she was led away.

She had spoken so quickly and so loudly that Ramirez hadn't been able to catch what she had said. His mind was still reeling from what Mezina had told him.

<Um... What things she say?> he asked Mezina.

The Huntress paused, unsure of what to say, but a familiar redhead stepped forward out of the crowd.

<She said you're nice,> Bao Sen lied.

<Bao Sen!> Ramirez cried. <What occurred? Alzoria is well?>

The lead Huntress took him by the elbow and gently led him away from the other vixens so she could talk to him with a little more privacy.

<Alzoria was attacked on her way home from the lodge,> Bao Sen told him slowly so he could keep up. <Three tods grabbed her.>

Ramirez swallowed in fear, his heart racing in his chest. <Well is the Alzoria?> he demanded in horrific Va'Shen, his distress making the Va'Shen vocabulary fly from his mind.

Bao Sen looked at him as if trying to decide how to best describe it.

<She has a few bruises,> she told him. <But they did not aim to beat her. I think they are there because she fought them.>

Ramirez shook his head, confused. <Slow,> he said. <Alzoria attacked, yes? But not hurt they to her?> He shook his head again. <What say you mean to that?>

<Rah-mee-raz,> Bao Sen said gently. <They took her hair.>

The Ranger was even more confused now, sure that his Va'Shen language skills here failing him. <Take... Take the hair?> he asked, pointing at the top of his head. <You mean to say what? Do not understand. Hair?>

<They cut her hair off,> Bao Sen repeated.

<Alzoria not hurt so?> he asked.

The Huntress knew she wasn't getting her point across. <They did not hurt her body,> he told her, to which Ramirez sighed in relief. <But they took her hair.>

<Not understand,> Ramirez said.

Bao Sen's tail was waving back and forth in frustration at the conversation, but she knew it wasn't his fault.

<They took her hair to tell her she is a bad vixen,> she said as plainly as she could. <Hair is important to us. They took it to tell her she is not a real vixen.>

Ramirez knew this wasn't getting them anywhere. <I see her?> he asked.

Bao Sen paused uncomfortably. <She does not want to see anybody,> she told him.

Ramirez gave up and marched to the door the other Huntresses were huddled around. Raising his fist, he knocked on the door, trying very hard to do so gently so as not to scare the vixen on the other side.

<Alzoria?> he called. <It John. I enter?>

<Go away, John,> a trembling voice called back, her words interspersed with hiccups. <You can't see me.>

<Alzoria,> he tried again. <I want see you unhurt. Please I enter?>

<I'm *shamed*, John!> she yelled back. <Please! Go away!>

He swallowed and took a step back. Alzoria must have sensed he was still there because she called out again in English.

"Sca-ram! Beat at!" she yelled. "No one homes!"

The Ranger took another step back and turned. Bao Sen was there, looking at him, but not in anger or judgement. She knew how Alzoria felt about Ramirez and at least sensed that Ramirez was close to Alzoria.

<Who?> he asked her.

* * *

As soon as he heard the news, Burgers knew exactly where to go and hoped he wasn't too late. Taking the key that hung with his dog tags from around his neck, he inserted it into the heavy lock on the steel door that led into the armory and opened it.

He found his friend standing there and sighed in relief. Ramirez was slapping a loaded magazine into an M-31 as he looked up and saw Burgers there.

Ramirez smiled. "Oh, hey Burgers!" he said casually as he slung the assault rifle over his shoulder.

"'Zup, buddy?" Burgers asked carefully as he took another step inside. The other Ranger was in full gear and looked like he was getting ready for a full-blown operation. "You... uh... heading somewhere?"

"Huh?" Ramirez asked. "Oh! Yeah! You know... thought I'd go to the range and squeeze off a few rounds, you know?"

"It's like zero-one in the morning," Burgers pointed out.

"Yeah, but the Chief's guys put up these new floodlights out there, so I figured I'd test them out."

"Uh huh," Burgers told him. He pointed to the black strands of heavy-duty plastic tucked into one of the MOLLE straps of his tactical vest. "So, what's the zip ties for?"

"Huh?" Ramirez asked. "Oh! Those! Those are for securing the targets."

"Uh huh," Burgers said gently. "Track'n... Track'n..." He paused for a moment before pointing at another item secured to the front of his friend's vest. "And the... um... the taser?"

"Oh, that!" Ramirez said as he opened a heavy metal box marked "DANGER: FLASH BANG GRENADES." "That's for... you know... in case the targets try to run away." He put a few of the cylindrical grenades into the pouches on his vest.

Burgers sighed. "Dude, you can't."

"The fuck I can't," Ramirez replied, his tone taking a much harder edge than before. "Alzoria managed to scratch one across the face. Make him real easy to find." He grunted as he replaced the now-half-empty box on the shelf where he found it. "Find him, give him a little juicey-juice from o'l Sparky here, get him to give up the other two... and then I take *their* hair."

"Along with some scalp?" Burgers asked.

Ramirez pointed at him and smiled. "See? Easy."

"Dude," Burgers said again gently. "You can't."

The other Ranger slammed his palms down on the stainless steel armorer's bench and looked at his friend.

"Burgers," he said plainly. "They basically stole her *honor*. They may as well have burned the word 'whore' into her forehead! It's the same thing!"

"I know, man," Burgers told him. "But you can't go after them."

"Why not? Huh?" Ramirez asked.

"Do you see what's happening here?" his friend asked him. "Why they did this to Alzoria and not one of *our* females?"

"Alzoria *is* one of our females," Ramirez growled at him.

"You know what I mean!" Burgers snapped back at him. "They did this to *her* because they want *you* to do exactly this! If they had done it to a female Ranger, we would be *justified* to go after them. Even the Va'Shen would have to accept that! But because they did it to Alzoria, it's none of our fucking business!"

"Well, they fucked up, because I'm making it my business," Ramirez hissed.

"And the story every Va'Shen will be telling each other tomorrow morning will be about how some human maniac beat the shit out of a bunch of poor Va'Shen guys!" Burgers shot back. "*Everything* everyone has done here... the caves, the *yarl*, the grain, the festival, the POWs... all of it... It *all* goes away! We go back to looking over our shoulders every minute of every day! That's what *they want!* Is that what you want?!"

"Of course not!"

"You think that's what *Alzoria* wants?!"

Ramirez didn't answer. He bit his lip and looked everywhere but at his friend's eyes. Finally, he slammed the rifle down on the bench in rage.

"MOTHERFUCKER!" he shouted. He finally turned back to Burgers. "So, what the fuck am I supposed to do?!"

Burgers stepped forward and put his finger in his friend's chest. "You go back to Alzoria's house and you *be there*. That's what you do. You be there for her."

"Goddammit, man," Ramirez muttered, turning away from him. "She doesn't even want to see me."

"Bullshit! She doesn't want *you* to see *her*! There's a difference." Ramirez said nothing, and Burgers went on. "There's gonna come a moment when she *will* want you there, and you don't want to miss it. Track'n?"

Ramirez bit his lip and nodded.

"Now, swear to me you're not going to do something... Ramirez-ish."

"I swear," the other Ranger said sullenly.

For the first time, Burgers sighed in relief. "Okay," he said. "Let's put this shit back, and I'll walk you back to her place. I'll talk to the Captain and let him know what you're up to, okay?"

Ramirez nodded again. "Okay."

"Okay."

* * *

Patricia couldn't help but note the somewhat more subdued mood in the chow hall during breakfast that morning. She, of course, knew why. It was a small FOB, and it was impossible to not hear about something unless a massive effort was made to conceal it. Alzoria was well-liked on the base. She was constantly seen hanging around Staff Sergeant Ramirez, himself very popular.

So, when one person heard she was attacked, almost every troop on the FOB knew almost instantly.

It wasn't just the fact that Alzoria had been the victim, however. Since their arrival here, crime in Pelle had been almost unheard of, let alone violent crime. It was a sharp left turn in how the humans on FOB Leonard had come to perceive the Va'Shen, and it made some of them, particularly the noncombat troops, nervous.

"Word gets around," she said quietly as she placed her tray on the table and sat down.

"Yeah, it does," Ben replied. Staff Sergeant Baird had told him about the attack personally and explained that Ramirez would need a few days to help Alzoria get through it. Given how much help the vixen had been to them, Ben had agreed instantly.

"Are you going to the *aderen* today?" Patricia asked as she picked at the scrambled eggs on her tray.

Ben sighed and shook his head. He absently stirred his coffee as he searched for a way to word his reasoning. The Ranger wasn't one hundred percent certain how Va'Shen justice worked, but it seemed that, in response to the attack, the village was holding an *aderen* to discuss it. Alacea had invited him to attend, but he had declined.

His reasoning was two-fold. First, this had been an episode of one Va'Shen, or three in this case, committing a crime against another. As such, he had no legal basis for interfering in the Pelle villagers' handling of the case. For another, everyone in the village knew about Ramirez and Alzoria's "relationship." Even if all he did was sit quietly at the *aderen* and listen, his presence would influence what the villagers might choose to say or argue, fearing retaliation from Ben for harming their "friend."

He explained this to Patricia, who, in the face of the logic, could only sadly nod.

"At least she wasn't physically hurt," Ben commented.

"The way I heard it discussed, it would have almost been better if she had been," Patricia told him.

Ben said nothing. There was another reason the issue weighed on his mind. The motive of the attack had obviously been because Alzoria and Ramirez were close. If some Va'Shen thought it had been so egregious that it warranted a violent response, did that mean that Alacea was also in danger?

He couldn't imagine anyone attacking the village religious leader, but, then again, until a day ago he had never imagined anyone attacking Alzoria.

"You're worried about Alacea?" Patricia asked as if reading his mind.

"A little," he admitted. "If someone tried the same thing with her... it would be my fault."

Patricia smiled reassuringly. "No, it wouldn't," she countered. "You couldn't blame yourself anymore than Ramirez should himself. If some asshole is going to do something, that's on them."

Ben gave a moment's thought to sending a Ranger or two to provide security at the temple, just in case. But he could only imagine the kind of message that would send, having armed troops standing outside the center of Pelle's religious world. His thoughts went back to the things Keyes had said to him, and he grit his teeth. He was pretty sure the way the Garan'Sel villagers had been treated and this attack had at least a tangential connection.

"You think we should visit Alzoria?" Patricia asked.

Ben sighed, once again haunted by the specter of the message that would send. Would that make the Huntress an even bigger target? He just didn't know.

"Let's see what comes of the *aderen* first," he suggested. "Then we can decide where to go from there."

* * *

Alacea sat in her usual spot at one end of the oval around which the members of the *aderen* sat and tried to consciously prevent her tail from moving. The subject of today's meeting hit very close to home for her, and she was naturally quite agitated by the whole affair.

She wasn't the only one, it seemed. Many of the villagers sitting around the oval appeared very concerned, their tails moving back and forth in deep thought, disturbed by the violence that had suddenly come to their community.

When she had heard of what happened to Alzoria, she had gone directly to the vixen's home. While the young girl was refusing to see anyone else, she could not refuse a visit from the Na'Sha, though Alacea would not have pressed the issue if she had asked her to go away.

She was thankful to see that Alzoria was, physically anyway, mostly unharmed. There were a few bruises on her knuckles and arms, wounds that occurred when she fought back, but it seemed that her attackers had one specific goal in mind and did not want to exacerbate the situation further by hurting her.

That said, the damage they did to her hair took Alacea's breath away. Most of it had been cut away in chunks, and the longest it was at any point was perhaps six inches, though there were some strands that had been missed and hung sadly down the side of her face. Alzoria had always had such beautiful hair, and it made Alacea physically sick to see what had become of it.

The two vixens spoke quietly, Alacea providing as much support for the girl as she could. Most of all she stressed that what had happened was *not* her fault. The two then prayed together, and Alacea left, hoping that she had done some good.

Lord Ramirez had been standing outside the house, though it seemed that Alzoria would not see him, and her mother would not let him wait inside. She offered him words of support as well, though she wasn't sure his Va'Shen was good enough for him to understand. She left him standing there, apparently having no intention of leaving anytime soon.

She knew that there were Va'Shen who would not be accepting of Alzoria's romantic intentions toward Lord Ramirez. The priestess, herself, had been accused by the very people she had sought to protect of demeaning herself and them by accepting her Tesho's taking of her... as complicated as that turned out to be.

Count Voro's harsh words came back to her as she stared at the temple floor. How he had accused her of selling her body to an alien invader. She took a quick look around the room and, just for a moment, wondered how many people in this room had considered taking *her* hair. The thought made her reach up and rub the tip of her purple braid between her fingers.

She looked up and to her left as Wenlin knelt next to her and took her place at Alacea's side. While the two villages integrated, both Pelle and Garan'Sel shared the responsibilities of the *aderen*, each sending their own representatives until such time as each side felt comfortable sending or accepting only one. There were exceptions, of course. Garan'Sel's *aderen* had a representative from their miners, a vocation Pelle did not have. And, so, one tod from Garan'Sel, Goto, held a spot alone. There were other changes as well. With the return of the Pelle commando, some positions were held by tods where, until just recently, they had been held by vixens.

One example was the Hunters. While her father, Bao Aren, had been away fighting in the war, his daughter, Bao Sen, had held that position and had done very well. But with the return of her elder brother, Dan Huun, Bao Sen had stepped aside, and he had permanently taken their fallen father's role.

<Welcome,> she greeted Wenlin.

<I apologize that I must intrude,> Wenlin said formally. She, of course, was not intruding. This was simply how it was done, but proper protocol had to be maintained. <How is the vixen?>

<Quite disturbed,> Alacea told her.

<Is it true that she sought to court a Dark One?> Wenlin asked her.

<It is true,> Alacea admitted openly. <I know the Dark One in question.> She turned as the door opened and three tods entered, one with a long scratch running down his left cheek. <He is better than some tods,> she finished darkly.

The three tods stood in the center of the oval, surrounded by the cummunity leaders of both villages, and waited as the opening ceremony of bowing and prayers was complete. Once that was done, it was time to get to business.

<This *aderen* is called upon to decide what punishment, if any, to inflict upon the tods Boso, Nadro and Boto,> Kasshas announced

from his position on the opposite side of the oval from Alacea and Wenlin. <The three were accused of, and have confessed to, an attack on the vixen, Alzoria, and forcibly cutting her hair. What have you to say for yourselves?>

The leader of the three, a tall Va'Shen with a brown ponytail, beard and mustache, stepped forward to speak on behalf of the others. <I am Nadro, community leaders,> he said rather uncertainly, adding a bow for politeness's sake. <We are not good with words, so we have asked our friend, Goto, to speak for us.>

There was some murmuring among the *aderen* as Goto stood up from his position and entered the center of the oval. Alacea sensed Wenlin leaning close to her just before the other vixen began to whisper to her.

<Goto is popular among the villagers,> Wenlin told her. <Many wanted him to become our new chieftain. His word is respected.>

<Why did you not recommend him?> Alacea whispered back. Garan'Sel never appointed a new chieftain after their last one was killed. If Goto was really popular enough to garner support from the community, it was odd that the Na'Sha would not recommend him, a hard and fast requirement for the chieftain's position.

Wenlin answered, her voice even and emotionless. <His views on how we should act on the issue of the Dark Ones is... complicated.>

Alacea's breath caught in her throat. It was a gentle euphemism, but as a Na'Sha herself she understood the hidden meaning. One thing a Na'Sha could never do would be to recommend a chieftain she believed would disobey the Emperor. A "complicated" view on the Dark Ones could only mean that not only did Goto believe the villagers should resist the invaders, but that he would act on this belief if given the opportunity.

<Be wary,> Wenlin continued before leaning away again. <He is educated... and angry.>

<*Aderen*,> Goto began. <I propose to you that this meeting serves no purpose and is wholly inappropriate as no crime has been committed.>

There was some hissing and a lot of tail-waving at this rather bold assertion.

<An interesting place Garan'Sel must be if three tods setting upon a lone vixen is so commonplace as to be considered legal,> Yasuren spoke up from behind her fan next to Kasshas.

Goto turned to her, his tail lazily moving back and forth. <I apologize,> he said. <I was not aware that the chieftain's myorin spoke for him in the *aderen*.>

<She speaks on behalf of the vixens of the community,> Kasshas told him pointedly. <It is unorthodox, but we find it works well.>

<Then it is she who should be thanking these three tods,> Goto continued, gesturing to the three Va'Shen men standing quietly in the oval. <The invasion of the Dark Ones has forced us to change many of our ways, but there remain limits as to acceptable behavior for both tods *and* vixens.> He paused a moment and looked around at the gathered villagers. <I have been told that this young vixen, Alzoria, openly sought courtship with a Dark One soldier. Is that true?>

As he asked this, he turned to where the Hunters Guild representative sat. Dan Huun met his gaze while, sitting next to him, Bao Sen glared daggers at the tod. <That is so,> Dan Huun answered calmly.

<Is there an Aru'Dace present?> Goto called.

Hestean began to stand up, but before she could, a voice from behind her spoke up.

<I am here,> Runa called from the back. She saw Hestean looking at her and put her hands over her mouth. <Apologies, Honored Aru'Dace!> she quickly said. <I am just used to answering to...>

<It is all right,> Hestean replied diplomatically. <If you can answer Goto's question, then please do.>

Goto waited for Hestean to sit down again before addressing the green-haired vixen. <Runa Aru'Dace, can you remind us of the penalties given four thousand years ago to Va'Shen found to have collaborated with the Dark Ones during their first invasion?>

Runa cleared her throat and began nervously. <Many collaborators managed to hide their associations from the Emperor's agents,> she said. <And so, very few collaborators were formally charged...>

<*Formally* charged,> Goto repeated. <That is not to say they were not punished.>

<N... No,> Runa replied. Her eyes darted around the *aderen* as she began to see the trap Goto was laying. <It fell to the communities themselves, those who had personally witnessed the collaboration... to... discipline them.>

<As they saw fit,> Goto finished for her.

<As... they saw fit, yes,> Runa repeated quietly.

<Your argument is invalid,> Yasuren announced. <Alzoria is not a collaborator. Everything she has done has been in accordance with the Emperor's will that we cooperate with the Dark One authorities.>

<The Emperor, in that same statement, commanded us to remain true to who we are, Va'Shen... the children of those who made all.> Goto looked around the room again. <To remain Va'Shen and to preserve our future. If Alzoria had succeeded in attracting a Dark One tesho, their children would be, not Va'Shen, but a mixture of the two races. And even if they could not have children, the kits they adopt and raise would be raised in the shadow of Dark One culture.>

The *aderen* was silent, seemingly enthralled by Goto's warning of this threat to their civilization, as if the actions of a single vixen could somehow single-handedly undo thousands of years of history.

<You see the threat now?> Goto asked them. <Four thousand years ago, the Dark Ones attempted to destroy us... through systematic slaughter... Today they attempt a new tactic. They destroy our culture... and they make us into their own image.>

Alacea couldn't believe what she was hearing. Goto made a young vixen's crush sound like a master plan formulated in a Dark One military headquarters on the other side of the galaxy.

If you did not know them as you do, a voice in her head pointed out, *would you not think such a thing possible?*

The priestess swallowed as she looked around and found many of the Va'Shen present were deep in thought, giving this ridiculous claim honest consideration.

<It is the responsibility of the community to hold its members to the good and proper path,> Goto continued. <So that such actions fail. So that others will not stray. These three...> He pointed at the tods in question. <... acted in the best interest of their community. If there is guilt anywhere, it is in the rest of us, who did not possess the courage to perform the duty ourselves.>

<Preposterous!> Yasuren cried angrily, her tail slapping her tesho so hard, he was leaning away from her to avoid it. <If there was such concern, they should have brought it to the *aderen*!>

<And how could they?> Goto asked her. He turned his eyes to Alacea, who froze in his gaze. <When our community leaders are unable to speak against such a thing.>

The movement of his eyes did not escape Yasuren's notice, nor did the message it was meant to convey. <Is that to mean a gang of tods should set upon the Na'Sha as well?> she demanded. This question seemed to momentarily turn the tide back as the Pelle villagers in the room became angry at the thought of Alacea being unfairly punished.

But Goto was ready for that as well.

<Of course not,> he said gently, turning to Alacea. *<No one could find fault with the Na'Sha's decisions, made in a time of desperation in order to save her own people. But an unfortunate side effect of her sacrifice and her efforts has been to make such unions* seem *possible... even beneficial. And in her position, how could she correct another vixen for doing the same thing she has done, if not for the same reasons?>*

Alacea was stunned. In the same breath, Goto had both supported and blamed her for the attack on Alzoria while excusing her for not stopping it in the first place.

<These tods did what they knew to be right,> Goto said, beginning to sum up his argument. <What we, upon deep reflection, also know to be right. In such circumstances, we cannot hold that a crime has been committed.>

With that final argument, Goto returned to his seat and knelt upon it, head held high and much calmer than most of the other Va'Shen around him.

<You see?> Wenlin whispered to the still-stunned Alacea. <There are times I wonder how a tod who spent most of his life underground could be so eloquent.>

<We will vote,> Kasshas announced. <Each member of the *aderen* will vote yes if they believe the three tods before us are guilty of a crime or no if they are not. If they are found to be guilty, we will then discuss punishment. The Farmers.>

On that prompt, the tod representing Pelle's farmers stood up and cast his vote, followed shortly by the representative of Garan'Sel's farmers. Alacea watched as each representative gave their vote in turn.

Hestean stood up. <The Mikorin vote yes.> The historian sat down again.

Although she was a key part of the *aderen*, Alacea was not a voting member. She was there as a representative of the community as a whole. If she voted, it was the same as saying the entire village agreed with her own opinion, and that simply did not make sense to the Va'Shen. Also, as Na'Sha, she would have to one day stand before the Gods and argue in support of whatever decision the *aderen* made, and she obviously would not be able to do that should any vote she make run counter to what the *aderen* ultimately decided.

Her eyes fell on Azarin, sitting next to his adopted father who represented the Craftsmen. She watched the older tod stand and vote yes.

But even then, the vote was extraordinarily closer, much closer, Alacea thought, than it really should be. Could Goto's argument truly have swayed so many? After everything the Pelle villagers have been through with her Tesho's people, could they really believe so easily in such a farfetched conspiracy?

The vote was tied when it reached the last representative, and Alacea had to stop herself from sighing in relief. The Hunters were the last representative to vote. It looked like Alzoria's attackers would be forced to face some measure of justice after all.

She quickly scolded herself for such a thought. It was the community who decided such things, not her. Even if they found the three guilt-free, she would have no choice but acknowledge and support that decision.

Dan Huun stood up. <The Hunters vote no.>

Alacea's ears shot straight up in shock, and she wasn't the only one. Kneeling next to Dan Huun, Bao Sen looked up at him absolutely flabbergasted.

<"No?!"> she demanded.

<No,> Dan Huun repeated, not even bothering to look at his sister. Everyone in the *aderen* began muttering, shocked at the unexpected turn. The three tods in the circle breathed a sigh of relief, their ears twitching in happiness.

Bao Sen shot to her feet. <The Huntresses demand a separate vote!> she cried.

Kasshas released a disappointed breath of his own, and his tail slapped the floor behind him. Sitting next to him, Yasuren appeared absolutely livid.

<I am sorry, Bao Sen, but you are no longer the representative of the Hunter's Guild. As such, you are not entitled to a separate vote,> Kasshas told her.

The crimson-haired vixen stood there in shock, utterly amazed at what her community had just done.

* * *

<How could you do such a thing?!> Bao Sen demanded the moment they set foot outside the temple. <*How could you?! Alzoria is one of our own!*>

Dan Huun refused to be shaken by his sister's emotional response and never even broke stride as they started down the main road through Pelle.

<Because Goto is right,> he told her. <Things have become muddled since the invasion.>

<And you think something like this makes them more clear?!> Bao Sen cried in response. <Alzoria...>

<Was trying to lay with a Dark One, Sister,> Dan Huun turned on her and hissed like an angry cobra. Now, finally, his emotions were coming out as his tail whipped back and forth and his ears pointed down at his sister. <That such a thought does not seem to faze you shows just how muddled things have become! They are not our friends! They are not our comrades! They are not fellow Va'Shen! They are *the enemy*! The *greatest* enemy we have ever faced! You, Alzoria, many of the other villagers here have all seemed to have forgotten that!>

<They are not the monsters we were told they were,> Bao Sen told him, trying to retain some semblance of calm. <They have done good things for us.>

<Do you know how Ten Sun died?> Dan Huun asked her suddenly. The mention of her youngest brother, barely fifteen when he left for the war, brought Bao Sen up short. <He never even saw the face of the enemy,> Dan Huun continued. <The Dark Ones sent a little flying machine that chased him through the forest like an animal until he was trapped and then gunned him down! Yun Do? He stepped on an explosive trap that *shredded* him into almost nothing! There wasn't even enough afterwards for us to *bury!*>

<I am not saying the war wasn't bad,> Bao Sen said calmly. <But it *is* over. By order of the Emperor himself. If I asked Rah-mee-raz about how some of his friends died, I'm sure I would hear very similar things. But he does not cling to his hatred.>

<My hatred kept me alive,> Dan Huun told her, his voice barely above a whisper. <And it will continue to do so.>

<Dan Huun, Bao Sen,>

They both turned at the interruption and found Azarin walking casually toward them.

Dan Huun bowed casually to him. <Blessed day, Azarin,> he said, his voice much friendlier than it was a moment ago.

<And eventful as well,> the former captain returned, offering the siblings a bow of his own.

<Yes,> the Hunter agreed much more sedately. <Is there something you require of us?> he asked.

<No,> Azarin said. <I just wanted to ask after Alzoria and see if she is all right.>

<She is...>

<She will be fine,> Dan Huun told him, interrupting his sister and receiving a dirty look and pointed ears in response.

<If I can help...> Azarin began.

Dan Huun cut him off. <We are thankful, but I am sure she just needs time, prayer and reflection.>

Azarin paused, noting the difference in auras between the two siblings. <Of course,> he agreed quietly.

As if an idea had suddenly occurred to him, Dan Huun's ears popped up. <Since you are here, however, I was wondering if you might be interested in coming to our home and having dinner with us sometime,> he said.

<You honor me,> Azarin replied. <I accept, of course.>

<Good,> Dan Huun told him. <I would love for my sister to get to know a valorous tod such as yourself.>

Bao Sen's ears popped up in surprise before pointing downward again in realization. Her brother, it seemed, was trying to set her up with his former captain.

<I shall look forward to it,> Azarin said without emotion. He bowed to emphasize his words.

<I must go,> Dan Huun said. <Excuse me.>

Before Bao Sen could say anything, the Hunter stepped off, leaving her alone with the one-eyed carpenter. She growled softly in anger... over a whole host of things.

<Are you alright?> Azarin asked her.

<Yes, I just had something in my throat,> Bao Sen told him coolly.

<No, I mean after all that,> Azarin said, nodding back at the temple where the vote had been held. <The outcome was very upsetting.>

<Yes, it was,> Bao Sen agreed quietly.

<Dan Huun, in his spirit, is a good tod,> Azarin told her. <But he does not always allow that goodness to have more influence in his decisions than his emotions.>

<Is that why he was not elected captain after my father died?> Bao Sen asked him pointedly.

<In part,> Azarin confessed reluctantly. <What will you do now?> he asked her.

Bao Sen's ears were still digging into her scalp as she thought. <Goto said that a message had to be sent,> she told him. <Perhaps we shall send one of our own.>

* * *

<We must celebrate,> Goto declared as he led the three other tods into his home and took a seat at the head of the table. The three tods, who had just barely evaded punishment, sat as well, their ears twitching happily.

<Did everything go well?> Posha asked as she came into the main room from the kitchen.

<Exactly as you said it would, Posha,> Goto told her. <Have we any *mura*?> he asked her.

<I think I managed to save one bottle,> the young vixen said happily. <I will fetch it!>

<And bring back a glass for yourself!> Goto called to her as she went into the kitchen. <We are celebrating!>

Nadro, Boso and Boto's ears fluttered even faster at the thought of *mura*. Boso, who wore his black hair short and wore only a mustache and no beard, looked across the table at Goto, curiosity written in the movement of his coal black tail.

<What did you mean by 'as you said it would?'> he asked him.

Goto's ears flickered in a proud grin. <My good friends, you have my niece to thank for your freedom. She helped me fashion the arguments to use today.>

"Helped" was an understatement. Posha had, in fact, practically written the script herself and even told Goto what to say should the debate turn to the Na'Sha.

<She did?> Boto, Bosa's brother, asked, stroking his short black beard. He was the one Alzoria had scarred during the fight, and it still ached.

<I say it often, but you still don't believe me,> Goto said smugly, his arms folded over his chest. <My sister's daughter is a genius.>

<Oh, Uncle, I am not,> Posha lightly scolded as she re-entered the room with a bottle and four glasses. She began to pour them their drinks as she faced the three defendants. <There were many debates in the city where I lived,> she explained. <I liked to watch them.>

<You do not give yourself enough credit, Niece,> Goto told her as he picked up his glass. He leaned across the table as if sharing a secret with the other three. <Were it not for her suggestions back in Garan'Sel, many more of us would have been killed in our fight with the Dark Ones.>

<Truly?> Nadro asked, eyeing Posha with much more appreciation than before.

<Keep your gaze down, my friend,> Goto ordered good-naturedly. <I'm not allowing my Posha to be taken by a dirt-worker like you or her uncle.>

<Uncle! Please!> Posha cried in embarrassment, her hand moving up to cover her ears.

Goto noticed that she had only brought four glasses. <You did not bring a glass for yourself?> he asked.

<I do not like the taste of *mura*,> she told him. <The three of you celebrate. I must go out and post a letter.>

<A letter?> Goto asked. He seemed to realize the answer to his own question a second later and added. <Of course.>

Since her arrival at Garan'Sel, his niece often wrote letters to her parents and sent them north. She told him that since she had not seen their bodies there was a chance they were still alive. Goto saw it more as a kind of therapeutic activity and so did not interfere. He had done the same thing and knew the desperate sliver of hope that compelled her.

<When I return, I shall cook a celebratory feast!> she announced happily.

<Thank you, Niece,> Goto said affectionately as he took a pull from his glass.

Posha returned to the kitchen, and her ears suddenly tensed as a slight scratching sound reached them. Checking over her shoulder and finding the four tods immersed in conversation, she went to the back and opened the door.

Turean stood there, his tail twitching nervously behind him.

<Hello, um... Posha,> he said with a bow. <I was... um... thinking you might want to... to... take a walk.>

The vixen's ears twitched a smile. <I would like that.>

Chapter 9

One month until contact...

Burgers flipped the page on the thick stack of printer paper and reached for his cup of coffee without looking. Dinner at the chow hall had officially ended an hour ago, but, having nothing else to do, the NCO had yet to leave, taking the moment of peace to catch up on some reading.

So engrossed with what he was reading, he didn't notice Mitchell approach with his own coffee cup and take the seat on the other side of the table from him.

"What'cha reading?" the infantryman asked.

"Fanfiction," Burgers replied, finally looking up. "You know that vidshow, SpaceKnight?"

"The one with the experimental space fighter?" Mitchell asked, taking a sip from his coffee.

"That's the one," Burgers told him, setting the papers aside. The Fuzz prevented people from watching vids, and old-fashioned books were prohibitively expensive. So, some of the more creative types on FOB Leonard had taken to borrowing some of the typewriters the Army had specially built for working on Va'Sh and started writing their own.

"Any good?" Mitchell asked.

"Eh," Burgers replied. "The writer *really* wants the two male leads to hook up, and the way she writes it... it kinda makes sense."

"This is what you Leonard folks do for fun, huh?" Mitchell asked.

Burgers sighed. No, not usually. But Ramirez was still waiting for Alzoria to see him, and Fletcher had some kind of medical issue to take care of, so he was at loose ends tonight.

"Just a slow night, I guess," Burgers said. "What are you doing tonight?"

Mitchell grinned. "I'm going off-base to get some cupcakes."

"Cupcakes?" Burgers asked, his face scrunched up in curiosity.

The other NCO nodded. "Some of the Va'Shy girls from Garan'Sel have a place on the end of the refugee shacks. Wanna come?" Burgers looked skeptical of marching across Pelle just for some baked treats. "I promise you, man, you're going to love it."

"They're that good?" Burgers asked.

Mitchell grinned like the cat that ate the canary. "Oh, yeah. Trust me."

Burgers took a breath, looked around at the empty chow hall and tapped the tabletop with his fingers. "Okay. Let's go eat cupcakes."

* * *

"Thanks for helping out, Ma'am. I really appreciate it," Fletcher said as she led Patricia into the examination room of the small FOB clinic in which she worked.

"It's no problem," the terp told her. "Kind of odd hours, though, isn't it?"

The corpsman shrugged. "Shit happens at any hour, I guess." She opened the curtain to reveal two vixens standing next to the exam table. One of them Patricia recognized. She had worked with Kastia before, and the green-haired Va'Shen healer could be prickly but also very professional.

The other vixen she didn't recognize. She had long, pale-gold hair that flowed down to her shoulders, and her green and white hanbok was clean and neat. Her ears were folded downward in a way that made her look sad, but it was honestly difficult to tell with the Va'Shen. Patricia guessed she was perhaps sixteen, and she was an absolute beauty.

When she realized the humans had entered the room, she jumped and turned toward them, but not in a welcoming way. It seemed more like someone who wanted to keep a dangerous animal in sight.

Fletcher bowed to the both of them and gestured to Patricia. "I asked Lieutenant Kim to come to make sure I understand everything. Is that all right?" She turned to the unknown vixen and added for her benefit, "She is also a vixen."

Patricia translated her words and saw the blonde vixen look down uncertainly, but Kastia bowed in assent.

<I know Lady Patricia,> she assured the other vixen. <You need not fear.>

<Very well,> the vixen said quietly. <I will trust the Healer's judgement.>

"What is the problem?" the corpsman asked.

Kastia answered for the other woman. <This vixen...> She paused and looked to the other Va'Shen woman, who must have given her some kind of sign because the healer continued without giving the vixen's name. <... came to me earlier this afternoon with symptoms I have not seen before. I want to be sure it is not the ray-dee-ay-shun.>

"What kind of symptoms?" Fletcher asked after listening to the translation.

Patricia translated the question and listened as Kastia explained further.

"Weird sores, she says," Patricia told the other woman. "In the vaginal area."

"Huh, okay," Fletcher said, taking out a pair of latex gloves and putting them on. "May I see?"

Patricia translated, and Kastia and the patient went back and forth for several moments. Fletcher looked to the terp for explanation.

"She's kind of embarrassed," Patricia explained.

"Please let her know I will be very quick, and only I will look."

Patricia broke into the aliens' conversation, and finally the vixen agreed. Fletcher gestured for the girl to sit on the table and lift the skirt of her hanbok. The terp and Kastia watched from a respectful distance as she examined the Va'Shen girl, who looked so embarrassed Patricia thought she might bolt from the room any second. She had turned away from them and shut her eyes tightly.

"Huh," the corpsman grunted. She took a short cotton swab from a sterile packet. "Tell her I'm going to touch them. If it hurts, please tell me."

Patricia translated, and the girl waited breathlessly until it was over. The lieutenant assumed it must not have hurt since the girl didn't cry out or say anything.

"Okay, I'm done," Fletcher said, standing up and giving the girl what, for a human, would be a reassuring smile. She stepped to another table and put the swab in a glass vial. As she did so, Kastia approached.

<Is it the illness?> she asked.

Mina poured a clear liquid into the vial and put a rubber topper on it. Holding it up to the light, she shook the vial up and down and watched as the liquid slowly turned a pale blue.

"Huh," Fletcher grunted again.

"She wants to know if it's radiation," Patricia said. "Is it?"

"No," the sailor said quietly. "It's not radiation." She turned to Kastia and paused, as if wondering how much she should say. "Tell her I have something that might help, but I don't know if it will work on Va'Shen."

Patricia and Kastia went back and forth as Fletcher went to the small dispensary and unlocked it. Filling a small white bottle with about ten small pills, she put the cap on and turned back to them.

"She says let's try it," Patricia said.

Fletcher held up the bottle for them to see. "Tell her she must swallow one of these per day for ten days. If she feels sick afterward, she must stop immediately."

Patricia nodded and translated for the two Va'Shen women. Kastia took the bottle and tried to open it, but the safety lock thwarted her. Fletcher took the bottle back and showed her.

"So children do not eat them by mistake," she explained to her.

Upon hearing the translation, Kastia looked at the bottle in admiration. She looked at the pills and sniffed them.

<You are certain it is not ray-dee-ay-shun?>

Fletcher nodded. <Yes,> she said in Va'Shen.

Kastia handed the bottle to the vixen and explained how to open it.

"Also!" Fletcher added suddenly, almost forgetting. "Tell her she should not be intimate with her husband until the sores are gone."

Patricia translated this as best she could, and Kastia's ears lowered. The other vixen looked away as if in shame.

"Something I said?" Fletcher asked Patricia.

Kastia said something in a curt tone that brooked no argument.

"She said it's not an issue," Patricia said. "She is not married."

"Well," Fletcher said quietly. "It's good to know anyway."

Kastia bowed to the two of them and led the young vixen out of the clinic.

"You're welcome," Patricia quietly called in the direction they had gone. She turned to the other woman. "So, not radiation. That's good."

"Yeah," Fletcher muttered distractedly, looking at the blue vial again.

"What is it?" Patricia asked.

The corpsman took a breath and shook the vial again, but the liquid inside stubbornly remained blue.

"It's just weird, is all," she told the terp. "I didn't think it could happen."

"What is it?" Patricia joked. "Is she pregnant?"

"No," Fletcher said, turning to her and holding up the vial.

"It's herpes."

* * *

There weren't many people out on the street at this time of night. Pelle, as a town, pretty much shut down once the sun went down, but there were still a few tods and vixens here and there rushing to conclude whatever business had brought them out that night.

Mitchell walked confidently down the street, his hand resting on the butt of his holstered pistol as if expecting to have to draw it at any second. Burgers followed him, and, although also armed, his hand never went near his own handgun. Waterlamps hanging from the fronts of shops and houses combined with the ever-present nighttime aurora gave the village an eerie light.

"Dude, what kind of bakery is open this time of night?" Burgers asked him as they walked.

"The best kind," Mitchell replied over his shoulder. "Don't worry about it, man. I don't want to spoil the surprise."

"Okay, whatever," Burgers muttered. As they entered the section of the village where the temp housing for the newcomers had been erected, the staff sergeant began to feel a strange vibe, like he was being watched through the scope of a rifle. His hand instinctively dropped to his weapon and rested there.

Mitchell's confident stride didn't change at all, however, and he continued to lead his old friend to a building on the end of the street.

Longer than some of the others and only one story, it looked like it was made to house perhaps three families. The front was made of white and tan composite materials like those found on the FOB while elements of Va'Shen architecture, such as the wood and tiled roof, could be seen here and there.

Mitchell stepped forward and slid the door open without knocking, and Burgers followed him inside.

What Burgers saw when he entered was exactly what he expected a bakery to look like. There was a polished wooden counter at the back of the room that was nice enough to be used as a bar at an Irish pub, on the other side of which stood wooden racks covered with cloth holding several loaves of dark brown bread. Burgers inhaled the smell and smiled at the scent of fresh baked bread. Perhaps Mitchell wasn't insane after all.

A vixen walked into the room from a door just to the left of where the counter ended, her long deep purple hair hanging down over the top half of the apron she wore over her hanbok.

"Mee-chill!" the vixen said with a welcoming bow. "You back so soon!"

"Hey there, Toki!" Mitchell said with a big smile. He put his arm around Burgers's shoulder. "This is my friend, Burgers. I told him how great your cupcakes were, and he would like to try one."

The vixen, Toki, bowed to Burgers and, for a moment, the NCO thought the Va'Shen woman was familiar.

"You will have usual, Mee-chill?" Toki asked.

"That sounds great, Toki," Mitchell replied. "And for my friend..." Mitchell trailed off and looked at Burgers critically, as if trying to pair his friend with a good wine.

"You choose from menu?" Toki suggested.

Before either of them could answer, the vixen went behind the counter and brought out a small wooden board with multi-colored rectangles pegged to it. There were a few spaces where it appeared that rectangles had been removed, and Burgers figured they were probably out of those flavors.

Toki removed a dark red rectangle and handed it to Mitchell before turning the board to Burgers and showing it to him expectantly.

"Um... I don't know," Burgers confessed. "I mean... I don't really know Va'Shen flavors. What's good?"

"It's *all* good, dude. Trust me," Mitchell told him with a grin.

"Er... okay." Burgers studied the board and pointed at a rectangle that was a very light green color. The Ranger knew the flavor probably wouldn't be the same, but the color made him think of mint and he had nothing else to go on.

Toki took the rectangle from the board and handed it to Burgers while Mitchell took a small sack of Va'Shen coins from his pocket and counted out the fee.

"Come," Toki said, beckoning them to follow her into the back.

Burgers gave his friend a questioning look, and Mitchell looked like he wanted to say something but held himself back with a grin.

"Just roll with it, brother. I'm telling you you're going to love it!"

The Ranger mentally shrugged and followed obediently, telling himself that, if nothing else, he'd learn a little about Va'Shen culture. Maybe there was a cupcake ceremony like the Japanese had with tea. He suddenly wondered if he was going to be treated to a show of a Va'Shen baker making his cupcake from scratch.

Toki stopped at a room with a closed paper door and opened it, bidding Burgers to go inside. The NCO stepped inside but was confused when the door began to shut behind him without Mitchell following him.

Mitchell gave him a thumbs up and a final, "Just roll with it!" Then, Burgers was alone.

"Oooo-kay," Burgers muttered as he looked around the small room. There was a tiny polished wooden table in the center with several Va'Shen sitting pillows around it. Water lamps hanging from the ceiling illuminated the room, but only just barely, giving the setting a candlelit appearance. But there was no oven or plates or napkins or anything to suggest that Burgers's original thought of a Va'Shen baking show was going to happen.

He blew a breath out between his lips as if to say "fuck it" and slapped his thighs before sitting down at the table and waiting.

Oddly enough, it was not long before the door slid open again, and a green-haired vixen in a red and black hanbok glided inside holding a tray upon which sat a small, round pastry. The vixen bowed to Burgers before doing something that shocked the Ranger.

The vixen *smiled*.

It wasn't a very natural smile. It was more like someone who had never done it had practiced it in a mirror... which, Burgers thought, was probably exactly the case.

"Hello," the vixen said. Burgers was still too shocked to reply, and the Va'Shen woman gently rested the tray with the cupcake on the table in front of him.

Burgers looked down at the pastry and paused. Once again, he hadn't been sure what to expect... but this hadn't been it.

The cupcake was, in a word, plain. It looked more like a muffin than a cupcake and was actually on the small side for one. There was no icing, and one of the top edges looked like it had uncooked flour on it.

"Um... This... This looks great," Burgers told the vixen uncertainly, hoping that the disappointment didn't show on his face.

The Va'Shen girl sat down right next to him, close enough for their legs to touch.

It was quite a different experience for Burgers. Usually, the Va'Shen didn't want to be close to a human, so this was way out of the ordinary. He was close enough to smell the vixen's perfume or possibly shampoo, a vaguely floral scent that reminded him of raspberries.

"So... um..." he began. <I am Burgers,> he said in Va'Shen. <What is your name?>

"You people car me 'Minty,'" she told him, hiding her mouth behind her hand.

Okay, this is getting weird...

He cleared his throat and turned his attention back to the sad little cake on the table. "So..."

The Ranger began asking the woman a question, turning to look over at her, when she suddenly crawled into his lap and enveloped him in her arms. Shocked, Burgers sat there frozen as the alien girl leaned in and began to lick at his neck.

"I yor virst Va'Shen?" the girl whispered.

"My first wha... What? Whoa!" Burgers cried, his brain finally catching up to the events happening to him. He scampered backward and took the girl by the arms, holding her away from him.

The vixen's tail thrashed about in shock, and her ears stood straight up.

Her *mint green* ears.

Burgers looked at the cupcake and then back at the girl, whose ears had now flattened in fear. He pulled the green rectangular block from his pocket and found it was roughly the same shade of green as the woman's hair.

"What in the hell?" Burgers whispered to himself. He stood up quickly, and the vixen fell to the floor with a cry. Burgers started for the door, and the Va'Shen girl got down on her knees and bowed, her forehead striking the floor with an audible *thump*.

"Please! I sorry!" she cried after him in stuttering English.

Burgers threw open the door and stalked down the hall toward the sound of two people muttering next door. Stopping at the door, he grabbed the handle and pulled it open to find Mitchell, his uniform top and t-shirt off and a vixen with dark red hair straddling him, the top of her hanbok pulled down off her shoulders exposing her small breasts.

The vixen cried out in surprise, and Mitchell looked at Burgers in surprised anger.

"Dude! What the fuck?!" Mitchell asked.

Burgers pointed his finger at him. "PUT YOUR FUCKING CLOTHES ON AND GET THE FUCK OUT HERE, SERGEANT!" he roared.

The NCO slammed the door shut and turned just as Toki, the green-haired girl and a new vixen with dark blue hair speckled with black spots approached from the direction he had just come.

The blue-haired woman was obviously in charge, leading the other two in a bow.

"I apologize, my lord," the vixen said in rather good English. "If Runa angered you, she shall be punished. Do you want another vixen?"

Burgers's eyes went to the green-haired girl, who was trembling and looked like she was about to collapse any moment.

"What is this place?" Burgers demanded.

"This is our bakery," the blue-haired vixen told him. "Your people pay, and we give them cake."

"Uh huh," Burgers said. "And the sex is just what? A nice bonus?"

The blue-haired vixen gave Burgers a fake forced smile just like the other girl had. "Vixens like big strong tod. We do not say they cannot be with big strong tod."

Before Burgers could reply, the door behind him slid open, and a confused and angry, but properly dressed Mitchell, stood there.

"Burgers, what the..."

"I recommend you shut the fuck up," Burgers told him, shutting the other man down. "What the fuck, man!?" he continued. "A fucking *brothel*!?"

"No," Mitchell replied evenly with a hint of conspiracy in his tone. "A *bakery* with a very *friendly* staff."

"Bullshit!" the staff sergeant roared. He pointed at the green-haired vixen, Runa, who was still shaking like a leaf. "She look like she's having a good time?! Grab your cover! We're leaving!"

"Yes, Staff Sergeant," Mitchell replied sullenly, glaring daggers at his now-probably-former friend.

Burgers looked up and down the hallway at the other doors. Suddenly, the place was silent as a tomb.

"And if anyone else in the sound of my voice is assigned to FOB Leonard," he shouted, "You have thirty seconds to get the hell out of here!"

He had hoped it was just a precaution but was shocked when two men in camouflage came out of two rooms and darted down the hall away from him. Burgers made to follow them but was brought up short by the vixen madame.

"You are displeased," the blue-haired woman stated. It wasn't a question. "Why?"

Burgers's jaw dropped as he suddenly remembered where he had seen these women before. His eyes went from the blue-haired woman to Runa to Toki and back again. They had all been in the same truck as Wenlin when he met them on the road. He had experienced several surprises tonight, but this one took the cake.

He turned to Mitchell aghast. "Holy shit," he breathed, pointing at the vixens. "Are these *Mikorin*!?" he asked. "You know they're basically nuns, right?!"

"I elect not to answer, Staff Sergeant," Mitchell replied woodenly.

Burgers grit his teeth and pointed at the door. "March!" he ordered.

* * *

Ben and the Va'Shen commando rolled over the cot and onto the hard-packed floor, landing with a thump that nearly drowned out the alarms and rifle fire outside. For a moment, he had the commando at a disadvantage, but suddenly found himself on his back, with the Va'Shen man's hands around his throat.

The Ranger tried to pry the alien's thin fingers from around his neck, but no matter what he tried, he couldn't free himself. Spots appeared before his eyes, obscuring his view of the commando on top of him, his face further hidden by shadows. As Ben gulped for air, he heard the sounds of mortars firing outside. He pushed at the alien, trying to find the commando's eyes with his fingers, but his vision was beginning to go black.

He heard another three mortar launches.

Then another three.

His eyes opened.

Darkness.

For a moment, he panicked, thinking he might actually be dead, but then he heard three knocks from nearby.

Ben took a deep breath and sat up, fumbling for the switch that would turn on the light in his hooch.

"Who's there?" he demanded in a gasp as the light came on and he rubbed his eyes. He looked at the clock and found it was near midnight.

"It's Staff Sergeant Baird, Sir," a deep but uncertain voice came back. "Sorry to wake you, but there's something you need to hear, and I didn't think it could wait."

Ben paused, trying to blink the sleep, the nightmare and the confusion from his brain all at once.

"Okay," he called back. "Just... give me two minutes."

"Yes, Sir."

The captain swung his legs over the side of his cot and rested his elbows on his knees, covering his face with his hands as he took a few deep breaths. Remembering some of the previous dreams, he quickly looked down at his crotch to see if he had pissed himself and said a silent prayer of thanks to find that he had not. He got up and quickly checked himself in the mirror before throwing on a tan uniform t-shirt and going to the door.

Opening it, Ben found Burgers standing there, sans sunglasses, with a very disturbed expression on his face.

"Come in, Staff Sergeant," Ben invited sleepily, turning and walking back into his hooch.

Burgers followed and, at Ben's invitation, sat in the pilfered office chair the captain kept for just such instances, taking a seat on the bed for himself.

"What's up?" Ben asked.

"Sir, I think we have a problem," Burgers began. "I just got back from the housing area for the Sector Six folks. One of the guys who was posted there brought me there, to what he called a 'bakery.' But it was actually a brothel."

Ben shut his eyes. "I'm sorry, Staff Sergeant. I'm going to need to hear that again."

Burgers quickly ran through the night's events, starting with Mitchell inviting him to get cupcakes and ending with his discovery in the Va'Shen 'bakery.'

"A brothel catering to humans?" Ben asked in disbelief.

Burgers nodded. "And it gets worse, Sir," he said. "The vixens working there... they're Mikorin."

Ben stared at him, shocked by this statement. "You're certain?" he asked skeptically.

The staff sergeant nodded. "I recognized some of them from when they arrived."

"You get any names?" Ben asked.

"Yeah," Burgers replied. "Toki was one. There was another one named Runa."

"Runa?" Ben repeated in surprise. "Short girl. Green hair?"

Burgers looked at him, surprised. "You know her?" he asked.

"She's the Garan'Sel Aru'Dace," Ben told him.

"Well, she brought me a cupcake and then tried to steal second base," Burgers told him.

Ben tried to reconcile the image of the mousy young priestess he had met at the temple with the working girl his NCO was describing.

"And, Sir," Burgers added, bringing Ben out of his thoughts, "I don't think this is something they do to work their way through community college, if you know what I mean. When I... um... 'refused service...' that little girl looked scared out of her mind. Like she expected to be punished because of it."

"You think she's there against her will?" Ben asked him seriously.

"I don't know about that," Burgers said. "But I don't think she liked being there either."

"What did Mitchell have to say for himself?" Ben asked.

"He thought I'd be into it," the NCO told him. "And when it became obvious I wasn't, he clammed up."

"How well do you know him?" Ben continued.

Burgers shrugged. "We were buddies in basic training," he said. "And went through Basic Infantry together, but that's it. After that, he went to Armor and I went to Infantry."

It was a pretty common story. Recruits often made life-long friends in basic training, even if they never saw each other again after that. Something about going through such a stressful and world-changing part of life together forged pretty strong bonds, but it didn't mean you knew everything about the friend you made. And sometimes you found out later that your buddy wasn't the kind of person you'd befriend if you had known more about them.

"What do you think, Sir?" Burgers asked him.

"Would you say this is something that was happening at Garan'Sel prior to the refugees coming here?" Ben asked.

Burgers nodded. "The girl, Toki, treated Mitchell like her best customer."

Ben sighed. "Shit." Every time he learned something about the happenings at Garan'Sel, it got worse. "I want to talk to the Sector Six folks," he told Burgers. "Tomorrow. All of them. One at a time."

"They may not want to say anything that could incriminate themselves," Burgers reminded him.

"Yeah," Ben agreed. "But you *can't* be the first person to see this and have a problem with it. *One* of them is going to tell us what's going on, if for no other reason than to avoid the hammer falling on *them*."

Burgers nodded. "I'll round them up and have them at the office first thing tomorrow. Should I tell them what it's about? Mitchell will have probably warned them by then."

"No, let 'em sweat a little," Ben said. "The guys he warns aren't the ones who are going to say anything anyway. Also, just so it's official, that place is banned for all FOB personnel as of now. Anyone walking into that place without a furry tail gets dragged directly to me. Copy?"

"Copy, Sir," Burgers said. "I'll draft up a notice and post it. What about the Va'Shen?"

Ben let out a long sigh. "I'll talk to them tomorrow after I hear from the Sector Six folks."

The NCO nodded again.

"Baird, thank you," Ben told him.

"For what, Sir?"

Ben looked him in the eye. "For being a decent human being."

Burgers smiled uncomfortably. "Thank you, Sir." He paused. "Sir? I don't know about you, but... the more I hear about these guys, the more sketch this all seems."

The captain nodded.

"It's not just you, Staff Sergeant."

Chapter 10

One month until contact…

The interviews began first thing in the morning.

Over breakfast, Ben filled Patricia in on what Burgers had reported, and Patricia updated him on what Fletcher had learned the previous night.

"Great," Ben sighed. "Alien STD epidemic. Let's throw that on the pile of shit we don't need."

"Any chance that it's *not* connected?" Patricia asked hopefully.

Ben gave her a look.

"Yeah, I didn't think so either," she sighed, looking down at her plate of rubbery scrambled eggs and exactly two pieces of bacon. "You gonna tell Kasshas?"

"I'm going to talk to Alacea first," Ben replied. "If this really is a Mikorin thing, she should have first crack."

As soon as they had finished breakfast and walked back to the office, Burgers brought the first Sector Six veteran in. Ben sat behind his desk, and Patricia pulled up a chair next to it, holding a notepad and pen. He sat the baby-faced private down and started by reading the soldier his Article 31 rights. He didn't want to give anyone an excuse to slip away later.

Unfortunately, it didn't come to much.

"I'm sorry, Sir," the private told him. "I haven't heard anything about it."

The interviews continued like that for more than an hour, and by that time Ben could begin to tell whom Mitchell had warned and who honestly didn't seem to know. It wasn't until a female specialist with a red bob entered and sat down across from him that they started to get somewhere.

"So, someone's finally going to do something about that place?" the soldier, Specialist McAllen, asked.

Ben leaned forward and put his elbows on the table. "You've been there?" he asked.

"No, Sir," she replied. "But everyone knows about it."

"Define 'everyone,'" Patricia prompted her.

"I mean *everyone*, Ma'am," the redhead told her. "It wasn't like it was a secret. At least, not a very good one."

"What can you tell me?" Ben asked her.

"Started up a couple of weeks after the Va'Shy temple burned down," McAllen said. "We had just started the Major's new 'Integrated Relations' plan, so there were a lot more troops actually in the village."

"'Integrated Relations?'" Ben asked. "What's that?"

"Well, Sir, the FOB had been taking a lot of fire from outside the wire. Lasers going through the hooch walls, hitting folks in their bunks and stuff. So, the Major had troops move into empty houses in the village. I guess figuring they could keep an eye on things better from there."

Ben made a note. Something about what McAllen said troubled him. "Go on," he said.

"Well, there was a little trouble with the villagers," McAllen said. "Some of the guys would try to talk up the female Va'Shies... One even got a little handsy, and a few villagers beat him up for it."

"What happened to the villagers?" Patricia asked.

McAllen turned to face her. "Punitive reprisals, Ma'am. We conducted midnight raids into a few homes suspected of smuggling weapons and contraband to let them know we were still in charge. Took the attackers into custody. We left it at that."

"Go on, Specialist," Ben prompted.

"So, a few days later, the 'bakery...'" McAllen made air quotes with her fingers. "... opened. Word started going around that if you wanted 'companionship...'" She made the air quotes again. "... that was where you went."

Ben leaned back in his chair and thought for a moment. "You said everyone knew about this," he told her. "Did that include Major Keyes and the rest of FOB leadership? Did they approve of their people frequenting such a place?"

"If you're asking me if there was a policy letter tacked on the bulletin board saying it was approved, then no, Sir," McAllen said. "I don't know exactly what Major Keyes knew or not, but..."

"But what?"

The Specialist licked her lips as she considered how much to say. "There was... an *understanding*."

"What kind of understanding?" Patricia asked her.

"Well... As long as the guys could get their rocks off at the bakery, there wasn't a need for them to mess with the Va'Shy girls," McAllen said. "And if they didn't mess with the Va'Shy girls, there was no need for the tods to step in. And if the tods didn't step in, there wasn't a need for midnight raids. And those raids did stop. So... I don't know how much Major Keyes knew, but that was how everyone I talked to saw it."

"Why didn't you report this?" Patricia asked her, shocked by what she was being told.

McAllen gave her a derisive snort. "Report it to *who*, Ma'am? The NCOs who were going to the bakery or the officers who may have made the deal in the first place? Me and the other females, we kept our mouths shut and waited for the deployment to be over. It just wasn't worth sabotaging our careers over."

McAllen was the only one who gave them any useful information. The rest claimed ignorance.

"That's the last one, Sir," Burgers said as he entered the office.

Ben threw his pen on the desk and leaned back in his office chair, hands behind his head in thought.

"Didn't hear noth'n, didn't see noth'n, don't know noth'n," the captain summed up.

"I thought McAllen's testimony was compelling," Patricia supplied helpfully. "Enough to get an investigation going, anyway."

"Yeah, but into whom?" Ben asked her.

"Mitchell and the others," she replied. Standing nearby, Burgers looked uncomfortable at the comment.

Ben saw the look and nodded at him. "You think that's a good idea, Staff Sergeant?" he asked. He wasn't putting him on the spot. Rather, Ben saw the same problem that Burgers did.

"Ma'am, with all due respect, just punishing the enlisted guys just shows them what they already think. The officers skate, and the enlisted take the fall."

"I get it, Staff Sergeant," Patricia told him. "But the sad truth is that, at the very least, we have witnesses who can put Mitchell at that brothel, one of them being *you*. Nothing we've heard from anyone can confirm that Sector Six leadership even knew what was going on."

"Which is bullshit, Ma'am," Burgers told her.

"Okay, let's stay focused here," Ben interjected. "The first order of business is to stop this thing here and now. I'm going to talk to Alacea and see how she wants to go about confronting Wenlin on it. Second order of business is making sure this doesn't blow back on *us*."

"You're worried we'll get the blame?" Patricia asked.

"No, I'm worried what the villagers are going to do when they find out our troops have been paying their religious icons for sex," Ben told her.

"You think they don't know already?" Patricia asked.

"I think if they did, there'd be a lot more bodies," Ben replied. "Third, we need to upchannel this to IG and maybe CID and get an investigation rolling. But for that, we're going to need Wenlin's cooperation."

"Think she'll testify against Keyes?" Patricia asked.

Ben wanted to reply with a positive, but he paused. He had seen the lengths the Va'Shen, particularly their religious caste, would go to protect their communities' honor. Would Wenlin really want to expose her Mikorin's actions to light of day, knowing that it would be impossible to further conceal what they did?

What would Alacea do in her place? He could see the gentle vixen accepting all the responsibility herself in the name of protecting her people and subjecting herself to any punishment she had to.

Once again, Ben had to keep himself from trying to predict the actions of the Va'Shen based on what he knew of humans.

The problem was that, in this case, he couldn't predict how his leadership would act either.

* * *

He found his friend leaning against the side of the barn that sat just fifty feet from the Va'Shen house, though it was smaller than the barns Burgers knew from growing up in Texas. It wasn't bright red or white, but a dark, brownish purple that made it look more like it had been stained than painted.

Seeing him approach, Ramirez raised his hand in greeting. Burgers jutted his chin at the barn behind the other Ranger.

"New digs?" he asked.

"Yeah, you like it?" Ramirez replied, looking up at the building he was calling home. "They let me sleep in here at night, and I can even pee behind it."

"Sounds like Alzoria's mom is warming up to you."

"Oh, totally," Ramirez said. "Every so often she comes out here, and we talk. This morning, when she came into the barn to work, I accidentally bumped my head on a support beam, and we had a little English lesson."

"What kind of English lesson?" Burgers asked.

As if on cue, the door to Alzoria's house opened, and an older vixen with deep burgundy hair gestured at the two of them, making shooing gestures with her hands. She began shouting at the two in Va'Shen, but Burgers couldn't make a lot of it out.

"*Utashi nada fomenda! Fomenda ne togashi, mahtherfahcker!*"

With that, she went back into the house and slammed the door shut. Burgers looked at Ramirez and shook his head.

"She says you're nice," Ramirez translated for him.

"Uh huh," Burgers noted. He reached into his assault pack and pulled out a white rectangular box about the size of a large book. "I brought you a box lunch from the chow hall."

"Bitch'n," Ramirez replied, taking the box from his friend and opening it. "Thanks."

"Any change?" Burgers asked him.

Ramirez took a bite from a tuna sandwich and shook his head. "She won't come out, but there's still a few Huntresses inside with her. The rest went off to do Huntress shit, I guess. How's things at the FOB?"

"Dude, you picked the best time to be out here," the other Ranger told him. He quickly gave Ramirez the entire story of what happened the night before and the interviews this morning.

"Holy shit, man," Ramirez commented at the end of it. "Think there'll be charges?"

Burgers shrugged. "I don't know. I think this is gonna end up being one of those grey areas where some JAG nitpicks at the details until they have an excuse not to go after an officer."

"Captain won't like that," Ramirez said. "He's got a soft spot for the Va'Shen. Especially the Mikorin."

"Kinda weird, isn't it?" Burgers asked.

"What do you mean?"

Burgers turned to him, his mirrored sunglasses concealing any hint of what he was really feeling. "I mean, here we are... barely a year after our planet gets blown up... three years of shooting at each other... and you're sitting outside a Va'Shen girl's house because you want to cheer her up, the captain is trying to get justice for a bunch of Va'Shen he hardly knows, and I'm wondering what the hell happened."

Ramirez thought about it for a minute. "Isn't this better, though?"

"I guess so," Burgers admitted. "With everything happening... I kinda wish it wasn't. It was a lot easier when... well... I didn't have to think of them as people."

Ramirez gave Burgers a lazy punch in the shoulder. "Damn, dude, you're getting all philosophical and shit. Save that bullshit for OCS, man."

"Fuck you, dude."

Ramirez grinned and held up the now-empty box. "Thanks for this."

"Anytime, man. I gotta jet. Tell Alzoria we're all pulling for her."

"If she comes out, sure."

Burgers started for the road and gave Ramirez one last lazy wave.

* * *

<Overlord, I offer greetings,> Sho Nan said darkly as she stood in the middle of the doorway. Her blue tail whipped back and forth almost menacingly, causing Ben to pause and wonder what he had done lately.

<I speak with Alacea Na'Sha?> he asked.

<Of course. Follow me.>

Whatever was bothering her, it must not have involved him. Sho Nan glided elegantly as ever down the polished hallway, and Ben followed at a respectful distance.

<You angry?> he asked her.

<Difficulties that do not require your assistance, Overlord,> Sho Nan told him stiffly.

<I accept your explanation,> he replied, the Va'Shen version of "okay then."

They stopped short as Alacea turned the corner and saw them. She changed course and approached, Sho Nan bowing to her, and Alacea bowing to Ben.

<I must speak at you,> Ben told her promptly, not even waiting for the formal greetings to conclude.

<Of course, Tesho,> she said. <We can speak in our den.>

<Thanks be to you, Sho Nan,> he said as the other Mikorin set off alone.

Ben followed Alacea down the hall to where the head priestess had her room.

<Sho Nan angry,> he commented.

<Indeed,> Alacea replied with a swish of her tail. <The Garan'Sel Ya'Jahar will not allow her to see their bakery, and she is quite angry about it.>

<I know why,> he told her as she stopped to open the door to her room.

She paused and looked at him, her ears bending toward him in interest. <You do?>

<Must speak,> he said, gesturing for her to go inside.

Now fully concerned about what her Tesho wanted to tell her, Alacea tentatively entered her room and sat down at the small table she kept there. Ben took a seat on the other side, not sparing a moment to note how natural it seemed to be in Alacea's room now.

<Big problem. Bad,> he said, getting right to the point.

It took more than twenty minutes for him to get the story across to her with his limited vocabulary and some hand gestures, some of which, by necessity, had to be a little more graphic than he would have liked. At the end of it, Alacea looked at him in complete shock, her face emotionless, but her tail whipping around behind her in agitation.

<You must be wrong,> she told him simply. <What you say... It is beyond comprehension for a Mikorin.>

It took Ben a moment to figure out what she had said, and he stood up, turning away to think of how he might convince her.

<Baird was there,> he said. <He told me. Runa Aru'Dace was there. Tried to ... um... do things with him.>

<Then Lord Baird must be wrong,> Alacea said. <No Mikorin would ever...>

<You would do.>

Alacea came up short at the implication that she would sell her body. Her ears pointed downward, and her tail moved faster.

<Tesho,> she said evenly. <That joke is not funny.>

He sat down across from her and looked her in the eye. <To protect Pelle,> he said quietly. <To protect Pelle people. You would do. Would you not?>

Alacea's eyes widened slightly, and her ears began to point to the sky as she remembered the things she had already done to protect her people from the Dark Ones. It was only a short step from there to remember the things she had been prepared to do as a result.

But none of those things had been necessary in the end. She had begun to think it was because her Tesho's people were, themselves, not as evil as the Dark Ones of their history, though she was still unwilling to speak openly of what she believed. But what if her Tesho was the exception and not the rule?

She took a breath. <Yes,> she admitted shamefully. <I might have done something similar if my people required it.>

<She must stop,> Ben told her. <Dangerous. Wrong. You help?>

<I shall address this with her,> Alacea promised him sadly. <But I shall pray it is all a mistake.>

<Thanks be to you,> Ben said with a sigh of relief. <Kasshas?> he asked.

The priestess took a quick breath. <No,> she answered. <This... this is something the Mikorin must deal with. If Kasshas knew... he would be compelled to answer it. And that would help no one.>

Ben listened and took her meaning. If the chieftain heard of it, he would be forced to either conceal it from his people or take some type of formal action. Once that happened, who could tell what the villagers might do? He sighed and buried his face in his hands, exhausted by it all.

Alacea saw this and watched him critically for a moment, her tail twitching. <Are you well, Tesho?> she asked.

He looked up at her and smiled tiredly. <Am well,> he replied.

Despite his assurances, Alacea did not think Ben *looked* well. And upon reflection, she found that there really was no reason for him to look or be well. In the past couple of months since his arrival, he'd been nearly killed by a *yarl*, eaten by a *toka*, fell from a roof, and been shot at by commandos. To say he'd been working hard would be a criminal understatement.

Alacea rose from her seat and circled behind him. Ben followed her with his eyes but said nothing as she rested her hands on his shoulders. Before he could protest, she raised her hands and took the tops of his ears between his fingers, rubbing them gently.

Ben didn't know how he was supposed to respond, so he said nothing and decided to let the priestess do as she pleased. It was obvious to him that whatever she was doing she was doing because she thought it would help him somehow.

As for Alacea, she continued to gently rub her Tesho's ears, remember a time when she was very small and watching her mother do the same for her father after a long day. It was one of the few memories she had that gave her any idea of what a myorin should do for her tesho.

<Feel good?> she asked quietly.

<Yes,> he replied simply as she continued to rub.

Alacea's mind went back to her conversation with Sho Nan and Pavastea in the bath. Although she had promised herself that she would use the first opportunity to nip him, she found herself shying away again. This time, however, she had a good reason. With everything happening, it didn't seem to be the appropriate time.

There was another part of her that hesitated. She had to admit that there was a certain element of fear in her reasoning. Having seen what they had done to Alzoria, the priestess was now anxious, wondering if there were tods out there waiting to take her hair as they had done the Huntress's.

On a few occasions, her marriage to the village Overlord had prompted some to scorn her, but none had ever gone as far as the three Garan'Sel tods. Now that they had and the results put on full display for her, the fear had naturally increased.

<You must find time to rest,> she told him gently.

<Rest does not help me,> he replied. At her questioning pause, he elaborated. <I see bad things when I asleep.>

<What do you see?> she asked, continuing to rub his earlobes. Their fleshiness and lack of fur felt alien in her hands, almost wrong, and she wondered suddenly if she were actually hurting him. The snoring incident had demonstrated just how differently the aliens' bodies worked.

Ben paused. He wasn't sure he wanted to share his dreams with Alacea. For one, they were his problem to deal with, not hers. For another, whining about dreams he had about killing one of her people didn't seem like the most sensitive thing to do.

But the rhythmic squeezing of his ears and his fatigue lulled him into a more suggestive state, and he closed his eyes.

<I kill Va'Shen... Early in fight,> he told her. <Close... With hands... He comes at night while asleep. We fight again and more.>

<This really happened to you?> she asked, seeking confirmation that she had understood his story correctly.

<Yes,> he admitted quietly. <Attacked one night. Many die. He came into my den while asleep. I woke. We fought. We fought hard. I kill him. Now see again every night. Make me fight every night.>

Alacea said nothing as he spoke, letting him get all of it out. She continued to gently rub his ears before she finally replied to his words.

<To kill so closely is an intimate act,> she told him softly. <When we die, a door to the Glade opens, and our souls go through it. Sometimes, when one does not wish to leave, the soul fights to stay. A part of it will cling to the nearest other soul, even if that soul belongs to the one trying to push it into death. It becomes a part of you.>

Ben fought his way through the translation until he thought he got her point. <I am trapped?> he asked her.

<No,> she assured him, her voice a comforting whisper. <The two of you will make peace one day. Just as we did.>

Her ears popped up as his hand reached up and took hers. She stopped rubbing as he gave her fingers a gentle squeeze.

<Thanks be to you,> he said quietly.

Alacea's ears twitched a smile. <You are welcome, Tesho.>

Ben stood up and picked up his hat. <Much to do. Must go.>

Alacea rose gracefully to her feet. <I will summon Wenlin directly and address this. I promise you.> She bowed, and he bowed back to her.

When Ben left, he felt oddly refreshed.

* * *

Only an hour or so had passed since her Tesho had left the temple, and Alacea sat alone in the Mikorin meeting room, her eyes closed in silent meditation. She knew that, in only a few moments, she would have to have the most uncomfortable conversation she had had since...

My wedding?

No, this would be even worse. If even half of what her Tesho had told her was accurate, then she was about to talk to a Mikorin who had risked dooming her entire temple to the Frost.

Humans said that the road to Hell was paved with good intentions, but for the Va'Shen this motto could be very literal. Assuming her Tesho was right *and* assuming that Wenlin did it to protect her people, the very best she could hope for would be to be declared *Zaishin*, the "noble damned."

In the Va'Shen's religion, there were no exceptions for good intentions. To do evil in the pursuit of good was still evil. To prevent evil from being done except in the most severe of circumstances, the Gods did not allow one to skate by. To be named *Zaishin* was the greatest sacrifice one could make to their community, greater than even sacrificing one's life. The *Zaishin* sacrificed their eternity in the Glade. Even if to protect others, even to save the entire community, the entire planet, the sacrifice must still be paid. If the good outweighed the bad by a large enough margin, it was possible to avoid the Frost, but no matter what they would be banned from the Glade and drift forever in the nothingness between the two worlds.

The *Dara Tang,* Va'Sh's secret police, frequently evoked *Zaishin*, declaring that their mission to preserve the integrity of the Empire trumped their own eternities. It was what allowed them to perform such cruel and deceitful actions without fear while also ensuring that only the most fanatical of the Emperor's supporters would enlist in their ranks.

She imagined that whoever had ordered the destruction of her Tesho's homeworld had probably considered themselves *Zaishin*, willing to spend forever in limbo to strike a futile but extreme blow against the enemy.

She remembered how Wenlin and her Mikorin had seemed reluctant to enter the temple, the reason now suddenly clear. To face the direct gaze of the Gods after what they had done must have felt very unpleasant. How could they feel they were proper Mikorin after what they had done?

There was a scratch at the door, and Alacea looked up to find Sho Nan standing in the doorway.

<Wenlin Na'Sha has arrived,> she stated.

<Please send her in, Sho Nan,> Alacea said. As the blue-haired vixen turned, Alacea called after her.

<Sho Nan Ya'Jahar.>

Sho Nan turned, her ears flattening. Alacea almost never addressed her by her rank. To do so meant that whatever she was about to order must be followed without fail.

<Yes, Na'Sha?> she asked respectfully.

<We must not be disturbed,> Alacea told her carefully. <We must not be *heard*. By *anyone*. Do you understand?>

Sho Nan bowed to her. <I shall see to it, Na'Sha. It will be as you say.>

<Thank you, Sho Nan.>

A few moments later, Wenlin appeared in the room without a sound, like a phantom, her dull green hanbok clashing with the bright, clean colors in the rest of the room. Sho Nan shut the door behind her, and Wenlin bowed.

<Greetings, Alacea Na'Sha.>

Alacea stood and returned her bow. <Welcome, Wenlin Na'Sha.> She held her hand out to the table before her. <Will you sit?>

Wenlin glided forward and knelt at the opposite side of the table as Alacea retook her seat, reaching forward to pour the other vixen a cup of tea.

<I have asked to speak with you because my Tesho has come to me in great concern,> Alacea began as she respectfully held the teacup out to Wenlin with both hands. <He has told me some very worrisome things about your bakery.>

Wenlin took a sip of the tea, her eyes cast downward at the table. <I have been told one of his corporals was displeased by its offerings,> she noted casually.

<A very gentle euphemism,> Alacea pointed out. <Considering the nature of his complaint.>

The raven-haired vixen put her tea down and locked eyes with the other Na'Sha. <Let us dispense with such euphemisms then,> she declared. <The Overlord's corporal did not like the vixen he was given. He was offered another, and he refused. Tell me what will satisfy the Overlord, and I will see it done.>

Alacea looked at her in shock, her tail slapping against the wooden floor in complete disbelief. <You do not deny it, then,> she whispered.

<It would do no good to deny it,> Wenlin told her. <The Overlord and his corporal are dissatisfied. That is all that matters.>

<That is not what I mean!> Alacea cried, jumping to her feet. She gazed down at her fellow Na'Sha, who looked calmly up at her. <You... You sell your Mikorin...> Alacea gasped out.

Wenlin's tail slapped the floor, her ears folded downward in anger. <You make it sound like I seek profit from it. Did you seek your marriage for your own benefit?>

Alacea slowly sat down as her heart and mind whirled. She didn't doubt her Tesho's word, but to hear a Na'Sha admit it so openly stunned her.

<Wenlin,> she whispered. <What have you done?>

The younger woman stood up and turned away from the table, gathering her thoughts as her hand went instinctively to the pouch on her belt. Her fingers stopped short, however, and curled into fists as her tail began to move back and forth faster and faster.

She turned to Alacea, her ears digging into the top of her skull. <I did what my community *needed* me to do!> she cried. <When Zenyua Na'Sha died, I was *elected* Na'Sha by the other Mikorin. I was not her planned successor! I did not seek the position! But of all the Mikorin, it was thought that *I* would best be able to do what our community wanted. To make it all go away.>

<What do you mean, 'go away?'> Alacea asked aghast.

<They didn't want any more violence!> Wenlin answered. <There were some tods who insisted on violating the Emperor's decree, on fighting the Dark Ones! And whenever they did, the punishment would come to the community as a whole! The chieftain tried to stop them, and he was killed for it! The Na'Sha tried to stop them... and she was killed for it. My mandate was simple: Make it all stop. And if I could not stop the tods, then perhaps I could stop the Dark Ones. So that is what we did.>

Alacea listened in silent horror as this Na'Sha, only a little younger than her, bled her story to her like pus from an infected wound.

<When some of those idiots found some weapons and shot into the Dark Ones' camp, the Overlord sent his troops to live in the village among us,> Wenlin told her. <So that they could not be shot without risking Va'Shen. *I* went to the villagers living in those houses and told them to leave, to make room for the soldiers! And when some tods beat a Dark One nearly to death, the Overlord came to me and asked for the names of the perpetrators. So, I gave him names.>

Wenlin looked away and took a shuddering breath.

<Alacea Na'Sha, I *had no idea* who had done it! I just gave him names so that the nightly attacks would stop! And I stood there and watched as his soldiers put those people into their vehicles and took them away, never to be seen again!>

<Wenlin...> Alacea said softly.

But the other woman wasn't finished.

<And when the soldiers began to harass our vixens,> she growled. <I had to make that go away too. I gave them a more... pleasing... alternative... and let it be known that it would continue as long as the Dark Ones did not bother the vixens anymore.>

She looked up at Alacea and hiccupped a cry of painful grief. <I became a collaborator, Alacea Na'Sha... because my people *wanted me* to be a collaborator.> She turned away again.

The two were silent for several moments, but Wenlin would not look back at her. The younger vixen's shoulders slumped, and her tail went slack.

<I both admire and hate you, Alacea Na'Sha,> she whispered. <I look at what you managed to purchase here for only a fraction of what we paid, and I resent you. I resent you because we paid so much more and received so much less in return. I do not fear the Frost. I am already there. It just hasn't started to snow yet.>

Rushing forward, Alacea grabbed the woman by the arm and whirled her around. Wenlin was stunned as the vixen wrapped her arms around her and hugged her tightly.

<I cannot imagine the burden placed on you,> Alacea told her sympathetically. <Such a thing should not be asked of anyone. I am so sorry I did not see it sooner.>

Guilt flooded through Alacea as she spoke these words. She had sensed something was off about the Garan'Sel Mikorin but was so focused on moving her relationship with her Tesho forward that she had failed to realize just how devastating their experiences had been. Hearing how much Wenlin had endured broke the priestess's heart, but also made her realize just how blessed Pelle had been. It could have just as easily have been her village forced to face such horrors.

Wenlin slowly pulled away from her. <We all do as we must,> she said philosophically. <You, yourself, have faced such horrors. And I will not allow you to face them alone.>

Alacea took the vixen's hands in her own and squeezed reassuringly. <Wenlin, you have based the situation here on false assumptions, and knowing what you have endured I can see why you would form them.>

<What do you mean?>

Alacea cleared her throat, and her tail twitched in embarrassment. <You assume that things are good here because I have made some great sacrifice. That is not the case. While I originally married the Overlord as a way of saving my people, I have since come to understand that it was never necessary to do so.>

<Our Overlord specialized in brute force,> Wenlin told her, her ears pointed skeptically at Alacea. <But I think yours is an expert on manipulation if he could make you believe that.>

<It is true.> Alacea released her hands and went back to the table. Wenlin watched her with great interest as Alacea seemed to debate with herself on how much she should say. <I have come to know them quite well. My Tesho came to me, not to complain about poor service, but to tell you to stop completely. By their rules and code of honor, you and your Mikorin should never have been allowed to make the sacrifices that you did, and he wants to punish those who inflicted these acts on you.>

Wenlin stared at her in shock. Her tail swished about in almost a panic as she tried to decipher what the other Na'Sha's words meant, what the Overlord could possibly stand to gain from them.

<I... do not understand,> she finally admitted shakily. <Are you saying... none of this was necessary?>

<I am *not* saying that!> Alacea replied quickly. She understood that, most likely, the only thing keeping the Garan'Sel Mikorin going was the knowledge that their sacrifices *meant* something. <You

protected your people! And I truly believe the Gods will *not* punish you for that, and when I meet them, I will argue as such. What I *am* saying is that your sacrifice should never have been necessary in the first place. That, even by the Dark Ones' standards, what happened in your village was a crime. And it is a crime my Tesho wants to investigate and punish.>

Wenlin looked at the floor, at the table, at the wall, anything but Alacea, as if she were trying to prove she was still in the real world.

<That is why Lord Baird was so upset,> Alacea continued. <He saw what was happening to your people. He was not angry at your Mikorin. He was angry *for them*. He was angry that his fellow soldiers had taken advantage of them. That is why my Tesho wants you to stop.>

<But... who will protect the vixens?> Wenlin asked in what, to Alacea, almost sounded like a child's voice.

Alacea reached out and embraced the young woman again, this time comforting her.

<We shall protect each other,> she promised.

Chapter 11

1 month until contact...

Azarin's ears picked up her approach long before the blue-haired woman appeared in the darkness of the dimly-lit road that led to the house he was building. The carpenter had been spending time after his normal day job to continue the construction of his sister and brother-in-law's new house and had lost track of time. Looking up at the moons, he saw it was now quite late, and only the moons' light, the aurora of The Blessing and some well-placed water lamps gave him enough illumination to continue working.

When Hestean finally came into the light of the lamps, Azarin was waiting for her in the front door. He offered a respectful bow, which she returned.

<Blessed evening, Hestean Aru'Dace,> he said. <You are out late in the evening.> There was a hint of disapproval in his voice. Although crime was low in Pelle, it wasn't unheard of, and Alzoria's recent experience had put many on edge.

<I wanted to see you and could not tolerate waiting,> she replied. <May I speak with you?>

Her tone was formal but not harsh, Azarin noted. His ears picked up the sound of regret in her voice, and he gave her another short bow. <Of course,> he said. <I have no tea or anything to offer inside, but...>

<Let us speak out here,> she said. At his assent, she began to speak. <I come to you tonight to discuss two topics. First... I apologize for what I said in our last meeting.>

Azarin's ears popped up at the statement. <There is nothing to forgive,> he assured her.

<I was out of line,> she told him. <After all you have been through and after all the years I have known you, it was not only insulting to insinuate heresy on your part, it was patently absurd. I

have never known a tod as good or as pious as you. Furthermore, as Aru'Dace, it is not my place to pass judgement on such statements, but only to record they have been made. I apologize.>

<I accept your apology,> he said formally, more to put her at ease than out of any feelings that he was owed one. <It is no longer worth speaking of. What is your next topic?>

Hestean took a few steps closer to him, her eyes on the floor and her tail waving about in subtle concern.

<I have come to ask you to do something, and you may, of course, refuse.>

<What is it?>

<I am concerned for Alzoria,> Hestean told him. <She has been shamed... and if her Dark One does not, in the end, take her, it will be very difficult, if not impossible, for her to find a worthy tesho. I would like you to consider taking her yourself.>

Azarin's ears were practically scraping the bottoms of Va'Sh's two moons at this point. <Me?> he asked in surprise.

Hestean looked away as if ashamed to be asking him for such a favor. <You are an accomplished craftsman,> she said. <A commando leader. You are certain to take over your father's place in the *aderen*. Your influence would negate any resentment the others may feel for her. What honor was taken from her, you can provide from a well of your own.>

<I see,> he said.

<And...>

Azarin cocked his head at her broken statement. <And?> he prompted.

Hestean looked at the ground again. <It would gladden me... to see you wed.>

Azarin saw the pain in the young vixen's ears and knew it came in two distinct shapes. Hestean had chosen the Mikorin and was intent to follow through on that, giving up the life of a typical vixen and all it entailed, including him. But in doing so, she did not wish to see Azarin deny himself the life of a typical tod.

He looked away for a moment. <Dan Huun, I think, would like to see me take Bao Sen,> he told her.

Hestean's face tightened momentarily. <Bao Sen is a good vixen,> she agreed. <The two of you would be a good match.>

<But you'd prefer I take Alzoria,> Azarin concluded.

<I want you to do whatever would make you happy,> she told him. <If you wish to take Bao Sen, you should take her. But, if you have no preference at all, it would serve the community best for you to take Alzoria.>

<You know my preference,> he told her simply.

<Your preference would damage the community,> she replied emotionlessly.

<The community does not concern me.>

<A selfish statement.>

He took a step toward her, and Hestean swallowed nervously.

<My preference,> he told her quietly, <Would harm *you*. That is why I do not pursue it. To take another... would also harm you. And so, I do not pursue it either.>

Hestean turned from him and began to walk back toward the road.

<Please consider what I have said,> she asked as she walked away.

Azarin watched her go, his ears drooping as the sound of her footsteps faded into nothingness.

* * *

As Hestean was walking away from Azarin, Ramirez was lying in the grass next to Alzoria's barn, looking up at the green and purple aurora that waved lazily in the sky above Va'Sh. He quietly blew a breath of air out between his lips as he came to the conclusion of a silent argument he had been having with himself for the last couple of hours.

It was time to go back to work.

He liked Alzoria. He liked Alzoria *a lot*.

But he was a soldier. He had known guys who had been ordered to pull duty while their kids were being born because "mission." Right now, someone else was back at the FOB doing his work. It wasn't right for him to stay camped out here after the vixen had told him point-blank she didn't want to see him.

This would be the last night. He'd make one more attempt in the morning and then go back to the FOB. He'd come back after duty, maybe even arrange to sleep here again, but he couldn't stand by anymore.

<John.>

"Holy..." He looked around and, seeing nothing in the grass around him, craned his neck to look straight up.

Kneeling on the edge of the barn roof like some kind of superhero and wrapped in a dark cloak was Alzoria, her eyes looking down at the Ranger.

"Hey, Alzoria," he called quietly. <How to arrive up in there?> he asked.

Her ears twitched under the cloak. <Not easily,> she told him.

"You look like a superhero," he told her. Seeing she didn't understand, he switched to Va'Shen again. <You appear like hunter for justice.>

Alzoria didn't say anything to that, just stared down at Ramirez sadly.

<You better than beforetime?> he asked her.

The vixen pulled the cloak down a little more, trying to hide more of her face.

<You shouldn't be here, John,> she told him.

<I want be here,> he replied.

<I'm shamed, John,> she said.

He tried a smile. <Alzoria... I always shamed. I do well so.>

She didn't say anything to that.

<I see?> he asked her gently.

Alzoria pulled the cloak around her even tighter. <Why?> she asked. <Why would you want to see my shame?>

<It not shame,> he told her. <It is you. Want see you.>

<If I show you... will you leave?> she asked.

<No,> he replied immediately.

Her eyes narrowed, and Ramirez could hear the sound of her tail thumping against the roof of the barn.

<You are impossible,> she muttered. <I am *shamed*.>

<I do not importance on that,> he told her, which was as close to "I don't care" as his limited vocabulary would allow.

<Fine, then I will show you!> she snapped at him. She lithely hopped down from the roof and landed next to him. Without even a pause to regain her footing, almost as if she were afraid to hesitate, she pulled the cloak off her head and exposed her ears.

In the moonlight, it was a little hard to see, so Ramirez brought out the mini-lantern he had brought with him, bathing her face and ears in a cold white light.

Her hair was a mess. Whoever had done it obviously wasn't even trying or else Alzoria's resistance had made caution impossible. Most of it had been cut to be no longer than her ears, but there were strands of it that was the original length, patches that they had missed.

<Well?> she demanded.

Ramirez pointed at his own shaved head. <Mine is shorter.>

<Is that all you have to say?> she asked with some heat.

<Happy they did not hurt you,> he told her. <Was... scared... they hurt you. Cut you or hit on you.>

<You are not supposed to say that!> she cried. <You're supposed to look at me with disgust just like everyone else will! You're supposed to be ashamed that you know me or spent time with me! You're supposed to be worried that people will think you're my friend or...>

She broke off and looked away.

The Ranger raised his hand and pulled up his left sleeve, exposing his wrist where a series of red and black beads circled it, held together with tight strands of gold and orange.

<Always wear,> he said, showing it to her. <Alzoria made for me. Always wear. Always show. Alzoria made. Give me honor.>

Alzoria hiccupped quietly and leaned against the side of the barn. <What do I do, John?> she asked quietly. It appeared she had finally given up on pushing him away. <I don't know what I should do now.>

Ramirez gave the question real thought. Finally, he stood straighter and looked down at her.

<Thing one,> he said. <Fix hair.>

<Fix it?> she asked. <Fix it how?> There were vixens in Pelle who cut and washed hair, but the emphasis for a vixen's hair was always on long and luxurious. Short styles were almost unheard of. The shortest hairstyle a vixen would tolerate would be a bob like Sho Nan's, and she only kept one to keep her hair from getting into her cooking.

<I have idea. You come to camp? Next day?> he asked.

<John...> Alzoria began sadly. <I don't want people to see me...>

<Important. We fix. Promise,> Ramirez said. <You come?>

Alzoria was silent for several moments, but finally looked up at the Ranger and into his eyes. Interpreting Dark One looks and gestures was still difficult for her, but something in his eyes told her it would be okay.

<Yes,> she said with a brief inclination of her head. <I will come. When?>

<Beyond mid-day eating.>

<I will come,> she promised.

Ramirez grinned and stroked her cheek with his fingers.

<No worry,> he said. <Me got this.>

* * *

Nadro looked up at the sun shining between the leaves in the trees, and his ears twitched happily. Garan'Sel was cooler, wetter, and it was home, but the area around Pelle was so beautiful he was already falling in love with it. The woods around Pelle that bordered the mountains in which the Pelle villagers had once hid from the Dark Ones was largely an untouched paradise.

And it was where Nadro intended to build his home.

<There is a stream not far from here,> Boto commented as he came up behind his friend. <Most likely a spring too.>

<Why build so far away?> his other friend, Boso, asked, looking around the small glade overgrowing with thick, red grass.

<The mountains are not far from here,> Nadro explained. <Pelle has no mines, but I think Goto wants to look for one. I don't want to hike from Pelle every day to get there.>

<What if there are no minerals?> Boto asked.

<Then I shall become a woodsman,> Nadro explained. <And harvest the trees.>

Boto looked around at the abundance of trees, and his ears twitched. <A good plan.>

Nadro's ears fluttered happily, and he walked up to a very large, purple tree at the edge of the small glade. The tree must have been ancient. The trunk was easily six feet around and towered over them. He looked up at the sound of a soft hiss. Sitting in the lowest branch of the tree, a blue-furred kashu glared down at him as if annoyed at his intrusion. The small, furry lizard creature hissed another warning at him.

Ignoring the creature's complaint, the former miner reached up and patted the side of the tree's trunk, resting his hand on it almost lovingly.

<Yes,> he said. <You shall make a fine house.>

He didn't feel the pain for a full second. For that second, he looked at his hand in confusion as the feathered fletching of an arrow rested against his knuckles, and his hand refused to move.

Then he felt the pain.

Nadro screamed as he reached up with his other hand, instinctively trying to pull the arrow out, but the shot had been so powerful that the arrow had sunk into the tree up to the feathers. Behind him, he heard Boto cry out, and he turned his head to see his friend, clutching at an arrow sticking out of his left kneecap. Only a moment later, Boso screamed and fell over, an arrow anchoring his foot to the ground.

The tod took hold of the feathered part of the arrow and broke it, freeing his hand. He fell to his knees, looking at the bloody hole in his hand in horror.

He should have been looking behind him.

Something looped around his neck from behind and pulled taut, squeezing the breath from him. His hands went automatically to the rope around his throat, and he felt a sharp blow strike him in the back of the knees, knocking him down. Nadro's face hit the soft grass, which did nothing to soften the blow, and stars appeared before his eyes. His hands were pulled behind his back and before he knew it, he was hogtied.

Shaking his head, he turned his eyes to his friends and found them nearby in much the same position. Two vixens with short, cropped hair were tying Boso up. Closer to him, a vixen with very short green hair had her knee in Boto's back as she pulled a rope tightly around the tod's neck.

A green rope.

It suddenly dawned on him why the rope around his neck didn't feel as coarse as regular rope. It was made of hair. The vixens attacking them were strangling them with their own hair...

The knee shoved into his back knocked the wind out of him, and a second later he felt cool steel against his throat, just above where the rope held his head up. He felt soft breath on his ears as the person behind him leaned closer.

<Listen well, kashu bait,> Bao Sen hissed into his ears. <You took my Huntress's honor, so we're taking something from you.>

Nadro gulped, the movement of his neck pushing against the blade causing a small cut that started bleeding.

Bao Sen sensed his discomfort, and her ears twitched. <No,> she assured him. <Not *that*. Not *this* time. But if you *ever* touch one of my Huntresses again, we will cut off your tod-hoods and nail them above our lodge door for luck. If you understand, squeak.>

Nadro let the tiniest bit of air pass his lips, afraid to move his neck anymore. Nearby, he could hear other Huntresses making the same promises to Boto and Boso.

<Good,> Bao Sen hissed. <Now, just to make sure you never forget it...>

The feeling of the knife disappeared from his neck, and he felt the Huntress violently take hold of his left ear. He cried out in pain as the knife sliced through it, and nearby, Boto and Boso screamed as well. He looked up and saw the bloody ear hit the grass in front of him.

<*Do not* touch my Huntresses again,> Bao Sen growled one last time. She got off him and grabbed the ear.

A second later the three tods were alone in the woods again, wounded and hogtied. Nearby, one of the brothers was hiccupping sobs.

Laying on his side, Nadro looked up and saw the kashu staring down at him again. The creature seemed to grin at him a moment before it turned and scurried back up the tree.

* * *

The two Dark Ones looked down at her critically, one of them rubbing her chin in thought. The other shook her head in awe.

"Damn, sweetie, they really did a number on you, didn't they?" Private First Class Rachel Jenkins commented.

"They sure didn't leave much to work with," Fletcher added, looking at the sides of Alzoria's head.

The vixen, sitting in a chair in FOB Leonard's small rec room, looked down at the ground in shame, unwilling to meet the alien women's eyes. She had come to the FOB just as Ramirez had asked, and he met her at the gate, taking the cloaked vixen straight to the rec room where the other two women were waiting.

Alzoria listened to their comments, understanding some words but not others. Her lack of comprehension caused her imagination to run wild, filling in the gaps with mocking insults.

"Can you do something with it?" Ramirez asked from behind them.

Va'Sh wasn't the only place where the length and style of hair was important. In the military there were still official and unofficial rules when it came to hairstyles. And while over the years the rules had eased, you still couldn't just come to work with whatever style you wanted. But at the same time, there wasn't always a barber available, particularly on far-flung FOBs like Leonard. But there was always at least one person who knew something about hair who would help you out. For men that was easy. You just had to do a buzz cut. For women, a little more knowledge and experience was required.

"Pixie cut?" Fletcher asked Rachel.

Rachel reached out and touched the vixen's hair, playing with it between her fingers. "Yeah, maybe feathered baby bangs or something. There might be enough left to do that."

"Definitely," Fletcher agreed.

Rachel smiled at Alzoria and brought out a bag packed with styling instruments.

"Don't you worry, sweetie, we're going to make you look shit-hot."

"We're going to do a pixie cut," Fletcher told Ramirez.

"Pig-see?" Alzoria asked nervously. "What is pig-see?"

Fletcher held her hands horizontally one six inches above the other. "A pixie is a tiny, beautiful girl about this high with short hair and wings on her back. She flies around and does magic."

Alzoria looked to Ramirez for a translation as she didn't catch all of that.

<Beauty girl... magic... short... short hair,> Ramirez told her.

<Magical?> Alzoria asked. She relaxed a little at the thought of having something positive to compare her hair to.

"Totes magical," Ramirez confirmed.

Rachel held up her scissors and smiled. "Let's get this party started!"

* * *

The air in the *aderen* was chilly as Bao Sen and five of her Huntresses stood defiantly in the center of the oval. All six of the vixens wore their hair short, barely coming past where the ears on a human woman would be. This had shocked the community leaders almost more than the acts that had brought them there in the first place.

It wasn't as if they had tried to hide it or run from their actions. Bao Sen herself had reported to Kasshas that Nadro, Boso and Boto were tied up in the woods and where to find them. It wasn't long after that that Alacea and Wenlin had been informed.

The three victims were sitting in the back of the room, bandages on their hands, heads, knees and feet. Alacea looked at them from her place at the end of the oval and felt a twinge of pity. It looked as if the Huntresses' anger had fully reared its head during the attack.

She looked around the oval and found that almost all of the representatives were the same as the last *aderen*. Goto was sitting in the same spot as before, his tail thumping the ground behind him in anger.

With the pre-*aderen* ceremonies and bowing concluded, Kasshas stood up and cleared his throat.

<This *aderen* is called upon to decide what punishment, if any, to inflict upon the vixens Bao Sen, Mezina, Ezeta, Benea, Wezeta and Ketra,> Kasshas announced from his position on the opposite side of the oval from Alacea and Wenlin. <The six were accused of, and have confessed to, an attack on the tods, Nadro, Boso and Boto and forcibly removing their ears. What have you to say for yourselves?>

Bao Sen took a step forward, speaking for the six of them. Her ears dug into her skull as she focused her anger on the task at hand.

<A few days ago, this *aderen* chose to send a message to the community,> Bao Sen told them. <You may have thought that message was something akin to 'the community must keep its people on the right path.' But the message that we heard was, 'we will not protect you.' The Huntresses have chosen to send a message of our own. That message is, 'We will.'>

<Just because you do not agree with the *aderen's* judgement does not give you the right to attack innocent tods,> Goto pronounced from his seat nearby.

Bao Sen turned her gaze toward him. <As friend and mentor to Alzoria, I have right of vengeance,> she announced.

<The Right of Vengeance is not meant to be a loophole around the *aderen*,> Yasuren told Bao Sen quietly, but without heat. <It is for when the justice of the *aderen* fails.>

Bao Sen's ears popped up in happiness. Yasuren could not have given her a better lead in, and Alacea wondered briefly if that was what the older vixen meant to do.

<I submit that that is exactly what happened here,> Bao Sen proclaimed loudly. <This *aderen*, influenced by their fear of the Dark Ones, failed to apply justice properly as had been in the past.>

The other members of the *aderen* whispered amongst themselves at the bold proclamation. Kasshas looked at Bao Sen with upturned ears, impressed and somewhat insulted at the same time.

<This is utter nonsense,> Goto complained, turning to Kasshas, but the chieftain cut him off.

<The *aderen* will hear the specifics of your charge, Bao Sen,> he told her.

Bao Sen stood straighter and began her pitch. <Long before the arrival of the Garan'Sel villagers, the Dark One, Rah-mee-raz and Alzoria underwent a shared trauma, their capture by the Kar'El commando. Following this trauma, a friendship developed, and Alzoria spent a fair amount of time with Rah-mee-raz. At one point, Alzoria's uncle approached the Overlord to propose an arranged marriage between the two.>

<What is the point of this argument?> Goto asked, his arms folded over his chest and his tail slapping the ground. <It does nothing but prove that the actions of Nadro, Boso and Boto to correct Alzoria were justified.>

<Except they were not justified,> Bao Sen retorted icily. <Not under the historical application of Pelle's justice.>

Alacea leaned forward. Having expected an emotional plea rather than a measured argument, she was suddenly very curious as to what magic the Huntress might perform here.

<Please explain your meaning, Bao Sen,> she prompted.

<Following the first Dark One invasion, Pelle, much like today, was fused with another village. When these new villagers arrived, there was a period of time where each side had to become acclimated to the other. During this time, there were several personal conflicts. Some of these conflicts had to do with matters that were not even considered controversial to the Pelle villagers before the arrival of the newcomers. The *aderen* at the time deemed that since it was the newcomers joining the Pelle villagers and not the other way around, matters that the Pelle community had previously settled would remain settled and not be reopened.>

<What does any of this have to do with your assault on three tods?!> Goto demanded.

Yasuren, quicker than some of the others, picked up on where Bao Sen was going, and her ears began to twitch.

Bao Sen ignored Goto and continued.

<As Pelle did not discipline or even declare Alzoria wrong before the arrival of the Garan'Sel, even after an *official* family attempt to form a union between her and the Dark One, the matter of whether she had behaved improperly should already have been considered closed and *not* open to reinterpretation by the new Garan'Sel villagers.> Bao Sen looked Kasshas in the eyes as she finished. <To be blunt, this community essentially *approved* of her courtship, and she therefore had no reason to believe she was doing anything wrong.>

<Just because a wrong was not corrected in the past does not mean it should not be corrected in the present,> Goto argued.

<And what I am telling you is that your argument is invalid as in the eyes of the village, *Alzoria committed no wrong,*> Bao Sen countered. <The Aru'Dace can confirm what I say is correct.>

This time, Hestean did not give Runa a chance to interject before her. She rose to her feet.

<Bao Sen's interpretation of Pelle's history is correct,> she announced. <The Pelle community's decisions made prior to the arrival of newcomers were considered closed. Actions taken after their arrival were eligible for scrutiny under the laws and customs of both villages.>

<If Alzoria had done something wrong, Pelle would have corrected her,> Bao Sen said. <Or will the *aderen* confess to not leading the community properly?>

An icy silence fell over the group. Goto looked between Bao Sen and Hestean, his ears digging down into his head.

<Did you come up with this argument all on your own?> he asked. He turned to Alacea and leveled a freezing glare at her. <Or did your Na'Sha direct you?>

Unlike last time, Goto had made no preparation prior to making his argument. He was shooting from the hip, and the hissing and angry glares from the Pelle members of the *aderen* all indicated that it was a fatal misstep.

Alacea returned the tod's glare with a steely one of her own. Wenlin watched as she rose to her feet and faced the old miner.

<Speak plainly, Goto,> she commanded with all the authority she could muster into her voice. <If you wish to accuse a Na'Sha of acting inappropriately, then do so, and I will make my arguments.>

Goto paused, and the *aderen* looked back and forth between the two. In the previous *aderen*, Goto had prepared his arguments carefully with Posha's help, and Alacea had not engaged directly. This time, he was flying blind, and the Na'Sha herself was demanding an answer.

The Va'Shen had a saying. "Only gods and fools argue with a Na'Sha."

<I will show truth in this matter,> Hestean said, raising her voice over the mutterings of the *aderen*. As Goto and Alacea continued their face-off, the historian began to speak. <Bao Sen came to me and made use of her right to seek information from the Mikorin. This is how she learned of Pelle's ancient laws.>

<Is your question answered?> Alacea asked Goto imperiously.

Goto snarled quietly to himself. <It is,> he muttered in reply.

<Then the community bids you to sit,> Alacea told him as if giving a command to a dog.

Kasshas cleared his throat. <We shall vote on whether the vixens shall be punished. The Farmers,> he prompted.

Alacea watched the vote carefully, counting each yes and no, and once again marveling at how close it actually was. It seemed to her that it really didn't matter what Bao Sen's argument had been, or even Goto's in the previous *aderen*. Each member was voting with their own feelings about the Dark Ones, not so much the matter itself. By the time it reached the last vote, it was once again tied.

<The Hunters,> Kasshas prompted.

Every eye and ear turned to Dan Huun. A week ago, the idea of a guild voting against one of its members in the *aderen* would be unthinkable, especially against a family member. But after the sudden twist in the last vote, no one was certain what the Hunter leader would do.

Bao Sen turned to her brother and glared, daring him to vote against her.

Dan Huun stood and held his head up high. <The Hunters vote no.>

There was an almost audible sigh of relief, not so much for the verdict but that the son and daughter of Bao Aren would not, it seemed, go to war today.

Kasshas rose to his feet. <The vote has been made. The vixens will not be punished.>

Everyone began to rise to their feet, but Goto's voice stopped everyone in their tracks.

<One last matter,> he said. Everyone turned to him, expecting some last-minute attack that would throw everything into chaos again.

<You may speak, Goto,> Kasshas told him.

<What did you do with the three tods' ears?> he asked Bao Sen. <Did you throw them in the garbage? Feed them to the *kashus*?>

It didn't really matter what the vixens had done with the ears, and it was obvious that Goto was only trying to make Bao Sen and her Huntresses look worse in the eyes of the community.

Bao Sen, however, was now beyond caring how they looked. She met Goto's gaze and put her hands on her hips, her tail waving about behind her in annoyance.

<I take offense to your question,> she said. <We are Huntresses. We would never condone such waste.> She held out her hand, and Mezina wordlessly placed something into it.

The *aderen* watched, eyes wide, as Bao Sen tossed the object at Goto's feet so he could see it. The tod snarled at what he saw and glared at Bao Sen, who explained for those who couldn't make out what it was.

<We sewed them together and made a coin purse,> she announced coldly. <Please don't tell Alzoria,> she asked. <We intend it as a wedding gift.>

The room was completely silent. Even Hestean and Yasuren, who had been rooting for the Huntresses from the beginning, looked ill.

<We are Huntresses,> Bao Sen reminded them. <We make use of every part of our prey.> She turned to Goto. <Remember that.>

* * *

Rachel brought a hand-held mirror up to Alzoria's face and smiled. "Ta-da!" she announced.

Alzoria looked at the image in the mirror and reached up, touching her delicate bangs and running her fingers along the hair on the sides that had been shaved short. There had been just enough hair in the front to give her almost a widow's peak and they hadn't had to shave too much from the sides to make it look good. If not for the ears and tail, Alzoria would not have looked in any way out of place on Earth or in the colonies.

The vixen continued to examine her hair silently, unsure of what to say or think. It was the shortest hair she had ever seen on a grown vixen, but at the same time it was styled and neat. It looked like something she had *chosen* to have done, not the result of someone taking her hair from her.

Her ears twitched at the sight.

Fletcher turned and gave Ramirez a thumbs up. The Ranger stepped forward and looked at the Huntress's new haircut.

<Think of it, you do?> he asked.

<I think… I like it,> Alzoria told him. She tossed her hair and watched as the widow's peak fluttered up and down. <I do not have to pin it out of the way when I clean a kill,> she remarked.

"Right?" Ramirez agreed supportively. <I think it look great beautiful for you.>

Alzoria turned away, the fur on her ears going stiff at the compliment.

"Shit hot," Rachel confirmed.

"Shet howt," Alzoria agreed. No, it wasn't the return of her gorgeous gold and orange hair, but it was something else. She looked at Ramirez, and her ears wiggled.

"I'm glad we could help your girlfriend out, Army," Fletcher told him with a grin and a pat on the shoulder.

Ramirez was about to correct her when Alzoria spoke up.

"'Garfend?'" she asked. "What is 'garfend?'"

"Um, well…" Ramirez began, but Fletcher cut him off.

"A girlfriend is a vixen," she explained slowly. "She is not myorin. But she will maybe be myorin later."

Alzoria's ears perked up, and she quickly grabbed Ramirez's arm, pulling him next to her.

"Garfend," she declared.

Ramirez gave Fletcher a look. "Why would you tell her that?" he asked.

Fletcher smiled at him. "Because," she said. "It's funny."

Chapter 12

Three weeks until contact...

Keyes wasn't in the outer office when Ben arrived, but a female lieutenant asked him to sit in one of the plush chairs reserved for the commander's visitors. Taking a seat, Ben put his patrol cap in his lap and took the opportunity to go over his report one more time.

In the days that had passed since Alacea had confronted Wenlin about the true nature of the bakery, Ben had focused on gathering what evidence he could on the events that occurred in Sector Six under Keyes's command. Despite everything that had happened, however, Wenlin had not been as helpful as Ben would have thought or liked. It seemed that although the Garan'Sel Na'Sha would like to see some form of justice done, her primary concern was seeing that further dishonor wasn't heaped upon her village or her Mikorin. That made things difficult.

However, he was hopeful about some of the troops who had served under Keyes and had sent some of them a few days before to give testimony to the JAG under oath. He had also sent a report directly to the CJTF commander and had requested an appointment to speak with him personally.

The lieutenant went into the general's office and came out a moment later.

"Sir, the general will see you now."

Ben stood up and walked into the office, the lieutenant closing the door behind him. Army Lieutenant General Alfred C. Walker sat behind his desk, his close-cropped gray hair and hawkish nose gave him an intimidating appearance, but that wasn't what worried Ben.

Keyes was sitting in a chair across from the general.

Shit.

Walker gestured to the empty chair next to Keyes. "Have a seat, Captain. I believe you already know Major Keyes." He nodded to his left. "As well as Dr. Sinclair."

Ben looked and was surprised to find Sinclair, the CJTF Cultural Advisor, sitting in a chair against the wall between a small table and a bookcase.

"It's good to see you again, Captain," Sinclair told him simply.

"You too, Sir," Ben replied as he uncomfortably sat down next to Keyes. It was good to at least have one friendly face in the room. Walker had just taken command from General Traxler, who had been more than satisfied by Ben's progress in Sector 13. Walker, however, barely knew Ben, having only spoken to him once, whereas he saw and talked to Keyes every day, giving Keyes a distinct home field advantage.

Ben didn't see a JAG in the room, and he had a feeling that was on purpose.

"Gentlemen," Walker began, his hands clasped together in front of him. "We're here to clear the air. Neither of you are under investigation. We're just having a conversation."

"With all due respect, Sir," Ben replied. "This 'conversation' includes some very serious breaches of Army regulations. I have to recommend that, at the very least, Major Keyes be made aware of his Article 31 rights."

"I don't think that's necessary, Captain," Walker told him.

"I have troops giving the JAG sworn depositions as we speak, Sir," Ben argued. The last thing he wanted was to give Keyes a loophole through which to slip away.

"No, Captain, you don't," Walker replied coolly. "That has been turned off."

Ben looked at the general in complete shock. "Sir?" was all he could think to ask.

"What we have here, Captain, is a failure on the part of all parties to properly communicate with one another," Walker said. "It was bound to happen with no way to instantaneously communicate up and down the chain. That's what this meeting is for. Now, I have read your report, and in it you make some rather startling claims about Major Keyes's command in Sector Six."

Walker paused a moment to flip through the report in question. "Now, Major Keyes assures me there are proper explanations for these."

"I would love to hear them, Sir," Ben deadpanned.

"For instance," Walker continued, "You claim that Major Keyes was somehow involved with forcing Va'Shen women into prostitution."

"My claim was that Major Keyes knew of the Garan'Sel Mikorins' activities and either condoned them or failed to keep tabs on the activities of his troops," Ben corrected.

Walker turned to Keyes. "Major? Do you have a response?"

"Yes, Sir," Keyes said calmly. "If I must choose one or the other, then I choose the former."

Ben blinked at the admission, stunned that Keyes would do so so casually.

Of course, there was more to it than that.

"When my people began to lodge inside the village proper, they were made aware of the... er... services... the villagers provide and made use of them," Keyes continued. "That included a culturally acceptable sex trade."

"Culturally acceptable?" Ben repeated angrily.

"I am told that the industry in Garan'Sel was run by their church, was it not?" Keyes countered. "Are they not the arbiters of what is and is not culturally acceptable to them?"

"They felt their backs were against the wall because their local women were being harassed by *your* troops," Ben spat. "None of them would have chosen to sell their bodies."

"But they did," Keyes replied. "If soldiers under my command act inappropriately, then the victims come to me and *I* handle it. If they don't do that, they can hardly complain that they had no other option, now, can they?"

"You know damn well that our positions in those sectors makes complaining to us difficult for them," Ben counterattacked. "They're scared to death of us."

"Not too scared to make money by having sex with us, though," Keyes pointed out.

"Even if you were one hundred percent right about their motivations," Ben said, "It is illegal for troops to participate in the sex industry of a military-occupied nation. It is illegal because in that situation, consent cannot be positively verified, and the sex workers in that situation could be the victims of human trafficking."

"Yes," Keyes agreed. "*Human* trafficking." Keyes took a breath, seeming to be frustrated at having to actually defend his actions. "This is a very unique situation where we must, if not defer, then be sensitive to the culture of the Va'Shen. The Va'Shen say my troops are welcome to their services. I say they must not participate. What message does that send to the Va'Shen? On Earth or one of the colonies, it wouldn't be an issue because there is a shared historical and cultural framework, but the Va'Shen may take it a different way. What if they believe it was forbidden because we don't view them as people or think them unclean? It sounds insane, I know, but are you telling me, Captain, that you've never made what seemed like a strange or insane command decision because of a concern of what the Va'Shen might do?"

Boom. There it was. Keyes had done his homework. And now he was going to use Ben's marriage to Alacea as a way to justify his own actions.

"That," Ben bit out. "Is different."

"Of course it is, Captain," Keyes replied, his voice laced with venomous sarcasm. "Your experiences with the Va'Shen are limited to the southern regions. In the north, I was losing men *every week*. If erring on the side of caution could save just one of them, I did it. And you, *Captain*, did the same exact thing. And if a cross-cultural miscommunication resulted in some Va'Shen being harmed, I am sorry... but so be it."

"That's enough, gentlemen," Walker broke in. He turned to Sinclair. "Doctor, what's your opinion here?"

"I am afraid there's not much I can add here, General," Sinclair said sheepishly. "The Va'Shen are a proud people. They do not openly discuss things like prostitution. I must say, however, that if the act is approved by the Mikorin of the village, it can't really be called illegal. Their motivations may not be completely sound, but... if they approve it as a solution to a problem then that would be considered the *appropriate* solution... to the Va'Shen, anyway."

"In other words, they may have hated doing it, but that's on them," Walker concluded.

"Quite."

Ben couldn't believe what he was hearing. In any other country on Earth, on any other planet where humans were in control, Keyes would be hauled up as a war criminal and thrown in the stockade.

"Something being acceptable in their culture does not automatically mean it is acceptable to our own," Ben shot back.

Walker sighed. "Listen to yourself, Captain," he said. "Imagine making that statement online or on the vid. Think of the pushback you would get for saying something so xenophobic. It's a more understanding world, Captain. We don't build gallows next to funeral pyres anymore."

"Was there more?" Keyes asked with a hint of triumph in his voice.

"What is this about you lodging your troops with the Va'Shen to prevent attacks?" Walker asked.

"Ah! Yes," Keyes replied. "We were taking fire from outside the FOB rather frequently. I felt our isolation from the Va'Shen we were there to protect made it impossible to develop positive relationships, so I moved several squads into the village as a way of integrating with the Va'Shen community."

"And the fact that it made the villagers de facto human shields had nothing to do with it, I guess," Ben spat.

Keyes sighed once again in frustration. "There is ample historical evidence that secluding troops from the populace alienates the two cultures from one another and actually feeds insurgencies. I believed that showing the Va'Shen that we are not monsters would deprive the insurgents of one of their recruiting tools and reduce the number of attacks."

"That is not how Wenlin describes it," Ben retorted.

"Yes, I'm sure Wenlin would have a different viewpoint," Keyes told him. "Here's the thing about Wenlin, Captain. Wenlin does what is best for *Wenlin*. It is no mere happenstance that both her chieftain and her previous Na'Sha died, leaving her in charge."

"It would be difficult to simply accept the word of a Va'Shen in this case, Captain," Walker told him, coming to Keyes's aid. "They have very strong motivations to undermine our ability to run this occupation."

"Does that mean we disregard their charges of wrongdoing?" Ben asked him.

"It means we remember whose team we're all on," Walker answered coldly. The general picked up the report and put it in the bottom drawer of his desk. "Thank you, Major, I think that will be all."

"Thank you, Sir," Keyes said, standing up. "I am sorry if my actions caused any confusion."

"I would like CID to determine just how much confusion there is," Ben spoke up.

"CID is not going to take this case, Captain," Walker told him.

"That's not the way it's supposed to work, Sir," Ben replied.

"It's how it works on Va'Sh," the general responded coolly. "You can go, Major."

Keyes gave Ben a nod and walked out the door, leaving the Ranger there to seethe at the events he had just witnessed.

"Now that that is over with, I'd like to discuss your other report," Walker told him.

"Sir, about Keyes," Ben tried again.

"That matter is closed, *Captain*."

In the military, *how* one is addressed can speak volumes as to where one stands with both their superiors and their subordinates. If an enlisted person calls a lieutenant "sir" or "ma'am," it denotes the normal and expected amount of respect for the rank. If they call them "Eltee," it is not just respect, but some degree of fondness. If an enlisted person calls them "lieutenant," that junior officer should watch their ass.

When a superior calls one by their rank with the tone Walker had just used with Ben, it had its own specific meaning.

Shut the fuck up.

So, Ben did.

Walker took another report from his desk and flipped through it. "This report from your Two concerning a previous interstellar conflict between the Va'Shen and another race is very interesting."

"Yes, Sir," Ben agreed dully.

"Doctor, what's your take?" the general asked Sinclair.

"None of the Va'Shen officials I have spoken to have mentioned anything of the sort," Sinclair replied. "And when I ask, they simply say that there are many legends and fairy tales about evil creatures from dark realms."

"We have those too, Doctor, but we generally don't train our military to fight them," Ben pointed out. "Apparently, the Va'Shen do."

"It would explain a great many things," Sinclair admitted. "But no one at the Imperial Court wants to discuss it."

"I would recommend looking outside the court," Ben told him. "Talk to some of the Aru'Dace in the communities outside the capital. They wouldn't have a reason to lie."

Sinclair looked to Walker, who nodded in approval. "Let me know where you want to go. I'll get you what you need."

The meeting ended there. An outsider might have called it a mixed victory. They were going to investigate the "Dark Things" but at the same time it looked like the fix was in as far as Keyes was concerned.

"Have a good day, gentlemen," Keyes remarked from his desk as Ben and Sinclair passed it on the way out. Ben said nothing. Once they were out of the general's office, Sinclair sighed and turned to Ben.

"I am sorry, Captain, that I could not be more helpful."

"Don't worry about it, Doctor," Ben sighed. "The outcome had already been decided."

* * *

When Ramirez and Alzoria arrived at the Huntress's lodge, there was no one outside, but the vixen could hear voices coming from within. She took a nervous breath, and the Ranger standing next to her squeezed her arm supportively.

<Do you think they will accept me back?> she asked.

Ramirez didn't understand the whole question, but he could tell by her voice she was nervous about seeing her fellow Huntresses again.

<I say they not like you be away,> he said as carefully as he could. <I say they want see Alzoria not sad.>

Hearing this, the Huntress stepped forward and rested her hand on the door handle. Pulling it open, she entered the lodge with Ramirez following behind her.

The Huntresses were gathered around a low table in what appeared to be an important discussion. There was something different about them, but it didn't click with Ramirez until after Alzoria spoke.

<You cut your hair,> she whimpered in shock.

The Huntresses turned to her and jumped to their feet, running up to her and crowding her with hugs.

Bao Sen stood at the rear of the pack, and Ramirez took in her new hairstyle. Her red hair now fell to her chin, but he had to admit it wasn't a bad look. By human standards anyway.

By now he had realized what the Huntresses had all done and why, and he smiled.

<What did you do to your hair?> one of the Huntresses asked Alzoria in awe.

<I was asking you the same thing!> Alzoria cried, looking around at all of them. <Why would you do this?>

Alzoria's friend and frequent partner in crime, Ketra, posed and put her hand under her newly cropped hair. <If one person cuts it, it's strange,> she said. <If everyone cuts it, it's stylish!>

Ramirez heard Alzoria hiccup, and the young vixen covered her ears with her hands, moved by the gesture. The Huntresses responded by crowding around her again.

<I did not think your hair would look like this,> one of the Huntresses told Alzoria. <I have never seen anything like it.>

Alzoria touched the side of her head where part of it had been shaved. <John's people cut it for me,> she said. <What do you think?>

The Huntresses were silent for a moment until another of Alzoria's friends, Mezina, stepped forward and examined Alzoria's haircut critically.

<I think it will keep your hair from getting into your kill when you gut it,> she said.

<I think so too,> Alzoria said in relief.

<I like how it has many parts,> another Huntress said. <It is shaved in some places and longer in others.>

<They had to work with what was left,> Alzoria replied sheepishly.

<They did very well,> Ketra told her.

<Better than we did,> Mezina noted, rubbing the strands of her short green hair between her fingers. As careful as they had been, all they had really done was take some shears and cut their hair off in one pass. They hadn't thought to try to style it.

Almost as one, all of the Huntresses' eyes turned to Ramirez.

The Ranger cleared his throat. "I guess Mina and Rachel are about to go into business together," he said.

* * *

Goto watched from the front door as Posha and the one-armed boy, Turean, conversed on the road in front of him. His niece's ears were fluttering happily as the boy's tail was a flurry of nervous movement. Goto remembered days like that, long forgotten after years of working underground.

He watched as the two gave short bows to each other, and Posha turned, trotting happily up to him. Turean left with an obvious spring in his step that somehow annoyed Goto.

Posha stopped and gave Goto a short bow. <Uncle Goto,> she said in greeting.

<Posha, I've noticed you spending a fair bit of time with that young tod,> he commented, trying to sound casual.

The young vixen's ears twitched a smile. <He is a nice person,> she said. <And quite attentive.>

<And crippled,> Goto added. <And a collaborator.>

Posha ignored him and stepped into the house, and Goto followed her.

<Though I am your guardian, you are not a miner's daughter,> he told her. <Your father was a bureaucrat. Your mother was a healer. You should not debase yourself by allowing a tod of lower standing to court you.>

Posha was looking through their stock of food, preparing to cook dinner. She didn't bother looking back as she answered. <Who would you suggest, then?> she asked casually, as if the discussion had nothing to do with her.

<The chieftain's son,> Goto told her immediately, telling Posha that he had been giving this some thought. <A son of a noblevixen, a valorous commando... The vixens I see waving their tails at him would be no match for you.>

<And his being the chieftain's son would benefit you as well,> she pointed out, but without disapproval.

Goto's tail went slack. <That is not what I aim for,> he told her. <I only want you to attain the best life you can. Were it not for those Dark Ones you would likely have been taken by now by a high-ranking bureaucrat, perhaps even a count! They stole that life from you just as they stole your parents! I would not see you reward that by lowering yourself to the level of one of their pets.>

Posha's ears twitched. <Your concern makes me happy, Uncle,> she told him.

He waited a moment for her to add some argument to his point, but she didn't. It was an aspect of his niece he did not like. She picked which battles she thought were worth fighting or could be won. If they weren't, she simply pretended they weren't happening.

It was aggravating in the extreme. She must have gotten that from her father.

<Would you at least be willing to speak to the chieftain's son?> he asked her.

<Of course,> she said. <I have not carved Turean's name in my bones.>

<Good,> Goto replied. <Perhaps I will speak to the chieftain and arrange a meeting.>

<If that is what you would like, Uncle,> Posha said.

She returned to preparing dinner, and Goto grunted, not as happy by the outcome of the conversation as he should be. Perhaps he should have a conversation with this Turean and let him know exactly where things stood.

* * *

Alacea was not yet an expert on human facial expressions, but she could tell her Tesho was troubled when he appeared at the temple door and asked to speak with her. She led him directly to her room where she had him sit at the small table in the corner as she heated some water for tea on the tiny stove. He said nothing as she worked, which made her quite certain something had gone awry for him.

It was only when she placed the cup of red tea in front of him and sat down that he finally spoke.

<I am sorry,> he told her quietly. <I did not find justice for Mikorin.>

<I see,> she said in disappointment.

<The soldier Keyes has many friends who are nobles also,> he told her. <They protect him.>

<These friends are your overlords?> she asked.

He nodded. <Yes,> he replied. <Grand Overlord.>

Her tail twitched as she thought on this.

Ben took a breath and quickly added. <I will continue,> he said. <Ask others for help.> He wasn't sure where to go with this, though. He could send a letter to the U.S. Colonial Command Inspector General, perhaps Big Army or even the combatant commander himself. If worse came to worst, he could write Congress. He didn't want to go to the media. They couldn't be trusted.

Alacea looked up and into his eyes, her ears pointed at him, and for a moment he thought she was mad at him. She had a right to be. He had promised to help the Garan'Sel Mikorin get justice for what had happened and had failed.

<You must stop,> she said simply.

Those three words puzzled him, and he had to study them to make sure he was hearing right. She wasn't asking if he would stop. She wasn't giving him permission to stop. She was telling him, *commanding him*, to stop.

<You *must* stop,> she repeated.

<Why stop?> he asked. <What happened is bad.>

<If you continue to fight this, Tesho, they could fight back.>

<I know,> he said. The old saying, "If you intend to kill a king then you *must* kill him," was also pretty apt when going after politically protected generals. As it was already, there was a good chance he would "strangely" be passed over for major when the promotion boards met.

She could see that he wasn't understanding her point. <They might take you away,> she elaborated. <If they do, will they send a person like you to replace you?> she asked. <Or will they send a person like Keyes?>

Ben felt his breath catch in his throat as he suddenly realized the threat his alien wife was worried about. It was certainly a possibility that, having caused a little consternation for the commander, the general would want to keep an eye on Ben by doing the same thing to him that he had done to Keyes, pulling him up to the headquarters to push papers and plan conferences where his every move could be monitored. Who would the HQ send to replace him? Hell, he could even see a scenario where Keyes, himself, was sent to Pelle, Walker citing his "experience" working with the Va'Shen. The irony of such a thing was enough to make Ben choke on his tea.

It would be horrible for Alacea's people, but his Rangers would also suffer. What would they do if faced with the kind of orders that Keyes had given his own people? He couldn't see Patricia, Ramirez, Baird or Warren following such orders and would probably end up sent to the more violent northern areas as a result. As for his junior soldiers... He wanted to believe they would refuse as well, but they were young and inexperienced. The Army had trained them to *trust* their leaders, and he could very well see most of them going along to get along, even if they didn't like it.

He sighed. It was possible this chain of feared events had already been put in motion by his behavior in Walker's office.

<Please, Tesho,> Alacea begged quietly. <I love that you have tried so hard, but do not pursue this further.>

He let out another breath and nodded. <I am sorry,> he said.

<Do not be sorry,> she told him. <I am proud to be the myorin of a tod who would do such a thing.>

For the first time this visit, Ben smiled, unsure of how to respond. Finally, he just decided to address the next issue.

<I must tell Wenlin,> he said.

<I will tell Wenlin,> Alacea replied.

<No,> he said firmly. <I tell her I do things, I fail. I must tell her I fail.> Alacea paused, her tail moving back and forth in concern. <That is bad?> Ben asked.

<No,> she answered immediately. <There is honor in it. I just...> She trailed off, not knowing how to tell him that he had done enough, that none of the Va'Shen had even expected him to go as far as he had.

<We go?> he asked.

Alacea's ears twitched once. <Let us finish our tea first. Bad news can wait a few minutes more.>

* * *

Burgers leaned against the front of the LTV parked outside the temple as he silently waited. He wasn't even sure she would be around here, and he didn't want to go up and knock on the door. Sure, the captain could do that, but he was just another grunt as far as the Mikorin were concerned.

Also, what he wanted to do might embarrass her, and he didn't want that. So, on a hunch, he waited.

He was amazed when he suddenly found his hunch had paid off. Coming up the road toward the temple was a familiar, petite, green-haired Va'Shen in a brown and white hanbok, her arms full of books. Burgers stood up straight and waited for her to get closer.

The girl caught sight of him and froze for a moment before quickly turning and starting down the road from whence she came.

"Hey! Wait!" he called. "Um..." <Wait still thank you!> he called.

The girl froze but didn't turn back to him, and Burgers trotted up to her.

Runa waited, her tail twitching spasmodically in worry as the Dark One approached. It would not be the first time a Dark One stopped her in the street. Many of her "clients" often tried to give her things or chat her up. She always tried to simply ignore them and walk away, but the Dark One soldiers often didn't like that and would berate her for doing so.

It was safer, she found, to wait, remain silent and simply endure whatever was to come. However, she was particularly nervous about this Dark One. He was the one who had gotten angry at her and caused a huge scene in the bakery as a result. She had not been punished afterward, but it was readily apparent that something she had done had caused a huge mess for the Mikorin.

Burgers slowed to a walk as he caught up to her and stepped in front of her, the massive man looking down at the tiny vixen.

<You Runa?> he asked.

The Aru'Dace cleared her throat nervously. <I am Runa,> she breathed fearfully.

<I want ask,> Burgers said in halting Va'Shen. <You are unhurt and okay?>

Runa didn't say anything, unsure of what to make of the question.

Burgers took her silence as him not speaking correctly. <I angry before,> he said slowly. <Surprise. Did not want hurt... you. Um... Did not want Mikorin hurt... from we.>

She didn't understand him. Not the words, she understood his butchered Va'Shen just fine. But *what* he was saying didn't make sense to her.

<Did you be'd hurted?> he asked.

<I don't understand you,> she whimpered.

<Do not hear,> he said apologetically.

<I said I don't understand you!> she suddenly screamed at him. Every Va'Shen head, ear and tail in the street turned toward them.

Burgers took a step back in surprise at the sudden outburst from the mousy girl. Her tail was whipping around angrily, and her delicate green ears were digging into her skull in rage.

<Why are you so confusing!?> she cried. <Why are you monsters one minute and nice the next?! *WHY CAN'T YOU JUST BE NICE ALL THE TIME!?*>

Before Burgers could react, Runa took off past him at a dead run, some of the books she had been carrying falling out of her arms and into the street.

The Ranger watched her go and took a sad breath. That did not go the way he had hoped.

* * *

Wenlin sat silently on the other side of the table as Ben explained what had happened at Jamieson Airfield. As soon as their conversation at the temple had concluded, Alacea walked with him to where Wenlin and her Mikorin had made their home in what was rapidly becoming the "Garan'Sel Quarter" of the village.

After knocking on the door of the bakery, which, since their after-hours activities had shut down, had continued on as a simple bakery, the Mikorin who answered showed them inside and went to get Wenlin.

Once they were taken to a private room, the Garan'Sel Na'Sha silently entered and bowed to him, her drab green and white hanbok as pristine as the young woman could make it.

<Greetings, Overlord,> she said in her slow, machine-like tone. <How may I serve today?>

They sat down, and Ben went through everything that had happened. Wenlin remained impassive and emotionless, barely even blinking.

Her behavior made Alacea study her. Once again, there was something off about her. The vixen who had broken down in her temple was nowhere to be seen. Instead, this statue of a beautiful young woman faced them, her ears and tail almost completely motionless.

She bowed to Ben as he finished his story. <I thank you for your consideration of our desires, Overlord,> he told him.

<I do not want remain as this,> he told her. <Want to make bad things right. Are things you need?>

The Na'Sha bowed to him again. <Your benevolence is more than enough, Overlord.>

<Stop,> Alacea interrupted suddenly, drawing both Wenlin's and her Tesho's eyes to her. She stared at Wenlin as if waiting for some signal or sign. <What is wrong with you?> she asked.

It wasn't like a human, "What's the matter with you?" admonishment. Alacea truly thought there was something wrong with the vixen in front of her. She could feel it.

<I feel no illness, Alacea Na'Sha,> Wenlin replied evenly.

<Myorin?> Ben asked her in a whisper.

Alacea and Wenlin continued to stare at each other, one vixen's tail and ears moving about in concern and the other's practically dead.

<It... It is nothing, Tesho,> Alacea finally said. <I apologize.> She decided to turn the conversation to something constructive. <Wenlin, you mentioned at one point that some of your people were... um... arrested. Perhaps, Tesho could assist in some way with that.>

For the first time, the other vixen seemed to respond, sitting up straighter. Her eyes pointed downward, almost as if she was looking within herself for some answer.

<That would be most helpful,> Wenlin allowed. <I shall write a list of their names and get it to Alacea Na'Sha to send to you.>

<You may come speak at me when you wish,> Ben told her. <You do not require permission.>

<I understand,> Wenlin replied without making any promise to actually do what Ben suggested.

<Yes, good,> Ben said. <I will do. More?> he asked.

<No, Overlord,> Wenlin told him. <Once again, I thank you for your kindness.> She bowed.

Ben returned her bow and looked to Alacea. <Myorin? You say things?>

<No, Tesho,> she said quietly. <I am sure there will be other opportunities to speak.>

With that, everyone stood and bowed, and a Mikorin showed Ben and Alacea out of the room, leaving Wenlin alone.

Tenzeta entered the room and stood next to Wenlin. <Do you think he spoke the truth?> the Ya'Jahar asked her.

<Would it matter if he had?> Wenlin asked in return.

<Alacea Na'Sha seems to place great trust in him,> Tenzeta told her.

<Yes, she does.>

Tenzeta took Wenlin by the arm and turned her around until they were face-to-face. <Na'Sha,> she hissed. <Wenlin... please stop taking that... that... potion! Every time you take it you appear more and more as if a doll!>

The Na'Sha looked at her, her ears remaining pointed at the ceiling. <It is the only way to face them,> she informed her friend. <If I show the Dark Ones weakness, they will use it against us. And I am no longer able to face them without the medicine's effects.>

Even after Alacea had told her her tesho was different, Wenlin could not bring herself to completely believe it. He was a monster. He might be more merciful than most, but he was still a monster. And even the thought of being in the same room with *any* of them made her quake. The medicine allowed her to function. And that was all that mattered.

Tenzeta's ears drooped, and she stepped back. Wenlin remained frozen where she was.

<How are the Mikorin Zaishin?> Wenlin asked her.

The Mikorin who had volunteered to accept the Dark Ones' "affections," the ones who had willingly damned themselves, had been both puzzled and relieved when they were told the bakery's nighttime activities would cease. But with the threat now alleviated, the true horror of what they had done was beginning to descend upon them.

<I watch them closely,> Tenzeta breathed. <I add *sora* root to their soup at dinner to ensure they sleep. Some of them do not wish to leave the bakery. They fear happening upon one of the Dark Ones they've entertained.>

<And how is Runa doing?> Wenlin asked.

Tenzeta sighed. Runa was one of their youngest Zaishin and held a higher post among the Mikorin. As such she was under an intense amount of pressure.

<She endures,> Tenzeta responded evenly. There was little more that could be said than that.

<Please continue to see to it that they *all* endure,> Wenlin instructed.

Tenzeta bowed.

<Yes, Na'Sha.>

Chapter 13

Two weeks until contact...

"Jeef, I go to launch," Turean announced, giving his boss a wave before grabbing the cloth bag on the shelf near the door.

Warren looked up from the inventory report he was reading and gave the boy a wave. "Okay, have a good lunch," he said, distractedly.

The Va'Shen boy saw the chief was busy and didn't try to pull him into a conversation. Instead, he went out the door and started down the FOB's main thoroughfare. As he walked, he swung his bag back and forth, enjoying the sunshine. Normally, he would take his lunch to the dining facility and eat with the other SeaBees, but today was different. He had a lot of thinking to do, and he couldn't do that in such a noisy place.

Not that he minded the noise. He loved eating with the SeaBees. They were good people who had always made him feel welcome, taking the time to teach him how to use their tools and how they built such amazing things. One of them had even cut holes in a yellow hard-hat so Turean could wear one without crushing his ears.

His close ties to the Dark One engineers, however, was also a problem.

The Va'Shen boy found an out-of-the-way area near the fuel storage area and sat down near one of the pumping stations. Large rubber bladders filled with helicopter and truck fuel lay in a row, though the refueling area was empty of vehicles today, giving him some privacy.

Reaching into his bag, he took out a small wooden box, and his ears fluttered. He didn't want to open it yet. He just wanted to look at it. It wasn't anything special to most eyes, just a regular box to hold some pickled vegetables and *lemess*. But the fact that it was Posha who had made the food inside this box made him happy. Posha, who had saw him walking to work and came out of her house to hand the sack lunch to him.

Most vixens wouldn't even look at Turean. That was simply how it was when you were a young cripple. It was assumed that you could not work and so no one expected you to. The community supported you, but they would not support you *and* your family. Vixens wanted a tod who could support them, and in Va'Shen eyes, that wasn't Turean.

But that seemed to be changing. Turean wasn't sitting at home with his mother anymore. He was going to work every day. He helped clean up work areas and repair equipment. He dug trenches and drove vehicles.

And he was the *only* tod who was doing that. No other tod was working with the Dark Ones like this, and he understood fully why. But as a result, he was the only one *learning* about how they did things, how their equipment worked, how to operate their vehicles.

Chief Warren had told him that, eventually, the number of Dark One soldiers here to do those kinds of jobs would go down, and they would have to hire Va'Shen to make up the difference. When that happened, it was possible Turean would get an actual job with a title and position.

It made him feel guilty sometimes. His father had died fighting the Dark Ones, and there were some in the village who could not believe he would willingly work with them. But his father had been a practical tod. He would have been the first to tell Turean that the war was over, and a tod did what a tod had to in order to support his family. He and his mother were alone now, and he knew that somewhere in the Glade, his father approved of what he was doing.

He quietly ate some pickled vegetables and decided to focus on his real problem.

Posha.

Turean liked Posha. He liked Posha *a lot*.

And Posha seemed to like him. They took walks together and talked late into the night outside her home. If he were not a cripple, he likely would have taken her by now.

But he *was* a cripple, and that made the situation much more difficult. For one thing, her uncle, Goto, was dead set against any such idea. He had spoken to Turean and let him know in no uncertain terms that he did not approve of him being around Posha.

Turean understood that, and he didn't want to bring dishonor to Posha or chain her to a life of having to support a cripple.

He had tried to explain to Goto what Chief Warren had said, how he might soon be able to get a better job than most of the tods in Pelle, but the older tod wouldn't hear of it. Talking about working with the Dark Ones only made the man angrier until he got to the point where he was shouting at Turean, calling him a "collaborator."

He wasn't sure what he was going to do.

Turean looked down at the box again, and his ears twitched again.

But he wasn't going to give up.

His resolve strengthened, he finished his lunch and prepared to go back to work. As he put the lunch box back in the bag, he heard it hit something solid, and he paused. There was something else in there. His ears fluttered at the thought that perhaps Posha had also given him a dessert or some kind of memento.

The Va'Shen boy reached inside the bag and took hold of the object, pulling it out, he held it up and examined the glass sphere, roughly the size of his fist.

There was a flash.

* * *

"Good afternoon, Sir. This is Sergeant Miles with the JDOG."

Ben had to strain to hear the voice on the corded, old fashioned phone that had taken the place of his holotop, tablet and satellite communications suite. The sergeant's voice sounded like he was talking to him through a hundred-yard-long metal pipe.

But this was the call he had been waiting for, so Ben didn't want to risk losing the connection entirely by asking him to call back.

"Thanks for calling, Sergeant Miles," Ben said, grabbing a notepad and pen in preparation for taking notes. "I'm assuming this is about my request?"

"Yes, Sir," Miles replied. "Colonel Ling asked me to look into it. Unfortunately, I don't have much to tell you. We have no records of any detainees coming to us from Sector Six. It's possible that they went to the British detention center at Camp Josey, but I'm still looking into that."

Ben felt a chill run up his back, and he absolutely hated it. This phone call should be a minor inconvenience, a matter of waiting a few more days and nothing more. Instead, he had to wonder if a fellow Army officer had merely sent some detainees to a different camp or if he secretly had them shot and dumped into a ditch.

"Thank you, Sergeant Miles," he said. "Please let me know what you find."

"Will-do, Sir. Have a good day."

"You too," Ben replied. "Out here."

He put the phone down in the cradle and sat back in his chair. From her desk, Patricia looked at him and put her pen down. "Bad news?" she asked.

"JDOG never got any detainees from Sector Six," Ben told her.

Patricia was silent for a good minute. "You think he killed them?"

Ben took a breath. Standard operating procedure for Va'Shen detained for suspected insurgent activities was to send them to a detention facility for interrogation and further processing. If Wenlin was being honest, and the villagers rounded up by Keyes were taken away, they should have shown up at Jamieson. That was the assigned detention facility for Sectors One through 20. The only reason they'd end up at Camp Josey is someone made a mistake.

Which was possible.

Under any other circumstances, probable.

But Ben didn't know, and that scared the shit out of him.

"Too early to jump to that conclusion," he told her. "Let's give Ling time to turn something up."

Patricia nodded.

Before the conversation could go any further, a loud siren ripped across the camp, growing louder and higher pitched as it went. Ben and Patricia looked at each other in shock and horror before quickly dashing to the cross-shaped racks behind their desks where they kept their armor, vests and helmets.

This was not the first time the two had heard the alarm on FOB Leonard. Ben made sure to run tests and drills regularly. But there were none scheduled for today, and that could only mean one thing.

The FOB was under attack.

Ben's thoughts went immediately to his dream, of the fenceline torn down, glassers being thrown all over, and his Rangers being overrun. Looking down at his hands as he zipped up his load-bearing vest, he found them shaking ever so slightly. Willing them to stop, he quickly finished putting on his equipment and went to help Patricia put on hers. The interpreter still wasn't used to putting on her equipment in a hurry and was just now putting on her helmet. Ben quickly helped her strap it in and slapped her on the shoulder to let her know she was all set.

"TOC," he ordered, and the two ran to the door and outside.

Outside the office, troops were running to their battlestations in various states of equipment and dress. Patricia almost stopped and laughed as one Ranger ran by her, soaking wet with a rifle in one hand and the other holding up the towel that was covering his waist.

The Tactical Operations Center was next door to their office, and it only took a few seconds to run there and get inside.

In a regular TOC, the walls would be filled with holoscreens or, barring that, flatscreen monitors showing live maps of the area, drone footage, gun cameras, personnel status lists and every and any other piece of information a commander might ever need to direct a battle. Thanks to the Fuzz, none of that would work. Here on FOB Leonard, there was a big map of the camp, divided by marker into different sectors with flags and tacks pinned to various points. Two white boards flanked the map with a single specialist standing next to it. That specialist would be the only person on the entire planet allowed to make changes to the board or the map. If anyone else tried, be it a lowly private or a four-star general, that specialist would jump dead in their shit. Continuity of information was too important to risk with different people moving things around.

Stationed directly in front of the board was a row of desks filled with clipboards and phones. Currently, there was only a single female Air Force staff sergeant sitting at the center desk, but other troops were running into the tiny building, grabbing chairs and checklists as they took their posts.

Ben made a beeline for the Air Force sergeant. Staff Sergeant Helena Bishop was in charge of coordinating information throughout the FOB, a job she had trained for and had six years of experience doing. Every movement she made was fluid, deliberate and calm, and Ben was once again thankful that he had managed to poach her from her bullshit duty on Jamieson, checking for people's reflective belts outside the rec center.

"What do you got?" Ben asked her, leaning over her shoulder and studying the board.

"Glasser detonation in Sector Three, near the fuel pumps," Bishop reported steadily. "No other contacts yet. QRF is out and responding. Gladius One and Two are rolling out of the sallyports now. One is heading north. Two is heading south. Three and Four are rolling inside the fenceline."

Ben looked at the map and the red "X" that marked where the glasser went off. He looked for the nearest fenceline and shook his head.

"That would be one hell of a throw," he commented. Even so, he had seen the Va'Shen use jerry-rigged launchers, most recently at Jamieson where a trio of Va'Shen agents had used a giant rubber band to launch glassers all over the barracks area.

A phone rang, and Bishop picked it up, not bothering to respond to Ben's comment.

"TOC," she said into the phone. She scribbled something on a notepad. "Copy. Out here." She put the phone down and looked up at the specialist at the board. "All guard towers report ready. No contacts." The specialist made some notes on the board in response.

"Any casualties?" Patricia asked from behind Ben.

"Nothing reported," Bishop said. "Watchtower said they think there's a glassed body at the blast site."

Ben bit his lip at the thought. Watchtower was the tallest tower in the FOB, tasked with overwatch for the entire camp. He kept two marksmen up there at all times. Along with keeping watch, they would also act as a communications hub with the two LTVs of troops sent out to search for the enemy outside the fenceline. Since radios didn't work, the LTV crews would hold up flags, each with different, but simple, meanings. Watchtower would see these and report them to the TOC. It was a pretty low-tech solution, but it was the best they had at the moment.

Minutes ticked by as Ben waited and Bishop received reports from various areas of the FOB, reporting readiness. Some commanders would feel the need to bark orders or urge his people to hurry with what they were doing, but Ben knew that was useless. He trained his people to be the best at what they did precisely so he *wouldn't* have to do that. His job was to make decisions and take the responsibility for them. Until it was time to do his job, he let them do theirs.

As soon as Bishop would put down the phone, it would ring again, and she would pick it up again. She never seemed frazzled by the constant activity, and Ben couldn't say he would act the same way.

"TOC," she said into the phone. She made a note. "Copy all. Out here." She put the phone down, and it began to ring, but this time she left it for someone else, looking up at the board. "Gladius One reports circuit complete, no contacts."

As soon as the specialist started making the notes on the board, another troop spoke up.

"Gladius Two reports circuit complete. No contacts."

"TOC," Bishop said again into the phone. Ben studied the board. It looked like the massive attack he had feared would not materialize. The two LTV patrols had found no signs in the areas immediately outside the FOB.

Bishop put the phone down. "Report from Watchtower," she announced. "Gladius Three and Four report no contacts." She turned to Ben. "All sectors report secure, Sir."

Ben took a breath, giving it a few moments thought. Thirty minutes had passed as the search teams had combed inside and outside the perimeter. "Bring us to Black."

"Yes, Sir." Bishop picked up the phone and quickly dialed a number from memory. "Watchtower, TOC. Alarm Black. Say again. Alarm Black."

The alarm outside, which had never stopped since the "battle" began, now changed to three separate blasts, a pause, three blasts, a pause, and continuing.

Alarm Black was the notification that the attack was over, but there could still be unexploded ordnance within the camp. Right now, designated personnel in each building were gearing up to go outside and check the immediate surroundings for undetonated glassers or other surprises. Two specialists inside the TOC did the same, and the door cracked open a moment later as they left to make their assigned circuit.

It was a little premature, but Ben was concerned about the damage to the fuel area. If there was a spill happening, that wasn't a problem that got better with time.

"Have the SeaBees send a team out to check the fuel area," he ordered Bishop. "Tell them to be careful. No heroics. I just want to know how bad we've been hit."

"Yes, Sir." Bishop picked up another phone. As she relayed the orders to Chief Warren, Ben studied the board again and tried to make sense of what just happened. Perhaps some young, angry tods had found a glasser somewhere and decided to strike a blow against the invaders. They must have launched it from outside, he thought, because if they had snuck in to deliver it, there were several other areas where they could have caused significantly more damage.

They waited as reports continued to come in, each one good news. No unexploded glassers found. All personnel accounted for. No surprises. The only unit left to report in were the SeaBees.

Ben checked the clock. Two hours had passed since the alarm had first sounded. The stress had made it seem longer. He let out a breath, relieved that his dream hadn't actually come pass. At least, not yet.

"TOC."

Ben tried to hear what was being said on the other side of the phone as Bishop held the device to her ear.

"Hold one." The Air Force NCO turned and held the phone out to him. "SeaBees for you, Sir."

The Ranger captain took the phone and put it to his ear, ready to, hopefully, hear a very mundane damage report and an estimated time to repair their facilities. "Gibson," he announced.

"Sir, it's Warren," he heard from the other end. The senior sailor sounded shook up, and for a moment Ben thought they must have been hit much harder than he first thought. "I'm at the fuel pumps. Sir, I think you better come down here and see this."

He could have demanded more information, but Ben could hear it in the man's voice. Whatever he wanted Ben to see, he *needed* Ben to see.

"I'm on my way."

* * *

Ben's first thought when he saw it was that it looked like a glass version of "The Thinker." Turean, looking down at the glass orb in his hand as if deep in thought. His face showed no fear, but that didn't say much when it came to Va'Shen facial expressions. At most, the Ranger could say that his ears and tail appeared to have been motionless at the time the bomb went off.

<I cannot make sense of it,> Yasuren breathed as she held herself, her ears folded down and back in grief. Kasshas put his arm around her and nuzzled her ears with his bearded face. It was late afternoon now. As soon as Chief Warren had shown him the body, Ben knew he needed to get Kasshas involved in this. He had sent Baird out in an LTV with orders to bring the chieftain back, but to be calm and respectful about it. The entire village must have heard the alarms, and so, they knew something was up.

The NCO had returned a half-hour later, not only with Kasshas, but his wife and son, Tasshas, who had refused to let his parents go into the human stronghold alone.

Ben had sent a separate LTV to find Alacea and bring her as well. He knew that she would have a role in whatever happened next. He expected the priestess to be standing nearby, but when he turned, he found her several paces away, standing next to Chief Warren.

Alacea took the SeaBee's hands in hers and said something softly to him. Ben was suddenly once again grateful for his alien wife's senses. He knew the chief and Turean had been close, but with everything going on, he had not had the opportunity to give him any emotional support.

Turean's "body" sat in the center of a ten-meter glass circle, which included some pipes and one of the pumping stations. Thankfully, whatever fuel had been in those pipes had also turned to glass, and nothing had spilled before the SeaBees were able to shut down the pumps and drain them.

There would have to be an investigation. Sergeant Carpenter was already there, taking measurements and notes. Normally, a holographer would come to the site and make a three-dimensional walk-around image of the scene, but that was obviously impossible.

Questions. So many questions.

What had this been, he wondered? A bolt-from-the-blue suicide attack from a would-be insurgent who had managed to infiltrate their ranks? An attack gone wrong? It would not be the first time a bomber had been killed by his own munitions. Could it have been some kind of weird accident? Maybe Turean found the glasser lying by the pumps and picked it up. But if so, who put it there and why didn't they just set it off themselves?

Striking upon an idea, he turned to Tasshas, who was helping his father comfort his mother.

<Tasshas commando, yes?> he asked. <You understand glass weapon?>

Yasuren turned quickly to him, her ears pointed at him in fear and anger. <Tasshas had nothing to do with this!> she proclaimed.

Ben held his hands up, realizing how his words might have been interpreted. <Tasshas not do. I know. I not understand glass weapon. Need Tasshas help.>

The former commando squeezed his mother's hand reassuringly and stepped toward Ben. <I do know these weapons quite well,> he admitted to the Ranger. <What of it?>

Ben motioned for Patricia to join them. She had been helping Alacea speak to Warren, and she quickly jogged over to join them. The captain gestured to Turean and the glassed area.

"Ask him what he makes of this," he ordered Patricia. "As a commando. What does his gut say happened here?"

Patricia had to think about how to word that request for a moment before turning and speaking to Tasshas.

The former commando listened and studied Turean's glassed form for a hard minute, his tail swaying back and forth in thought.

<It is difficult to know,> he confessed. <He does not have the look of a tod about to die. Glass grenades are very versatile weapons that require much training before one can use them safely. It is possible that he made a mistake while arming it.>

Ben listened as Patricia recounted the tod's statement and arched an eyebrow. <Do you not just pick up and toss?> He illustrated this with a tossing motion of his hand.

Tasshas's tail slapped the ground. <No,> he said. <The lights on the sphere must be aligned in a certain way to get the effect you want.> Tasshas took a breath as he tried to remember just how many settings there were. <There are many ways to use them.>

As Patricia translated, Ben held up a hand and interrupted her. "Wait, wait," he said. "What lights? What is he talking about?"

Patricia asked the questions, and Tasshas replied.

<The different colored lights on the sphere,> Tasshas told him. He looked confused at Ben's question.

The terp stepped in to help. <Glass grenades we have seen have no lights upon them,> she said. <Just glass.>

<I do not know how that can be,> Tasshas said. <You need the lights to arm the weapon.>

Patricia translated this, and Ben gave it some thought.

It was Chief Warren who proposed the answer that made the most sense.

"Maybe they only appear to the Va'Shen," he said, walking up to them. "They may only show up in a spectrum of light they can see, and we can't."

"That would explain it," Patricia agreed. "I've seen Va'Shen walking around with different colored sunglasses. Maybe they're not sunglasses. Maybe they're actually corrective."

"Okay," Ben said, getting the group back on track. "Turean comes here, eats his lunch. He either takes out a glasser or finds one on the ground. He picks it up..." He trailed off for a minute. "... Then he either sets it off deliberately or by accident."

"We know the Va'Shen don't seem to have a taboo when it comes to suicide," Patricia added softly, her eyes going to the chief in concern.

"No way," Warren told them flatly. "Not Turean. He wouldn't do that. And let's say for a minute he *did* want to attack us... Why come here and do it? He could have rolled it into the DFAC and taken out a good twenty or thirty of us instead. This stuff..." He gestured to the pumps. "We'll be up and running again in two hours. There's nothing to gain from it."

"What do you think, Senior Chief?" Ben asked him.

"I think someone set him up," Warren replied, folding his arms over his chest.

"Why?" Patricia asked. "They could just sneak in and toss glassers all over the place. Why try to set up Turean?"

"I don't know," Warren admitted. "But I know for a *fact*..." He pointed at Turean's body. "... That boy *did not* intend to do this."

<What are you saying, please?> Kasshas politely broke in. The humans had naturally held their debate in English, leaving the Va'Shen out of the conversation.

Patricia quickly brought the Va'Shen up to speed on the debate.

<Want know why Turean do this,> Ben told them.

Kasshas took a breath, and his tail moved slowly back and forth. <I do not know, Overlord.> He bowed low to the human commander. <I apologize to you for what has happened and once again offer my head as compensation.>

<Father!> Tasshas cried.

"He said..." Patricia began.

"Yeah, I know, kill him if I wanna," Ben sighed. <Stand please.> Kasshas rose again. The Ranger looked hard at the Va'Shen man. "You know, one day you're going to say that and I'm going to actually take you up on it."

<Overlord?> Kasshas asked, not understanding.

<Not important,> Patricia hastily assured him. <Leader of fighters just say need not offer your death so much easy.>

"What now?" Warren asked.

Ben took a deep breath and blew it out through his mouth in dread. "Now we gotta tell the family."

"He has a mother," Warren told him. "Dad died in the war."

Ben turned to Kasshas. <Must speak Turean mother. Tell her what is happened.>

<You do not need to do that, Overlord,> Kasshas assured him. <We will tell her for you.>

<No,> Ben replied firmly. <Turean like my fighter. I must tell. It is how the thing is done.>

<Kasshas,> Alacea said gently. <For them it is a matter of honor. If he is not there to tell her, it would be a moral cowardice.>

<I see,> Kasshas relented. <I will take you to her.>

<Thank you.>

<I will go as well,> Alacea assured him.

"Patricia, I might need you too," Ben told her. The terp nodded in response.

"Me too."

Ben looked at Warren, whose expression told him that no argument to the contrary would be accepted. He nodded to the man. "Of course." He turned to Carpenter, who was still taking measurements. "Sergeant Carpenter!"

"Sir!"

"We're going to tell the family," Ben told him. "Please take care not to... break... the remains."

"Yes, Sir."

* * *

They walked silently to the house Turean shared with his mother. With so many important village and Dark One officials marching down the street, many of the villagers came outside, watching curiously from their doorways.

Ben walked out front, Alacea in her place of honor just behind him and to the left. Warren and Patricia walked as part of that group while Kasshas, his wife and his son walked a few paces behind.

There was almost no sound in the village, as if everyone just somehow knew that something terrible had happened. Out of habit, Ben walked with his hand close to the butt of his pistol, his eyes checking open windows and doorways as he went, wondering if there was another glasser waiting to be chucked out toward them.

The sun was about to go down by the time they arrived at Basilla's house. Alacea stepped up to the door and scratched gently at it. A moment later, the older vixen's face appeared as the door opened.

She saw everyone gathered there, and her tail fell to the floor. <Why are you here?> she asked. She looked around the group and followed up with another question. <Where is Turean?>

Ben stepped forward and bowed to Basilla. <I am sorry,> he said gently. <There was a thing today. Turean has died.>

Basilla looked around in confusion, her eyes finally landing on Alacea. <Na'Sha?> she asked. <What is he saying?>

Alacea took her hands in hers. <Turean has passed into the Glade, Basilla,> she told her quietly. <We do not know for sure what happened yet, but he was caught in a glass grenade explosion and...>

Basilla's ears folded down into her head, and she hiccupped. <What did you do to him?!> she yelled over Alacea's head at the humans. <You promised he wouldn't be hurt!>

Warren flinched, stunned at the accusation.

Ben stood still, willing himself to turn to stone, to shut off his emotions. This part of his job was always the worst, always the most emotionally bruising.

<What did you do to him?!> Basilla wailed, physically launching herself toward the humans, but Alacea caught her in a strong embrace and held her as the vixen began hiccupping uncontrollably. She wailed loudly, her cries of grief echoing through the silent village and into the ears of the villagers who were still standing by their doors, watching the scene unfold.

<Overlord,> Kasshas said gently. <You should leave now. There is no more good your presence can do here.>

Ben turned his head to him. He understood enough of what the chieftain had said and agreed.

"Chief, Eltee, let's go." He bowed one more time to the assembled Va'Shen, and the three humans started back down the road, leaving the screaming vixen behind them.

* * *

<Where did he get the glass grenade?>

It was already dark by the time Kasshas, Yasuren and Tasshas had started back to their home. Alacea would stay with Basilla to pray with the woman and comfort her as best she could. Yasuren had promised to fill in the other Mikorin on their way home so they could provide support as well.

Kasshas's question hung in the air as they walked. Although his son said nothing, Kasshas's gaze turned toward him. <Was there anything you did not tell the Overlord?> he asked.

Pelle's chieftain might look like a simple man, but he was anything but. He could tell his son was troubled by more than just the day's events. Yasuren, who had always spoiled Tasshas a little too much, could never believe he was hiding something, but Kasshas had once been a young tod and could always tell what was on his son's mind.

Tasshas continued walking, but he did turn toward his parents, his ears folded back in worry. <I do not know where he got the weapon,> he assured them. <But... I have been approached by some tods from Garan'Sel in the last week, asking about how I felt about the Dark Ones, what it was like to fight them... if I *still* wanted to fight them.>

<What did you say?> Yasuren breathed.

<I told them the truth,> Tasshas replied. <I am bound by oath to obey the Emperor and *not* fight them.> He was quiet a moment before continuing. <Two days later, a different tod asked what I would do if others fought them instead. Would I join in or stand aside? He also, very carefully, tried to find out if I was willing to teach others how to fight them if I could not fight them myself.>

<They want to fight the Dark Ones?> Yasuren gasped, her tail twitching urgently.

<They were careful not to come out and say as much,> Tasshas told them. <But it was obvious they were thinking about it. I know I am not the only commando they've approached.>

<Azarin?> Kasshas asked him.

<I do not believe so,> Tasshas answered. <He is related to the Dark Ones through his sister. And he is the kind that would not tolerate such a threat.>

<Dan Huun, then?> Kasshas asked.

Tasshas took a breath, and his ears twitched an affirmative. <Very likely.> He paused. <If they are asking such things, it is possible they approached Turean as well and recruited him to their cause.>

<He would not agree to such a thing,> Yasuren told him.

<Do not be so sure, Mother,> Tasshas replied. <Young tods are easy to manipulate into a fight. Fill their heads with talk of honor and valor, use the ghosts of their fathers and grandfathers to shame them, and you find an otherwise gentle tod ready to kill. I know,> he told her. <I know because *I* have done this. To prepare young and frightened commandos to stand and fight when they should have run.> He turned away from them and looked down at the shadow-filled road ahead of them. <They do not understand until it is too late.>

He stopped as Yasuren suddenly grabbed hold of the young tod and hugged him tightly.

<You are strong,> she told him quietly. <So strong that I forget sometimes how difficult things have been for you. I will not forget again.>

Tasshas hugged her in return and looked up at his father. <What will you do?> he asked him.

<That, my son, is a very difficult question,> Kasshas said. <What will I do?>

* * *

Turean's funeral was the next day. As carefully and as solemnly as they could, the SeaBees had cut the glass statue of the tod some still believed to be their friend out of the ground and transported him to the Mikorin temple where the ceremony would take place.

Ben, Patricia and Warren attended, but out of consideration for the family and the Va'Shen, stood away from the others, close enough to observe, but far enough to not be a distraction.

Basilla, dressed in a deep red robe, stood silently, her tail and ears practically dead, only twitching when she heard her son's name spoken. Ben watched as Alacea, Wenlin, and two other Mikorin performed a ceremony over the wooden coffin that contained the young tod's body, ending as they raised their hands up to either side of their head and praying to the Va'Shen gods.

Before they knew it, the funeral was over. The crowd began to break up. Alacea was walking with Basilla toward her home.

"Okay, show's over," Ben breathed as he turned to go.

"Sir."

He turned and saw Warren hadn't moved. "I'd like to go pay my respects, if that's all right."

Ben nodded. "Watch yourself," he warned. "Emotions are likely pretty high right now."

"Yes, Sir." The engineer saluted him, and Ben saluted back, before he turned started down the road after Basilla.

"Should we go with him?" Patricia asked.

Ben shook his head. "No, if we're there we'll just make it awkward for everyone." He started back toward the FOB. Patricia hesitated a moment before following him.

Warren could tell he was getting dirty looks as he walked down the road toward Basilla's house, but he ignored them. The Va'Shen were going to believe what they were going to believe no matter what anyone actually said or did, so fuck 'em. But he couldn't just go back to work without telling Basilla, himself, how sorry he was.

Turean had been like a long lost nephew to him. He wanted to see the tod succeed despite the loss of his arm, to take that success and shove it into the faces of anyone who had ever doubted him. He could have done it too. Warren was certain of that. The kid had had a good feel for the job, for building and fixing things. All he needed was a little mentorship, and Warren wanted to give him that.

And now he was gone.

The engineer didn't want to believe that Turean had been trying to attack the base. But there was doubt. "Green on Blue," where a supposed local ally betrayed the people who had been sent to help them, wasn't a rare occurrence in situations like this. He just never thought Turean could have that in him, and if he was wrong, then that just made him stupid.

Warren had a lot of reasons to kick himself.

He arrived at the small yellow house and knocked gently on the red door. A few moments later, it opened and Alacea was standing there.

<Expert Engineer Wo-Ren,> she greeted with a bow.

<Blessed day to you,> Warren told her, giving her a short bow of his own. <Um... Come to say Turean's mother... Um...> He found himself blinking tears out of his eyes. <Want to say... bad feel... for thing that happen.>

Alacea could see the pain in the man, her experience with her Tesho giving her a better sense of human emotions than most Va'Shen. She took his hand. <Please, come inside,> she asked, pulling him gently into the house.

The inside of Basilla's house was simple but clean and neat. A small iron stove sat in the corner, and a low table just big enough for three or four people took up the center of the room. Basilla was at the stove, stirring a pot with a wooden spoon.

<Basilla,> Alacea said. <Expert Engineer Wo-Ren has come to pay his respects.>

Warren braced himself, expecting the woman to explode and lash out at him the way she did yesterday, but the explosion did not come. She put the spoon down without facing them and wiped her hands on a towel.

She finally turned to him and stepped forward, bowing very low to him from the waist.

"Senor Jeef," she said in greeting. <I apologize for my behavior yesterday.>

Warren wanted to cry.

<You... I...> He didn't know what to say to a grieving mother apologizing to him after he failed to take care of her son.

<He... loved you,> Basilla said, still not rising from her bow. <He loved you... and I should not have yelled at you.>

"Ma'am, you don't bow to me. You don't have to..." He turned desperately to Alacea. <You tell to her. Do not bow for me. Please not to ever bows to at me! I...> The Va'Shen words, falling out of his mouth in a jumble suddenly stopped. He couldn't go on.

Alacea squeezed his hand. <I told her what happened,> she said to him. <And that you defended Turean's honor. You were his friend. She feels guilt as you do. Please, accept her apology.>

He nodded. <I... Yes,> he said.

Basilla stood back up. <You will eat with us?> she asked.

At Alacea's pointed look, Warren nodded. <Yes.>

<Good,> the grieving woman replied. She turned back to the stove. <Turean bought this pot for me,> she said. <He was very proud when he brought it home.>

<Turean... good tod,> Warren said as Basilla brought the pot to the table and gestured for him to sit down.

<Yes,> Basilla agreed woodenly as she took her seat.

A scratching at the door drew their attention, and Alacea stood up to get it. She opened the door and froze in surprise.

Goto stood there with Posha next to him. A few other Garan'Sel villagers stood nearby, some holding a variety of articles like boxes, blankets, pots and pans.

Alacea bowed to them. <Blessed day,> she said in greeting.

<Blessed day, Na'Sha,> Goto returned. <We would like to pay our respects to Basilla.>

Basilla had heard this and stood up, walking to the door to see who had come. She bowed to Goto, who bowed back to her.

After Goto rose to his full height, he began speaking again. <Basilla, we have come to show our respect and appreciation for your son's sacrifice.> He gestured to the other villagers. <We have brought gifts to help aid you through this difficult time.>

<Gifts?> Basilla asked. <For what?>

Goto's ears fluttered a smile. Next to him, Posha remained silent, her eyes cast downward at the floor.

<Your son's courage calls for a reward,> he said. <We cannot thank him, so we offer these to you instead.>

Alacea caught onto what Goto meant, and her ears folded downward. <Goto, perhaps this is not the best time to...>

<To give one's life to bloody the Dark Ones is an act of great honor, Basilla,> Goto went on, ignoring Alacea's warning. <What your son did will never be forgotten. We should instead honor him by taking his example to heart.>

Basilla stared at him, her eyes wide, her tail moving faster and faster. Alacea watched as her ears began to fold downward into her skull.

<What,> she asked quietly, <Are you talking about? Do... Do you think my son... He...>

Alacea put a hand on Basilla's shoulder. <Basilla, let us...>

<Get out of here!> Basilla ordered, pushing Goto with both hands. <Get out of here!> she yelled at the group. <Is that what you think of my son?!> she cried. <You think my son so honorless and deceitful that he would betray people who befriended him?!>

<Your son is a martyr,> Goto said, trying to calm the woman. <Even with his handicap, he fought the Dark Ones when no one else would! He is a hero!> Goto paused for a moment as Warren stepped into view behind the vixens, his voice beginning to ice over. <Or would you remember him as a Dark One pet?>

<Goto!> Alacea snapped.

<Is something the matter?>

Every eye turned to the one-eyed tod who had asked that question. Azarin strolled casually up the lane toward Basilla's house, locking his eye onto Goto who was, himself, on the receiving end of Alacea's angry glare.

<We were just bringing Basilla our condolences,> Goto told him. <In appreciation for her son's sacrifice.>

<If you have done so, then you should leave the vixen to her grief,> Azarin said reasonably. <After all, you mean not to bring her anymore pain than she must already endure, yes?>

Goto glared at him, but the other villagers in his group looked distinctly uncomfortable with the direction their visit had gone. Azarin's words had cut straight to the heart of that awkwardness, making them feel guilty for remaining.

<Uncle, he is quite right,> Posha told Goto gently. <We meant well, but this is becoming its own source of pain.>

Goto looked around and saw he had no more allies in the group. He took a breath and cleared his throat.

<Very well,> he said. <We shall leave these here for you,> he told Basilla.

<Your generosity is appreciated,> Alacea told him stiffly.

<Of course,> Goto replied. He bowed to Basilla, and the group, after depositing the gifts near Basilla's door, turned and walked away.

Azarin watched them go before approaching the door.

<Thank you, Brother, for your aid,> Alacea told him in relief.

<You are welcome,> Azarin said. He bowed to Basilla. <Basilla, I came to tell you how sorry I am.>

<Thank you, Azarin,> Basilla replied.

Azarin saw Warren there and realized that Goto had interrupted something even before he arrived.

<I do not wish to interrupt,> he announced with a bow. <I shall pray for Turean and for you.>

Basilla bowed. <Thank you.>

<Thank you, Brother.>

They watched as Azarin walked away, and Alacea turned to Basilla and Warren. <Come,> she said. <Let us eat soup and remember the Turean we knew.>

* * *

As Azarin made his way up the hill toward the incomplete house he was building for his sister, he sensed movement and froze. He strained his ears and heard the barest sound of breath several feet to his right. The former commando relaxed as he recognized it.

<You should not try to surprise a commando,> he said casually as he continued toward the house. <Most of us do not consider it enjoyable.>

<I apologize,> a familiar voice said as the bushes near the house rustled. Azarin looked over and saw a flash of red as Bao Sen stepped into view. <I was not sure you would want to be seen with me.>

<Nonsense,> Azarin replied. <My friends' daughter and sister is always welcome in my eyes.>

Bao Sen's ears twitched in relief.

Azarin gestured to her head. <You changed your hair again,> he noted.

The Huntress's hand went up to the back of her head. Thanks to Ramirez's friends, the rough chop job she had done with her hunting knife had been replaced with an inverted bob. It still stuck out as being short, but at least it looked like it had been a style choice.

<Yes,> she said. <It is a new style for Huntresses.>

<So I've heard,> he said as he stepped through the still doorless entryway to the house. <Would you like some *mura*?>

<Thank you,> she said, stepping into the house after him. The incomplete house was lit by water lamps placed in the corners. Two saw-horses sat nearby next to a pile of lumber ready to be cut and nailed into place.

He poured some *mura* from a small jug into a wooden cup and handed it to her, taking his own pull from the jug itself.

<Why are you here?> he asked with his own typical frankness.

<I came to apologize,> she said before taking a sip from her cup.

<For what?>

<I know my brother was trying to set up a marriage between us,> she said. <He recently said you had rejected the proposal. I assume it was because of what happened in the *aderen*.>

Azarin took a breath as he realized what she was talking about. Dan Huun *had* approached him a couple of days ago to seriously inquire if he had any interest in joining their two families, and he had politely declined.

<Is that what your brother said?> Azarin asked her.

<Not as a certainty,> Bao Sen told him. <But he seemed to assume so. I regret if my actions made such a thing inconvenient.>

<It had nothing to do with that,> Azarin assured her. <What you did for Alzoria... I would have done the same for any of my commandos.>

<Thank you,> Bao Sen told him.

Azarin studied the Huntress for a moment before asking. <Are you disappointed I declined?> he asked.

Her tail thumped the wood floor in embarrassment. <Not... truly,> she said cautiously. <Were the situation reversed, however, I would not have so quickly declined.>

Azarin silently kicked himself as he realized the mistake he had made. By immediately shutting Dan Huun's suggestion down, he had made Bao Sen wonder if there was something wrong with her. He had never considered the Huntress a particularly insecure vixen before, but he imagined such a curt rejection might wound any vixen's pride.

<You are a fine vixen,> he said. <My answer to your brother had nothing to do with you. I am simply not prepared to marry anyone.>

<May I ask why?> she prodded, genuinely curious. Despite the tod's modesty, Bao Sen knew the vixens of Pelle, along with quite a few from Garan'Sel, thought highly of Azarin and most would not reject him if he showed up to take them.

He thought about her question for a few seconds.

<No,> he finally answered.

<I see,> Bao Sen said, taking a sip from her cup.

<How is Alzoria?> he asked, trying to change the subject.

<Doing much better,> she replied. <I hate to have to admit it, but Rahmeeraz is a much better tod than some tods I know.>

<I know how you feel,> Azarin told her. <The Dark Ones... are not what we were told they were.>

She considered his statement carefully. <There have been times that I have felt the same,> she replied noncommittally.

<I think it important that we judge by the facts we see rather than those that have been presented to us,> Azarin said, once again very careful not to say anything... heretical.

Bao Sen finished her *mura* and put the cup down on the floor. <Thank you for the drink,> she said. <I take my leave.>

<A blessed evening to you, then,> he told her.

<And to you.>

He watched her walk out the door and into the brush, avoiding the road completely. A few seconds later, he could detect no sign of her. He grunted in respect. Her brothers, Hunters all, had all shown similar proficiency in stealthy movement.

Not that it had done them much good in the end.

It wasn't but a few minutes later that he heard more movement coming his way, but, unlike Bao Sen, this visitor may as well have come singing a marching song. He looked out the door and saw his brother approaching the house.

<Greetings, Brother,> he said casually, taking another pull from the *mura* jug.

<Blessed evening,> Ben said, stopping outside the door and looking in. <Forgive please. Not much able to help in recents.>

<Have you come to help now?> Azarin asked, one ear folding down in thought.

<Some,> Ben said. <Need think. Hammer time help think.>

<I see,> Azarin replied. <Would you like some *mura*?> he asked, holding the jug out.

Ben shook his head. With everything happening he didn't want to be caught under the influence should an emergency occur. <No. Thanks be to you.>

<You didn't come here to think,> Azarin told him. <What is it you want to ask me?>

Ben was silent for several moments. He had hoped to be a little more subtle, to let the topic come up naturally. But his brother-in-law was a little more on-the-ball than he would have liked.

<You believe Turean meant attack for us?> he asked.

Ben had heard what Alacea, Kasshas, Yasuren and Tasshas had said, but all of them had different motivations, different places from which their points of view were formed. For some reason, he felt that Azarin would give him a more concrete answer.

He was right.

<No,> Azarin told him simply, taking another pull from the jug.

<Why?> Ben asked.

<Because he knew you,> Azarin said, turning his single eye toward the Ranger. <He knew you were not monsters. He knew you as people. He was not the kind to betray people.>

Ben thought about this. <His father die in war,> he pointed out.

<I knew his father,> Azarin told him. <He was worth more than some pipes. Turean would have felt the same way. If he wanted revenge, this would be a much different visit.> He turned to Ben. <It is more likely that Turean would have tried to stop an attack than to lead one.>

Ben silently digested this.

<Who then?> he asked Azarin.

<Are you asking me to tell you who you should punish?> Azarin asked.

<I ask for you to help before bad thing becomes big bad thing,> Ben replied. <I tell you I did not want again war. Some want again war. Help me stop.>

<How?> Azarin asked. <What would you have me do? Stand up at an *aderen* and tell everyone the Dark Ones are our friends now?> He looked Ben in the eye. <I've spoken with the Garan'Sel villagers. I know what happened there. They are *entitled* to their hatred. Do you think they would believe me?>

Ben turned away and let out an exasperated breath. <You can hate someone,> he said slowly, making sure he got the words right. <And you can live beside them also. Alacea tell you I have Myorin before she?>

Azarin's ears popped up. <She did not.>

<She die,> Ben said. <Va'Shen kill her. Many others die by side her.> He turned around and sat down on the front step. <When I meet Alacea, Alacea try say she kill my Myorin. Say to make me angry. Make me hate Alacea. Say so I kill her. Not kill Pelle people.>

The commando listened intently, never having heard this story about his sister and her alien husband.

<She say that to me,> Ben continued. <And I want to kill her. Feel hate.> He turned and looked Azarin in the eye. <However but... not make things good again.>

<There are many stories like that one,> Azarin commented. <Nothing makes things right in the end.>

<Then just make better,> Ben begged him.

* * *

Tenzeta pulled the cloak tighter around herself as she walked down the road that ran through the Garan'Sel Quarter. Clouds covered the sky, blocking out the usual aurora that offered some illumination this late at night. There were a few sprinkles of rain here and there, and the Mikorin was grateful for them. It meant less people would be outside.

It had taken weeks to find out who it was that made the Na'Sha's "medicine." She knew it wasn't the Garan'Sel healer. For some time, she suspected Pelle's healer, Kastia, had been making it for her out of ignorance. One night she saw Wenlin going out long after everyone was asleep. Seizing on a hunch, Tenzeta followed her. She was no Huntress, but neither was Wenlin, and she didn't seem to suspect that she was being followed.

When she stopped outside Goto's home, Tenzeta wasn't sure what to think. But sneaking closer, she overheard Wenlin speaking, not to the miner, but his niece, Posha.

The vixen from the city, the one who never really seemed to fit in with the rest of the village, knew how to make a potion that deadened the Na'Sha's emotions. At her age, it was an amazing feat.

A feat on which Tenzeta intended to confront her.

At least, that was her initial desire. She wanted to commit violence on this idiot vixen for what she had done to Wenlin. It didn't matter if Wenlin was asking her. It didn't matter that she thought it was helping the Na'Sha. Tenzeta had watched as more and more of her friend began to fade, replaced by a vixen made of stone, whose tail and ears never moved.

But the nightmares stopped her.

Not hers.

Those of the Mikorin Zaishin. The first night she intended to go and face Posha, she was stopped as she passed by one of the Mikorin's rooms. The cries and hiccups from inside made her stop and enter, and she ended up spending several hours with the vixen trying to comfort her.

Sora root, the ingredient she had been adding to their soup to make them sleep worked very well. But its effect faded over time. What did not fade were the intense feelings of guilt and shame the Mikorin Zaishin were experiencing. All of them had volunteered, but none of them could realistically have known what to expect. Some of their Dark One customers may have been kind, but others weren't. And even a little kindness could not overwrite the shame of what they had done.

They had painted their faces. Practiced looking in a mirror and contorting their faces to match the Dark Ones' expressions. Learned just enough of their language to flatter them. And learned how not to cry out.

That was, thankfully, over. But the wounds in the vixens' souls refused to scab over. And now Tenzeta, once so angry at Posha for what she had done, was now on her way to beg that same vixen for help.

If the drug could deaden Wenlin's fear... perhaps it could deaden shame too.

When she arrived at Posha's home, she hesitated outside the door. She was so preoccupied by what she was doing that she had given no thought to *how* she would do it. What was she supposed to do? Ask for a gallon of drugs like she was ordering a new bucket at the mercantile?

She was about to turn and go when the door suddenly opened, catching Tenzeta in the light coming from the lamps inside. Posha stopped short, looking at the woman with skyward ears. Catching herself, she quickly bowed.

<Tenzeta Ya'Jahar,> she greeted. <A blessed evening.>

<And... And to you, Posha,> Tenzeta said.

<If you have come to see my uncle...>

<No, actually, I would like to see you,> Tenzeta interrupted. <About something you do for the Na'Sha.>

Recognition flashed across the younger vixen's eyes. <I see. Come to the door in the back. I will let you in there.>

Before Tenzeta could reply, the door shut in her face. Relieved that she had managed this first stage without it blowing up in her face, the Mikorin quickly circled the long building and found her way to the rear entrance. As if hearing her footsteps approaching, Posha opened the door and let her inside.

Once inside Posha's room, Tenzeta pulled back her hood and let her ears free. Looking around the small, dimly lit room, the Mikorin saw pestles, glass and clay jars filled with different colored herbs as well as a short row of glass bottles with different types of stoppers. It was hardly the bedroom of a typical young vixen.

<What would you ask of me, Honored Ya'Jahar?> Posha asked respectfully.

Tenzeta took another cautious look around, suddenly hesitant. <You make a potion for the Na'Sha,> she said, half question, half accusation. <One that deadens her emotions.>

Posha regarded Tenzeta carefully, as if unsure of the footing over an icy lake before taking a first step. <I do,> she admitted, believing it better to speak the truth to a Mikorin than attempt to lie.

<I need some as well,> Tenzeta told her.

The younger vixen seemed surprised by the request. <You suffer a similar... er... ailment... as the Na'Sha?> she asked.

<No,> Tenzeta said, her tail suddenly moving about nervously. <It is not for me...>

<It can be dangerous if too much is taken at once,> Posha told her. <I need to know who it is for, how large they are, tod or vixen...>

<It is for eight vixens.>

<*Eight*?!> Posha cried.

<Yes,> Tenzeta said quickly. <They are young vixens from fifteen to twenty years old.>

<Why would so many vixens need such a drug?> Posha demanded.

<I cannot tell you that,> Tenzeta replied firmly.

<Then I cannot make it for you,> Posha told her just as firmly. <It is dangerous.>

<Please, Posha,> Tenzeta begged. <I would not ask if it were not important.>

<What is happening to the Mikorin?> Posha asked her sympathetically. <What evil could have befallen so many of you to need a drug so potent? Tell me. I want to help.>

Tenzeta was silent as she pondered what to do. The Bakery and its true purpose were a closely-guarded secret among the Mikorin. Wenlin had told Alacea about it, yes, but even she understood what might happen if the village at large found out. Such a reaction would undermine the entire purpose of the Bakery in the first place. And so it remained the Mikorins' private shame, shared only with other Mikorin.

But Tenzeta needed help, and she didn't know where else to turn. Wenlin obviously trusted Posha to a certain extent. Perhaps Tenzeta could as well.

<What I am going to tell you,> she said quietly, <Must remain in the strictest of confidence.>

Posha took the Mikorin's hands in her own and gave them a gentle squeeze. <I understand.>

Tenzeta told her everything.

Chapter 14

4 days until contact...

Ben took off his boots, one after the other, and tossed them into the corner of his hooch before falling back on his bed and letting out an exhausted breath. His initial report on the "attack" on FOB Leonard went out with a convoy that passed through that afternoon. In the end, he couldn't say for certain what the motive behind the attack had been or even if it had been an attack. All he could do was give the timeline as he knew it.

In the end, he knew, it would make little difference. Someone at the HQ would take his report, read over it, and add a few numbers into a spreadsheet. Turean, his motives and ambitions, the root causes, the grieving on his side of the fenceline and the Va'Shen's, all of it would be condensed into a few tick marks added to the total of Va'Shen attacks on Coalition bases. If there was anything that would distinguish it from the others, it would be that it was probably the first recorded "Green on Blue" attack to occur on Va'Sh.

But no one would give a thought as to why. It was just another Va'Shen attack.

He put this depressing thought on hold as a slight scratching from his door reached his ears. Sitting up and putting his feet back on the ground, he called out.

<Enter, please.>

The door cracked open, and Alacea peeked her head inside.

<Am I disturbing your rest, Tesho?> she asked.

He shook his head. <No. Please. Enter.>

She entered almost cautiously, pausing to remove her grey leather boots before walking in and standing before him.

<You bothered by coming into this place?> he asked.

<Bothered?> she asked.

<At entrance,> he specified, pointing at the wall in the direction the FOB's main gate was situated. He imagined that, in the aftermath of the attack, the sentries would be on edge and Sergeant Carpenter may have increased the scrutiny he showed Va'Shen visitors.

<No,> she said. <I am known to them. May I sit?> she asked nervously.

<Yes, good,> he replied. He watched as she sat down on the floor opposite of him. She seemed more skittish than normal. <You are well?> he asked.

<Yes, Tesho.>

<Basilla well?> he asked.

<She will be,> Alacea replied. <She has lost much.>

<Yes,> Ben agreed. He paused before asking his next question. <Garan'Sel Mikorin? They are well?>

Alacea knew without asking which Mikorin he was referring to.

<Wenlin's Mikorin and our own are caring for them,> she said. <They have deep scars.>

<You need help? I help? Need things?>

<One of them mentioned a medicine Lady Mina had given them,> she said. <She said it worked well and wondered if they might get more.>

Ben nodded as he remembered Fletcher's report on discovering one of the vixens had contracted herpes. He was glad to hear the medicine that worked so well on humans was also effective on the Va'Shen.

<I make certain you receive,> he said.

<Thank you, Tesho,> Alacea replied. The beautiful alien woman looked away from him, her side-braid falling in front of her shoulder.

<More things?> he asked.

<I... do not want to insult you,> she said.

<Then I will not feel insults,> he told her.

Her ears twitched a faint smile before slowly folding downward. <I spoke to some of them,> she said. <They described their experiences.> She looked up at them. <Is... the matrimonial act really bad for your people?> she asked.

Ben had to think through her words pretty hard. In her nervousness, Alacea had resorted to more formal language.

"Matrimony act?" he thought. *Does... Does she mean sex?*

He cleared his throat. <You mean... um... tod and vixen... make baby act?> he asked stupidly.

The fur on Alacea's ears stiffened, and her tail thumped against the floor. <The way they described it. It sounds... awful.>

Yes, he imagined the Mikorin who had been on the other end of those particular business transactions didn't have very fond memories of it.

<No,> he said simply. <Can be very good.> Trying to think of a way to explain it to an alien woman who was already sheltered enough in how her own species made love, forget humans, he looked up at the ceiling and searched for inspiration.

Finally, he took a breath and looked at her. <Tesho... want give good to myorin... And want give good to tesho... then it is very good,> he said. <When tesho or myorin... um... just want take... just want good for them... not want give good, just want take... it is bad.>

Alacea thought on his words for several moments. <Then... care must be shown by both,> she concluded. <Or it does not work right?>

<Um... yes, good,> he said, thinking she was getting a good grasp on it.

Alacea reached up and took her braid in her hand, rubbing it between her fingers as she thought about it.

<I... am uneducated... in these things,> she admitted quietly. <But... you would show me care, Tesho?>

Ben swallowed back a nervous lump in his throat upon hearing this and struggled to come up with something to say. It wasn't that the topic hadn't come up before. After all, Alacea, at one point, told him that Va'Shen tradition said they had to have a baby sooner rather than later. But even then, the focus on that conversation was more the end result than the act itself.

Alacea was a very beautiful woman, one of the most beautiful Ben had ever seen, human or Va'Shen. And while some people considered sex with the Va'Shen as near the same as sex with an animal, Ben wasn't one of them. As a matter of fact, he had sworn testimony and eye-witness accounts that told him some humans had found sex with a vixen worth paying for.

As for Alacea, she only realized what she had said after she had said it. After hearing such heart-wrenching stories from the Garan'Sel Mikorin, her fear had prompted her to seek some kind of assurance from him. Now that the question had been asked, she felt embarrassed at asking it.

<Will not do,> he said carefully. <Things you do not want do. Promise.>

Alacea looked down at the ground, ashamed that she felt the need for such an assurance in the first place. <Thank you,> she mumbled. After everything that happened between them, it was foolish to think he would harm her or do something that *might* harm her without at least warning her.

A few weeks ago, she was getting her first nip from this man. With everything happening, she never did get an opportunity to nip him back.

<Myorin...>

She looked up at the change in her Tesho's tone. He sounded much more solemn than before, but also uncertain.

<Yes, Tesho?> she asked.

<You know... we are not the Dark Things. Yes?>

Alacea said nothing. She had heard about the argument that had erupted between Hestean and Azarin in Patricia's presence. She had managed to console her fellow Mikorin and make a convincing argument that there were any number of innocent explanations.

<Dark *Ones,*> she corrected.

<Dark *Ones,*> he repeated.

<And yes... I know you are not them.>

<Why you think not?> he asked, curious.

She thought carefully about how to reply. <When Voro captured me,> she said, looking up at him, <There were many things you could have done, things a true Dark One would have done in your place.> She paused for a moment, shyly looking away from him. <No Dark One would have come after me,> she continued. <No Dark One... would have treated my wounds... or carried me home even as he suffered.>

Ben listened and found himself almost blushing like a schoolboy at her words.

But when she looked back at him, her eyes and ears told him she was deathly serious. <I do not know how this... error... occurred, Tesho,> she said. <But you must not take lightly the meaning the Emperor's word has for us. I, myself, have prayed long and hard over what this means, and I still remain greatly concerned.>

He tried to find something to say to that, something that might alleviate her concern. But with his limited Va'Shen language skills, the best he could do was...

<It be well.>

Alacea looked at him, her right ear turned downward like an arched eyebrow on a human. She rose to her feet. <It is late, Tesho. I must go.>

He started to stand in order to show her out, but stopped as her hands went to his shoulders, holding him in place. Looking up at her, he found her staring down at him, her tail thrashing about.

In a flash of movement, she suddenly bent down and bit his left ear, causing him to cry out. His hand went to his ear, but before he could say anything, she was already out the door and gone. He looked at the bit of blood on his fingers.

"What the..."

He looked at the half-open door and smiled as he remembered their moment in the garden, the last time she had run away from him. Shaking his head, he stood up and went to the door, closing it.

Sometimes, Alacea was just too damn cute, he thought.

* * *

Once again, Tenzeta found herself lurking around the Garan'Sel Quarter of Pelle in the middle of the night. Three days had passed since she had met Posha and requested the medicine for the Mikorin Zaishin. Upon hearing the Mikorin's story of why the medicine was needed, Posha, shocked to her core, had agreed to make a large enough supply for the suffering vixens, but it would take time. She told Tenzeta to return in three days, and she would have enough made.

Tenzeta was not sure how much "enough" would be, but she hoped it was compact enough for her to bring it back to the bakery in one trip. She could not ask anyone else to help her carry it, and the more trips she made, the more likely it would be that she would be spotted and asked uncomfortable questions.

Even now she was worried. The night was cloudless and The Blessing and the two moons of Va'Sh shone brightly overhead, illuminating the street in a bright enough green glow to cast shadows on the ground. To this end, Tenzeta remained near the walls of buildings, using the natural Va'Shen skill of stealth to conceal her movements.

Posha's home was in sight. There were no lights on, and she easily circled around to the back, approaching the rear door silently. When she arrived, she reached up and gently scratched at the door.

The door opened, and Tenzeta stepped into the dimly lit room to find Posha standing on the opposite side of the room near her worktable. It took a moment before Tenzeta realized that, from her position, the aqua-haired vixen could not have opened the door. It only dawned on her when the door shut behind her and she turned to see a tall, brown-haired and grim-faced tod staring down at her.

She turned again as the door that led to the living area of the house opened, and Goto and two other tods entered the room. Shocked, Tenzeta looked to Posha, who looked down at the floor in shame.

<I am sorry, Ya'Jahar,> Posha said quietly. <I could not remain silent about such a horrendous crime. Please forgive me.>

Tenzeta turned to Goto to demand to know what he was doing when the tod behind her took her shoulders in an iron grip and immobilized her.

Goto, his ears digging into his scalp in fury, stared at her as if trying to look through her.

<Let us speak, Honored Ya'Jahar,> he growled.

* * *

Alacea looked up from her place of honor at the end of the *aderen's* oval as Wenlin entered the room and walked straight toward her, the skirt of her green and white hanbok rippling as she walked. It was not the patient and graceful glide Mikorin typically strove for, and it made Alacea immediately think that something must be wrong.

She and Hestean had been the first to arrive, a perk of holding the community meetings within the temple, though she was still in the dark as to the nature of the meeting. Yasuren had come to her and said that Goto had requested an emergency meeting of the *aderen* but gave no details. She didn't know what the prickly tod wanted now, but Alacea, so far, had not been impressed by him. He seemed to *want* conflict, to root for it and was constantly seeking ways to give it form.

Wenlin approached her and, instead of taking her seat next to Alacea, looked down at the other Na'Sha instead.

<Alacea Na'Sha,> she began. <Have you spoken to Tenzeta today? Is she, by chance, in your temple?>

Alacea's ears popped up in surprise at the question. <I have not seen the Ya'Jahar,> she said. <I am afraid we have had very little to speak of. It is possible, however, that she is working together with Sho Nan on some issue. Shall I call her?>

<If you would, please,> Wenlin said, her tail moving about in concern. <It is not like her to disappear without telling anyone.>

Alacea rose to her feet and beckoned for the other Mikorin to follow her. The two headed for the doorway that led further into the temple. <Tenzeta seems a very responsible Ya'Jahar. I am sure whatever she is doing is quite important.>

Wenlin didn't reply immediately. When she did, her voice was quiet. <She is my friend,> she shared. <She cares for our Zaishin,> she added in a whisper. <I do not know what I would do without her.>

The two entered the kitchen where Sho Nan was preparing dinner for the Mikorin. Seeing the two Na'Shas, she turned away from the humongous stewpot and bowed to them.

<Greetings, Na'Shas,> she said. <How may I serve?>

<Sho Nan, have you seen Tenzeta today?> Alacea asked her.

<I have not,> Sho Nan answered curtly. The blue-haired priestess was still somewhat miffed at having been refused entry into the Garan'Sel's bakery. Alacea had been unable to tell her the truth about the place. Among the Pelle Mikorin, the less who knew, the better. She did not want to put Sho Nan into the uncomfortable

position of knowing such a secret if it was not necessary. She had asked Sho Nan to let the bakery matter rest, and she had. But Sho Nan liked to hold a grudge.

Wenlin's tail moved a little faster as her worry shifted up into a higher gear. Alacea rested her hand on the young vixen's shoulder.

<After the *aderen*, we shall all go and look for her,> she assured the Na'Sha. She turned back to Sho Nan. <Thank you, Sho Nan.>

Sho Nan bowed in response and returned to her cooking while Alacea and Wenlin left the kitchen.

<How have you been feeling?> Alacea asked as they made their way back to the meeting hall. The priestess's tone carried a little extra weight with this question. She was still unnerved by the way Wenlin could seem like a normal vixen one moment and then become like a heartless marionette the next. It seemed that, for the moment anyway, Alacea was speaking to the former.

<I am well, Na'Sha,> Wenlin told her. A moment later, Wenlin stopped walking, prompting Alacea to do the same. They were almost to the doors to the meeting hall. <Alacea,> she continued with some trepidation. <I... cannot thank you enough for your support.>

<My Tesho has done more than I have,> Alacea told her, trying to deflect gratitude she did not feel she had earned.

<Without you, I do not believe he would have helped us at all,> Wenlin told her, aware that she was being somewhat insulting, but it was what she believed.

<I do not believe that to be true,> Alacea told her diplomatically. <Wenlin... I know you and your people have suffered greatly. And I know it will take time before you learn what we in Pelle have. But I promise you that one day you *and* your Mikorin will see happier days.>

<I want to believe that to be true,> Wenlin told her. <And if it happens, it will be in no small part thanks to your efforts.>

Alacea's ears twitched a smile. <Come,> she said, holding her hand out to her friend. <Let us attend the *aderen* and then search for your friend.>

Wenlin took her hand, and the two entered the meeting hall. More of the community's leaders had arrived, and the assigned spaces were quickly filling.

Hestean saw them enter and made her way to them. <Na'Shas,> she said with a quick bow in greeting.

<Blessed evening, Hestean,> Alacea said.

<Kastia asked me to inform you that she would not be able to attend,> Hestean said. <Young Horas has a fever, so she is at their home tending to him.>

<I see,> Alacea said. <I will be sure to pass on anything she needs to know. Anything else?>

<By chance, Na'Sha, do you know what this is about?> Hestean asked. <It is all quite... unsettling.>

It was Wenlin who answered this time. <Goto has called this meeting,> she said. <Which means, I am sure, he has discovered someone has not been sufficiently pious or patriotic for his liking.>

Alacea felt a growl form in her throat. Ever since the episode outside Basilla's house, the priestess had decided to be much more wary of the old miner. The fact that he had managed to gather so many people to accompany him to Basilla's home that day worried her, however. If Goto wanted to be belligerent and unreasonable, that was one thing. But to lead others into belligerence was something else entirely.

She looked out at the group and found Goto speaking to Kasshas, who did not look pleased. Alacea thought the chieftain may have been pressing Goto for a reason he called this *aderen*, and Goto was refusing to elaborate.

It didn't matter much anyway as now that everyone had arrived, it was time to begin. Alacea and Wenlin took their seats at the head of the oval while everyone else sat down.

At the other end of the oval, Kasshas looked up at Alacea and began the ceremonies. <We shall begin the *aderen*,> he said. <Alacea Na'Sha, Wenlin Na'Sha, how do the Gods see our community?>

The two Mikorin rose and bowed. <The sun shines. The water is clean. Our people are healthy. They see us with love in their hearts,> Alacea told him.

<Then let us serve our community,> Kasshas replied. He turned to Goto. <Goto of the Miners has requested this emergency meeting. I now ask him to speak.>

Goto stood up and adjusted his white and black monpei. Alacea watched him warily as he stepped into the middle of the oval and looked around the meeting hall as if taking attendance. His eyes fell on Alacea and Wenlin and froze there for a moment before he began to speak.

<Community leaders of Garan'Sel and Pelle,> he began. <I have called us together this evening to share with you information I have found that a horrendous crime has taken place within our community.>

Tails swished back and forth but without urgency. By now most knew of Goto's penchant for hyperbole.

<Not long ago I stood before you and warned you of the Dark Ones' wickedness and their targeting of our vixens,> Goto went on. <But not even I fully appreciated the extent of the insult and damage they were prepared to do.> He turned to the Na'Shas. <For I have learned that the Dark One soldiers have been violating the virtue of our Mikorin.>

Alacea's ears popped up as the members of the *aderen* cried out in shock at this accusation. She looked to her left and found Wenlin staring at Goto fearfully, her hands, folded in her lap, were shaking uncontrollably.

Kasshas stood up from his spot at the head of the *aderen*. <If you are referring to the Overlord's marriage to our Na'Sha...>

Goto angrily cut him off. <No!> he snapped. <Though that violation is enough to turn the ears of any Va'Shen... What I have discovered is much worse. Our Mikorin... our beautiful and chaste representatives of our community before the Gods... have been selling their bodies to the Dark Ones in a misguided attempt to purchase peace and stability.>

It was Yasuren who now stood up to challenge the miner. <These charges are incredibly explosive,> she chided. <I hope you have more evidence to show than to simply ask us to accept your word.>

<That I do,> Goto growled. He raised his voice and called to the entrance. <Bring her!>

The *aderen* erupted as the doors opened and Tenzeta entered, flanked by four Garan'Sel miners... four Garan'Sel miners armed with hardlight rifles.

Alacea stood up. <How dare you!?> she cried. <How *dare you* bring weapons into the *aderen*?!>

<These tods are armed for our protection!> Goto replied, not to Alacea, but to the other members of the *aderen*. <For now that their secret is exposed, we face incredible peril!>

<Tenzeta,> Wenlin whispered in a hiccup.

The Ya'Jahar, who did not appear to have been physically harmed, looked down at the floor. <I am sorry, Wenlin,> she croaked. <I had no choice.>

Goto raised his hands, and as if a dog obeying its master, the *aderen* fell silent.

<Tell them,> he instructed Tenzeta. <Tell them what you told us.>

Tenzeta looked to Wenlin in fear, and the Garan'Sel Na'Sha looked down at her lap in shame. Her hand slowly went to the pocket of her hanbok.

<Please, Tenzeta Ya'Jahar,> Kasshas prompted. <If you can provide evidence, you are obligated to the community to do so.>

Tenzeta took a breath and shut her eyes. <The Dark Ones... were beginning to prey upon our vixens,> she said. <They would... harass them... or attempt to convince them to be alone with them... One was assaulted, and a group of tods beat the Dark One to near death.> She paused and looked around at the shocked Pelle villagers, who had never experienced such things since their occupation began. <The situation was becoming dangerous for the entire village, so...> She stopped and looked at Wenlin, begging the young woman with her eyes for forgiveness. <So... the Mikorin asked for volunteers... to give themselves to sate the Dark Ones' lusts... in exchange for restraint against the other village vixens.>

The *aderen* erupted in angry shouts. Some refused to believe what they were hearing. Others took it as the final evidence they needed to justify their continuing resistance against the human invaders.

<How many?> Goto prompted Tenzeta, his tone harsh.

Tenzeta swallowed. <Eight,> she replied.

Kasshas stood up and called for silence, and the community leaders gradually calmed down enough for his voice to be heard.

<Alacea Na'Sha, Wenlin Na'Sha... Is this true?> he asked.

Wenlin stood up, her tail trembling as if gripped in a cold terror. She would not look up into the eyes of her community as she responded.

<It is true,> she whispered.

The shouting began again as a wave of fury began to swell and crest over the attendees. Seeing this, Alacea stood up and threw herself into the fray.

<The story is incomplete!> she cried.

Hearing her speak, the Pelle villagers in the hall quieted down, but it took a few moments before the Garan'Sel villagers would.

<The story is incomplete,> she repeated.

<How so?> Goto challenged her. <Oh!> he said as if some great truth had suddenly occurred to him. <You must mean that once we arrived in the domain of your *master*, the selling of our Mikorin stopped, correct?>

Alacea froze, realizing she had walked into a trap.

<Except it did *not* stop,> Goto hissed. <It continued!>

Every eye turned to Alacea, waiting for her to counter Goto's argument. The priestess rolled her shoulders and steadied herself.

<It continued,> she admitted.

Half the crowd erupted, the Garan'Sel half. The other half, the one made up of Pelle villagers, were shocked into total silence at the admission. Alacea pressed into the storm once again.

<Until my Tesho learned of it!> she shouted. <And it was he who ended it!>

But by now no one could... or would... hear her.

Goto raised his arms over his head, bidding for quiet again. <We now see what our community has been forced to endure,> he said. <We now see the futility behind our own cowardice! Had we continued to fight, as some of us had in Garan'Sel, as the hero Turean fought here, this may have been averted!>

Alacea heard the crack of glass breaking and turned her head to the sound. Wenlin still stood there, her eyes cast downward, and in her right hand a mixture of blood and some green substance leaked between her fingers and onto the meeting hall's polished wood floor.

<We! Must! FIGHT!> Goto loudly proclaimed. <Until this injustice is accounted for!> He turned to Wenlin and addressed her directly, a hush falling over the room. <Wenlin Na'Sha,> he said gently. <I cannot imagine what you and your Mikorin have gone

through. But surely you must see now that your efforts to buy peace have failed.>

Wenlin grit her teeth at the accusation.

<I now ask you for your sanction,> Goto announced. <Give the community the Na'Sha's blessing to bring the people together and fight the Dark Ones as one!>

<We are loyal subjects of the Emperor!> Alacea angrily cried. <We are bound by his orders, and his orders are *to cooperate!*>

Goto turned on her like an angry *toka*. <I am not speaking to the Overlord's pet!> he thundered.

Several of the Pelle villagers hissed at Goto. In the corner of her eye, she saw Azarin, sitting behind his foster father, tensing as if ready to leap on the man.

Goto ignored them, turning back to Wenlin. <You have failed,> he told her. <But there is time to make it right. Give us your sanction. Lead us in this fight. We will drive the Dark Ones from this place and bring your Mikorin justice!>

The eyes that were on Alacea before now turned to Wenlin. The young vixen stood frozen for a few moments before taking a breath.

<Alacea,> she whispered, catching the other Na'Sha's attention. <Forgive me. I must make this right.>

<Wenlin,> Alacea breathed. <Please...>

The Garan'Sel Na'Sha stepped into the oval, and Goto's ears fluttered in victory. He raised his hands in prayer, prepared to accept the Na'Sha's sanction and approval from the Gods that his cause was just.

Wenlin approached and stood before him. She was a head shorter than the miner, and she had to look up to see his face, his eyes closed in solemn prayer.

<May the Gods forgive me,> Wenlin whispered.

Without another word, her right hand flashed upward and across Goto's throat, the broken glass from the medicine vial opening a gash in the tod's neck that he immediately and futiley tried to close with his hands. Red blood gushed from between his fingers as he fell to his knees in front of Wenlin, looking up at her in complete shock at what she had done. He tried to speak, but only a faint burbling could be heard as blood bubbled up to his lips.

A vixen screamed, and as if it were a signal, someone from behind the oval dived at one of Goto's armed entourage. The sharp hums of hardlight rifles began to fill the meeting hall as the armed tods reflexively tried to protect themselves.

Alacea took a step forward after Wenlin, but she was tackled to the ground.

<Stay down!> Azarin hissed into her ears.

There were a few more shots, many more screams, and then silence. It had all lasted only a few seconds, but when Azarin lifted himself off her, Alacea was presented with a horrific scene.

Many of the attendees had fled the room. A few remained, shocked into paralysis or standing over the dead or unconscious bodies of Goto's bodyguards. Tasshas stood over one of them, the tod's hardlight rifle in his hands.

Alacea looked to the center of the oval and saw Wenlin laying facedown next to Goto's still-bleeding body. She crawled on her hands and knees to her, not even bothering to take the time to stand up.

<Wenlin!> she cried. <Wenlin!> Taking the woman by the arm, she rolled the other Na'Sha onto her back. Wenlin's dead eyes stared up at her, a neat, nearly completely cauterized hole dripping a tiny amount of blood from above her right eye.

<Wenlin!> Alacea heard someone cry, and a moment later Tenzeta was kneeling next to her, holding her friend's body in her arms and wailing.

Alacea looked at the dead Mikorin for another moment before looking up and seeing many more tods and vixens on the ground, moaning in pain.

<Kastia,> she whispered. <We need Kastia!> She stood up and rushed to the nearest wounded tod, a merchant who ran a feed shop in the village. <Hestean!> she cried. <Fetch Kastia! We need her!> Another tod came and started to help the man. She turned to shout again, to make sure Hestean had heard her. <Heste...>

She broke off as her eyes went to where the Aru'Dace usually sat. She saw someone lying face up on the ground there, their legs slowly moving as if trying to climb back up.

<Hestean!> Alacea screamed. She rushed to her friend's side, followed a moment later by Azarin, who leapt over fallen bodies from the other side of the room to get there.

Alacea knelt next to the blue-haired woman. Hestean looked back up at her, her breathing coming in rapid gasps.

<N... Na'Sha...> she gasped out.

<Don't talk,> Azarin ordered as he checked her over. There was a burnt hole the size of a quarter in her midsection, an almost textbook perfect shot. <Just breathe, Hestean,> he said, his trembling voice now beginning to betray just how badly the woman had been hurt.

By now, Mikorin from within the temple led by Sho Nan had rushed in, stopping at the gory sight that met them.

<Sho Nan!> Alacea screamed. <Find Kastia!>

The other Mikorin didn't reply, instead racing out the door to search for the healer.

Alacea turned back to Hestean, whose breathing was becoming faster and unsteady. She squeezed her friend's hand.

<Just look at me, Hestean,> Alacea begged. <Kastia will come and take care of you. Just wait.>

Hestean's eyes turned to Azarin, who looked down at her in hopeless worry. The Mikorin released Alacea's hand and reached over, taking Azarin's right hand instead.

Azarin let her take his hand, squeezing it gently, unable to say anything.

Hestean squeezed his hand and then pulled it up to her lips. Putting the fleshy part of his palm between her teeth, she bit down as hard as the weakening woman could, until two tiny rivulets of blood dripped onto her lips.

Azarin stared down at her in complete shock. <Hestean...>

She released his hand and let her head fall back to the floor.

<I shall... await you... in... the Glade... Tesho...> she breathed to him.

And then she stopped.

<Hestean?> Alacea whimpered. <Hestean?!> she cried. Getting no response, the Na'Sha began to wail and hiccup, burying her face into her fallen friend's chest.

Azarin stared down at her for several moments and then climbed to his feet. Turning, he found Tasshas standing there, his ears bent backwards in grief.

<Azarin,> he said. <I am sorry...>

The carpenter said nothing. He surveyed the scene with his good eye before looking back at his friend.

<You have their rifles?> he asked.

<Yes,> Tasshas confirmed.

<Who are our four best remaining marksmen?> Azarin asked.

Tasshas didn't respond immediately, not sure what it was exactly his friend expected to do with that information.

<Corporal!> Azarin prompted in a furious hiss.

<Um... Portas... Konoro... Deshin and Webas, Captain,> Tasshas answered, reflexively addressing his friend by his military rank.

By this point, Kasshas had joined them. Yasuren was tending to a wounded vixen nearby.

<Give a rifle to each and have them position themselves on the roofs of houses near the entrances to the village,> Azarin ordered. <If a Garan'Sel villager attempts to leave and one of us isn't with them, shoot them.>

<Azarin?> Kasshas gasped.

<Shoot them,> Azarin repeated.

<What do you intend to do, Azarin?> Kasshas demanded.

<I am going to cut out this disease,> Azarin told him quietly. <Tonight. I need the portrait of the Emperor you have in your home, Chieftain.> Without waiting for an answer he turned to Tasshas again. <Once those riflemen are in place, assemble the commando in the plaza. As many as you can find in one hour.>

<Yes, Captain,> Tasshas said. The commando turned and bade two other tods holding rifles to follow him.

<Azarin, what are you going to do?> Kasshas asked again.

<Chieftain,> Azarin began, turning to him. <I am going to take the commando into the village, and I am going to make every Garan'Sel villager swear on the Emperor's visage to submit to the Dark Ones. And anyone who doesn't, I intend to shoot.>

Kasshas was shocked back a step. <You would do that?> he asked in a haunted whisper.

<Look around you,> Azarin told him. <You *will* see this scene again if we do not excise this tumor in our community now. If we do not do it, the Dark Ones eventually will themselves, and when that happens Pelle will become the same nightmare Garan'Sel did.>

Kasshas looked back toward his wife, who had overheard everything. Her tail thumped against the floor twice. Yasuren was a noblevixen, trained from birth to know when to make hard decisions.

He turned back to Azarin. <You will need the Na'Sha's sanction,> he reminded him quietly. <Otherwise, the community may split further.>

Azarin slowly turned to his sister, who was still hiccupping over Hestean's body.

<Na'Sha,> he began quietly.

<You have my sanction,> Alacea told him, not even looking up at him. <The war is over. I will lose no more of our community to it.>

Azarin turned back to Kasshas, who gave him a short bow. <The commando is yours to command,> he said. <Go with the community's sanction.>

The commando officer started for the door. <I'll be back in an hour,> he said.

<Where are you going?> Kasshas asked.

<To speak to my brother,> Azarin told him.

* * *

Ben was typing up his latest progress report on the overly-hi-tech typewriter an aerospace defense firm back on Earth had built for the DoD on Va'Sh at a million dollars a pop. The sun was beginning to set outside, and he had sent Patricia home for the day, leaving him alone to catch up on some work. A few more paragraphs and he intended to call it a day himself, hit the chow hall, maybe take a walk around the perimeter for some air.

While he typed, his eyes moved up, just for a half-second, at the door. It actually took him a few more moments of typing before he realized that he had seen a silhouette in the doorway. Looking up again, he found Azarin standing there, looking at him, his ears folded down in anger and grief.

Ben warily stood up, not sure what was about to happen and, on instinct, found his right hand slowly dropping to the butt of his pistol.

But Azarin made no offensive moves.

<Azarin?> Ben asked. <Things well?> His tone was cautious. He couldn't say he knew the tod intimately, but he knew him well enough to see that the alien man was not his usual self.

The tod stepped further into the office and stopped a few paces from his human brother-in-law.

<I must speak with you,> Azarin told him.

<Yes, good,> Ben replied cautiously.

<There was violence at the *aderen*,> Azarin said simply. <Many have been hurt. Some have died.>

Ben, as a good Army officer, could have said a hundred different things in response.

Do you need medical assistance?

Is everyone all right?

How can we assist you?

<Alacea well?> he asked instead, his voice only betraying a little of the fear he felt.

<She is well,> Azarin assured him calmly. <The violence came from Garan'Sel villagers who were attempting to gain support to fight you.>

Ben worked through his words in his mind before replying. <I understand.>

<These tods... They accused the Mikorin... and you... of selling Mikorin girls for your men's pleasure,> Azarin said, taking a step forward. <Is it true?>

The Ranger wasn't sure if the truth would cause the former commando to rush forward and stab him, but he knew lying about it would only make it worse.

<Truth,> he said. <They do at Garan'Sel. Come here, they do again. We, Alacea, discover. Make them stop.>

Azarin turned away, considering his brother's words. Alacea had said something similar in the *aderen*, though no one was really listening anymore at that point.

<You need healer help?> Ben asked. <We send healer?>

The commando officer turned his eye to Ben. <No,> he said firmly. He stepped toward the Ranger. <Your people must not leave your base until morning,> he decreed.

Ben's eyes narrowed, unsure if he was being threatened or not. <Why this?> he asked.

But it wasn't a threat. Far from it.

<I am taking the commando into the village,> Azarin told him. <I will make every villager from Garan'Sel stand before the Emperor's image and take the same oath you gave to us.>

<They do not do?> Ben asked, a sinking feeling in his gut.

<I will shoot them,> Azarin replied as casually as if telling Ben what he was having for dinner.

<Cannot let you do,> Ben told him, shaking his head.

Azarin looked at him and let out a breath. <Hestean... is dead,> he told him quietly. <Your myorin, right now, weeps over her body.>

Ben shut his eyes for a moment in sympathy and sadness. He liked Hestean. She had always been kind to them, even in the early days when everyone else looked at them with suspicion.

He reached out and rested his hand on Azarin's shoulder. In that moment, he didn't see Azarin. It was like he was looking at himself. He had been here, where Azarin now stood, the knowledge that someone special to him was now dead still so new as to seem unreal, like a dream. The tod's immediate future was not a bright one. It would be filled with cold nights of self-reproach, guilt, what-ifs, anger, hatred, self-revulsion and a grief that nothing could quite stop.

<I am sorry,> he told the tod quietly.

<I am not asking my Overlord for permission,> Azarin told him firmly. <I am telling my brother what he must do to keep his people and his family safe. Violence has been made against us and more will come if it is not rooted out and dealt with now. This... is not a matter for your people.>

<Cannot let you do,> Ben repeated quietly.

Azarin stepped back, regarding his brother with amused ears. <And what would you do to stop it?> he asked. <You will send your troops to fight us? Imprison us like we were before? You must know there is no way for you to involve your forces without making things worse for them.>

Ben paused, racking his brain for a way to prove his brother wrong, but he couldn't. History was filled with instances of U.S. forces pushing their way into factional conflicts only to end up becoming the targets of both sides. If he sent his Rangers into the village to stop what was about to happen, the would-be insurgents would not be grateful. They would not halt whatever plans they had to attack them. If anything, it would be seen as weakness, and the commandos that Ben had come to know, with whom he had built fragile relationships, would see his actions as a betrayal and resent his interference in their affairs.

There was no good outcome for this. No happy ending. And in war, despite what the vids and video games might show, it was sadly typical. No right or wrong choice. Just bad or worse.

<You once told me that if we betrayed you, if we attacked your people, you would kill us all,> Azarin reminded him. <I believe you. By luck and the will of the Gods, my home never became a battleground. I will not lose it now for the sake of some idiot tods who want to pretend to be commandos. This will end tonight. Do not come between us.>

He turned and started for the door.

<Azarin,> Ben called after him.

The Va'Shen stopped in the doorway but did not look back.

<Be alive,> the Ranger said.

Without another word or even a look, Azarin walked out.

* * *

The two Rangers manning Tower Seven practically jumped to attention when they heard someone climbing up the ladder toward them. Everyone had heard about what happened to the two sentries who had been caught sleeping on duty, and no one wanted to be the next two guys. They weren't sure who was coming. Most likely it was Sergeant Carpenter doing a spot check, but they were surprised to find Captain Gibson stick his head up over the top of the ladder and make his way inside.

"Good evening, Rangers," Ben said.

"Good evening, Sir," the two greeted in return. Neither saluted. As the guard towers were the most likely to be targeted by enemy snipers, it was procedure to not salute anyone inside them, lest they give would-be commando marksmen ideas.

Ben took a look at the village spread out before him. Tower Seven was the closest to Pelle and could give him the best view of what was happening there. Aside from some lit windows, he couldn't see much.

"Anything happening out there?" he asked the sentries.

It had been five hours since he spoke to Azarin. He had confined everyone to base and gave orders to give extra scrutiny to any Va'Shen coming near the fence. Ben had been waiting for news in his office, but when nothing came, he had moved to the TOC. When nothing of note came to the TOC, he decided to try to see for himself what was going on.

One of the sentries, a thin Hispanic specialist named Thompson, answered the question.

"Some sporadic weapons fire," he reported. "A few screams. No contacts near us, Sir."

Ben nodded. Not the massacre he was fearing then. At least... not yet.

He looked over his shoulder at the two men. "You get chow yet?" he asked.

"No, Sir," they both answered.

"Go get something to eat," he ordered. "I'll watch things here."

The two looked at each other, momentarily wondering if this was a trap, but they nodded to the captain in thanks.

"We'll be right back, Sir," Thompson promised.

"No rush," Ben assured them, taking a seat behind the M-270 machine gun.

The two Rangers climbed down the ladder, leaving Ben alone with his thoughts and the village below. He saw a flash from somewhere in the Garan'Sel Quarter, the familiar bluish light that signaled a hardlight rifle being fired from a distance.

He heard the sound of steps on the ladder and prepared himself to chastise the two sentries for rushing back when they didn't have to, but it wasn't a helmeted figure that appeared before him. Patricia was climbing unsteadily into the guard tower with him, taking a moment to dust off her knees and remove her patrol cap.

"Anything big?" she asked.

He shook his head. "Some shooting," he told her. "Not a lot."

She nodded and sat down in the other chair, looking out at the village just as he had.

"It looks peaceful," she commented quietly.

"Sure does."

He had fully briefed Patricia on what was happening and had told her to get some sleep in case they ended up needing to work in shifts. The terp had apparently chosen to ignore that order.

She was looking at him in concern. Taking a nervous breath, as if psyching herself up, she paused a moment before speaking her mind.

"You know this isn't your fault, right?" she asked.

He turned and regarded her for a moment before turning back to the village that was *his* responsibility.

"Isn't it?" he asked. "I could have stopped this."

"Could you have?" she asked. "I mean, seriously? Or could you have just dragged it out longer?"

He gave her question thought. His reasoning for not intervening before still made sense now. But doubt gnawed at him. Maybe it hadn't been a matter of troops. Maybe if he had been able to bring Keyes to some kind of justice, the Garan'Sel villagers would have been appeased. Maybe if he had taken a more hands-on role in the unification between the two villages, he could have headed some of this off before it got to this point.

"It's a Va'Shen problem," Patricia told him firmly. "Just like the attack on Alzoria. It is something *they* have to deal with. The only thing we can do is meddle and make it worse for them." When he didn't reply, her expression softened. "You did everything in your power to keep this from happening. But you can't take away the Va'Shen's agency. They have to be able to solve their own problems. Their way."

"Their way," Ben huffed. "Because it's their culture?" he asked.

Patricia didn't reply. She knew where he was going with this. The culture argument was what Keyes used to justify letting the Mikorin's brothel continue.

"General Walker said something to me," Ben told her. "He said, 'we don't build gallows next to funeral pyres anymore.'"

Patricia's faced scrunched up in confusion. "Is that something we used to do?" she asked.

"He was referencing something that happened in India back when the British were occupying it," Ben explained. "A British general, Charles Napier, learned that it was tradition in his AO that when a man died, his widow would throw herself on his burning funeral pyre. And if she didn't want to, the villagers would throw her on it themselves."

"Holy shit," Patricia replied in awe.

Ben nodded. "Napier ordered the practice discontinued, but the local priests refused. They said it was a part of their cultural traditions, and he had no right to interfere. So, Napier said, 'Fine. Back in Britain, when people burn a woman to death, we hang them. So, you build your pyres, and we'll build our gallows, and we'll both celebrate our traditions together.'" Ben paused before concluding. "The practice stopped."

"Good on him," Patricia remarked.

"Would we do that today?" Ben asked her seriously. "Could we?" he asked. "We preach cultural sensitivity, but is there a point where we say 'no, you're not doing this because it's wrong?'"

Patricia was actually becoming angry at this point. "Stop it," she ordered. "I see what you're doing. You're thinking that because you aren't going down there, guns blazing, you're on the same moral ground as Keyes for letting his people get away with what they did! Well, it's different!"

"Is it?" he asked.

"Yes, it is!" Patricia scolded him. "The difference is that you give a shit, and Keyes didn't. You weighed the options, looked at the consequences of action and inaction, and you made the best call you could under shitty circumstances. You think Keyes sat up at night worrying about what was happening to those vixens? You think he gave one shit about what it would do to their community when word got out?"

Ben looked at her, considering her words.

"Look, I'm just a staff lieutenant," she said. "I'm not some hard-charging, high-speed operator with a thousand battles under my belt, but even I can see the difference between now and then. And if you just need someone to say it, I will. *You did the right thing.*"

The captain took a breath and tapped the butt of the machine gun with his fingers in thought.

"Thanks, Patricia," he said.

The woman smiled. "Anytime, Sir."

"Go get some sleep," ordered. "Just in case this spills over onto us."

"Yes, Sir."

Ben didn't watch her leave, his eyes went back to the village. *What is happening down there?*

* * *

Azarin listened as Tasshas gave his report. The two were in the center of the Garan'Sel quarter, a portrait of the Emperor sitting upon an easel behind them. His commandos would find Garan'Sel villagers, bring them to the center of the quarter whether they wanted to go or not, and Azarin would tell them what had happened and give them a choice.

They could take the oath, or he could shoot them.

Most were taking the oath. The first time a trio of miners were brought to him who had refused, Azarin had taken Tasshas's rifle from his hands and pointed it at the leader's head. He hadn't hesitated and fully intended to follow through on his threat, but in the half second between aiming and activating the trigger, Tasshas had put his hand on the rifle, stopping him.

<It will cause more problems,> Tasshas told him firmly. <We don't have to kill them. We should banish them from the village instead. If they do not want to comply with the will of the community, then they do not have to be a part of it.>

Azarin said nothing. He continued to stare down the barrel of the rifle at the dull-green-haired tod, whose tail had puffed up to three times its size in panic. The tod, who had probably suffered under the humans in Garan'Sel, most likely thought the commando captain had been bluffing. But the cold look in Azarin's eye showed him now that he wasn't.

The captain considered his friend's words. One of the reasons Azarin had made Tasshas his second-in-command was that he knew more about politics than most Va'Shen thanks to his mother's influence. He had the ability to look downriver in time, to see how their actions would impact life in the village a week, a month, a year from now. Tasshas wasn't a weak-hearted tod. If he thought killing these tods was the right thing to do, he would do it without hesitating. That was what made Azarin pause now. Tasshas would not recommend it if he didn't honestly believe it.

The captain slowly raised the rifle, and the three would-be insurgents let out a relieved breath. Azarin turned to one of his nearby commandos and beckoned him over.

<Take these tods to the other side of the bridge and let them go,> he ordered. <If you see them in the village again, kill them.>

<Yes, Captain,> the commando replied. He gestured with his rifle for the three tods to precede him, and they did, not wanting to risk Azarin's wrath by asking him about their belongings or their families. They knew they were getting away with their lives and, even then, just barely.

Some, however, did not. They didn't wait to be brought to Azarin. When they saw the commandos approaching, they had simply fought. Some had bows and rifles and others had only knives. Azarin's orders to his commandos had been simple. If a villager wanted to fight, fight them. It was they, he thought, that had decided it was worth their lives to do so.

<That is most of them,> Tasshas concluded his report. <Should we do the same to our people?> he asked.

Azarin took a breath. Could he do the same to the villagers of Pelle? Force them out at gunpoint and make them take an oath?

Before he could answer that question, two commandos approached with a familiar aqua-haired vixen between them.

Tasshas, thinking this was simply the next villager in line, approached. <Place your hands up in prayer and...>

<Captain, wait please,> one of the commandos, a tod who had served in Dan Huun's corporalship, Able Guardsman Udo, said. <This one is... different.>

Azarin took a step toward them. <Different how?>

Posha said nothing as the two commandos looked at each other. Udo turned to Azarin and answered him.

<When we found her, she was writing a letter,> he said, holding up a piece of parchment.

<Why is that strange?> Azarin asked as Tasshas took the letter from the commando, reading over it.

Udo gestured to Tasshas as if to say, "you'll see," and the captain turned to him.

<We also found glassers in the home, Sir,> the other commando said.

Probably Goto's, Azarin thought.

<Buried under the vixen's bedding.>

One of Azarin's ears folded down at this new information, and he looked at Posha as if suddenly meeting an entirely different person.

<It's gibberish,> Tasshas announced, holding the letter up. <It doesn't say anything.>

Azarin looked at Posha while taking the letter from his friend, a cold ball of steel taking shape in his stomach. He looked over the letter, and his ears began to fold down into his head in anger.

<It's not gibberish,> he said, turning back to the vixen. <It's *code*.>

Tasshas looked at Posha in shock.

Azarin held the letter in front of the vixen's eyes. <Who would a miner's niece be writing coded letters to?> he asked her. Posha said nothing, her ears folded down in absolute rage as her eyes bored into Azarin as if trying to kill him with her gaze.

<But you're not a miner's niece, are you?> Azarin continued. <Are you?> he repeated.

<What do you mean?> Tasshas asked him.

He answered the question as he continued to address Posha. <You are *Dara Tang*... aren't you?> he demanded.

<You are serious?> Tasshas gasped.

<What did you do?> Azarin asked her. <Take the real Posha's place and use Goto to agitate your village into acting against the Dark Ones? Or was he *Dara Tang* too?>

Posha's ears flickered in dry amusement. <Goto,> she said quietly, <Was a convenient idiot. He had the anger, just not the intelligence to do what was necessary.>

<And Turean?> Azarin asked her. <Was he 'convenient' as well?>

The vixen gave him a look of disgust. <Do not presume to judge me,> she growled at him. <Everything I have done, I have done for my Emperor. If you had done the same, my presence would not be necessary in the first place.>

<The Emperor ordered us to cooperate,> Tasshas pointed out.

<And are you the kind of tod who gives his Emperor what he asks for or what he *wants*?> she shot back.

<A convenient philosophy,> Tasshas replied dryly.

<One a coward like you could never understand,> she hissed at him. She turned her scorn on Azarin. <I know about you, collaborator,> she proclaimed. <Your cowardice is already known throughout the capital. Who are you to judge me?>

Azarin knew the answer to that question already. Taking a step forward, his hand moved so fast that no one actually saw him draw the dagger that he plunged into Posha's midsection.

Even she seemed surprised, her eyes going wide and her blue-green ears popping toward the sky. She looked up at the commando who was practically standing on her feet, his hand pushing the knife as far into her as it would go.

<I am tesho to a murdered myorin,> he hissed into her ears. <And I claim Right of Vengeance. Go now and *freeze*.>

He pulled the knife from her, and Posha collapsed in front of him, her hands futilely clutching the bleeding wound, made in the same spot that Hestean had been shot. She looked up at the commandos surrounding her while her hanbok darkened with blood, as if expecting one of them to help her.

Azarin glared down at her. He had watched Va'Shen bleed out before, forced to stand by helplessly while their commando's healer tried to prevent them from dying. He knew about how long it took.

He counted the seconds as Posha bled and shivered as the warmth began to leave her body, refusing to take his eyes off the deceitful agitator until he was sure she would never be able to harm his people again.

She died exactly when he thought she would.

Chapter 15

16 hours until contact…

"Given what you've told me, I don't believe there was anything else you could have done that would not have severely undermined the relationships you had already built," the staticky voice on the other end of the line said. "It was hardly an ideal situation, but I think, culturally speaking, your choice of strategic forbearance was the correct one."

Ben wanted to sigh in relief, but there was still that nagging bit of guilt that told him that letting Azarin run wild would haunt him for the rest of his life, no matter what Dr. Sinclair said.

"Thank you, Doctor," he told the older man over the phone.

Three days had passed since that night. Ben had spent most of them working on the report of the night's events, including what Azarin had told him afterwards. News that the Va'Shen secret police had had an agent in his area of operations was unsettling, but hopefully, now that she was gone, things would return to some semblance of normal.

He had not had a chance to see Alacea in those three days other than a brief meeting he had insisted on to make sure she was unharmed. Hestean and Wenlin's deaths had, of course, affected her deeply. He wanted to console her, to be there for his Myorin, but her duties and his wouldn't allow it. News of, what was essentially, an armed, if mostly peaceful, pogrom taking place in his sector had just about every directorate chief at the CJTF headquarters ringing his phone off the hook, demanding "an update." The commander's office even called, and hearing Keyes's voice on the other side of the line to schedule the tele-meeting made Ben want to throw the phone to the other side of the room.

Then, there were the funerals.

Those who had opposed Azarin as well as Goto and the entourage who had shot up the *aderen* didn't receive one. The Va'Shen attitude was that those villagers had chosen to defy the community's will and so were unworthy of the usual funeral rites.

Apparently, the village didn't have much tolerance for people who cause the death of two Mikorin.

Those two Mikorin, however, received what amounted to a state funeral, one that Ben, Patricia and his senior staff had been invited to attend. Unlike Turean's funeral, Kasshas and Alacea had insisted the humans stand among the rest of the mourners instead of off to the side and out of the way. Ben understood the message that was being sent to anyone among the Garan'Sel who might still be thinking of stirring up trouble. "The humans are part of the community. If you don't like it, leave."

Wenlin and Hestean's bodies had been placed in coffins made of polished purple wood. Vines of red flowers had been weaved into their hair. Even in death, the two vixens looked beautiful and regal. The entirety of both villages had attended, many making the strange hiccupping sounds the Va'Shen made when crying.

And at the head of the group, standing between the two coffins, had been Alacea, her eyes closed and her hands up in prayer. She did not cry. She was the Na'Sha, and her duties to the people and the two dead Mikorin made it impossible for her to submit to her grief and weep for them.

Ben had watched her the entire time, waiting for the moment she might break, the moment she would look to him for help. He had resolved to go to her side and help her if it came to that. He had buried friends. He knew what she was going through.

Once the funeral was over, the bodies of the Mikorin were carried to the top of a hill overlooking the temple and buried. Afterward, Alacea and the rest of the Mikorin disappeared into the temple. Kasshas and Yasuren had told him that the Mikorin would grieve amongst themselves and either determine or welcome the women's successors. As Na'Sha, Wenlin's "successor" would naturally be Alacea. But there was apparently some concern about Runa succeeding Hestean.

And so, with all that, Ben hadn't spent more than fifteen minutes with his alien wife in three days, and to say he was concerned for her was an understatement.

"Captain? Did we get disconnected?"

Ben shook the thoughts away and replied. "Sorry, Doctor. I got distracted for a moment."

"Understandable," Sinclair told him. "I can't imagine things there are exactly run of the mill."

Surprisingly, they were quickly returning that way, but Ben didn't tell Sinclair that.

"How has your research been going?" Ben asked him. "Any luck learning about the Dark Ones?"

"Actually, I have learned some," Sinclair told him. "I followed your advice and went to some temples in the other provinces. At first, I received a very negative reception..."

"Let me guess," Ben said. "You tried telling them we *weren't* the Dark Ones and they acted like you were trying to tell them water wasn't wet."

"Precisely," Sinclair grumbled, and Ben could just see the older man rolling his eyes. "I changed tactics, however, and began to ask what they knew of the Dark Ones, claiming that our knowledge of what happened back then was... um... incomplete."

"Not quite a lie, but not quite the truth," Ben remarked. "Very Va'Shen."

"Isn't it just?" Sinclair bantered. His tone turned serious as he went on, however. "I'll be circulating a complete report as soon as I'm done, but there was one interaction that stood out."

"What was that?" Ben asked.

"One of the Mikorin asked *me* a question," Sinclair said. "She asked me, 'why did your people leave?'"

Ben chewed on that as Sinclair went on.

"It would seem, Captain, that the Va'Shen and 'Great Ones' never actually *defeated* the Dark Ones," Sinclair said. "From what the Mikorin told me, one day they apparently just got into their ships and left. No explanation. No final climactic battle. The Va'Shen woke up one day and watched them go."

"That... is somehow really terrifying," Ben commented.

"Agreed," the cultural advisor said. "I'm not a great expert on war, but usually you don't just up and leave one unless you have something more important to do... or someone more dangerous to face."

"Great," Ben said. "So now there's potentially *three* unknown hostile powers we know nothing about."

"Funny how the universe suddenly got so much smaller, isn't?" Sinclair quipped.

"Doctor," the Ranger replied, "I have a feeling that before long, we're going to start wishing we were alone out here again."

* * *

<Na'Sha, Azarin has arrived.>

Alacea lowered her tea cup and placed it on the small table in front of her. The meeting room she had chosen was small, but warmly lit. This conversation was going to be uncomfortable, and she was looking for any way to make it less so.

<Thank you, Sho Nan,> she said. <Please show him in.>

<Yes, Na'Sha,> Sho Nan replied. Like Alacea, the blue-haired vixen's hanbok was made up of deep reds, the Va'Shen color of mourning. The Mikorin would wear red for the next month in honor of Wenlin and Hestean, after which they would return to wearing

their usual dresses, silently telling the community it was time for life to continue forward.

The blue-haired woman disappeared, and a moment later Azarin stepped into the room. He, too, wore red, but not being as well off as some other Va'Shen, he had to make do with a red shirt and brown trousers.

He bowed to her in respect. <Blessed morning, Alacea Na'Sha,> he told her.

<Blessed morning,> she replied, standing up and giving her own bow. <Thank you for coming to see me.>

Azarin slightly bowed his head again in acknowledgement of her thanks.

She motioned for him to sit, and he knelt at the other side of the table. <I must speak to you first as your Na'Sha,> she told him.

<As you wish,> he replied.

<First, I wanted to inform you that, after much meditation on the matter, I believe you have no reason to feel any guilt about what happened the other night.>

<I feel no guilt,> he told her. <And... I feel all of it as well.>

Alacea's ears bent downward sadly. <To be more specific,> she said, <I mean in regards to your calling forth the commando without permission of the Emperor. Your oath to the Overlord specified as such, did it not?>

<It did,> he told her. <But... am I a tod who gives his Emperor what he asks for... or what he wants?>

<It is my feeling as well,> she said. <In such an emergency, with the approval of the Chieftain, the Na'Sha and the Overlord, it is reasonable to assume the Emperor would have approved of your call to action.>

He bowed to her. <Thank you for your assurance, Na'Sha,> he said formally.

<Second,> she began more hesitantly. <Second... I stress that I am speaking as your Na'Sha, and I ask that you not take offense.>

<I will not,> he promised dryly.

Alacea swallowed and looked down at her reflection in her tea cup. <What Hestean did... on her deathbed... was improper.>

Azarin's eartips pointed to her in interest.

<It is understandable,> Alacea went on quietly. <But... in doing so... she denied you the chance to seek out a myorin... To have a family and children of your own.> She paused a moment, feeling every bit the villain as she spoke of her friend this way. <As such... if you wish for an Exception, I shall apply for one on your behalf. Under the circumstances, I believe it would be granted fully and without conditions.>

The commando cleared his throat, trying to will away the emotions he felt.

<It was the only time in her life she ever did something for herself,> Azarin told her. <And I will not take that from her. She was my Myorin.>

<Even if only for a few moments?> Alacea asked. <Please think carefully, Azarin. I know Hestean would not ask you to deny yourself the chance for happiness just for her sake.>

<'Moments?'> Azarin repeated. He looked down at the table for a few seconds in thought before raising his eye back to her. <No,> he continued quietly. <She was my Myorin.> He pointed at his chest. <In here...> His finger moved to his head. <And in here... She was *always* my Myorin.>

<I understand,> Alacea replied, her voice beginning to break. <I now wish to speak to you as your sister.> This time she didn't wait for his approval. <I am so sorry, Brother!> she cried, letting a soft hiccup escape her throat. <I am so sorry!>

Azarin rounded the table and embraced his sister, and together, the two siblings wept.

* * *

Two more weregoblins crawled out of the holes in the cave floor, bringing the total to twenty. Fighting with their backs to each other, it seemed that the three adventurers were killing one weregoblin just to see two more take its place, and the cavern, which once seemed big enough to play racquetball in, was now much more cramped.

The Dark Knight swung his broadsword down and cleaved another goblin completely in two. Looking up and seeing the odds against them, the tall warrior called out to his friends.

"Okay, guys!" he said. "I'ma use my coupon!"

To his left, his fairy companion zapped another monster with her wand before turning her head to him. "Yor *coupon*?" she asked.

"Yeah," the knight said, swinging his sword again. "Got it in that chest awhile back. One free spell..."

"Dat's a spell scowoll, nawt a coupon!" the fairy corrected him.

"Look!" the knight shot back angrily, "It gives me one free spell without having to spend anything, right?! Coupon!"

To his right, their cleric bashed another weregoblin in the head with her staff. "Wait, wasn't that scroll for a *flare* spell?"

"Oh, do *nawt* use dat in here!" the fairy cried. "Yow'll blind us too!"

"C'mon, what are the odds of that?" the knight asked.

"You have to roll a fifteen or higher to *not* blind us with them!" the cleric shouted.

"I was promised there would be no math," the knight said. "Here I go!"

"Dow't do et!" the fairy yelled.

"FLARE COUPON!"

* * *

The blue twenty-sided die rolled to a stop in the middle of the table, a very distinct white number "1" facing straight up at the ceiling.

Ramirez looked at the die and pursed his lips. "Huh..." he remarked. "That didn't go like I expected it."

"You asshole," Fletcher commented, her eyes narrowing at him.

"YOU FOCKED US ALL!" Burgers cried in his fairy voice.

"Oh c'mon, it's not that bad!" Ramirez cried, turning to the specialist at the end of the table for help.

Specialist Denham, the assigned dungeon master for their game, gave him a disapproving look. "The spell blinds everyone in your party for two turns, and the weregoblins are not affected at all."

"YOU FOCKED US ALL!" Burgers cried again.

"Yep," Ramirez confirmed with a nod. "It sure does seem that way..."

"What you do?"

The four of them all turned to find a familiar, short-haired Va'Shen looking at them from not far away. Over the past several days, Alzoria had grown into her new look, and it almost felt like the hair-cutting incident had never happened. Other Va'Shen in the village sometimes gave her disapproving looks, but many more sympathized with her and commented on how nice her new hairstyle looked whether they personally approved of her relationship with Ramirez or not.

"Oh, hey Alzoria," Ramirez said in greeting. "We're playing a game."

"You are bad at?" she asked him. Sensing the disapproval of the other humans around him, she continued. "You look bad at."

"Yes," Burgers and Fletcher replied in unison.

Ramirez turned and gave his friends an utter look of betrayal.

"Super bad," Burgers added.

"Good," Alzoria declared. "Then you come."

"Come where?" Ramirez asked as he stood up from his chair, the fact that he was going with her seemingly already decided.

"I cook for you," Alzoria said. "You come to my house."

"Oh," Ramirez replied with just a hint of nervousness. "Is your... um... mother going to be there?"

"No!" Alzoria cried angrily. "She told me you teach her 'motherfucker!' I know what that means! You stay away from mother!"

Burgers and Fletcher erupted in laughter while Ramirez grabbed his hat. "Okay, I'm good with that!"

"Good," Alzoria said, turning away with a huff. "Come. We bounce."

"Good luck, guys!" Ramirez called to his friends as he unapologetically left them in the lurch.

"That asshole," Fletcher remarked again.

* * *

The fairy and the cleric watched helplessly as twenty weregoblins fell upon the Dark Knight and hacked him into tiny pieces with their rusted knives and swords.

"Oh no," the cleric remarked deadpan. "Ramiro the Dark Knight is slain."

"Yeh," the fairy agreed. "Anyway..."

The two turned and ran for the exit, taking advantage of Ramiro's noble sacrifice to make their escape.

As they turned the final corner, a tall figure stepped into their path and called out to them.

* * *

"Staff Sergeant Baird?" the armored sentry asked.

Burgers looked up from the table at him. "Yeah?" he replied casually.

"I think you have a visitor at ECP One, Staff Sergeant," the sentry said.

"You *think* I have a visitor?" Burgers replied, standing up and grabbing his patrol cap off the table.

"Well, Staff Sergeant, it's this Va'Shy girl," the sentry explained. "She came up and asked for 'the dark skin man who yells.'"

"Yeah, that's you," Fletcher agreed.

"I don't yell that much," Burgers protested quietly, seemingly hurt by the description. But, sighing, he decided to go anyway. "I don't know how long this will be," he said to Fletcher apologetically.

"That's okay," she said, starting to pack up her own things. "It's my turn with the 'SpaceKnight' fanfiction."

"All right," Burgers said to the medic and the DM. "I'll catch y'all tomorrow."

He followed the sentry out of the dining facility and toward the entry control point. The sun was just now going down, giving the FOB a quiet, almost tranquil appearance.

As they approached the front gate, the sentry pointed to a short, green-haired vixen awkwardly standing as far from the guard shack as she could without actually leaving the FOB. Burgers recognized her immediately and started toward her while the sentry broke off and went back to the guard shack.

<Blessed evening,> he called to her.

Runa looked up at him, her tail suddenly moving faster as he approached. In her tiny hands she clutched a small sack made of delicate white cloth.

<Blessed evening,> she replied, bowing to him.

<You are Runa, yes?> Burgers asked as he came to a stop a few steps from her. He didn't want to crowd her and make her uncomfortable, so he decided to keep a respectful distance.

The Mikorin looked away for a moment but then seemed to gather her courage and looked up at him. <I... I have been named Mikorin Aru'Dace for Pelle,> she informed him.

<Good, yes?> Burgers asked. <Um... I... am... feel good... of... you.>

<Th... Thank you,> she said. <I... I know that... if it were not for you... we might still be...> She broke off, seemingly not wanting to say anymore. Instead, she held the sack out to him. <I wanted to give this to you!> she finished quickly.

Burgers cleared his throat and slowly stepped forward, gently taking the bag from her as if she might turn and run off if he startled her.

<Thank you!> she cried before turning and running off down the road toward the village exactly as he thought she would.

Burgers watched her go for a moment before carefully opening the bag and looking inside. He broke out into a wide grin and reached inside, carefully removing its contents.

A small cake, obviously carefully made, topped with green frosting and a bright violet berry, sat in the large man's hand.

"Now *this*..." he said appreciatively. "... is a cupcake."

* * *

Ben collapsed onto his bunk and groaned. It was already past nine o'clock, and he had finally gotten off the phone he had been chained to all day only ten minutes ago.

Reports, reviews, "good ideas," back-briefings, whatever the directorates wanted to call them, that's what he had been stuck doing. The intelligence directorate wanted to know more about the *Dara Tang*. Operations wanted to know how the situation in Pelle was going to affect convoy movements. Logistics and security wanted to know if they needed to give convoys additional security when going through Sector 13. Plans wanted a complete "lessons learned" document. Communications... well, network and comms were out anyway, so they didn't even bother to call. The Surgeon General's office wanted to know more about the spread of herpes from human to Va'Shen.

Now, *that one*, Ben had been eager to talk about, promising them a full report on it, including *how* such transmissions were able to occur in the first place. If General Walker wanted to cover for Keyes, fine. But *he* could justify it to the rest of the headquarters. Ben wasn't going to sugarcoat anything for leadership's sake. Let them fight it out.

In the end, he never got a chance to check on Alacea.

Tomorrow, he promised himself. *Tomorrow I'll go the temple and...*

He sighed. It sounded so hollow, like the kind of promise made by a man who knew he had somehow screwed up.

But I haven't...

Have I?

Alacea had her own business to attend to, just like he did.

Alacea wasn't expecting him to come see her while he was busy, just like he wasn't expecting her to come to him.

Alacea...

"Fuck it," he said, getting up and out of bed.

* * *

Alacea stood in the garden and looked up at The Blessing, its bands of green and purple waving at her from the Heavens. And just below it was the hilltop on which she had buried her friend.

Why did it turn out like this? Barely two months before, she was walking down the street with her, gently chiding her and enduring a little subtle revenge as a result.

And Azarin...

He spent so long as a commando, fighting far away from his village. Two months after he returned and the vixen he had loved, had loved from the day they had met, was dead.

It simply wasn't fair.

She bit her lip, the pain unable to subdue the guilt.

He protected me, she thought. *When the shooting began, Azarin protected me instead of Hestean. Did he consciously make that choice? Because I am his sister? Because I am the Na'Sha? Or did he only realize it after Hestean was dead?*

The thought that her brother might be wrestling with such guilt made her heart hurt.

She felt lonely.

Her Tesho had not come to see her lately. She understood why. What had happened in the village had certainly drawn the attention of the Grand Overlord, her Tesho's liege lord. She had been grateful, actually. With everything she had had to do over the past few days, she didn't really have time to...

No, that wasn't it.

It was because she knew what would have happened if they had found time alone together.

She would have thrown herself into his arms and wept. Wept and beat on his chest with her fists in pure frustration, sadness and anger. She would have bit at him, tore his shirt and chest to shreds with her fingernails as she howled in fury at the Gods.

Alacea would have done those things, as horrible as they were, because she knew he would have taken it. He was the kind of person who endured for others. He endured for her.

She was the Na'Sha. She was the community. She wasn't permitted the luxury of breaking down into a screaming mess. If any of the villagers ever saw such a thing, they would think the world was coming to an end, that their community was coming unraveled.

It was only with him she could ever do such things.

<I will await you in the Glade, Tesho...>

She buried her face in her hands as her friend's final words came back to her. All that time... All that time they could have been happy together... wasted. It was all wasted, lost to honor and custom until the very last moment.

If you were going to defy custom by marking him, why did you wait until it was too late?!

She thought this as she looked at the hilltop. Hestean and her brother could have run away together years ago. Half the village already knew about them. Tasshas had suggested as much to Azarin and even offered to help get them to another village.

A much younger Sho Nan, in her own Sho Nan way, had even pointed out to Hestean that if they did, it would be Jemenista's job to justify it to the Gods, not hers. Jemenista, she had reminded Hestean, was very good at her job. It was as close as an acolyte could get to suggesting blasphemy and not be thrown out of the temple.

Sho Nan had always been very good at walking that line.

But Hestean was a Mikorin. She had given her life to the Gods. In the end, it was only after she knew she would no longer be able to serve them that she allowed herself that one selfish moment.

Her ears twitched as she heard the sound of footfalls coming from outside the garden. Turning, she could see the road that led from town toward the temple, though in the darkness it was hard to see much except for whatever happened to wander into the glow of the waterlamps.

But in the light of one of those lamps, her Tesho stopped and looked up at her.

They looked at one another for a moment. Then Ben started forward again, eschewing the front entrance of the temple and rounding the building to enter the garden directly.

Alacea watched him approach without a word, saying nothing until he was right next to her.

<Tesho,> she said quietly in greeting.

<Myorin,> he replied. <I am... sad... for Hestean... for you,> he said awkwardly. <Want say to you. Want help... But...>

<You had your duties as I had mine,> she told him, injecting as much dignity into her voice as she could.

She looked up at him, her ears slowly flattening. He reached out and touched her shoulder, and she stepped into him, letting him envelop her in his arms.

The feelings from earlier welled up in her again as if to remind her that she had been waiting for this. She could weep. She could cry out her fury and beat upon him. But the thoughts died away as he held her. The anger, frustration and sadness were still there, but it was if they were being drawn from her body like poison from a wound.

Ben wasn't sure how long they stayed like that. He had simply held her, reaching up and gently stroking her hair so she could just cry or scream or whatever else she needed.

Without a word or warning, she pulled away from him and grabbed his hand, leading him to the doorway into the temple.

<Myorin?> he asked quietly. <You well?>

<Come with me, Tesho,> she replied. She led him down the darkened corridors of the temple, passing no one as they made the turn toward her room.

She let him inside and turned, shutting the door. Her hand rested on the doorframe for a moment as she looked down at her feet. Ben stood in the center of the room, watching her closely, unsure of what she intended to say or do.

<I...> She broke off and said nothing for several moments, her tail moving back and forth in confusion and nervousness. Ben waited patiently, wanting to be there for her however she needed him and willing to wait for her to gather the strength to say whatever she needed to say.

<Tesho,> she finally began again. <I... I don't want to hesitate anymore. I don't want... I don't want to meet the Gods... and...> She shut her eyes in self-reproach.

<Myorin,> he said gently. <It will be well. Promise. It will be well again. Hurts. I know.>

Her Tesho didn't know what she was talking about, what she feared and felt. But his words reminded her what kind of tod he was and that she didn't have to feel fear in his presence.

<Will you care for me?> she asked. <Like... Like we talked about?>

Ben still couldn't see her face, but his own was starting to redden. There was only one talk they had where she had used those words.

<You... um...> he began nervously. <You want...>

<I want to mark you,> she said, the fear in her voice now gone. <You are my Tesho. I want you to *be* my Tesho. And I want everyone to know you are my Tesho.>

Ben cleared his throat. "Um... Okay," he said, unconsciously dropping back into English. <Um... Yes, good,> he replied.

<Sit, please,> she said.

Ben looked around and took a seat at the small table in her room.

<On the bedding please,> she corrected him quietly.

"Yeah," he said as he shuffled onto the futon in the corner. "Yeah, that makes more sense."

She turned to him, and for the first time in a long time, Ben couldn't tell what she was thinking based on her ears and tail. Her face was, in human terms, expressionless. But when she started toward him, it was obvious that she was nervous and straining to hold back panic.

<You tell me,> he said. <What you want do. I do.>

She didn't answer immediately, kneeling next to him on his right side.

<Remove your shirt, please,> she whispered. Hearing her say that in that breathy whisper gave him goosebumps, and he, as casually as he could, removed his uniform top and placed it nearby.

<Now this, please,> she said, pulling at the short sleeve of his sand-colored T-shirt.

The Ranger removed his shirt, and Alacea looked at his bare chest, at the scars on his left shoulder from where the *toka* had bit him. At the slash the commando from his dreams had made during the war.

She reached up and touched the right side of his chest with her fingers, looking for the spot she had once found while treating his wounds. They stopped at a point halfway between his nipple and the top of his shoulder.

There... she told herself, finding what she was looking for.

<How you...> Ben began, but before he could finish, Alacea's head darted toward his chest, her teeth latching onto him and biting *hard*.

The Ranger gritted his teeth and pounded the futon with his left hand as fire bloomed on his entire right side. His right arm came up and wrapped around the vixen's head, but instead of trying to pull the alien woman away, he pulled her closer to him.

It seemed to last for hours. She didn't pull at him like she would if she were trying to tear out a chunk of flesh, but she made no move to release him either. Spots began to blossom before Ben's eyes.

And then, the pain eased as her teeth released him. He continued to hold her head against him, and he felt her gently licking the wound she had made on his chest.

Carefully, almost as if he was afraid she would go after the other side of his chest, Ben moved his arm away, and Alacea sat up. She reached up and demurely wiped the blood from her lips with her fingers. He looked at her in a whole new light, not as the dignified priestess of her village, but as a woman.

She turned her eyes toward the bite she had made and touched it gently with her fingertips. <Now, everyone will know you are mine,> she whispered. <No other vixen will ever be more than a mistress. When you die and go to the Glade, it will be the only scar you carry there.>

<Alacea,> he breathed. <Myorin...>

<Does it hurt greatly?> she asked, and something in her voice made him think she *wanted* it to hurt, as if she were proud of that fact.

<It does,> he told her, but without heat or complaint.

<Good,> she said, confirming his hunch. <Then you will not soon forget.>

Ben cleared his throat, unsure of what was supposed to happen next. <Um... I bite to you now?> he asked.

Suddenly, it looked as if the old Alacea was coming back, and she demurely turned her head away.

<A Tesho marks his Myorin in a... less visible... but no less permanent way...>

Ben worked the words of her riddle in his mind and swallowed nervously as the answer came to him like a bolt of lightning from above.

Her virginity.

He reached out and brushed his fingers against her cheek. She closed her eyes and leaned into it, moving her ears closer to him. Pulling her close, he bent down and gave the tip of her ear a little bite, feeling her tense and then relax in his arms.

<Mark me and I will be yours,> she whispered to him. <Now and forever.>

Slowly and gently, Ben pulled her down onto the futon.

Epilogue

Contact

Alarms blared and gunshots rang out in the night. Through the plastic walls of the tent, the shadows of troops running to their battle stations broke up the light illuminating the Va'Shen commando standing only a few feet from him. Despite the shadows, Ben could see the gleam of light reflecting off the razor-sharp blade the alien carried low in his right hand.

Unlike his usual dream, he wasn't in his bunk. He was standing, facing the commando. He looked to his right and saw his belt and sidearm hanging from the end of his bed, just inside his reach.

He turned back to the commando, his face obscured and hidden from him. The Va'Shen soldier seemed to be waiting for him to do something, to react to him.

Ben regarded him for a moment as the screams of people being killed pierced the night around him.

"I don't want to do this anymore," he told the commando sadly.

The alien didn't reply. He charged forward, his knife flashing toward Ben's neck.

* * *

Ben opened his eyes and gasped. The commando, as usual, was gone, but the sight of the open skylight above him was unusual, and it took him a moment to remember where he was.

He turned his head to the right and found Alacea stirring next to him. Her eyes opened sleepily, and she looked at him, moving her body closer to his.

The warmth and softness of her body felt good against him, and he took a comforting breath as her delicate ears brushed against his face.

<A dream?> she asked softly.

<Yes,> he replied calmly, looking up through the skylight at the eerie green aurora and the stars twinkling behind it.

He almost jumped when he felt tiny bites assault his right shoulder. Looking down, he found his alien wife nibbling on him.

<I am with you,> she whispered between bites. <You are not alone.>

He smiled and pulled her closer to him, giving her ear a little nibble which caused her to squeak adorably.

All of this, he knew, complicated things. He knew there was no option now of him simply leaving Va'Sh and the two of them going their own ways. He wasn't going to leave her. Either he had to find a way to stay on Va'Sh past his deployment or bring her with him when he left. He doubted she would want to do that, but the first option would be damn near impossible if the Army didn't want it.

But he did. What he was feeling now, he realized, was something he had been searching for, and was now something he didn't want to live without.

As if she were reading his thoughts, she nuzzled his shoulder and whispered. <Thank you, Tesho.>

<Why?> he asked.

<For showing me care.>

He smiled. <Always will care,> he promised.

<Even if you have to leave?> she asked. There was no sadness in her voice. She had already accepted the fact that he would very likely be sent to fight another war for his liege lord eventually.

<Yes,> he said. <And then come back.>

Her eyes looked up into his. <Come back?> she asked.

<Yes,> he said. <I come back.>

Her ears twitched, tickling his cheek. <Then I will be expecting you.>

<Book,> he whispered. Her ears twitched again at their inside joke. He held her close and looked up at the sky again.

It was going to be difficult, a Grade A pain in the ass to make happen, but he meant it. He would find a way back. He'd volunteer for whatever shitty staff position he had to. Even if that didn't work, eventually the military would open the planet for civilian visitors. The occupation would end at some point, but even then the Coalition wouldn't just leave them to their own devices. They would work with the Va'Shen until, as he had told Azarin, enemies became friends.

Then the war would be over.

He smiled, wondering if he could actually live the rest of his life in a place with no electricity, net or any of the other technological comforts an American could normally take for granted.

Hasn't been that bad so far, he had to admit.

The human took a breath and watched the stars.

And then the sky lit up.

Ben shook his head, wondering if he was dreaming, but no. A bright flash and then a ring of light was expanding in the sky. For a moment, it could almost be mistaken for the coming dawn.

Alacea sat up and looked at the sky, further confirming to him that what was happening was real.

<Gods!> she breathed. <Gods! What is it?!>

Ben frowned as he watched the light fade again. He knew what it was. There was only one thing it could be.

"That was the *Neil Armstrong*," he told her, slipping back into English.

She looked at him, not understanding his words.

He glared at the sky, no longer a comforting presence but a source of new danger.

"Someone just blew up our ship."

To be concluded...